The Lone Star Ranger

The Lone Star Ranger

by

Zane Grey

LARGE PRINT EDITION

Sastrugi Press Classics
Jackson, WY

Sastrugi Press Classics edition of *The Lone Star Ranger* © 2019

The Lone Star Ranger by Zane Grey (Large Print Edition)

All rights reserved. No part of this publication may be distributed, reproduced, or transmitted in any form or by any means, including recording, photocopying, or other electronic or mechanical methods, without the prior written permission of the publisher, except in the case of brief quotations embodied in critical reviews and certain other non-commercial uses permitted by copyright law.

For permission requests, write to the publisher, addressed "Attention: Permissions Coordinator' Sastrugi Press, P.O. Box 1297, Jackson, WY 83001, United States.

www.sastrugipress.com
CIP Data available
Grey, Zane
The Lone Star Ranger / Zane Grey - Reprint 1st United States edition
p. cm.
1. Texas 2. Cowboy 3. History
Summary: Set in Texas, this classic western novel follows the life of Buck Duane who becomes an outlaw and sets out to clear his name.

ISBN-13: 978-1-944986-61-2 (hardback)
ISBN-13: 978-1-944986-62-9 (paperback)
ISBN-13: 978-1-64922-021-9 (paperback large print)
ISBN-13: 978-1-64922-039-4 (hardback large print)
813-dc22

Sastrugi Press Classics
00155
Printed in the United States of America when purchased in the United States
The Lone Star Ranger was first published in 1915.

10 9 8 7 6 5 4 3 2 1

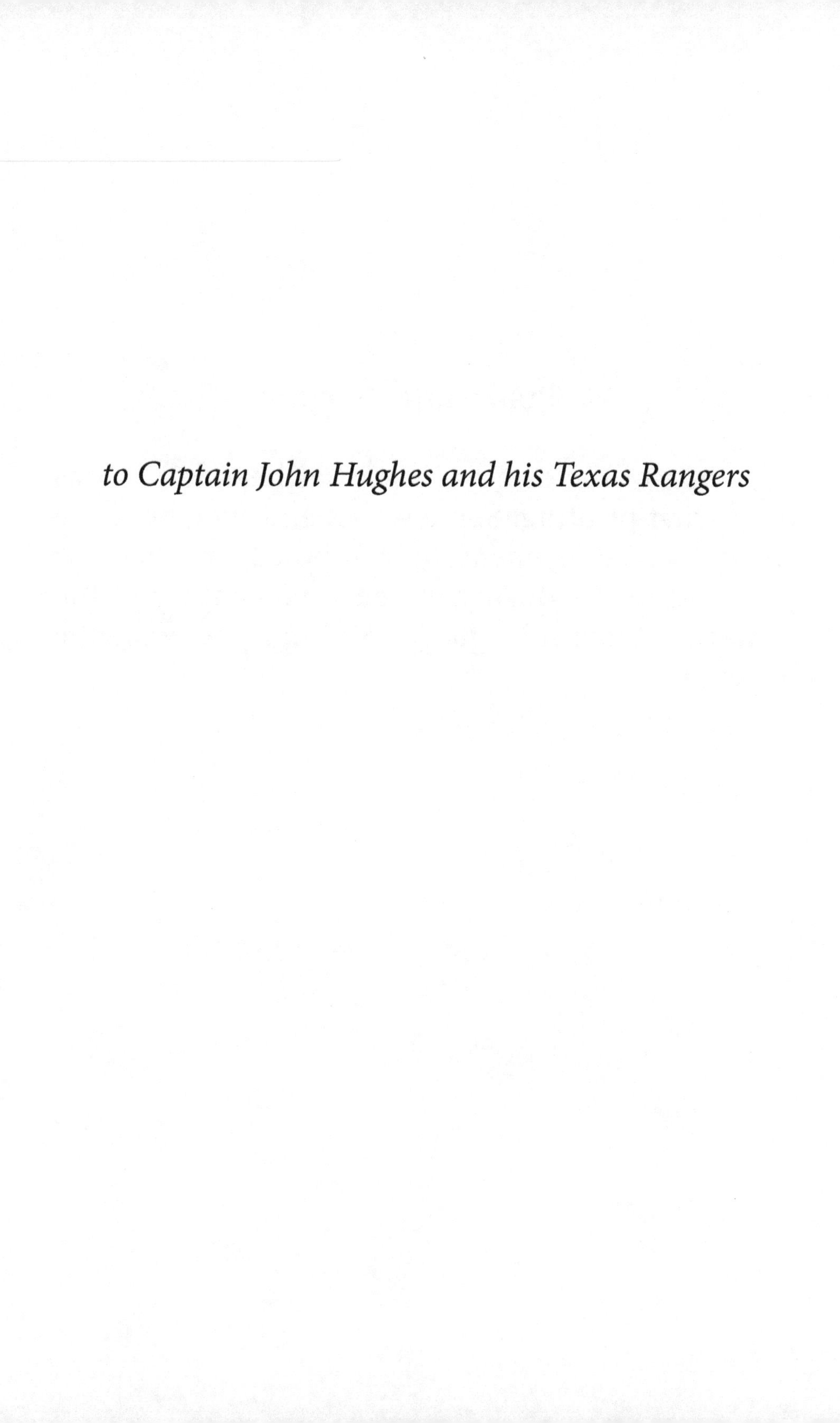

to Captain John Hughes and his Texas Rangers

Publishing Note

The text of the original book has been left as was in the first printing. Some words and spellings have since changed, hyphenated, combined, or otherwise gone out of use during the ensuing century in the American English language. We hope you enjoy the experience.

ORIGINAL FOREWORD

It may seem strange to you that out of all the stories I heard on the Rio Grande I should choose as first that of Buck Duane—outlaw and gunman.

But, indeed, Ranger Coffee's story of the last of the Duanes has haunted me, and I have given full rein to imagination and have retold it in my own way. It deals with the old law—the old border days—therefore it is better first. Soon, perchance, I shall have the pleasure of writing of the border of to-day, which in Joe Sitter's laconic speech, "Shore is 'most as bad an' wild as ever!"

In the North and East there is a popular idea that the frontier of the West is a thing long past, and remembered now only in stories. As I think of this I remember Ranger Sitter when he made that remark, while he grimly stroked an unhealed bullet wound. And I remember the giant Vaughn, that typical son of stalwart Texas, sitting there quietly with bandaged head, his thoughtful eye boding ill to the outlaw who had ambushed him. Only a few months have passed since then—when I had my memorable sojourn with you—and yet, in that short time, Russell and Moore have crossed the Divide, like Rangers.

Gentlemen,—I have the honor to dedicate this book to you, and the hope that it shall fall to my lot to tell the world the truth about a strange, unique, and misunderstood body of men—the Texas Rangers—who made the great Lone Star State habitable, who never know peaceful rest and sleep, who are passing, who surely will not be forgotten and will some day come into their own.

ZANE GREY.
June, 1915.

BOOK I
THE OUTLAW

CHAPTER I

So it was in him, then—an inherited fighting instinct, a driving intensity to kill. He was the last of the Duanes, that old fighting stock of Texas. But not the memory of his dead father, nor the pleading of his soft-voiced mother, nor the warning of this uncle who stood before him now, had brought to Buck Duane so much realization of the dark passionate strain in his blood. It was the recurrence, a hundred-fold increased in power, of a strange emotion that for the last three years had arisen in him.

"Yes, Cal Bain's in town, full of bad whisky an' huntin' for you," repeated the elder man, gravely.

"It's the second time," muttered Duane, as if to himself.

"Son, you can't avoid a meetin'. Leave town till Cal sobers up. He ain't got it in for you when he's not drinkin'."

"But what's he want me for?" demanded Duane. "To insult me again? I won't stand that twice."

"He's got a fever that's rampant in Texas these days, my boy. He wants gun-play. If he meets you he'll try to kill you."

Here it stirred in Duane again, that bursting gush of blood, like a wind of flame shaking all his inner being, and subsiding to leave him strangely chilled.

"Kill me! What for?" he asked.

"Lord knows there ain't any reason. But what's that to do with most of the shootin' these days? Didn't five cowboys over to Everall's kill one another dead all because they got to jerkin' at a quirt among themselves? An' Cal has no reason to love you. His girl was sweet on you."

"I quit when I found out she was his girl."

"I reckon she ain't quit. But never mind her or reasons. Cal's here, just drunk enough to be ugly. He's achin' to kill somebody. He's one of them four-flush gun-fighters. He'd like to be thought bad. There's a lot of wild cowboys who're ambitious for a reputation. They talk about how quick they are on the draw. They ape Bland an' King Fisher an' Hardin an' all the big outlaws. They make threats about joinin' the gangs along the Rio Grande. They laugh at the sheriffs an' brag about how they'd fix the rangers. Cal's sure not much for you to bother with, if you only keep out of his way."

"You mean for me to run?" asked Duane, in scorn.

"I reckon I wouldn't put it that way. Just avoid him. Buck, I'm not afraid Cal would get you if you met down there in town. You've your father's eye an' his slick hand with a gun. What I'm most afraid of is that you'll kill Bain."

Duane was silent, letting his uncle's earnest words sink in, trying to realize their significance.

"If Texas ever recovers from that fool war an' kills off these outlaws, why, a young man will have a lookout," went on the uncle. "You're twenty-three now, an' a powerful sight of a fine fellow, barrin' your temper. You've a chance in life. But if you go gun-fightin', if you kill a man, you're ruined. Then you'll kill another. It'll be the same old story. An' the rangers would make you an outlaw. The rangers mean law an' order for Texas. This even-break business doesn't work with them. If you resist arrest they'll kill you. If you submit to arrest, then you go to jail, an' mebbe you hang."

"I'd never hang," muttered Duane, darkly.

"I reckon you wouldn't," replied the old man. "You'd be like your father. He was ever ready to draw—too ready. In times like these, with the Texas rangers enforcin' the law, your Dad would have been driven to the river. An', son, I'm afraid you're a chip off the old block. Can't you hold in—keep your temper—run away from trouble? Because it'll only result in you gettin' the worst of it in the end. Your father was killed in a street-fight. An' it was told of him that he shot twice after a bullet had passed through his heart. Think of the terrible nature of a man to be able to do that. If you have any such blood in you, never give it a chance."

"What you say is all very well, uncle," returned Duane, "but the only way out for me is to run, and I won't do it. Cal Bain and his outfit have already made me look like a coward. He says I'm afraid to come out and face him. A man simply can't stand that in this country. Besides, Cal would shoot me in the back some day if I didn't face him."

"Well, then, what're you goin' to do?" inquired the elder man.

"I haven't decided—yet."

"No, but you're comin' to it mighty fast. That damned spell is workin' in you. You're different to-day. I remember how you used to be moody an' lose your temper an' talk wild. Never was much afraid of you then. But now you're gettin' cool an' quiet, an' you think deep, an' I don't like the light in your eye. It reminds me of your father."

"I wonder what Dad would say to me to-day if he were alive and here," said Duane.

"What do you think? What could you expect of a man who never wore a glove on his right hand for twenty years?"

"Well, he'd hardly have said much. Dad never talked. But he would have done a lot. And I guess I'll go down-town and let Cal Bain find me."

Then followed a long silence, during which Duane sat with downcast eyes, and the uncle appeared lost in sad thought of the future. Presently he turned to Duane with an expression that denoted resignation, and yet a spirit which showed wherein they were of the same blood.

"You've got a fast horse—the fastest I know of in this country. After you meet Bain hurry back home. I'll have a saddle-bag packed for you and the horse ready."

With that he turned on his heel and went into the house, leaving Duane to revolve in his mind his singular speech. Buck wondered presently if he shared his uncle's opinion of the result of a meeting between himself and Bain. His thoughts were vague. But on the instant of final decision, when he had settled with himself that he would meet Bain, such a storm of passion assailed him that he felt as if he was being shaken with ague. Yet it was all internal, inside his breast, for his hand was like a rock and, for all he could see, not a muscle about him quivered. He had no fear of Bain or of any other man; but a vague fear of himself, of this strange force in him, made him ponder and shake his head. It was as if he had not all to say in this matter. There appeared to have been in him a reluctance to let himself go, and some voice, some spirit from a distance, something he was not accountable for, had compelled him. That hour of Duane's life was like years of actual living, and in it he became a thoughtful man.

He went into the house and buckled on his belt and gun. The gun was a Colt .45, six-shot, and heavy, with an ivory handle. He had packed it, on and off, for five years. Before that it had been used by his father. There were a number of notches filed in the bulge of the ivory handle. This gun was the one his father had fired twice after being shot through the heart, and his hand had stiffened so tightly upon it in the death-grip that his fingers had to be pried open. It had never been drawn upon any man since it had come into Duane's possession. But the cold, bright polish of the weapon showed how it had been used. Duane could draw it with inconceivable rapidity, and at twenty feet he could split a card pointing edgewise toward him.

Duane wished to avoid meeting his mother. Fortunately, as he thought, she was away from home. He went out and down the path toward the gate. The air was full of the fragrance of blossoms and the melody of birds. Outside in the road a neighbor woman stood talking to a countryman in a wagon; they spoke to him; and he heard, but did not reply. Then he began to stride down the road toward the town.

Wellston was a small town, but important in that unsettled part of the great state because it was the trading-center of several hundred miles of territory. On the main street there were perhaps fifty buildings, some brick, some frame, mostly adobe, and one-third of the lot, and by far the most prosperous, were saloons. From the road Duane turned into this street. It was a wide thoroughfare lined by hitching-rails and saddled horses and vehicles of various kinds. Duane's eye ranged down the street, taking in all at a glance, particularly persons moving leisurely up and down. Not a cowboy was in sight. Duane slackened his stride, and by the time he reached Sol White's place, which was the first saloon, he was walking slowly. Several people spoke to him and turned to look back after they had passed. He paused at the door of White's saloon, took a sharp survey of the interior, then stepped inside.

The saloon was large and cool, full of men and noise and smoke. The noise ceased upon his entrance, and the silence ensuing presently broke to the clink of Mexican silver dollars at a monte table. Sol White, who was behind the bar, straightened up when he saw Duane; then, without speaking, he bent over to rinse a glass. All eyes except those of the Mexican gamblers were turned upon Duane; and these glances were keen, speculative, questioning. These men knew Bain was looking for trouble; they probably had heard his boasts. But what did Duane intend to do? Several of the cowboys and ranchers present exchanged glances. Duane had been weighed by unerring Texas instinct, by men who all packed guns. The boy was the son of his father. Whereupon they greeted him and returned to their drinks and cards. Sol White stood with his big red hands out upon the bar; he was a tall, raw-boned Texan with a long mustache waxed to sharp points.

"Howdy, Buck," was his greeting to Duane. He spoke carelessly and averted his dark gaze for an instant.

"Howdy, Sol," replied Duane, slowly. "Say, Sol, I hear there's a gent in town looking for me bad."

"Reckon there is, Buck," replied White. "He came in heah aboot an hour ago. Shore he was some riled an' a-roarin' for gore. Told me confidential a certain party had given you a white silk scarf, an' he was hell-bent on wearin' it home spotted red."

"Anybody with him?" queried Duane.

"Burt an' Sam Outcalt an' a little cowpuncher I never seen before. They-all was coaxin' trim to leave town. But he's looked on the flowin' glass, Buck, an' he's heah for keeps."

"Why doesn't Sheriff Oaks lock him up if he's that bad?"

"Oaks went away with the rangers. There's been another raid at Flesher's ranch. The King Fisher gang, likely. An' so the town's shore wide open."

Duane stalked outdoors and faced down the street.

He walked the whole length of the long block, meeting many people—farmers, ranchers, clerks, merchants, Mexicans, cowboys, and women. It was a singular fact that when he turned to retrace his steps the street was almost empty. He had not returned a hundred yards on his way when the street was wholly deserted. A few heads protruded from doors and around corners. That main street of Wellston saw some such situation every few days. If it was an instinct for Texans to fight, it was also instinctive for them to sense with remarkable quickness the signs of a coming gun-play. Rumor could not fly so swiftly. In less than ten minutes everybody who had been on the street or in the shops knew that Buck Duane had come forth to meet his enemy.

Duane walked on. When he came to within fifty paces of a saloon he swerved out into the middle of the street, stood there for a moment, then went ahead and back to the sidewalk. He passed on in this way the length of the block. Sol White was standing in the door of his saloon.

"Buck, I'm a-tippin' you off," he said, quick and low-voiced. "Cal Bain's over at Everall's. If he's a-huntin' you bad, as he brags, he'll show there."

Duane crossed the street and started down. Notwithstanding White's statement Duane was wary and slow at every door. Nothing happened, and he traversed almost the whole length of the block without seeing a person. Everall's place was on the corner.

Duane knew himself to be cold, steady. He was conscious of a strange fury that made him want to leap ahead. He seemed to long for this encounter more than anything he had ever wanted. But, vivid as were his sensations, he felt as if in a dream.

Before he reached Everall's he heard loud voices, one of which was raised high. Then the short door swung outward as if impelled by a vigorous hand. A bow-legged cowboy wearing wooley chaps burst out upon the sidewalk. At sight of Duane he seemed to bound into the air, and he uttered a savage roar.

Duane stopped in his tracks at the outer edge of the sidewalk, perhaps a dozen rods from Everall's door.

If Bain was drunk he did not show it in his movement. He swaggered forward, rapidly closing up the gap. Red, sweaty, disheveled, and hatless, his face distorted and expressive of the most malignant intent, he was a wild and sinister figure. He had already killed a man, and this showed in his demeanor. His hands were extended before him, the right hand a little lower than the left. At every step he bellowed his rancor in speech mostly curses. Gradually he slowed his walk, then halted. A good twenty-five paces separated the men.

"Won't nothin' make you draw, you—!" he shouted, fiercely.

"I'm waitin' on you, Cal," replied Duane.

Bain's right hand stiffened—moved. Duane threw his gun as a boy throws a ball underhand—a draw his father had taught him. He pulled twice, his shots almost as one. Bain's big Colt boomed while it was pointed downward and he was falling. His bullet scattered dust and gravel at Duane's feet. He fell loosely, without contortion.

In a flash all was reality for Duane. He went forward and held his gun ready for the slightest movement on the part of Bain. But Bain lay upon his back, and all that moved were his breast and his eyes. How strangely the red had left his face—and also the distortion! The devil that had showed in Bain was gone. He was sober and conscious. He tried to speak, but failed. His eyes expressed something pitifully human. They changed—rolled—set blankly.

Duane drew a deep breath and sheathed his gun. He felt calm and cool, glad the fray was over. One violent expression burst from him. "The fool!"

When he looked up there were men around him.

"Plumb center," said one.

Another, a cowboy who evidently had just left the gaming-table, leaned down and pulled open Bain's shirt. He had the ace of spades in his hand. He laid it on Bain's breast, and the black figure on the card covered the two bullet-holes just over Bain's heart.

Duane wheeled and hurried away. He heard another man say:

"Reckon Cal got what he deserved. Buck Duane's first gunplay. Like father like son!"

CHAPTER II

A thought kept repeating itself to Duane, and it was that he might have spared himself concern through his imagining how awful it would be to kill a man. He had no such feeling now. He had rid the community of a drunken, bragging, quarrelsome cowboy.

When he came to the gate of his home and saw his uncle there with a mettlesome horse, saddled, with canteen, rope, and bags all in place, a subtle shock pervaded his spirit. It had slipped his mind—the consequence of his act. But sight of the horse and the look of his uncle recalled the fact that he must now become a fugitive. An unreasonable anger took hold of him.

"The d—d fool!" he exclaimed, hotly. "Meeting Bain wasn't much, Uncle Jim. He dusted my boots, that's all. And for that I've got to go on the dodge."

"Son, you killed him—then?" asked the uncle, huskily.

"Yes. I stood over him—watched him die. I did as I would have been done by."

"I knew it. Long ago I saw it comin'. But now we can't stop to cry over spilt blood. You've got to leave town an' this part of the country."

"Mother!" exclaimed Duane.

"She's away from home. You can't wait. I'll break it

to her—what she always feared."

Suddenly Duane sat down and covered his face with his hands.

"My God! Uncle, what have I done?" His broad shoulders shook.

"Listen, son, an' remember what I say," replied the elder man, earnestly. "Don't ever forget. You're not to blame. I'm glad to see you take it this way, because maybe you'll never grow hard an' callous. You're not to blame. This is Texas. You're your father's son. These are wild times. The law as the rangers are laying it down now can't change life all in a minute. Even your mother, who's a good, true woman, has had her share in making you what you are this moment. For she was one of the pioneers—the fightin' pioneers of this state. Those years of wild times, before you was born, developed in her instinct to fight, to save her life, her children, an' that instinct has cropped out in you. It will be many years before it dies out of the boys born in Texas."

"I'm a murderer," said Duane, shuddering.

"No, son, you're not. An' you never will be. But you've got to be an outlaw till time makes it safe for you to come home."

"An outlaw?"

"I said it. If we had money an' influence we'd risk a trial. But we've neither. An' I reckon the scaffold or jail is no place for Buckley Duane. Strike for the wild country, an' wherever you go an' whatever you do-be a man. Live honestly, if that's possible. If it isn't, be as honest as you can. If you have to herd with outlaws try not to become bad. There are outlaws who 're not all bad—many who have been driven to the river by such a deal as this you had. When you get among these men avoid brawls. Don't drink; don't gamble. I needn't tell you what to do if it comes to gun-play, as likely it will. You can't come home. When this thing is lived down, if that time ever comes, I'll get word into the unsettled country. It'll reach you some day. That's all. Remember, be a man. Goodby."

Duane, with blurred sight and contracting throat, gripped his uncle's hand and bade him a wordless farewell. Then he leaped astride the black and rode out of town.

As swiftly as was consistent with a care for his steed, Duane put a distance of fifteen or eighteen miles behind him. With that he slowed up, and the matter of riding did not require all his faculties. He passed several ranches and was seen by men. This did not suit him, and he took an old trail across country. It was a flat region with a poor growth of mesquite and prickly-pear cactus. Occasionally he caught a glimpse of low hills in the distance. He had hunted often in that section, and knew where to find grass and water. When he reached this higher ground he did not, however, halt at the first favorable camping-spot, but went on and on. Once he came out upon the brow of a hill and saw a considerable stretch of country beneath him. It had the gray sameness characterizing all that he had traversed. He seemed to want to see wide spaces—to get a glimpse of the great wilderness lying somewhere beyond to the southwest. It was sunset when he decided to camp at a likely spot he came across. He led the horse to water, and then began searching through the shallow valley for a suitable place to camp. He passed by old camp-sites that he well remembered. These, however, did not strike his fancy this time, and the significance of the change in him did not occur at the moment. At last he found a secluded spot, under cover of thick mesquites and oaks, at a goodly distance from the old trail. He took saddle and pack off the horse. He looked among his effects for a hobble, and, finding that his uncle had failed to put one in, he suddenly remembered that he seldom used a hobble, and never on this horse. He cut a few feet off the end of his lasso and used that. The horse, unused to such hampering of his free movements, had to be driven out upon the grass.

Duane made a small fire, prepared and ate his supper. This done, ending the work of that day, he sat down and filled his pipe. Twilight had waned into dusk. A few wan stars had just begun to show and brighten. Above the low continuous hum of insects sounded the evening carol of robins. Presently the birds ceased their singing, and then the quiet was more noticeable. When night set in and the place seemed all the more isolated and lonely for that Duane had a sense of relief.

It dawned upon him all at once that he was nervous, watchful, sleepless. The fact caused him surprise, and he began to think back, to take note of his late actions and their motives. The change one day had wrought amazed him. He who had always been free, easy, happy, especially when out alone in the open, had become in a few short hours bound, serious, preoccupied. The silence that had once been sweet now meant nothing to him except a medium whereby he might the better hear the sounds of pursuit. The loneliness, the night, the wild, that had always been beautiful to him, now only conveyed a sense of safety for the present. He watched, he listened, he thought. He felt tired, yet had no inclination to rest. He intended to be off by dawn, heading toward the southwest. Had he a destination? It was vague as his knowledge of that great waste of mesquite and rock bordering the Rio Grande. Somewhere out there was a refuge. For he was a fugitive from justice, an outlaw.

This being an outlaw then meant eternal vigilance. No home, no rest, no sleep, no content, no life worth the living! He must be a lone wolf or he must herd among men obnoxious to him. If he worked for an honest living he still must hide his identity and take risks of detection. If he did not work on some distant outlying ranch, how was he to live? The idea of stealing was repugnant to him. The future seemed gray and somber enough. And he was twenty-three years old.

Why had this hard life been imposed upon him?

The bitter question seemed to start a strange iciness that stole along his veins. What was wrong with him? He stirred the few sticks of mesquite into a last flickering blaze. He was cold, and for some reason he wanted some light. The black circle of darkness weighed down upon him, closed in around him. Suddenly he sat bolt upright and then froze in that position. He had heard a step. It was behind him—no—on the side. Some one was there. He forced his hand down to his gun, and the touch of cold steel was another icy shock. Then he waited. But all was silent—silent as only a wilderness arroyo can be, with its low murmuring of wind in the mesquite. Had he heard a step? He began to breathe again.

But what was the matter with the light of his camp-fire? It had taken on a strange green luster and seemed to be waving off into the outer shadows. Duane heard no step, saw no movement; nevertheless, there was another present at that camp-fire vigil. Duane saw him. He lay there in the middle of the green brightness, prostrate, motionless, dying. Cal Bain! His features were wonderfully distinct, clearer than any cameo, more sharply outlined than those of any picture. It was a hard face softening at the threshold of eternity. The red tan of sun, the coarse signs of drunkenness, the ferocity and hate so characteristic of Bain were no longer there. This face represented a different Bain, showed all that was human in him fading, fading as swiftly as it blanched white. The lips wanted to speak, but had not the power. The eyes held an agony of thought. They revealed what might have been possible for this man if he lived—that he saw his mistake too late. Then they rolled, set blankly, and closed in death.

That haunting visitation left Duane sitting there in a cold sweat, a remorse gnawing at his vitals, realizing the curse that was on him. He divined that never would he be able to keep off that phantom. He remembered how his father had been eternally pursued by the furies of accusing guilt, how he had never been able to forget in work or in sleep those men he had killed.

The hour was late when Duane's mind let him sleep, and then dreams troubled him. In the morning he bestirred himself so early that in the gray gloom he had difficulty in finding his horse. Day had just broken when he struck the old trail again.

He rode hard all morning and halted in a shady spot to rest and graze his horse. In the afternoon he took to the trail at an easy trot. The country grew wilder. Bald, rugged mountains broke the level of the monotonous horizon. About three in the afternoon he came to a little river which marked the boundary line of his hunting territory.

The decision he made to travel up-stream for a while was owing to two facts: the river was high with quicksand bars on each side, and he felt reluctant to cross into that region where his presence alone meant that he was a marked man. The bottom-lands through which the river wound to the southwest were more inviting than the barrens he had traversed. The rest or that day he rode leisurely upstream. At sunset he penetrated the brakes of willow and cottonwood to spend the night. It seemed to him that in this lonely cover he would feel easy and content. But he did not. Every feeling, every imagining he had experienced the previous night returned somewhat more vividly and accentuated by newer ones of the same intensity and color.

In this kind of travel and camping he spent three more days, during which he crossed a number of trails, and one road where cattle—stolen cattle, probably—had recently passed. Thus time exhausted his supply of food, except salt, pepper, coffee, and sugar, of which he had a quantity. There were deer in the brakes; but, as he could not get close enough to kill them with a revolver, he had to satisfy himself with a rabbit. He knew he might as well content himself with the hard fare that assuredly would be his lot.

Somewhere up this river there was a village called Huntsville. It was distant about a hundred miles from Wellston, and had a reputation throughout southwestern Texas. He had never been there. The fact was this reputation was such that honest travelers gave the town a wide berth. Duane had considerable money for him in his possession, and he concluded to visit Huntsville, if he could find it, and buy a stock of provisions.

The following day, toward evening, he happened upon a road which he believed might lead to the village. There were a good many fresh horse-tracks in the sand, and these made him thoughtful. Nevertheless, he followed the road, proceeding cautiously. He had not gone very far when the sound of rapid hoof-beats caught his ears. They came from his rear. In the darkening twilight he could not see any great distance back along the road. Voices, however, warned him that these riders, whoever they were, had approached closer than he liked. To go farther down the road was not to be thought of, so he turned a little way in among the mesquites and halted, hoping to escape being seen or heard. As he was now a fugitive, it seemed every man was his enemy and pursuer.

The horsemen were fast approaching. Presently they were abreast of Duane's position, so near that he could hear the creak of saddles, the clink of spurs.

"Shore he crossed the river below," said one man.

"I reckon you're right, Bill. He's slipped us," replied another.

Rangers or a posse of ranchers in pursuit of a fugitive! The knowledge gave Duane a strange thrill. Certainly they could not have been hunting him. But the feeling their proximity gave him was identical to what it would have been had he been this particular hunted man. He held his breath; he clenched his teeth; he pressed a quieting hand upon his horse. Suddenly he became aware that these horsemen had halted. They were whispering. He could just make out a dark group closely massed. What had made them halt so suspiciously?

"You're wrong, Bill," said a man, in a low but distinct voice.

"The idee of hearin' a hoss heave. You're wuss'n a ranger. And you're hell-bent on killin' that rustler. Now I say let's go home and eat."

"Wal, I'll just take a look at the sand," replied the man called Bill.

Duane heard the clink of spurs on steel stirrup and the thud of boots on the ground. There followed a short silence which was broken by a sharply breathed exclamation.

Duane waited for no more. They had found his trail. He spurred his horse straight into the brush. At the second crashing bound there came yells from the road, and then shots. Duane heard the hiss of a bullet close by his ear, and as it struck a branch it made a peculiar singing sound. These shots and the proximity of that lead missile roused in Duane a quick, hot resentment which mounted into a passion almost ungovernable. He must escape, yet it seemed that he did not care whether he did or not. Something grim kept urging him to halt and return the fire of these men. After running a couple of hundred yards he raised himself from over the pommel, where he had bent to avoid the stinging branches, and tried to guide his horse. In the dark shadows under mesquites and cottonwoods he was hard put to it to find open passage; however, he succeeded so well and made such little noise that gradually he drew away from his pursuers. The sound of their horses crashing through the thickets died away. Duane reined in and listened. He had distanced them. Probably they would go into camp till daylight, then follow his tracks. He started on again, walking his horse, and peered sharply at the ground, so that he might take advantage of the first trail he crossed. It seemed a long while until he came upon one. He followed it until a late hour, when, striking the willow brakes again and hence the neighborhood of the river, he picketed his horse and lay down to rest. But he did not sleep. His mind bitterly revolved the fate that had come upon him. He made efforts to think of other things, but in vain.

Every moment he expected the chill, the sense of loneliness that yet was ominous of a strange visitation, the peculiarly imagined lights and shades of the night—these things that presaged the coming of Cal Bain. Doggedly Duane fought against the insidious phantom. He kept telling himself that it was just imagination, that it would wear off in time. Still in his heart he did not believe what he hoped. But he would not give up; he would not accept the ghost of his victim as a reality.

Gray dawn found him in the saddle again headed for the river. Half an hour of riding brought him to the dense chaparral and willow thickets. These he threaded to come at length to the ford. It was a gravel bottom, and therefore an easy crossing. Once upon the opposite shore he reined in his horse and looked darkly back. This action marked his acknowledgment of his situation: he had voluntarily sought the refuge of the outlaws; he was beyond the pale. A bitter and passionate curse passed his lips as he spurred his horse into the brakes on that alien shore.

He rode perhaps twenty miles, not sparing his horse nor caring whether or not he left a plain trail.

"Let them hunt me!" he muttered.

When the heat of the day began to be oppressive, and hunger and thirst made themselves manifest, Duane began to look about him for a place to halt for the noon-hours. The trail led into a road which was hard packed and smooth from the tracks of cattle. He doubted not that he had come across one of the roads used by border raiders. He headed into it, and had scarcely traveled a mile when, turning a curve, he came point-blank upon a single horseman riding toward him. Both riders wheeled their mounts sharply and were ready to run and shoot back. Not more than a hundred paces separated them. They stood then for a moment watching each other.

"Mawnin', stranger," called the man, dropping his hand from his hip.

"Howdy," replied Duane, shortly.

They rode toward each other, closing half the gap, then they halted again.

"I seen you ain't no ranger," called the rider, "an' shore I ain't none."

He laughed loudly, as if he had made a joke.

"How'd you know I wasn't a ranger?" asked Duane, curiously. Somehow he had instantly divined that his horseman was no officer, or even a rancher trailing stolen stock.

"Wal," said the fellow, starting his horse forward at a walk, "a ranger'd never git ready to run the other way from one man."

He laughed again. He was small and wiry, slouchy of attire, and armed to the teeth, and he bestrode a fine bay horse. He had quick, dancing brown eyes, at once frank and bold, and a coarse, bronzed face. Evidently he was a good-natured ruffian.

Duane acknowledged the truth of the assertion, and turned over in his mind how shrewdly the fellow had guessed him to be a hunted man.

"My name's Luke Stevens, an' I hail from the river.

Who're you?" said this stranger.

Duane was silent.

"I reckon you're Buck Duane," went on Stevens. "I heerd you was a damn bad man with a gun."

This time Duane laughed, not at the doubtful compliment, but at the idea that the first outlaw he met should know him. Here was proof of how swiftly facts about gun-play traveled on the Texas border.

"Wal, Buck," said Stevens, in a friendly manner, "I ain't presumin' on your time or company. I see you're headin' fer the river. But will you stop long enough to stake a feller to a bite of grub?"

"I'm out of grub, and pretty hungry myself," admitted Duane.

"Been pushin' your hoss, I see. Wal, I reckon you'd better stock up before you hit thet stretch of country."

He made a wide sweep of his right arm, indicating the southwest, and there was that in his action which seemed significant of a vast and barren region.

"Stock up?" queried Duane, thoughtfully.

"Shore. A feller has jest got to eat. I can rustle along without whisky, but not without grub. Thet's what makes it so embarrassin' travelin' these parts dodgin' your shadow. Now, I'm on my way to Mercer. It's a little two-bit town up the river a ways. I'm goin' to pack out some grub."

Stevens's tone was inviting. Evidently he would welcome Duane's companionship, but he did not openly say so. Duane kept silence, however, and then Stevens went on.

"Stranger, in this here country two's a crowd. It's safer. I never was much on this lone-wolf dodgin', though I've done it of necessity. It takes a damn good man to travel alone any length of time. Why, I've been thet sick I was jest achin' fer some ranger to come along an' plug me. Give me a pardner any day. Now, mebbe you're not thet kind of a feller, an' I'm shore not presumin' to ask. But I just declares myself sufficient."

"You mean you'd like me to go with you?" asked Duane.

Stevens grinned. "Wal, I should smile. I'd be particular proud to be braced with a man of your reputation."

"See here, my good fellow, that's all nonsense," declared Duane, in some haste.

"Shore I think modesty becomin' to a youngster," replied Stevens. "I hate a brag. An' I've no use fer these four-flush cowboys thet 're always lookin' fer trouble an' talkin' gun-play. Buck, I don't know much about you. But every man who's lived along the Texas border remembers a lot about your Dad. It was expected of you, I reckon, an' much of your rep was established before you thronged your gun. I jest heerd thet you was lightnin' on the draw, an' when you cut loose with a gun, why the figger on the ace of spades would cover your cluster of bullet-holes. Thet's the word thet's gone down the border. It's the kind of reputation most sure to fly far an' swift ahead of a man in this country. An' the safest, too; I'll gamble on thet. It's the land of the draw. I see now you're only a boy, though you're shore a strappin' husky one. Now, Buck, I'm not a spring chicken, an' I've been long on the dodge. Mebbe a little of my society won't hurt you none. You'll need to learn the country."

There was something sincere and likable about this outlaw.

"I dare say you're right," replied Duane, quietly. "And I'll go to Mercer with you."

Next moment he was riding down the road with Stevens. Duane had never been much of a talker, and now he found speech difficult. But his companion did not seem to mind that. He was a jocose, voluble fellow, probably glad now to hear the sound of his own voice. Duane listened, and sometimes he thought with a pang of the distinction of name and heritage of blood his father had left to him.

CHAPTER III

Late that day, a couple of hours before sunset, Duane and Stevens, having rested their horses in the shade of some mesquites near the town of Mercer, saddled up and prepared to move.

"Buck, as we're lookin' fer grub, an' not trouble, I reckon you'd better hang up out here," Stevens was saying, as he mounted. "You see, towns an' sheriffs an' rangers are always lookin' fer new fellers gone bad. They sort of forget most of the old boys, except those as are plumb bad. Now, nobody in Mercer will take notice of me. Reckon there's been a thousand men run into the river country to become outlaws since yours truly. You jest wait here an' be ready to ride hard. Mebbe my besettin' sin will go operatin' in spite of my good intentions. In which case there'll be—"

His pause was significant. He grinned, and his brown eyes danced with a kind of wild humor.

"Stevens, have you got any money?" asked Duane.

"Money!" exclaimed Luke, blankly. "Say, I haven't owned a two-bit piece since—wal, fer some time."

"I'll furnish money for grub," returned Duane. "And for whisky, too, providing you hurry back here—without making trouble."

"Shore you're a downright good pard," declared Stevens, in admiration, as he took the money. "I give my word, Buck, an' I'm here to say I never broke it yet. Lay low, an' look fer me back quick."

With that he spurred his horse and rode out of the mesquites toward the town. At that distance, about a quarter of a mile, Mercer appeared to be a cluster of low adobe houses set in a grove of cottonwoods. Pastures of alfalfa were dotted by horses and cattle. Duane saw a sheep-herder driving in a meager flock.

Presently Stevens rode out of sight into the town. Duane waited, hoping the outlaw would make good his word. Probably not a quarter of an hour had elapsed when Duane heard the clear reports of a Winchester rifle, the clatter of rapid hoof-beats, and yells unmistakably the kind to mean danger for a man like Stevens. Duane mounted and rode to the edge of the mesquites.

He saw a cloud of dust down the road and a bay horse running fast. Stevens apparently had not been wounded by any of the shots, for he had a steady seat in his saddle and his riding, even at that moment, struck Duane as admirable. He carried a large pack over the pommel, and he kept looking back. The shots had ceased, but the yells increased. Duane saw several men running and waving their arms. Then he spurred his horse and got into a swift stride, so Stevens would not pass him. Presently the outlaw caught up with him. Stevens was grinning, but there was now no fun in the dancing eyes. It was a devil that danced in them. His face seemed a shade paler.

"Was jest comin' out of the store," yelled Stevens.

"Run plumb into a rancher—who knowed me. He opened up with a rifle. Think they'll chase us."

They covered several miles before there were any signs of pursuit, and when horsemen did move into sight out of the cottonwoods Duane and his companion steadily drew farther away.

"No hosses in thet bunch to worry us," called out Stevens.

Duane had the same conviction, and he did not look back again. He rode somewhat to the fore, and was constantly aware of the rapid thudding of hoofs behind, as Stevens kept close to him. At sunset they reached the willow brakes and the river. Duane's horse was winded and lashed with sweat and lather. It was not until the crossing had been accomplished that Duane halted to rest his animal. Stevens was riding up the low, sandy bank. He reeled in the saddle. With an exclamation of surprise Duane leaped off and ran to the outlaw's side.

Stevens was pale, and his face bore beads of sweat. The whole front of his shirt was soaked with blood.

"You're shot!" cried Duane.

"Wal, who 'n hell said I wasn't? Would you mind givin' me a lift—on this here pack?"

Duane lifted the heavy pack down and then helped Stevens to dismount. The outlaw had a bloody foam on his lips, and he was spitting blood.

"Oh, why didn't you say so!" cried Duane. "I never thought. You seemed all right."

"Wal, Luke Stevens may be as gabby as an old woman, but sometimes he doesn't say anythin'. It wouldn't have done no good."

Duane bade him sit down, removed his shirt, and washed the blood from his breast and back. Stevens had been shot in the breast, fairly low down, and the bullet had gone clear through him. His ride, holding himself and that heavy pack in the saddle, had been a feat little short of marvelous. Duane did not see how it had been possible, and he felt no hope for the outlaw. But he plugged the wounds and bound them tightly.

"Feller's name was Brown," Stevens said. "Me an' him fell out over a hoss I stole from him over in Huntsville. We had a shootin'-scrape then. Wal, as I was straddlin' my hoss back there in Mercer I seen this Brown, an' seen him before he seen me. Could have killed him, too. But I wasn't breakin' my word to you. I kind of hoped he wouldn't spot me. But he did—an' fust shot he got me here. What do you think of this hole?"

"It's pretty bad," replied Duane; and he could not look the cheerful outlaw in the eyes.

"I reckon it is. Wal, I've had some bad wounds I lived over. Guess mebbe I can stand this one. Now, Buck, get me some place in the brakes, leave me some grub an' water at my hand, an' then you clear out."

"Leave you here alone?" asked Duane, sharply.

"Shore. You see, I can't keep up with you. Brown an' his friends will foller us across the river a ways. You've got to think of number one in this game."

"What would you do in my case?" asked Duane, curiously.

"Wal, I reckon I'd clear out an' save my hide," replied Stevens.

Duane felt inclined to doubt the outlaw's assertion. For his own part he decided his conduct without further speech. First he watered the horses, filled canteens and water bag, and then tied the pack upon his own horse. That done, he lifted Stevens upon his horse, and, holding him in the saddle, turned into the brakes, being careful to pick out hard or grassy ground that left little signs of tracks. Just about dark he ran across a trail that Stevens said was a good one to take into the wild country.

"Reckon we'd better keep right on in the dark—till I drop," concluded Stevens, with a laugh.

All that night Duane, gloomy and thoughtful, attentive to the wounded outlaw, walked the trail and never halted till daybreak. He was tired then and very hungry. Stevens seemed in bad shape, although he was still spirited and cheerful. Duane made camp. The outlaw refused food, but asked for both whisky and water. Then he stretched out.

"Buck, will you take off my boots?" he asked, with a faint smile on his pallid face.

Duane removed them, wondering if the outlaw had the thought that he did not want to die with his boots on. Stevens seemed to read his mind.

"Buck, my old daddy used to say thet I was born to be hanged. But I wasn't—an' dyin' with your boots on is the next wust way to croak."

"You've a chance to-to get over this," said Duane.

"Shore. But I want to be correct about the boots—an' say, pard, if I do go over, jest you remember thet I was appreciatin' of your kindness."

Then he closed his eyes and seemed to sleep.

Duane could not find water for the horses, but there was an abundance of dew-wet grass upon which he hobbled them. After that was done he prepared himself a much-needed meal. The sun was getting warm when he lay down to sleep, and when he awoke it was sinking in the west. Stevens was still alive, for he breathed heavily. The horses were in sight. All was quiet except the hum of insects in the brush. Duane listened awhile, then rose and went for the horses.

When he returned with them he found Stevens awake, bright-eyed, cheerful as usual, and apparently stronger.

"Wal, Buck, I'm still with you an' good fer another night's ride," he said. "Guess about all I need now is a big pull on thet bottle. Help me, will you? There! thet was bully. I ain't swallowin' my blood this evenin'. Mebbe I've bled all there was in me."

While Duane got a hurried meal for himself, packed up the little outfit, and saddled the horses Stevens kept on talking. He seemed to be in a hurry to tell Duane all about the country. Another night ride would put them beyond fear of pursuit, within striking distance of the Rio Grande and the hiding-places of the outlaws.

When it came time for mounting the horses Stevens said, "Reckon you can pull on my boots once more." In spite of the laugh accompanying the words Duane detected a subtle change in the outlaw's spirit.

On this night travel was facilitated by the fact that the trail was broad enough for two horses abreast, enabling Duane to ride while upholding Stevens in the saddle.

The difficulty most persistent was in keeping the horses in a walk. They were used to a trot, and that kind of gait would not do for Stevens. The red died out of the west; a pale afterglow prevailed for a while; darkness set in; then the broad expanse of blue darkened and the stars brightened. After a while Stevens ceased talking and drooped in his saddle. Duane kept the horses going, however, and the slow hours wore away. Duane thought the quiet night would never break to dawn, that there was no end to the melancholy, brooding plain. But at length a grayness blotted out the stars and mantled the level of mesquite and cactus.

Dawn caught the fugitives at a green camping-site on the bank of a rocky little stream. Stevens fell a dead weight into Duane's arms, and one look at the haggard face showed Duane that the outlaw had taken his last ride. He knew it, too. Yet that cheerfulness prevailed.

"Buck, my feet are orful tired packin' them heavy boots," he said, and seemed immensely relieved when Duane had removed them.

This matter of the outlaw's boots was strange, Duane thought. He made Stevens as comfortable as possible, then attended to his own needs. And the outlaw took up the thread of his conversation where he had left off the night before.

"This trail splits up a ways from here, an' every branch of it leads to a hole where you'll find men—a few, mebbe, like yourself—some like me—an' gangs of no-good hoss-thieves, rustlers, an' such. It's easy livin', Buck. I reckon, though, that you'll not find it easy. You'll never mix in. You'll be a lone wolf. I seen that right off. Wal, if a man can stand the loneliness, an' if he's quick on the draw, mebbe lone-wolfin' it is the best. Shore I don't know. But these fellers in here will be suspicious of a man who goes it alone. If they get a chance they'll kill you."

Stevens asked for water several times. He had forgotten or he did not want the whisky. His voice grew perceptibly weaker.

"Be quiet," said Duane. "Talking uses up your strength."

"Aw, I'll talk till—I'm done," he replied, doggedly. "See here, pard, you can gamble on what I'm tellin' you. An' it'll be useful. From this camp we'll—you'll meet men right along. An' none of them will be honest men. All the same, some are better'n others. I've lived along the river fer twelve years. There's three big gangs of outlaws. King Fisher—you know him, I reckon, fer he's half the time livin' among respectable folks. King is a pretty good feller. It'll do to tie up with him ant his gang. Now, there's Cheseldine, who hangs out in the Rim Rock way up the river. He's an outlaw chief. I never seen him, though I stayed once right in his camp. Late years he's got rich an' keeps back pretty well hid. But Bland—I knowed Bland fer years. An' I haven't any use fer him. Bland has the biggest gang. You ain't likely to miss strikin' his place sometime or other. He's got a regular town, I might say. Shore there's some gamblin' an' gun-fightin' goin' on at Bland's camp all the time. Bland has killed some twenty men, an' thet's not countin' greasers."

Here Stevens took another drink and then rested for a while.

"You ain't likely to get on with Bland," he resumed, presently. "You're too strappin' big an' good-lookin' to please the chief. Fer he's got women in his camp. Then he'd be jealous of your possibilities with a gun. Shore I reckon he'd be careful, though. Bland's no fool, an' he loves his hide. I reckon any of the other gangs would be better fer you when you ain't goin' it alone."

Apparently that exhausted the fund of information and advice Stevens had been eager to impart. He lapsed into silence and lay with closed eyes. Meanwhile the sun rose warm; the breeze waved the mesquites; the birds came down to splash in the shallow stream; Duane dozed in a comfortable seat. By and by something roused him. Stevens was once more talking, but with a changed tone.

"Feller's name—was Brown," he rambled. "We fell out—over a hoss I stole from him—in Huntsville. He stole it fuss. Brown's one of them sneaks—afraid of the open—he steals an' pretends to be honest. Say, Buck, mebbe you'll meet Brown some day—You an' me are pards now."

"I'll remember, if I ever meet him," said Duane.

That seemed to satisfy the outlaw. Presently he tried to lift his head, but had not the strength. A strange shade was creeping across the bronzed rough face.

"My feet are pretty heavy. Shore you got my boots off?"

Duane held them up, but was not certain that Stevens could see them. The outlaw closed his eyes again and muttered incoherently. Then he fell asleep. Duane believed that sleep was final. The day passed, with Duane watching and waiting. Toward sundown Stevens awoke, and his eyes seemed clearer. Duane went to get some fresh water, thinking his comrade would surely want some. When he returned Stevens made no sign that he wanted anything. There was something bright about him, and suddenly Duane realized what it meant.

"Pard, you—stuck—to me!" the outlaw whispered.

Duane caught a hint of gladness in the voice; he traced a faint surprise in the haggard face. Stevens seemed like a little child.

To Duane the moment was sad, elemental, big, with a burden of mystery he could not understand.

Duane buried him in a shallow arroyo and heaped up a pile of stones to mark the grave. That done, he saddled his comrade's horse, hung the weapons over the pommel; and, mounting his own steed, he rode down the trail in the gathering twilight.

CHAPTER IV

Two days later, about the middle of the forenoon, Duane dragged the two horses up the last ascent of an exceedingly rough trail and found himself on top of the Rim Rock, with a beautiful green valley at his feet, the yellow, sluggish Rio Grande shining in the sun, and the great, wild, mountainous barren of Mexico stretching to the south.

Duane had not fallen in with any travelers. He had taken the likeliest-looking trail he had come across. Where it had led him he had not the slightest idea, except that here was the river, and probably the inclosed valley was the retreat of some famous outlaw.

No wonder outlaws were safe in that wild refuge! Duane had spent the last two days climbing the roughest and most difficult trail he had ever seen. From the looks of the descent he imagined the worst part of his travel was yet to come. Not improbably it was two thousand feet down to the river. The wedge-shaped valley, green with alfalfa and cottonwood, and nestling down amid the bare walls of yellow rock, was a delight and a relief to his tired eyes. Eager to get down to a level and to find a place to rest, Duane began the descent.

The trail proved to be the kind that could not be descended slowly. He kept dodging rocks which his horses loosed behind him. And in a short time he reached the valley, entering at the apex of the wedge. A stream of clear water tumbled out of the rocks here, and most of it ran into irrigation-ditches. His horses drank thirstily. And he drank with that fullness and gratefulness common to the desert traveler finding sweet water. Then he mounted and rode down the valley wondering what would be his reception.

The valley was much larger than it had appeared from the high elevation. Well watered, green with grass and tree, and farmed evidently by good hands, it gave Duane a considerable surprise. Horses and cattle were everywhere. Every clump of cottonwoods surrounded a small adobe house. Duane saw Mexicans working in the fields and horsemen going to and fro. Presently he passed a house bigger than the others with a porch attached. A woman, young and pretty he thought, watched him from a door. No one else appeared to notice him.

Presently the trail widened into a road, and that into a kind of square lined by a number of adobe and log buildings of rudest structure. Within sight were horses, dogs, a couple of steers, Mexican women with children, and white men, all of whom appeared to be doing nothing. His advent created no interest until he rode up to the white men, who were lolling in the shade of a house. This place evidently was a store and saloon, and from the inside came a lazy hum of voices.

As Duane reined to a halt one of the loungers in the shade rose with a loud exclamation:

"Bust me if thet ain't Luke's hoss!"

The others accorded their interest, if not assent, by rising to advance toward Duane.

"How about it, Euchre? Ain't thet Luke's bay?" queried the first man.

"Plain as your nose," replied the fellow called Euchre.

"There ain't no doubt about thet, then," laughed another, "fer Bosomer's nose is shore plain on the landscape."

These men lined up before Duane, and as he coolly regarded them he thought they could have been recognized anywhere as desperadoes. The man called Bosomer, who had stepped forward, had a forbidding face which showed yellow eyes, an enormous nose, and a skin the color of dust, with a thatch of sandy hair.

"Stranger, who are you an' where in the hell did you git thet bay hoss?" he demanded. His yellow eyes took in Stevens's horse, then the weapons hung on the saddle, and finally turned their glinting, hard light upward to Duane.

Duane did not like the tone in which he had been addressed, and he remained silent. At least half his mind seemed busy with curious interest in regard to something that leaped inside him and made his breast feel tight. He recognized it as that strange emotion which had shot through him often of late, and which had decided him to go out to the meeting with Bain. Only now it was different, more powerful.

"Stranger, who are you?" asked another man, somewhat more civilly.

"My name's Duane," replied Duane, curtly.

"An' how'd you come by the hoss?"

Duane answered briefly, and his words were followed by a short silence, during which the men looked at him. Bosomer began to twist the ends of his beard.

"Reckon he's dead, all right, or nobody'd hev his hoss an' guns," presently said Euchre.

"Mister Duane," began Bosomer, in low, stinging tones, "I happen to be Luke Stevens's side-pardner."

Duane looked him over, from dusty, worn-out boots to his slouchy sombrero. That look seemed to inflame Bosomer.

"An' I want the hoss an' them guns," he shouted.

"You or anybody else can have them, for all I care. I just fetched them in. But the pack is mine," replied Duane. "And say, I befriended your pard. If you can't use a civil tongue you'd better cinch it."

"Civil? Haw, haw!" rejoined the outlaw. "I don't know you. How do we know you didn't plug Stevens, an' stole his hoss, an' jest happened to stumble down here?"

"You'll have to take my word, that's all," replied Duane, sharply.

"I ain't takin' your word! Savvy thet? An' I was Luke's pard!"

With that Bosomer wheeled and, pushing his companions aside, he stamped into the saloon, where his voice broke out in a roar.

Duane dismounted and threw his bridle.

"Stranger, Bosomer is shore hot-headed," said the man Euchre. He did not appear unfriendly, nor were the others hostile.

At this juncture several more outlaws crowded out of the door, and the one in the lead was a tall man of stalwart physique. His manner proclaimed him a leader. He had a long face, a flaming red beard, and clear, cold blue eyes that fixed in close scrutiny upon Duane. He was not a Texan; in truth, Duane did not recognize one of these outlaws as native to his state.

"I'm Bland," said the tall man, authoritatively. "Who're you and what're you doing here?"

Duane looked at Bland as he had at the others. This outlaw chief appeared to be reasonable, if he was not courteous. Duane told his story again, this time a little more in detail.

"I believe you," replied Bland, at once. "Think I know when a fellow is lying."

"I reckon you're on the right trail," put in Euchre. "Thet about Luke wantin' his boots took off—thet satisfies me. Luke hed a mortal dread of dyin' with his boots on."

At this sally the chief and his men laughed.

"You said Duane—Buck Duane?" queried Bland. "Are you a son of that Duane who was a gunfighter some years back?"

"Yes," replied Duane.

"Never met him, and glad I didn't," said Bland, with a grim humor. "So you got in trouble and had to go on the dodge? What kind of trouble?"

"Had a fight."

"Fight? Do you mean gun-play?" questioned Bland. He seemed eager, curious, speculative.

"Yes. It ended in gun-play, I'm sorry to say," answered Duane.

"Guess I needn't ask the son of Duane if he killed his man," went on Bland, ironically. "Well, I'm sorry you bucked against trouble in my camp. But as it is, I guess you'd be wise to make yourself scarce."

"Do you mean I'm politely told to move on?" asked Duane, quietly.

"Not exactly that," said Bland, as if irritated. "If this isn't a free place there isn't one on earth. Every man is equal here. Do you want to join my band?"

"No, I don't."

"Well, even if you did I imagine that wouldn't stop Bosomer. He's an ugly fellow. He's one of the few gunmen I've met who wants to kill somebody all the time. Most men like that are fourflushes. But Bosomer is all one color, and that's red. Merely for your own sake I advise you to hit the trail."

"Thanks. But if that's all I'll stay," returned Duane. Even as he spoke he felt that he did not know himself.

Bosomer appeared at the door, pushing men who tried to detain him, and as he jumped clear of a last reaching hand he uttered a snarl like an angry dog. Manifestly the short while he had spent inside the saloon had been devoted to drinking and talking himself into a frenzy. Bland and the other outlaws quickly moved aside, letting Duane stand alone. When Bosomer saw Duane standing motionless and watchful a strange change passed quickly in him. He halted in his tracks, and as he did that the men who had followed him out piled over one another in their hurry to get to one side.

Duane saw all the swift action, felt intuitively the meaning of it, and in Bosomer's sudden change of front. The outlaw was keen, and he had expected a shrinking, or at least a frightened antagonist. Duane knew he was neither. He felt like iron, and yet thrill after thrill ran through him. It was almost as if this situation had been one long familiar to him. Somehow he understood this yellow-eyed Bosomer. The outlaw had come out to kill him. And now, though somewhat checked by the stand of a stranger, he still meant to kill. Like so many desperadoes of his ilk, he was victim of a passion to kill for the sake of killing. Duane divined that no sudden animosity was driving Bosomer. It was just his chance. In that moment murder would have been joy to him. Very likely he had forgotten his pretext for a quarrel. Very probably his faculties were absorbed in conjecture as to Duane's possibilities.

But he did not speak a word. He remained motionless for a long moment, his eyes pale and steady, his right hand like a claw.

That instant gave Duane a power to read in his enemy's eyes the thought that preceded action. But Duane did not want to kill another man. Still he would have to fight, and he decided to cripple Bosomer. When Bosomer's hand moved Duane's gun was spouting fire. Two shots only—both from Duane's gun—and the outlaw fell with his right arm shattered. Bosomer cursed harshly and floundered in the dust, trying to reach the gun with his left hand. His comrades, however, seeing that Duane would not kill unless forced, closed in upon Bosomer and prevented any further madness on his part.

CHAPTER V

Of the outlaws present Euchre appeared to be the one most inclined to lend friendliness to curiosity; and he led Duane and the horses away to a small adobe shack. He tied the horses in an open shed and removed their saddles. Then, gathering up Stevens's weapons, he invited his visitor to enter the house.

It had two rooms—windows without coverings—bare floors. One room contained blankets, weapons, saddles, and bridles; the other a stone fireplace, rude table and bench, two bunks, a box cupboard, and various blackened utensils.

"Make yourself to home as long as you want to stay," said Euchre. "I ain't rich in this world's goods, but I own what's here, an' you're welcome."

"Thanks. I'll stay awhile and rest. I'm pretty well played out," replied Duane.

Euchre gave him a keen glance.

"Go ahead an' rest. I'll take your horses to grass." Euchre left Duane alone in the house. Duane relaxed then, and mechanically he wiped the sweat from his face. He was laboring under some kind of a spell or shock which did not pass off quickly. When it had worn away he took off his coat and belt and made himself comfortable on the blankets. And he had a thought that if he rested or slept what difference would it make on the morrow? No rest, no sleep could change the gray outlook of the future. He felt glad when Euchre came bustling in, and for the first time he took notice of the outlaw.

Euchre was old in years. What little hair he had was gray, his face clean-shaven and full of wrinkles; his eyes were half shut from long gazing through the sun and dust. He stooped. But his thin frame denoted strength and endurance still unimpaired.

"Hey a drink or a smoke?" he asked.

Duane shook his head. He had not been unfamiliar with whisky, and he had used tobacco moderately since he was sixteen. But now, strangely, he felt a disgust at the idea of stimulants. He did not understand clearly what he felt. There was that vague idea of something wild in his blood, something that made him fear himself.

Euchre wagged his old head sympathetically. "Reckon you feel a little sick. When it comes to shootin' I run. What's your age?"

"I'm twenty-three," replied Duane.

Euchre showed surprise. "You're only a boy! I thought you thirty anyways. Buck, I heard what you told Bland, an' puttin' thet with my own figgerin', I reckon you're no criminal yet. Throwin' a gun in self-defense—thet ain't no crime!"

Duane, finding relief in talking, told more about himself.

"Huh," replied the old man. "I've been on this river fer years, an' I've seen hundreds of boys come in on the dodge. Most of them, though, was no good. An' thet kind don't last long. This river country has been an' is the refuge fer criminals from all over the states. I've bunked with bank cashiers, forgers, plain thieves, an' out-an'-out murderers, all of which had no bizness on the Texas border. Fellers like Bland are exceptions. He's no Texan—you seen thet. The gang he rules here come from all over, an' they're tough cusses, you can bet on thet. They live fat an' easy. If it wasn't fer the fightin' among themselves they'd shore grow populous. The Rim Rock is no place for a peaceable, decent feller. I heard you tell Bland you wouldn't join his gang. Thet'll not make him take a likin' to you. Have you any money?"

"Not much," replied Duane.

"Could you live by gamblin'? Are you any good at cards?"

"No."

"You wouldn't steal hosses or rustle cattle?"

"No."

"When your money's gone how'n hell will you live? There ain't any work a decent feller could do. You can't herd with greasers. Why, Bland's men would shoot at you in the fields. What'll you do, son?"

"God knows," replied Duane, hopelessly. "I'll make my money last as long as possible—then starve."

"Wal, I'm pretty pore, but you'll never starve while I got anythin'."

Here it struck Duane again—that something human and kind and eager which he had seen in Stevens. Duane's estimate of outlaws had lacked this quality. He had not accorded them any virtues. To him, as to the outside world, they had been merely vicious men without one redeeming feature.

"I'm much obliged to you, Euchre," replied Duane. "But of course I won't live with any one unless I can pay my share."

"Have it any way you like, my son," said Euchre, good-humoredly. "You make a fire, an' I'll set about gettin' grub. I'm a sourdough, Buck. Thet man doesn't live who can beat my bread."

"How do you ever pack supplies in here?" asked Duane, thinking of the almost inaccessible nature of the valley.

"Some comes across from Mexico, an' the rest down the river. Thet river trip is a bird. It's more'n five hundred miles to any supply point. Bland has mozos, greaser boatmen. Sometimes, too, he gets supplies in from down-river. You see, Bland sells thousands of cattle in Cuba. An' all this stock has to go down by boat to meet the ships."

"Where on earth are the cattle driven down to the river?" asked Duane.

"Thet's not my secret," replied Euchre, shortly. "Fact is, I don't know. I've rustled cattle for Bland, but he never sent me through the Rim Rock with them."

Duane experienced a sort of pleasure in the realization that interest had been stirred in him. He was curious about Bland and his gang, and glad to have something to think about. For every once in a while he had a sensation that was almost like a pang. He wanted to forget. In the next hour he did forget, and enjoyed helping in the preparation and eating of the meal. Euchre, after washing and hanging up the several utensils, put on his hat and turned to go out.

"Come along or stay here, as you want," he said to Duane.

"I'll stay," rejoined Duane, slowly.

The old outlaw left the room and trudged away, whistling cheerfully.

Duane looked around him for a book or paper, anything to read; but all the printed matter he could find consisted of a few words on cartridge-boxes and an advertisement on the back of a tobacco-pouch. There seemed to be nothing for him to do. He had rested; he did not want to lie down any more. He began to walk to and fro, from one end of the room to the other. And as he walked he fell into the lately acquired habit of brooding over his misfortune.

Suddenly he straightened up with a jerk. Unconsciously he had drawn his gun. Standing there with the bright cold weapon in his hand, he looked at it in consternation. How had he come to draw it? With difficulty he traced his thoughts backward, but could not find any that was accountable for his act. He discovered, however, that he had a remarkable tendency to drop his hand to his gun. That might have come from the habit long practice in drawing had given him. Likewise, it might have come from a subtle sense, scarcely thought of at all, of the late, close, and inevitable relation between that weapon and himself. He was amazed to find that, bitter as he had grown at fate, the desire to live burned strong in him. If he had been as unfortunately situated, but with the difference that no man wanted to put him in jail or take his life, he felt that this burning passion to be free, to save himself, might not have been so powerful. Life certainly held no bright prospects for him. Already he had begun to despair of ever getting back to his home. But to give up like a white-hearted coward, to let himself be handcuffed and jailed, to run from a drunken, bragging cowboy, or be shot in cold blood by some border brute who merely wanted to add another notch to his gun—these things were impossible for Duane because there was in him the temper to fight. In that hour he yielded only to fate and the spirit inborn in him. Hereafter this gun must be a living part of him. Right then and there he returned to a practice he had long discontinued—the draw. It was now a stern, bitter, deadly business with him. He did not need to fire the gun, for accuracy was a gift and had become assured. Swiftness on the draw, however, could be improved, and he set himself to acquire the limit of speed possible to any man. He stood still in his tracks; he paced the room; he sat down, lay down, put himself in awkward positions; and from every position he practiced throwing his gun—practiced it till he was hot and tired and his arm ached and his hand burned. That practice he determined to keep up every day. It was one thing, at least, that would help pass the weary hours.

Later he went outdoors to the cooler shade of the cottonwoods. From this point he could see a good deal of the valley. Under different circumstances Duane felt that he would have enjoyed such a beautiful spot. Euchre's shack sat against the first rise of the slope of the wall, and Duane, by climbing a few rods, got a view of the whole valley. Assuredly it was an outlaw settle meet. He saw a good many Mexicans, who, of course, were hand and glove with Bland. Also he saw enormous flat-boats, crude of structure, moored along the banks of the river. The Rio Grande rolled away between high bluffs. A cable, sagging deep in the middle, was stretched over the wide yellow stream, and an old scow, evidently used as a ferry, lay anchored on the far shore.

The valley was an ideal retreat for an outlaw band operating on a big scale. Pursuit scarcely need be feared over the broken trails of the Rim Rock. And the open end of the valley could be defended against almost any number of men coming down the river. Access to Mexico was easy and quick. What puzzled Duane was how Bland got cattle down to the river, and he wondered if the rustler really did get rid of his stolen stock by use of boats.

Duane must have idled considerable time up on the hill, for when he returned to the shack Euchre was busily engaged around the camp-fire.

"Wal, glad to see you ain't so pale about the gills as you was," he said, by way of greeting. "Pitch in an' we'll soon have grub ready. There's shore one consolin' fact round this here camp."

"What's that?" asked Duane.

"Plenty of good juicy beef to eat. An' it doesn't cost a short bit."

"But it costs hard rides and trouble, bad conscience,

and life, too, doesn't it?"

"I ain't shore about the bad conscience. Mine never bothered me none. An' as for life, why, thet's cheap in Texas."

"Who is Bland?" asked Duane, quickly changing the subject. "What do you know about him?"

"We don't know who he is or where he hails from," replied Euchre. "Thet's always been somethin' to interest the gang. He must have been a young man when he struck Texas. Now he's middle-aged. I remember how years ago he was soft-spoken an' not rough in talk or act like he is now. Bland ain't likely his right name. He knows a lot. He can doctor you, an' he's shore a knowin' feller with tools. He's the kind thet rules men. Outlaws are always ridin' in here to join his gang, an' if it hadn't been fer the gamblin' an' gun-play he'd have a thousand men around him."

"How many in his gang now?"

"I reckon there's short of a hundred now. The number varies. Then Bland has several small camps up an' down the river. Also he has men back on the cattle-ranges."

"How does he control such a big force?" asked Duane. "Especially when his band's composed of bad men. Luke Stevens said he had no use for Bland. And I heard once somewhere that Bland was a devil."

"Thet's it. He is a devil. He's as hard as flint, violent in temper, never made any friends except his right-hand men, Dave Rugg an' Chess Alloway. Bland'll shoot at a wink. He's killed a lot of fellers, an' some fer nothin'. The reason thet outlaws gather round him an' stick is because he's a safe refuge, an' then he's well heeled. Bland is rich. They say he has a hundred thousand pesos hid somewhere, an' lots of gold. But he's free with money. He gambles when he's not off with a shipment of cattle. He throws money around. An' the fact is there's always plenty of money where he is. Thet's what holds the gang. Dirty, bloody money!"

"It's a wonder he hasn't been killed. All these years on the border!" exclaimed Duane.

"Wal," replied Euchre, dryly, "he's been quicker on the draw than the other fellers who hankered to kill him, thet's all."

Euchre's reply rather chilled Duane's interest for the moment. Such remarks always made his mind revolve round facts pertaining to himself.

"Speakin' of this here swift wrist game," went on Euchre, "there's been considerable talk in camp about your throwin' of a gun. You know, Buck, thet among us fellers—us hunted men—there ain't anythin' calculated to rouse respect like a slick hand with a gun. I heard Bland say this afternoon—an' he said it serious-like an' speculative—thet he'd never seen your equal. He was watchin' of you close, he said, an' just couldn't follow your hand when you drawed. All the fellers who seen you meet Bosomer had somethin' to say. Bo was about as handy with a gun as any man in this camp, barrin' Chess Alloway an' mebbe Bland himself. Chess is the captain with a Colt—or he was. An' he shore didn't like the references made about your speed. Bland was honest in acknowledgin' it, but he didn't like it, neither. Some of the fellers allowed your draw might have been just accident. But most of them figgered different. An' they all shut up when Bland told who an' what your Dad was. 'Pears to me I once seen your Dad in a gunscrape over at Santone, years ago. Wal, I put my oar in to-day among the fellers, an' I says: 'What ails you locoed gents? Did young Duane budge an inch when Bo came roarin' out, blood in his eye? Wasn't he cool an' quiet, steady of lips, an' weren't his eyes readin' Bo's mind? An' thet lightnin' draw—can't you-all see thet's a family gift?'"

Euchre's narrow eyes twinkled, and he gave the dough he was rolling a slap with his flour-whitened hand. Manifestly he had proclaimed himself a champion and partner of Duane's, with all the pride an old man could feel in a young one whom he admired.

"Wal," he resumed, presently, "thet's your introduction to the border, Buck. An' your card was a high trump. You'll be let severely alone by real gun-fighters an' men like Bland, Alloway, Rugg, an' the bosses of the other gangs. After all, these real men are men, you know, an' onless you cross them they're no more likely to interfere with you than you are with them. But there's a sight of fellers like Bosomer in the river country. They'll all want your game. An' every town you ride into will scare up some cowpuncher full of booze or a long-haired four-flush gunman or a sheriff—an' these men will be playin' to the crowd an' yellin' for your blood. Thet's the Texas of it. You'll have to hide fer ever in the brakes or you'll have to KILL such men. Buck, I reckon this ain't cheerful news to a decent chap like you. I'm only tellin' you because I've taken a likin' to you, an' I seen right off thet you ain't border-wise. Let's eat now, an' afterward we'll go out so the gang can see you're not hidin'."

When Duane went out with Euchre the sun was setting behind a blue range of mountains across the river in Mexico. The valley appeared to open to the southwest. It was a tranquil, beautiful scene. Somewhere in a house near at hand a woman was singing. And in the road Duane saw a little Mexican boy driving home some cows, one of which wore a bell. The sweet, happy voice of a woman and a whistling barefoot boy—these seemed utterly out of place here.

Euchre presently led to the square and the row of rough houses Duane remembered. He almost stepped on a wide imprint in the dust where Bosomer had confronted him. And a sudden fury beset him that he should be affected strangely by the sight of it.

"Let's have a look in here," said Euchre.

Duane had to bend his head to enter the door. He found himself in a very large room inclosed by adobe walls and roofed with brush. It was full of rude benches, tables, seats. At one corner a number of kegs and barrels lay side by side in a rack. A Mexican boy was lighting lamps hung on posts that sustained the log rafters of the roof.

"The only feller who's goin' to put a close eye on you is Benson," said Euchre. "He runs the place an' sells drinks. The gang calls him Jackrabbit Benson, because he's always got his eye peeled an' his ear cocked. Don't notice him if he looks you over, Buck. Benson is scared to death of every new-comer who rustles into

Bland's camp. An' the reason, I take it, is because he's done somebody dirt. He's hidin'. Not from a sheriff or ranger! Men who hide from them don't act like Jackrabbit Benson. He's hidin' from some guy who's huntin' him to kill him. Wal, I'm always expectin' to see some feller ride in here an' throw a gun on Benson. Can't say I'd be grieved."

Duane casually glanced in the direction indicated, and he saw a spare, gaunt man with a face strikingly white beside the red and bronze and dark skins of the men around him. It was a cadaverous face. The black mustache hung down; a heavy lock of black hair dropped down over the brow; deep-set, hollow, staring eyes looked out piercingly. The man had a restless, alert, nervous manner. He put his hands on the board that served as a bar and stared at Duane. But when he met Duane's glance he turned hurriedly to go on serving out liquor.

"What have you got against him?" inquired Duane, as he sat down beside Euchre. He asked more for something to say than from real interest. What did he care about a mean, haunted, craven-faced criminal?

"Wal, mebbe I'm cross-grained," replied Euchre, apologetically. "Shore an outlaw an' rustler such as me can't be touchy. But I never stole nothin' but cattle from some rancher who never missed 'em anyway. Thet sneak Benson—he was the means of puttin' a little girl in Bland's way."

"Girl?" queried Duane, now with real attention.

"Shore. Bland's great on women. I'll tell you about this girl when we get out of here. Some of the gang are goin' to be sociable, an' I can't talk about the chief."

During the ensuing half-hour a number of outlaws passed by Duane and Euchre, halted for a greeting or sat down for a moment. They were all gruff, loud-voiced, merry, and good-natured. Duane replied civilly and agreeably when he was personally addressed; but he refused all invitations to drink and gamble. Evidently he had been accepted, in a way, as one of their clan. No one made any hint of an allusion to his affair with Bosomer. Duane saw readily that Euchre was well liked. One outlaw borrowed money from him: another asked for tobacco.

By the time it was dark the big room was full of outlaws and Mexicans, most of whom were engaged at monte. These gamblers, especially the Mexicans, were intense and quiet. The noise in the place came from the drinkers, the loungers. Duane had seen gambling-resorts—some of the famous ones in San Antonio and El Paso, a few in border towns where license went unchecked. But this place of Jackrabbit Benson's impressed him as one where guns and knives were accessories to the game. To his perhaps rather distinguishing eye the most prominent thing about the gamesters appeared to be their weapons. On several of the tables were piles of silver—Mexican pesos—as large and high as the crown of his hat. There were also piles of gold and silver in United States coin. Duane needed no experienced eyes to see that betting was heavy and that heavy sums exchanged hands. The Mexicans showed a sterner obsession, an intenser passion. Some of the Americans staked freely, nonchalantly, as befitted men to whom money was nothing. These latter were manifestly winning, for there were brother outlaws there who wagered coin with grudging, sullen, greedy eyes. Boisterous talk and laughter among the drinking men drowned, except at intervals, the low, brief talk of the gamblers. The clink of coin sounded incessantly; sometimes just low, steady musical rings; and again, when a pile was tumbled quickly, there was a silvery crash. Here an outlaw pounded on a table with the butt of his gun; there another noisily palmed a roll of dollars while he studied his opponent's face. The noises, however, in Benson's den did not contribute to any extent to the sinister aspect of the place. That seemed to come from the grim and reckless faces, from the bent, intent heads, from the dark lights and shades. There were bright lights, but these served only to make the shadows. And in the shadows lurked unrestrained lust of gain, a spirit ruthless and reckless, a something at once suggesting lawlessness, theft, murder, and hell.

"Bland's not here to-night," Euchre was saying. "He left today on one of his trips, takin' Alloway an' some others. But his other man, Rugg, he's here. See him standin' with them three fellers, all close to Benson. Rugg's the little bow-legged man with the half of his face shot off. He's one-eyed. But he can shore see out of the one he's got. An', darn me! there's Hardin. You know him? He's got an outlaw gang as big as Bland's. Hardin is standin' next to Benson. See how quiet an' unassumin' he looks. Yes, thet's Hardin. He comes here once in a while to see Bland. They're friends, which's shore strange. Do you see thet greaser there—the one with gold an' lace on his sombrero? Thet's Manuel, a Mexican bandit. He's a great gambler. Comes here often to drop his coin. Next to him is Bill Marr—the feller with the bandana round his head. Bill rode in the other day with some fresh bullet-holes. He's been shot more'n any feller I ever heard of. He's full of lead. Funny, because Bill's no troublehunter, an', like me, he'd rather run than shoot. But he's the best rustler Bland's got—a grand rider, an' a wonder with cattle. An' see the tow-headed youngster. Thet's Kid Fuller, the kid of Bland's gang. Fuller has hit the pace hard, an' he won't last the year out on the border. He killed his sweetheart's father, got run out of Staceytown, took to stealin' hosses. An' next he's here with Bland. Another boy gone wrong, an' now shore a hard nut."

Euchre went on calling Duane's attention to other men, just as he happened to glance over them. Any one of them would have been a marked man in a respectable crowd. Here each took his place with more or less distinction, according to the record of his past wild prowess and his present possibilities. Duane, realizing that he was tolerated there, received in careless friendly spirit by this terrible class of outcasts, experienced a feeling of revulsion that amounted almost to horror. Was his being there not an ugly dream? What had he in common with such ruffians? Then in a flash of memory came the painful proof—he was a criminal in sight of Texas law; he, too, was an outcast.

For the moment Duane was wrapped up in painful reflections; but Euchre's heavy hand, clapping with a warning hold on his arm, brought him back to outside things.

The hum of voices, the clink of coin, the loud laughter had ceased. There was a silence that manifestly had followed some unusual word or action sufficient to still the room. It was broken by a harsh curse and the scrape of a bench on the floor. Some man had risen.

"You stacked the cards, you—!"

"Say that twice," another voice replied, so different in its cool, ominous tone from the other.

"I'll say it twice," returned the first gamester, in hot haste. "I'll say it three times. I'll whistle it. Are you deaf? You light-fingered gent! You stacked the cards!"

Silence ensued, deeper than before, pregnant with meaning. For all that Duane saw, not an outlaw moved for a full moment. Then suddenly the room was full of disorder as men rose and ran and dived everywhere.

"Run or duck!" yelled Euchre, close to Duane's ear. With that he dashed for the door. Duane leaped after him. They ran into a jostling mob. Heavy gun-shots and hoarse yells hurried the crowd Duane was with pell-mell out into the darkness. There they all halted, and several peeped in at the door.

"Who was the Kid callin'?" asked one outlaw.

"Bud Marsh," replied another.

"I reckon them fust shots was Bud's. Adios Kid. It was comin' to him," went on yet another.

"How many shots?"

"Three or four, I counted."

"Three heavy an' one light. Thet light one was the

Kid's.38. Listen! There's the Kid hollerin' now. He ain't cashed, anyway."

At this juncture most of the outlaws began to file back into the room. Duane thought he had seen and heard enough in Benson's den for one night and he started slowly down the walk. Presently Euchre caught up with him.

"Nobody hurt much, which's shore some strange," he said. "The Kid—young Fuller thet I was tellin' you about—he was drinkin' an' losin'. Lost his nut, too, callin' Bud Marsh thet way. Bud's as straight at cards as any of 'em. Somebody grabbed Bud, who shot into the roof. An' Fuller's arm was knocked up. He only hit a greaser."

CHAPTER VI

Next morning Duane found that a moody and despondent spell had fastened on him. Wishing to be alone, he went out and walked a trail leading round the river bluff. He thought and thought. After a while he made out that the trouble with him probably was that he could not resign himself to his fate. He abhorred the possibility chance seemed to hold in store for him. He could not believe there was no hope. But what to do appeared beyond his power to tell.

Duane had intelligence and keenness enough to see his peril—the danger threatening his character as a man, just as much as that which threatened his life. He cared vastly more, he discovered, for what he considered honor and integrity than he did for life. He saw that it was bad for him to be alone. But, it appeared, lonely months and perhaps years inevitably must be his. Another thing puzzled him. In the bright light of day he could not recall the state of mind that was his at twilight or dusk or in the dark night. By day these visitations became to him what they really were—phantoms of his conscience. He could dismiss the thought of them then. He could scarcely remember or believe that this strange feat of fancy or imagination had troubled him, pained him, made him sleepless and sick.

That morning Duane spent an unhappy hour wrestling decision out of the unstable condition of his mind. But at length he determined to create interest in all that he came across and so forget himself as much as possible. He had an opportunity now to see just what the outlaw's life really was. He meant to force himself to be curious, sympathetic, clear-sighted. And he would stay there in the valley until its possibilities had been exhausted or until circumstances sent him out upon his uncertain way.

When he returned to the shack Euchre was cooking dinner.

"Say, Buck, I've news for you," he said; and his tone conveyed either pride in his possession of such news or pride in Duane. "Feller named Bradley rode in this mornin'. He's heard some about you. Told about the ace of spades they put over the bullet holes in thet cowpuncher Bain you plugged. Then there was a rancher shot at a water-hole twenty miles south of Wellston. Reckon you didn't do it?"

"No, I certainly did not," replied Duane.

"Wal, you get the blame. It ain't nothin' for a feller to be saddled with gun-plays he never made. An', Buck, if you ever get famous, as seems likely, you'll be blamed for many a crime. The border'll make an outlaw an' murderer out of you. Wal, thet's enough of thet. I've more news. You're goin' to be popular."

"Popular? What do you mean?"

"I met Bland's wife this mornin'. She seen you the other day when you rode in. She shore wants to meet you, an' so do some of the other women in camp. They always want to meet the new fellers who've just come in. It's lonesome for women here, an' they like to hear news from the towns."

"Well, Euchre, I don't want to be impolite, but I'd rather not meet any women," rejoined Duane.

"I was afraid you wouldn't. Don't blame you much. Women are hell. I was hopin', though, you might talk a little to thet poor lonesome kid."

"What kid?" inquired Duane, in surprise.

"Didn't I tell you about Jennie—the girl Bland's holdin' here—the one Jackrabbit Benson had a hand in stealin'?"

"You mentioned a girl. That's all. Tell me now," replied Duane, abruptly.

"Wal, I got it this way. Mebbe it's straight, an' mebbe it ain't. Some years ago Benson made a trip over the river to buy mescal an' other drinks. He'll sneak over there once in a while. An' as I get it he run across a gang of greasers with some gringo prisoners. I don't know, but I reckon there was some barterin', perhaps murderin'. Anyway, Benson fetched the girl back. She was more dead than alive. But it turned out she was only starved an' scared half to death. She hadn't been harmed. I reckon she was then about fourteen years old. Benson's idee, he said, was to use her in his den sellin' drinks an' the like. But I never went much on Jackrabbit's word. Bland seen the kid right off and took her—bought her from Benson. You can gamble Bland didn't do thet from notions of chivalry. I ain't gainsayin, however, but thet Jennie was better off with Kate Bland. She's been hard on Jennie, but she's kept

Bland an' the other men from treatin' the kid shameful. Late Jennie has growed into an all-fired pretty girl, an' Kate is powerful jealous of her. I can see hell brewin' over there in Bland's cabin. Thet's why I wish you'd come over with me. Bland's hardly ever home. His wife's invited you. Shore, if she gets sweet on you, as she has on—Wal, thet 'd complicate matters. But you'd get to see Jennie, an' mebbe you could help her. Mind, I ain't hintin' nothin'. I'm just wantin' to put her in your way. You're a man an' can think fer yourself. I had a baby girl once, an' if she'd lived she be as big as Jennie now, an', by Gawd, I wouldn't want her here in Bland's camp."

"I'll go, Euchre. Take me over," replied Duane. He felt Euchre's eyes upon him. The old outlaw, however, had no more to say.

In the afternoon Euchre set off with Duane, and soon they reached Bland's cabin. Duane remembered it as the one where he had seen the pretty woman watching him ride by. He could not recall what she looked like. The cabin was the same as the other adobe structures in the valley, but it was larger and pleasantly located rather high up in a grove of cottonwoods. In the windows and upon the porch were evidences of a woman's hand. Through the open door Duane caught a glimpse of bright Mexican blankets and rugs.

Euchre knocked upon the side of the door.

"Is that you, Euchre?" asked a girl's voice, low, hesitatingly. The tone of it, rather deep and with a note of fear, struck Duane. He wondered what she would be like.

"Yes, it's me, Jennie. Where's Mrs. Bland?" answered Euchre.

"She went over to Deger's. There's somebody sick," replied the girl.

Euchre turned and whispered something about luck. The snap of the outlaw's eyes was added significance to Duane.

"Jennie, come out or let us come in. Here's the young man I was tellin' you about," Euchre said.

"Oh, I can't! I look so—so—"

"Never mind how you look," interrupted the outlaw, in a whisper. "It ain't no time to care fer thet. Here's young Duane. Jennie, he's no rustler, no thief. He's different. Come out, Jennie, an' mebbe he'll—"

Euchre did not complete his sentence. He had spoken low, with his glance shifting from side to side.

But what he said was sufficient to bring the girl quickly. She appeared in the doorway with downcast eyes and a stain of red in her white cheek. She had a pretty, sad face and bright hair.

"Don't be bashful, Jennie," said Euchre. "You an' Duane have a chance to talk a little. Now I'll go fetch Mrs. Bland, but I won't be hurryin'."

With that Euchre went away through the cottonwoods.

"I'm glad to meet you, Miss—Miss Jennie," said Duane. "Euchre didn't mention your last name. He asked me to come over to—"

Duane's attempt at pleasantry halted short when Jennie lifted her lashes to look at him. Some kind of a shock went through Duane. Her gray eyes were beautiful, but it had not been beauty that cut short his speech. He seemed to see a tragic struggle between hope and doubt that shone in her piercing gaze. She kept looking, and Duane could not break the silence. It was no ordinary moment.

"What did you come here for?" she asked, at last.

"To see you," replied Duane, glad to speak.

"Why?"

"Well—Euchre thought—he wanted me to talk to you, cheer you up a bit," replied Duane, somewhat lamely. The earnest eyes embarrassed him.

"Euchre's good. He's the only person in this awful place who's been good to me. But he's afraid of Bland. He said you were different. Who are you?"

Duane told her.

"You're not a robber or rustler or murderer or some bad man come here to hide?"

"No, I'm not," replied Duane, trying to smile.

"Then why are you here?"

"I'm on the dodge. You know what that means. I got in a shooting-scrape at home and had to run off. When it blows over I hope to go back."

"But you can't be honest here?"

"Yes, I can."

"Oh, I know what these outlaws are. Yes, you're different." She kept the strained gaze upon him, but hope was kindling, and the hard lines of her youthful face were softening.

Something sweet and warm stirred deep in Duane as he realized the unfortunate girl was experiencing a birth of trust in him.

"O God! Maybe you're the man to save me—to take me away before it's too late."

Duane's spirit leaped.

"Maybe I am," he replied, instantly.

She seemed to check a blind impulse to run into his arms. Her cheek flamed, her lips quivered, her bosom swelled under her ragged dress. Then the glow began to fade; doubt once more assailed her.

"It can't be. You're only—after me, too, like Bland—like all of them."

Duane's long arms went out and his hands clasped her shoulders. He shook her.

"Look at me—straight in the eye. There are decent men. Haven't you a father—a brother?"

"They're dead—killed by raiders. We lived in Dimmit County. I was carried away," Jennie replied, hurriedly. She put up an appealing hand to him. "Forgive me. I believe—I know you're good. It was only—I live so much in fear—I'm half crazy—I've almost forgotten what good men are like, Mister Duane, you'll help me?"

"Yes, Jennie, I will. Tell me how. What must I do? Have you any plan?"

"Oh no. But take me away."

"I'll try," said Duane, simply. "That won't be easy, though. I must have time to think. You must help me. There are many things to consider. Horses, food, trails, and then the best time to make the attempt. Are you watched—kept prisoner?"

"No. I could have run off lots of times. But I was afraid. I'd only have fallen into worse hands. Euchre has told me that. Mrs. Bland beats me, half starves me, but she has kept me from her husband and these other dogs. She's been as good as that, and I'm grateful. She hasn't done it for love of me, though. She always hated me. And lately she's growing jealous. There was' a man came here by the name of Spence—so he called himself. He tried to be kind to me. But she wouldn't let him. She was in love with him. She's a bad woman. Bland finally shot Spence, and that ended that. She's been jealous ever since. I hear her fighting with Bland about me. She swears she'll kill me before he gets me. And Bland laughs in her face. Then I've heard Chess Alloway try to persuade Bland to give me to him. But Bland doesn't laugh then. Just lately before Bland went away things almost came to a head. I couldn't sleep. I wished Mrs. Bland would kill me. I'll certainly kill myself if they ruin me. Duane, you must be quick if you'd save me."

"I realize that," replied he, thoughtfully. "I think my difficulty will be to fool Mrs. Bland. If she suspected me she'd have the whole gang of outlaws on me at once."

"She would that. You've got to be careful—and quick."

"What kind of woman is she?" inquired Duane.

"She's—she's brazen. I've heard her with her lovers. They get drunk sometimes when Bland's away. She's got a terrible temper. She's vain. She likes flattery. Oh, you could fool her easy enough if you'd lower yourself to—to—"

"To make love to her?" interrupted Duane.

Jennie bravely turned shamed eyes to meet his.

"My girl, I'd do worse than that to get you away from here," he said, bluntly.

"But—Duane," she faltered, and again she put out the appealing hand. "Bland will kill you."

Duane made no reply to this. He was trying to still a rising strange tumult in his breast. The old emotion—the rush of an instinct to kill! He turned cold all over.

"Chess Alloway will kill you if Bland doesn't," went on Jennie, with her tragic eyes on Duane's.

"Maybe he will," replied Duane. It was difficult for him to force a smile. But he achieved one.

"Oh, better take me off at once," she said. "Save me without risking so much—without making love to Mrs. Bland!"

"Surely, if I can. There! I see Euchre coming with a woman."

"That's her. Oh, she mustn't see me with you."

"Wait—a moment," whispered Duane, as Jennie slipped indoors. "We've settled it. Don't forget. I'll find some way to get word to you, perhaps through Euchre. Meanwhile keep up your courage. Remember I'll save you somehow. We'll try strategy first. Whatever you see or hear me do, don't think less of me—"

Jennie checked him with a gesture and a wonderful gray flash of eyes.

"I'll bless you with every drop of blood in my heart," she whispered, passionately.

It was only as she turned away into the room that Duane saw she was lame and that she wore Mexican sandals over bare feet.

He sat down upon a bench on the porch and directed his attention to the approaching couple. The trees of the grove were thick enough for him to make reasonably sure that Mrs. Bland had not seen him talking to Jennie. When the outlaw's wife drew near Duane saw that she was a tall, strong, full-bodied woman, rather good-looking with a fullblown, bold attractiveness. Duane was more concerned with her expression than with her good looks; and as she appeared unsuspicious he felt relieved. The situation then took on a singular zest.

Euchre came up on the porch and awkwardly introduced Duane to Mrs. Bland. She was young, probably not over twenty-five, and not quite so prepossessing at close range. Her eyes were large, rather prominent, and brown in color. Her mouth, too, was large, with the lips full, and she had white teeth.

Duane took her proffered hand and remarked frankly that he was glad to meet her.

Mrs. Bland appeared pleased; and her laugh, which followed, was loud and rather musical.

"Mr. Duane—Buck Duane, Euchre said, didn't he?" she asked.

"Buckley," corrected Duane. "The nickname's not of my choosing."

"I'm certainly glad to meet you, Buckley Duane," she said, as she took the seat Duane offered her. "Sorry to have been out. Kid Fuller's lying over at Deger's. You know he was shot last night. He's got fever to-day. When Bland's away I have to nurse all these shot-up boys, and it sure takes my time. Have you been waiting here alone? Didn't see that slattern girl of mine?"

She gave him a sharp glance. The woman had an extraordinary play of feature, Duane thought, and unless she was smiling was not pretty at all.

"I've been alone," replied Duane. "Haven't seen anybody but a sick-looking girl with a bucket. And she ran when she saw me."

"That was Jen," said Mrs. Bland. "She's the kid we keep here, and she sure hardly pays her keep. Did Euchre tell you about her?"

"Now that I think of it, he did say something or other."

"What did he tell you about me?" bluntly asked Mrs. Bland.

"Wal, Kate," replied Euchre, speaking for himself, "you needn't worry none, for I told Buck nothin' but compliments."

Evidently the outlaw's wife liked Euchre, for her keen glance rested with amusement upon him.

"As for Jen, I'll tell you her story some day," went on the woman. "It's a common enough story along this river. Euchre here is a tender-hearted old fool, and Jen has taken him in."

"Wal, seein' as you've got me figgered correct," replied Euchre, dryly, "I'll go in an' talk to Jennie if I may."

"Certainly. Go ahead. Jen calls you her best friend," said Mrs. Bland, amiably. "You're always fetching some Mexican stuff, and that's why, I guess."

When Euchre had shuffled into the house Mrs. Bland turned to Duane with curiosity and interest in her gaze.

"Bland told me about you."

"What did he say?" queried Duane, in pretended alarm.

"Oh, you needn't think he's done you dirt Bland's not that kind of a man. He said: 'Kate, there's a young fellow in camp—rode in here on the dodge. He's no criminal, and he refused to join my band. Wish he would. Slickest hand with a gun I've seen for many a day! I'd like to see him and Chess meet out there in the road.' Then Bland went on to tell how you and Bosomer came together."

"What did you say?" inquired Duane, as she paused.

"Me? Why, I asked him what you looked like," she replied, gayly.

"Well?" went on Duane.

"Magnificent chap, Bland said. Bigger than any man in the valley. Just a great blue-eyed sunburned boy!"

"Humph!" exclaimed Duane. "I'm sorry he led you to expect somebody worth seeing."

"But I'm not disappointed," she returned, archly. "Duane, are you going to stay long here in camp?"

"Yes, till I run out of money and have to move. Why?"

Mrs. Bland's face underwent one of the singular changes. The smiles and flushes and glances, all that had been coquettish about her, had lent her a certain attractiveness, almost beauty and youth. But with some powerful emotion she changed and instantly became a woman of discontent, Duane imagined, of deep, violent nature.

"I'll tell you, Duane," she said, earnestly, "I'm sure glad if you mean to bide here awhile. I'm a miserable woman, Duane. I'm an outlaw's wife, and I hate him and the life I have to lead. I come of a good family in Brownsville. I never knew Bland was an outlaw till long after he married me. We were separated at times, and I imagined he was away on business. But the truth came out. Bland shot my own cousin, who told me. My family cast me off, and I had to flee with Bland. I was only eighteen then. I've lived here since. I never see a decent woman or man. I never hear anything about my old home or folks or friends. I'm buried here—buried alive with a lot of thieves and murderers. Can you blame me for being glad to see a young fellow—a gentleman—like the boys I used to go with? I tell you it makes me feel full—I want to cry. I'm sick for somebody to talk to. I have no children, thank God! If I had I'd not stay here. I'm sick of this hole. I'm lonely—"

There appeared to be no doubt about the truth of all this. Genuine emotion checked, then halted the hurried speech. She broke down and cried. It seemed strange to Duane that an outlaw's wife—and a woman who fitted her consort and the wild nature of their surroundings—should have weakness enough to weep. Duane believed and pitied her.

"I'm sorry for you," he said.

"Don't be SORRY for me," she said. "That only makes me see the—the difference between you and me. And don't pay any attention to what these outlaws say about me. They're ignorant. They couldn't understand me. You'll hear that Bland killed men who ran after me. But that's a lie. Bland, like all the other outlaws along this river, is always looking for somebody to kill. He SWEARS not, but I don't believe him. He explains that gunplay gravitates to men who are the real thing—that it is provoked by the four-flushes, the bad men. I don't know. All I know is that somebody is being killed every other day. He hated Spence before Spence ever saw me."

"Would Bland object if I called on you occasionally?" inquired Duane.

"No, he wouldn't. He likes me to have friends. Ask him yourself when he comes back. The trouble has been that two or three of his men fell in love with me, and when half drunk got to fighting. You're not going to do that."

"I'm not going to get half drunk, that's certain," replied Duane.

He was surprised to see her eyes dilate, then glow with fire. Before she could reply Euchre returned to the porch, and that put an end to the conversation.

Duane was content to let the matter rest there, and had little more to say. Euchre and Mrs. Bland talked and joked, while Duane listened. He tried to form some estimate of her character. Manifestly she had suffered a wrong, if not worse, at Bland's hands. She was bitter, morbid, overemotional. If she was a liar, which seemed likely enough, she was a frank one, and believed herself. She had no cunning. The thing which struck Duane so forcibly was that she thirsted for respect. In that, better than in her weakness of vanity, he thought he had discovered a trait through which he could manage her.

Once, while he was revolving these thoughts, he happened to glance into the house, and deep in the shadow of a corner he caught a pale gleam of Jennie's face with great, staring eyes on him. She had been watching him, listening to what he said. He saw from her expression that she had realized what had been so hard for her to believe. Watching his chance, he flashed a look at her; and then it seemed to him the change in her face was wonderful.

Later, after he had left Mrs. Bland with a meaning "Adios—manana," and was walking along beside the old outlaw, he found himself thinking of the girl instead of the woman, and of how he had seen her face blaze with hope and gratitude.

CHAPTER VII

That night Duane was not troubled by ghosts haunting his waking and sleeping hours. He awoke feeling bright and eager, and grateful to Euchre for having put something worth while into his mind. During breakfast, however, he was unusually thoughtful, working over the idea of how much or how little he would confide in the outlaw. He was aware of Euchre's scrutiny.

"Wal," began the old man, at last, "how'd you make out with the kid?"

"Kid?" inquired Duane, tentatively.

"Jennie, I mean. What'd you An' she talk about?"

"We had a little chat. You know you wanted me to cheer her up."

Euchre sat with coffee-cup poised and narrow eyes studying Duane.

"Reckon you cheered her, all right. What I'm afeared of is mebbe you done the job too well."

"How so?"

"Wal, when I went in to Jen last night I thought she was half crazy. She was burstin' with excitement, an' the look in her eyes hurt me. She wouldn't tell me a darn word you said. But she hung onto my hands, an' showed every way without speakin' how she wanted to thank me fer bringin' you over. Buck, it was plain to me thet you'd either gone the limit or else you'd been kinder prodigal of cheer an' hope. I'd hate to think you'd led Jennie to hope more'n ever would come true."

Euchre paused, and, as there seemed no reply forthcoming, he went on:

"Buck, I've seen some outlaws whose word was good. Mine is. You can trust me. I trusted you, didn't I, takin' you over there an' puttin' you wise to my tryin' to help thet poor kid?"

Thus enjoined by Euchre, Duane began to tell the conversations with Jennie and Mrs. Bland word for word. Long before he had reached an end Euchre set down the coffee-cup and began to stare, and at the conclusion of the story his face lost some of its red color and beads of sweat stood out thickly on his brow.

"Wal, if thet doesn't floor me!" he ejaculated, blinking at Duane. "Young man, I figgered you was some swift, an' sure to make your mark on this river; but I reckon I missed your real caliber. So thet's what it means to be a man! I guess I'd forgot. Wal, I'm old, an' even if my heart was in the right place I never was built fer big stunts. Do you know what it'll take to do all you promised Jen?"

"I haven't any idea," replied Duane, gravely.

"You'll have to pull the wool over Kate Bland's eyes, ant even if she falls in love with you, which's shore likely, thet won't be easy. An' she'd kill you in a minnit, Buck, if she ever got wise. You ain't mistaken her none, are you?"

"Not me, Euchre. She's a woman. I'd fear her more than any man."

"Wal, you'll have to kill Bland an' Chess Alloway an' Rugg, an' mebbe some others, before you can ride off into the hills with thet girl."

"Why? Can't we plan to be nice to Mrs. Bland and then at an opportune time sneak off without any gun-play?"

"Don't see how on earth," returned Euchre, earnestly. "When Bland's away he leaves all kinds of spies an' scouts watchin' the valley trails. They've all got rifles. You couldn't git by them. But when the boss is home there's a difference. Only, of course, him an' Chess keep their eyes peeled. They both stay to home pretty much, except when they're playin' monte or poker over at Benson's. So I say the best bet is to pick out a good time in the afternoon, drift over careless-like with a couple of hosses, choke Mrs. Bland or knock her on the head, take Jennie with you, an' make a rush to git out of the valley. If you had luck you might pull thet stunt without throwin' a gun. But I reckon the best figgerin' would include dodgin' some lead an' leavin' at least Bland or Alloway dead behind you. I'm figgerin', of course, thet when they come home an' find out you're visitin' Kate frequent they'll jest naturally look fer results. Chess don't like you, fer no reason except you're swift on the draw—mebbe swifter 'n him. Thet's the hell of this gun-play business. No one can ever tell who's the swifter of two gunmen till they meet. Thet fact holds a fascination mebbe you'll learn some day. Bland would treat you civil onless there was reason not to, an' then I don't believe he'd invite himself to a meetin' with you. He'd set Chess or Rugg to put you out of the way. Still Bland's no coward, an' if you came across him at a bad moment you'd have to be quicker 'n you was with Bosomer."

"All right. I'll meet what comes," said Duane, quickly. "The great point is to have horses ready and pick the right moment, then rush the trick through."

"Thet's the ONLY chance fer success. An' you can't do it alone."

"I'll have to. I wouldn't ask you to help me. Leave you behind!"

"Wal, I'll take my chances," replied Euchre, gruffly. "I'm goin' to help Jennie, you can gamble your last peso on thet. There's only four men in this camp who would shoot me—Bland, an' his right-hand pards, an' thet rabbit-faced Benson. If you happened to put out Bland and Chess, I'd stand a good show with the other two. Anyway, I'm old an' tired—what's the difference if I do git plugged? I can risk as much as you, Buck, even if I am afraid of gun-play. You said correct, 'Hosses ready, the right minnit, then rush the trick.' Thet much 's settled. Now let's figger all the little details."

They talked and planned, though in truth it was Euchre who planned, Duane who listened and agreed. While awaiting the return of Bland and his lieutenants it would be well for Duane to grow friendly with the other outlaws, to sit in a few games of monte, or show a willingness to spend a little money. The two schemers were to call upon Mrs. Bland every day—

Euchre to carry messages of cheer and warning to Jennie, Duane to blind the elder woman at any cost. These preliminaries decided upon, they proceeded to put them into action.

No hard task was it to win the friendship of the most of those good-natured outlaws. They were used to men of a better order than theirs coming to the hidden camps and sooner or later sinking to their lower level. Besides, with them everything was easy come, easy go. That was why life itself went on so carelessly and usually ended so cheaply. There were men among them, however, that made Duane feel that terrible inexplicable wrath rise in his breast. He could not bear to be near them. He could not trust himself. He felt that any instant a word, a deed, something might call too deeply to that instinct he could no longer control. Jackrabbit Benson was one of these men. Because of him and other outlaws of his ilk Duane could scarcely ever forget the reality of things. This was a hidden valley, a robbers' den, a rendezvous for murderers, a wild place stained red by deeds of wild men. And because of that there was always a charged atmosphere. The merriest, idlest, most careless moment might in the flash of an eye end in ruthless and tragic action. In an assemblage of desperate characters it could not be otherwise. The terrible thing that Duane sensed was this. The valley was beautiful, sunny, fragrant, a place to dream in; the mountaintops were always blue or gold rimmed, the yellow river slid slowly and majestically by, the birds sang in the cottonwoods, the horses grazed and pranced, children played and women longed for love, freedom, happiness; the outlaws rode in and out, free with money and speech; they lived comfortably in their adobe homes, smoked, gambled, talked, laughed, whiled away the idle hours—and all the time life there was wrong, and the simplest moment might be precipitated by that evil into the most awful of contrasts. Duane felt rather than saw a dark, brooding shadow over the valley.

Then, without any solicitation or encouragement from Duane, the Bland woman fell passionately in love with him. His conscience was never troubled about the beginning of that affair. She launched herself. It took no great perspicuity on his part to see that. And the thing which evidently held her in check was the newness, the strangeness, and for the moment the all-satisfying fact of his respect for her. Duane exerted himself to please, to amuse, to interest, to fascinate her, and always with deference. That was his strong point, and it had made his part easy so far. He believed he could carry the whole scheme through without involving himself any deeper.

He was playing at a game of love—playing with life and deaths Sometimes he trembled, not that he feared Bland or Alloway or any other man, but at the deeps of life he had come to see into. He was carried out of his old mood. Not once since this daring motive had stirred him had he been haunted by the phantom of Bain beside his bed. Rather had he been haunted by Jennie's sad face, her wistful smile, her eyes. He never was able to speak a word to her. What little communication he had with her was through Euchre, who carried short messages. But he caught glimpses of her every time he went to the Bland house. She contrived somehow to pass door or window, to give him a look when chance afforded. And Duane discovered with surprise that these moments were more thrilling to him than any with Mrs. Bland. Often Duane knew Jennie was sitting just inside the window, and then he felt inspired in his talk, and it was all made for her. So at least she came to know him while as yet she was almost a stranger. Jennie had been instructed by Euchre to listen, to understand that this was Duane's only chance to help keep her mind from constant worry, to gather the import of every word which had a double meaning.

Euchre said that the girl had begun to wither under the strain, to burn up with intense hope which had flamed within her. But all the difference Duane could see was a paler face and darker, more wonderful eyes. The eyes seemed to be entreating him to hurry, that time was flying, that soon it might be too late. Then there was another meaning in them, a light, a strange fire wholly inexplicable to Duane. It was only a flash gone in an instant. But he remembered it because he had never seen it in any other woman's eyes. And all through those waiting days he knew that Jennie's face, and especially the warm, fleeting glance she gave him, was responsible for a subtle and gradual change in him. This change he fancied, was only that through remembrance of her he got rid of his pale, sickening ghosts.

One day a careless Mexican threw a lighted cigarette

up into the brush matting that served as a ceiling for Benson's den, and there was a fire which left little more than the adobe walls standing. The result was that while repairs were being made there was no gambling and drinking. Time hung very heavily on the hands of some two-score outlaws. Days passed by without a brawl, and Bland's valley saw more successive hours of peace than ever before. Duane, however, found the hours anything but empty. He spent more time at Mrs. Bland's; he walked miles on all the trails leading out of the valley; he had a care for the condition of his two horses.

Upon his return from the latest of these tramps Euchre suggested that they go down to the river to the boat-landing.

"Ferry couldn't run ashore this mornin'," said Euchre. "River gettin' low an' sand-bars makin' it hard fer hosses. There's a greaser freight-wagon stuck in the mud. I reckon we might hear news from the freighters. Bland's supposed to be in Mexico."

Nearly all the outlaws in camp were assembled on the riverbank, lolling in the shade of the cottonwoods. The heat was oppressive. Not an outlaw offered to help the freighters, who were trying to dig a heavily freighted wagon out of the quicksand. Few outlaws would work for themselves, let alone for the despised Mexicans.

Duane and Euchre joined the lazy group and sat down with them. Euchre lighted a black pipe, and, drawing his hat over his eyes, lay back in comfort after the manner of the majority of the outlaws. But

Duane was alert, observing, thoughtful. He never missed anything. It was his belief that any moment an idle word might be of benefit to him. Moreover, these rough men were always interesting.

"Bland's been chased across the river," said one.

"New, he's deliverin' cattle to thet Cuban ship," replied another.

"Big deal on, hey?"

"Some big. Rugg says the boss hed an order fer fifteen thousand."

"Say, that order'll take a year to fill."

"New. Hardin is in cahoots with Bland. Between 'em they'll fill orders bigger 'n thet."

"Wondered what Hardin was rustlin' in here fer."

Duane could not possibly attend to all the conversation among the outlaws. He endeavored to get the drift of talk nearest to him.

"Kid Fuller's goin' to cash," said a sandy-whiskered little outlaw.

"So Jim was tellin' me. Blood-poison, ain't it? Thet hole wasn't bad. But he took the fever," rejoined a comrade.

"Deger says the Kid might pull through if he hed nursin'."

"Wal, Kate Bland ain't nursin' any shot-up boys these days. She hasn't got time."

A laugh followed this sally; then came a penetrating silence. Some of the outlaws glanced good-naturedly at Duane. They bore him no ill will. Manifestly they were aware of Mrs. Bland's infatuation.

"Pete, 'pears to me you've said thet before."

"Shore. Wal, it's happened before."

This remark drew louder laughter and more significant glances at Duane. He did not choose to ignore them any longer.

"Boys, poke all the fun you like at me, but don't mention any lady's name again. My hand is nervous and itchy these days."

He smiled as he spoke, and his speech was drawled; but the good humor in no wise weakened it. Then his latter remark was significant to a class of men who from inclination and necessity practiced at gun-drawing until they wore callous and sore places on their thumbs and inculcated in the very deeps of their nervous organization a habit that made even the simplest and most innocent motion of the hand end at or near the hip. There was something remarkable about a gun-fighter's hand. It never seemed to be gloved, never to be injured, never out of sight or in an awkward position.

There were grizzled outlaws in that group, some of whom had many notches on their gun-handles, and they, with their comrades, accorded Duane silence that carried conviction of the regard in which he was held.

Duane could not recall any other instance where he had let fall a familiar speech to these men, and certainly he had never before hinted of his possibilities. He saw instantly that he could not have done better.

"Orful hot, ain't it?" remarked Bill Black, presently. Bill could not keep quiet for long. He was a typical Texas desperado, had never been anything else. He was stoop-shouldered and bow-legged from much riding; a wiry little man, all muscle, with a square head, a hard face partly black from scrubby beard and red from sun, and a bright, roving, cruel eye. His shirt was open at the neck, showing a grizzled breast.

"Is there any guy in this heah outfit sport enough to go swimmin'?" he asked.

"My Gawd, Bill, you ain't agoin' to wash!" exclaimed a comrade.

This raised a laugh in which Black joined. But no one seemed eager to join him in a bath.

"Laziest outfit I ever rustled with," went on Bill, discontentedly. "Nuthin' to do! Say, if nobody wants to swim maybe some of you'll gamble?"

He produced a dirty pack of cards and waved them at the motionless crowd.

"Bill, you're too good at cards," replied a lanky outlaw.

"Now, Jasper, you say thet powerful sweet, an' you look sweet, er I might take it to heart," replied Black, with a sudden change of tone.

Here it was again—that upflashing passion. What Jasper saw fit to reply would mollify the outlaw or it would not. There was an even balance.

"No offense, Bill," said Jasper, placidly, without moving.

Bill grunted and forgot Jasper. But he seemed restless and dissatisfied. Duane knew him to be an inveterate gambler. And as Benson's place was out of running-order, Black was like a fish on dry land.

"Wal, if you-all are afraid of the cairds, what will you

bet on?" he asked, in disgust.

"Bill, I'll play you a game of mumbly peg fer two bits." replied one.

Black eagerly accepted. Betting to him was a serious matter. The game obsessed him, not the stakes. He entered into the mumbly peg contest with a thoughtful mien and a corded brow. He won. Other comrades tried their luck with him and lost. Finally, when Bill had exhausted their supply of two-bit pieces or their desire for that particular game, he offered to bet on anything.

"See thet turtle-dove there?" he said, pointing. "I'll bet he'll scare at one stone or he won't. Five pesos he'll fly or he won't fly when some one chucks a stone. Who'll take me up?"

That appeared to be more than the gambling spirit of several outlaws could withstand.

"Take thet. Easy money," said one.

"Who's goin' to chuck the stone?" asked another.

"Anybody," replied Bill.

"Wal, I'll bet you I can scare him with one stone," said the first outlaw.

"We're in on thet, Jim to fire the darnick," chimed in the others.

The money was put up, the stone thrown. The turtle-dove took flight, to the great joy of all the outlaws except Bill.

"I'll bet you-all he'll come back to thet tree inside of five minnits," he offered, imperturbably.

Hereupon the outlaws did not show any laziness in their alacrity to cover Bill's money as it lay on the grass. Somebody had a watch, and they all sat down, dividing attention between the timepiece and the tree. The minutes dragged by to the accompaniment of various jocular remarks anent a fool and his money. When four and three-quarter minutes had passed a turtle-dove alighted in the cottonwood. Then ensued an impressive silence while Bill calmly pocketed the fifty dollars.

"But it hadn't the same dove!" exclaimed one outlaw, excitedly. "This 'n'is smaller, dustier, not so purple."

Bill eyed the speaker loftily.

"Wal, you'll have to ketch the other one to prove thet. Sabe, pard? Now I'll bet any gent heah the fifty I won thet I can scare thet dove with one stone."

No one offered to take his wager.

"Wal, then, I'll bet any of you even money thet you CAN'T scare him with one stone."

Not proof against this chance, the outlaws made up a purse, in no wise disconcerted by Bill's contemptuous allusions to their banding together. The stone was thrown. The dove did not fly. Thereafter, in regard to that bird, Bill was unable to coax or scorn his comrades into any kind of wager.

He tried them with a multiplicity of offers, and in vain. Then he appeared at a loss for some unusual and seductive wager. Presently a little ragged Mexican boy came along the river trail, a particularly starved and poor-looking little fellow. Bill called to him and gave him a handful of silver coins. Speechless, dazed, he went his way hugging the money.

"I'll bet he drops some before he gits to the road,"

declared Bill. "I'll bet he runs. Hurry, you four-flush gamblers."

Bill failed to interest any of his companions, and forthwith became sullen and silent. Strangely his good humor departed in spite of the fact that he had won considerable.

Duane, watching the disgruntled outlaw, marveled at him and wondered what was in his mind. These men were more variable than children, as unstable as water, as dangerous as dynamite.

"Bill, I'll bet you ten you can't spill whatever's in the bucket thet peon's packin'," said the outlaw called Jim.

Black's head came up with the action of a hawk about to swoop.

Duane glanced from Black to the road, where he saw a crippled peon carrying a tin bucket toward the river. This peon was a half-witted Indian who lived in a shack and did odd jobs for the Mexicans. Duane had met him often.

"Jim, I'll take you up," replied Black.

Something, perhaps a harshness in his voice, caused Duane to whirl. He caught a leaping gleam in the outlaw's eye.

"Aw, Bill, thet's too fur a shot," said Jasper, as Black rested an elbow on his knee and sighted over the long, heavy Colt. The distance to the peon was about fifty paces, too far for even the most expert shot to hit a moving object so small as a bucket.

Duane, marvelously keen in the alignment of sights, was positive that Black held too high. Another look at the hard face, now tense and dark with blood, confirmed Duane's suspicion that the outlaw was not aiming at the bucket at all. Duane leaped and struck the leveled gun out of his hand. Another outlaw picked it up.

Black fell back astounded. Deprived of his weapon, he did not seem the same man, or else he was cowed by Duane's significant and formidable front. Sullenly he turned away without even asking for his gun.

CHAPTER VIII

What a contrast, Duane thought, the evening of that day presented to the state of his soul!

The sunset lingered in golden glory over the distant Mexican mountains; twilight came slowly; a faint breeze blew from the river cool and sweet; the late cooing of a dove and the tinkle of a cowbell were the only sounds; a serene and tranquil peace lay over the valley.

Inside Duane's body there was strife. This third facing of a desperate man had thrown him off his balance. It had not been fatal, but it threatened so much. The better side of his nature seemed to urge him to die rather than to go on fighting or opposing ignorant, unfortunate, savage men. But the perversity of him was so great that it dwarfed reason, conscience. He could not resist it. He felt something dying in him. He suffered. Hope seemed far away. Despair had seized upon him and was driving him into a reckless mood when he thought of Jennie.

He had forgotten her. He had forgotten that he had promised to save her. He had forgotten that he meant to snuff out as many lives as might stand between her and freedom. The very remembrance sheered off his morbid introspection. She made a difference. How strange for him to realize that! He felt grateful to her.

He had been forced into outlawry; she had been stolen from her people and carried into captivity. They had met in the river fastness, he to instil hope into her despairing life, she to be the means, perhaps, of keeping him from sinking to the level of her captors. He became conscious of a strong and beating desire to see her, talk with her.

These thoughts had run through his mind while on his way to Mrs. Bland's house. He had let Euchre go on ahead because he wanted more time to compose himself. Darkness had about set in when he reached his destination. There was no light in the house. Mrs. Bland was waiting for him on the porch.

She embraced him, and the sudden, violent, unfamiliar contact sent such a shock through him that he all but forgot the deep game he was playing. She, however, in her agitation did not notice his shrinking. From her embrace and the tender, incoherent words that flowed with it he gathered that Euchre had acquainted her of his action with Black.

"He might have killed you," she whispered, more clearly; and if Duane had ever heard love in a voice he heard it then. It softened him. After all, she was a woman, weak, fated through her nature, unfortunate in her experience of life, doomed to unhappiness and tragedy. He met her advance so far that he returned the embrace and kissed her. Emotion such as she showed would have made any woman sweet, and she had a certain charm. It was easy, even pleasant, to kiss her; but Duane resolved that, whatever her abandonment might become, he would not go further than the lie she made him act.

"Buck, you love me?" she whispered.

"Yes—yes," he burst out, eager to get it over, and even as he spoke he caught the pale gleam of Jennie's face through the window. He felt a shame he was glad she could not see. Did she remember that she had promised not to misunderstand any action of his? What did she think of him, seeing him out there in the dusk with this bold woman in his arms? Somehow that dim sight of Jennie's pale face, the big dark eyes, thrilled him, inspired him to his hard task of the present.

"Listen, dear," he said to the woman, and he meant his words for the girl. "I'm going to take you away from this outlaw den if I have to kill Bland, Alloway, Rugg—anybody who stands in my path. You were dragged here. You are good—I know it. There's happiness for you somewhere—a home among good people who will care for you. Just wait till—"

His voice trailed off and failed from excess of emotion. Kate Bland closed her eyes and leaned her head on his breast. Duane felt her heart beat against his, and conscience smote him a keen blow. If she loved him so much! But memory and understanding of her character hardened him again, and he gave her such commiseration as was due her sex, and no more.

"Boy, that's good of you," she whispered, "but it's too late. I'm done for. I can't leave Bland. All I ask is that you love me a little and stop your gun-throwing."

The moon had risen over the eastern bulge of dark mountain, and now the valley was flooded with mellow light, and shadows of cottonwoods wavered against the silver.

Suddenly the clip-clop, clip-clop of hoofs caused Duane to raise his head and listen. Horses were coming down the road from the head of the valley. The hour was unusual for riders to come in. Presently the narrow, moonlit lane was crossed at its far end by black moving objects. Two horses Duane discerned.

"It's Bland!" whispered the woman, grasping Duane with shaking hands. "You must run! No, he'd see you. That 'd be worse. It's Bland! I know his horse's trot."

"But you said he wouldn't mind my calling here," protested Duane. "Euchre's with me. It'll be all right."

"Maybe so," she replied, with visible effort at self-control. Manifestly she had a great fear of Bland. "If I could only think!"

Then she dragged Duane to the door, pushed him in. "Euchre, come out with me! Duane, you stay with the girl! I'll tell Bland you're in love with her. Jen, if you give us away I'll wring your neck."

The swift action and fierce whisper told Duane that Mrs. Bland was herself again. Duane stepped close to Jennie, who stood near the window. Neither spoke, but her hands were outstretched to meet his own. They were small, trembling hands, cold as ice. He held them close, trying to convey what he felt—that he would protect her. She leaned against him, and they looked out of the window. Duane felt calm and sure of himself. His most pronounced feeling besides that for the frightened girl was a curiosity as to how Mrs. Bland would rise to the occasion. He saw the riders dismount down the lane and wearily come forward. A boy led away the horses. Euchre, the old fox, was talking loud and with remarkable ease, considering what he claimed was his natural cowardice.

"—that was way back in the sixties, about the time of the war," he was saying. "Rustlin' cattle wasn't nuthin' then to what it is now. An' times is rougher these days. This gun-throwin' has come to be a disease. Men have an itch for the draw same as they used to have fer poker. The only real gambler outside of greasers we ever had here was Bill, an' I presume Bill is burnin' now."

The approaching outlaws, hearing voices, halted a rod or so from the porch. Then Mrs. Bland uttered an exclamation, ostensibly meant to express surprise, and hurried out to meet them. She greeted her husband warmly and gave welcome to the other man. Duane could not see well enough in the shadow to recognize Bland's companion, but he believed it was Alloway.

"Dog-tired we are and starved," said Bland, heavily. "Who's here with you?"

"That's Euchre on the porch. Duane is inside at the window with Jen," replied Mrs. Bland.

"Duane!" he exclaimed. Then he whispered low—something Duane could not catch.

"Why, I asked him to come," said the chief's wife. She spoke easily and naturally and made no change in tone. "Jen has been ailing. She gets thinner and whiter every day. Duane came here one day with Euchre, saw Jen, and went loony over her pretty face, same as all you men. So I let him come."

Bland cursed low and deep under his breath. The other man made a violent action of some kind and apparently was quieted by a restraining hand.

"Kate, you let Duane make love to Jennie?" queried Bland, incredulously.

"Yes, I did," replied the wife, stubbornly. "Why not? Jen's in love with him. If he takes her away and marries her she can be a decent woman."

Bland kept silent a moment, then his laugh pealed out loud and harsh.

"Chess, did you get that? Well, by God! what do you think of my wife?"

"She's lyin' or she's crazy," replied Alloway, and his voice carried an unpleasant ring.

Mrs. Bland promptly and indignantly told her husband's lieutenant to keep his mouth shut.

"Ho, ho, ho!" rolled out Bland's laugh.

Then he led the way to the porch, his spurs clinking, the weapons he was carrying rattling, and he flopped down on a bench.

"How are you, boss?" asked Euchre.

"Hello, old man. I'm well, but all in."

Alloway slowly walked on to the porch and leaned against the rail. He answered Euchre's greeting with a nod. Then he stood there a dark, silent figure.

Mrs. Bland's full voice in eager questioning had a tendency to ease the situation. Bland replied briefly to her, reporting a remarkably successful trip.

Duane thought it time to show himself. He had a feeling that Bland and Alloway would let him go for the moment. They were plainly non-plussed, and Alloway seemed sullen, brooding. "Jennie," whispered Duane, "that was clever of Mrs. Bland. We'll keep up the deception. Any day now be ready!"

She pressed close to him, and a barely audible "Hurry!" came breathing into his ear.

"Good night, Jennie," he said, aloud. "Hope you feel better to-morrow."

Then he stepped out into the moonlight and spoke. Bland returned the greeting, and, though he was not amiable, he did not show resentment.

"Met Jasper as I rode in," said Bland, presently. "He told me you made Bill Black mad, and there's liable to be a fight. What did you go off the handle about?"

Duane explained the incident. "I'm sorry I happened to be there," he went on. "It wasn't my business."

"Scurvy trick that 'd been," muttered Bland. "You did right. All the same, Duane, I want you to stop quarreling with my men. If you were one of us—that'd be different. I can't keep my men from fighting. But I'm not called on to let an outsider hang around my camp and plug my rustlers."

"I guess I'll have to be hitting the trail for somewhere," said Duane.

"Why not join my band? You've got a bad start already, Duane, and if I know this border you'll never be a respectable citizen again. You're a born killer. I know every bad man on this frontier. More than one of them have told me that something exploded in their brain, and when sense came back there lay another dead man. It's not so with me. I've done a little shooting, too, but I never wanted to kill another man just to rid myself of the last one. My dead men don't sit on my chest at night. That's the gun-fighter's trouble. He's crazy. He has to kill a new man—he's driven to it to forget the last one."

"But I'm no gun-fighter," protested Duane. "Circumstances made me—"

"No doubt," interrupted Bland, with a laugh. "Circumstances made me a rustler. You don't know yourself. You're young; you've got a temper; your father was one of the most dangerous men Texas ever had. I don't see any other career for you. Instead of going it alone—a lone wolf, as the Texans say—why not make friends with other outlaws? You'll live longer."

Euchre squirmed in his seat.

"Boss, I've been givin' the boy egzactly thet same line of talk. Thet's why I took him in to bunk with me. If he makes pards among us there won't be any more trouble. An' he'd be a grand feller fer the gang. I've seen Wild Bill Hickok throw a gun, an' Billy the Kid, an' Hardin, an' Chess here—all the fastest men on the border. An' with apologies to present company, I'm here to say Duane has them all skinned. His draw is different. You can't see how he does it."

Euchre's admiring praise served to create an effective little silence. Alloway shifted uneasily on his feet, his spurs jangling faintly, and did not lift his head. Bland seemed thoughtful.

"That's about the only qualification I have to make me eligible for your band," said Duane, easily.

"It's good enough," replied Bland, shortly. "Will you consider the idea?"

"I'll think it over. Good night."

He left the group, followed by Euchre. When they reached the end of the lane, and before they had exchanged a word, Bland called Euchre back. Duane proceeded slowly along the moonlit road to the cabin and sat down under the cottonwoods to wait for Euchre. The night was intense and quiet, a low hum of insects giving the effect of a congestion of life. The beauty of the soaring moon, the ebony canyons of shadow under the mountain, the melancholy serenity of the perfect night, made Duane shudder in the realization of how far aloof he now was from enjoyment of these things. Never again so long as he lived could he be natural. His mind was clouded. His eye and ear henceforth must register impressions of nature, but the joy of them had fled.

Still, as he sat there with a foreboding of more and darker work ahead of him there was yet a strange sweetness left to him, and it lay in thought of Jennie. The pressure of her cold little hands lingered in his. He did not think of her as a woman, and he did not analyze his feelings. He just had vague, dreamy thoughts and imaginations that were interspersed in the constant and stern revolving of plans to save her.

A shuffling step roused him. Euchre's dark figure came crossing the moonlit grass under the cottonwoods. The moment the outlaw reached him Duane saw that he was laboring under great excitement. It scarcely affected Duane. He seemed to be acquiring patience, calmness, strength.

"Bland kept you pretty long," he said.

"Wait till I git my breath," replied Euchre. He sat silent a little while, fanning himself with a sombrero, though the night was cool, and then he went into the cabin to return presently with a lighted pipe.

"Fine night," he said; and his tone further acquainted Duane with Euchre's quaint humor. "Fine night for love-affairs, by gum!"

"I'd noticed that," rejoined Duane, dryly.

"Wal, I'm a son of a gun if I didn't stand an' watch Bland choke his wife till her tongue stuck out an' she got black in the face."

"No!" ejaculated Duane.

"Hope to die if I didn't. Buck, listen to this here yarn. When I got back to the porch I seen Bland was wakin' up. He'd been too fagged out to figger much. Alloway an' Kate had gone in the house, where they lit up the lamps. I heard Kate's high voice, but Alloway never chirped. He's not the talkin' kind, an' he's damn dangerous when he's thet way. Bland asked me some questions right from the shoulder. I was ready for them, an' I swore the moon was green cheese. He was satisfied. Bland always trusted me, an' liked me, too, I reckon. I hated to lie black thet way. But he's a hard man with bad intentions toward Jennie, an' I'd double-cross him any day.

"Then we went into the house. Jennie had gone to her little room, an' Bland called her to come out. She said she was undressin'. An' he ordered her to put her clothes back on. Then, Buck, his next move was some surprisin'. He deliberately thronged a gun on Kate. Yes sir, he pointed his big blue Colt right at her, an' he says:

"'I've a mind to blow out your brains.'

"'Go ahead,' says Kate, cool as could be.

"'You lied to me,' he roars.

"Kate laughed in his face. Bland slammed the gun down an' made a grab fer her. She fought him, but wasn't a match fer him, an' he got her by the throat. He choked her till I thought she was strangled. Alloway made him stop. She flopped down on the bed an' gasped fer a while. When she come to them hard-shelled cusses went after her, trying to make her give herself away. I think Bland was jealous. He suspected she'd got thick with you an' was foolin' him. I reckon thet's a sore feelin' fer a man to have—to guess pretty nice, but not to BE sure. Bland gave it up after a while. An' then he cussed an' raved at her. One sayin' of his is worth pinnin' in your sombrero: 'It ain't nuthin' to kill a man. I don't need much fer thet. But I want to KNOW, you hussy!'

"Then he went in an' dragged poor Jen out. She'd had time to dress. He was so mad he hurt her sore leg. You know Jen got thet injury fightin' off one of them devils in the dark. An' when I seen Bland twist her—hurt her—I had a queer hot feelin' deep down in me, an' fer the only time in my life I wished I was a gun-fighter.

"Wal, Jen amazed me. She was whiter'n a sheet, an' her eyes were big and stary, but she had nerve. Fust time I ever seen her show any.

"'Jennie,' he said, 'my wife said Duane came here to see you. I believe she's lyin'. I think she's been carryin' on with him, an' I want to KNOW. If she's been an' you tell me the truth I'll let you go. I'll send you out to Huntsville, where you can communicate with your friends. I'll give you money.'

"Thet must hev been a hell of a minnit fer Kate Bland. If evet I seen death in a man's eye I seen it in Bland's. He loves her. Thet's the strange part of it.

"'Has Duane been comin' here to see my wife?' Bland asked, fierce-like.

"'No,' said Jennie.

"'He's been after you?'

"'Yes.'

"'He has fallen in love with you? Kate said thet.'

"'I—I'm not—I don't know—he hasn't told me.'

"'But you're in love with him?'

"'Yes,' she said; an', Buck, if you only could have seen her! She thronged up her head, an' her eyes were full of fire. Bland seemed dazed at sight of her. An' Alloway, why, thet little skunk of an outlaw cried right out. He was hit plumb center. He's in love with Jen. An' the look of her then was enough to make any feller quit. He jest slunk out of the room. I told you, mebbe, thet he'd been tryin' to git Bland to marry Jen to him. So even a tough like Alloway can love a woman!

"Bland stamped up an' down the room. He sure was dyin' hard.

"'Jennie,' he said, once more turnin' to her. 'You swear in fear of your life thet you're tellin' truth. Kate's not in love with Duane? She's let him come to see you? There's been nuthin' between them?'

"'No. I swear,' answered Jennie; an' Bland sat down

like a man licked.

"'Go to bed, you white-faced—' Bland choked on some word or other—a bad one, I reckon—an' he positively shook in his chair.

"Jennie went then, an' Kate began to have hysterics. An' your Uncle Euchre ducked his nut out of the door an' come home."

Duane did not have a word to say at the end of Euchre's long harangue. He experienced relief. As a matter of fact, he had expected a good deal worse. He thrilled at the thought of Jennie perjuring herself to save that abandoned woman. What mysteries these feminine creatures were!

"Wal, there's where our little deal stands now," resumed Euchre, meditatively. "You know, Buck, as well as me thet if you'd been some feller who hadn't shown he was a wonder with a gun you'd now be full of lead. If you'd happen to kill Bland an' Alloway, I reckon you'd be as safe on this here border as you would in Santone. Such is gun fame in this land of the draw."

CHAPTER IX

Both men were awake early, silent with the premonition of trouble ahead, thoughtful of the fact that the time for the long-planned action was at hand. It was remarkable that a man as loquacious as Euchre could hold his tongue so long; and this was significant of the deadly nature of the intended deed. During breakfast he said a few words customary in the service of food. At the conclusion of the meal he seemed to come to an end of deliberation.

"Buck, the sooner the better now," he declared, with a glint in his eye. "The more time we use up now the less surprised Bland'll be."

"I'm ready when you are," replied Duane, quietly, and he rose from the table.

"Wal, saddle up, then," went on Euchre, gruffly. "Tie on them two packs I made, one fer each saddle. You can't tell—mebbe either hoss will be carryin' double. It's good they're both big, strong hosses. Guess thet wasn't a wise move of your Uncle Euchre's—bringin' in your hosses an' havin' them ready?"

"Euchre, I hope you're not going to get in bad here. I'm afraid you are. Let me do the rest now," said Duane.

The old outlaw eyed him sarcastically.

"Thet 'd be turrible now, wouldn't it? If you want to know, why, I'm in bad already. I didn't tell you thet

Alloway called me last night. He's gettin' wise pretty quick."

"Euchre, you're going with me?" queried Duane, suddenly divining the truth.

"Wal, I reckon. Either to hell or safe over the mountain! I wisht I was a gun-fighter. I hate to leave here without takin' a peg at Jackrabbit Benson. Now, Buck, you do some hard figgerin' while I go nosin' round. It's pretty early, which 's all the better."

Euchre put on his sombrero, and as he went out Duane saw that he wore a gun-and-cartridge belt. It was the first time Duane had ever seen the outlaw armed.

Duane packed his few belongings into his saddlebags, and then carried the saddles out to the corral. An abundance of alfalfa in the corral showed that the horses had fared well. They had gotten almost fat during his stay in the valley. He watered them, put on the saddles loosely cinched, and then the bridles. His next move was to fill the two canvas water-bottles. That done, he returned to the cabin to wait.

At the moment he felt no excitement or agitation of any kind. There was no more thinking and planning to do. The hour had arrived, and he was ready. He understood perfectly the desperate chances he must take. His thoughts became confined to Euchre and the surprising loyalty and goodness in the hardened old outlaw. Time passed slowly. Duane kept glancing at his watch. He hoped to start the thing and get away before the outlaws were out of their beds. Finally he heard the shuffle of Euchre's boots on the hard path.

The sound was quicker than usual.

When Euchre came around the corner of the cabin Duane was not so astounded as he was concerned to see the outlaw white and shaking. Sweat dripped from him. He had a wild look.

"Luck ours—so-fur, Buck!" he panted.

"You don't look it," replied Duane.

"I'm turrible sick. Jest killed a man. Fust one I ever killed!"

"Who?" asked Duane, startled.

"Jackrabbit Benson. An' sick as I am, I'm gloryin' in it. I went nosin' round up the road. Saw Alloway goin' into Deger's. He's thick with the Degers. Reckon he's askin' questions. Anyway, I was sure glad to see him away from Bland's. An' he didn't see me. When I dropped into Benson's there wasn't nobody there but Jackrabbit an' some greasers he was startin' to work. Benson never had no use fer me. An' he up an' said he wouldn't give a two-bit piece fer my life. I asked him why.

"'You're double-crossin' the boss an' Chess,' he said.

"'Jack, what 'd you give fer your own life?' I asked him.

"He straightened up surprised an' mean-lookin'. An' I let him have it, plumb center! He wilted, an' the greasers run. I reckon I'll never sleep again. But I had to do it."

Duane asked if the shot had attracted any attention outside.

"I didn't see anybody but the greasers, an' I sure looked sharp. Comin' back I cut across through the cottonwoods past Bland's cabin. I meant to keep out of sight, but somehow I had an idee I might find out if Bland was awake yet. Sure enough I run plumb into Beppo, the boy who tends Bland's hosses. Beppo likes me. An' when I inquired of his boss he said Bland had been up all night fightin' with the Senora. An', Buck, here's how I figger. Bland couldn't let up last night. He was sore, an' he went after Kate again, tryin' to wear her down. Jest as likely he might have went after Jennie, with wuss intentions. Anyway, he an' Kate must have had it hot an' heavy. We're pretty lucky."

"It seems so. Well, I'm going," said Duane, tersely.

"Lucky! I should smiler Bland's been up all night after a most draggin' ride home. He'll be fagged out this mornin', sleepy, sore, an' he won't be expectin' hell before breakfast. Now, you walk over to his house. Meet him how you like. Thet's your game. But I'm suggestin', if he comes out an' you want to parley, you can jest say you'd thought over his proposition an' was ready to join his band, or you ain't. You'll have to kill him, an' it 'd save time to go fer your gun on sight. Might be wise, too, fer it's likely he'll do thet same."

"How about the horses?"

"I'll fetch them an' come along about two minnits behind you. 'Pears to me you ought to have the job done an' Jennie outside by the time I git there. Once on them hosses, we can ride out of camp before Alloway or anybody else gits into action. Jennie ain't much heavier than a rabbit. Thet big black will carry you both."

"All right. But once more let me persuade you to

stay—not to mix any more in this," said Duane, earnestly.

"Nope. I'm goin'. You heard what Benson told me. Alloway wouldn't give me the benefit of any doubts. Buck, a last word—look out fer thet Bland woman!"

Duane merely nodded, and then, saying that the horses were ready, he strode away through the grove. Accounting for the short cut across grove and field, it was about five minutes' walk up to Bland's house. To Duane it seemed long in time and distance, and he had difficulty in restraining his pace. As he walked there came a gradual and subtle change in his feelings. Again he was going out to meet a man in conflict. He could have avoided this meeting. But despite the fact of his courting the encounter he had not as yet felt that hot, inexplicable rush of blood. The motive of this deadly action was not personal, and somehow that made a difference.

No outlaws were in sight. He saw several Mexican herders with cattle. Blue columns of smoke curled up over some of the cabins. The fragrant smell of it reminded Duane of his home and cutting wood for the stove. He noted a cloud of creamy mist rising above the river, dissolving in the sunlight.

Then he entered Bland's lane.

While yet some distance from the cabin he heard loud, angry voices of man and woman. Bland and Kate still quarreling! He took a quick survey of the surroundings. There was now not even a Mexican in sight. Then he hurried a little. Halfway down the lane he turned his head to peer through the cottonwoods.

This time he saw Euchre coming with the horses. There was no indication that the old outlaw might lose his nerve at the end. Duane had feared this.

Duane now changed his walk to a leisurely saunter. He reached the porch and then distinguished what was said inside the cabin.

"If you do, Bland, by Heaven I'll fix you and her!" That was panted out in Kate Bland's full voice.

"Let me looser I'm going in there, I tell you!" replied Bland, hoarsely.

"What for?"

"I want to make a little love to her. Ha! ha! It'll be fun to have the laugh on her new lover."

"You lie!" cried Kate Bland.

"I'm not saying what I'll do to her AFTERWARD!" His voice grew hoarser with passion. "Let me go now!"

"No! no! I won't let you go. You'll choke the—the truth out of her—you'll kill her."

"The TRUTH!" hissed Bland.

"Yes. I lied. Jen lied. But she lied to save me. You needn't—murder her—for that."

Bland cursed horribly. Then followed a wrestling sound of bodies in violent straining contact—the scrape of feet—the jangle of spurs—a crash of sliding table or chair, and then the cry of a woman in pain.

Duane stepped into the open door, inside the room. Kate Bland lay half across a table where she had been flung, and she was trying to get to her feet. Bland's back was turned. He had opened the door into Jennie's room and had one foot across the threshold. Duane caught the girl's low, shuddering cry. Then he called out loud and clear.

With cat-like swiftness Bland wheeled, then froze on the threshold. His sight, quick as his action, caught Duane's menacing unmistakable position.

Bland's big frame filled the door. He was in a bad place to reach for his gun. But he would not have time for a step. Duane read in his eyes the desperate calculation of chances. For a fleeting instant Bland shifted his glance to his wife. Then his whole body seemed to vibrate with the swing of his arm.

Duane shot him. He fell forward, his gun exploding as it hit into the floor, and dropped loose from stretching fingers. Duane stood over him, stooped to turn him on his back. Bland looked up with clouded gaze, then gasped his last.

"Duane, you've killed him!" cried Kate Bland, huskily. "I knew you'd have to!"

She staggered against the wall, her eyes dilating, her strong hands clenching, her face slowly whitening. She appeared shocked, half stunned, but showed no grief.

"Jennie!" called Duane, sharply.

"Oh—Duane!" came a halting reply.

"Yes. Come out. Hurry!"

She came out with uneven steps, seeing only him, and she stumbled over Bland's body. Duane caught her arm, swung her behind him. He feared the woman when she realized how she had been duped. His action was protective, and his movement toward the door equally as significant.

"Duane," cried Mrs. Bland.

It was no time for talk. Duane edged on, keeping Jennie behind him. At that moment there was a pounding of iron-shod hoofs out in the lane. Kate Bland bounded to the door. When she turned back her amazement was changing to realization.

"Where 're you taking Jen?" she cried, her voice like a man's. "Get out of my way," replied Duane. His look perhaps, without speech, was enough for her. In an instant she was transformed into a fury.

"You hound! All the time you were fooling me! You made love to me! You let me believe—you swore you loved me! Now I see what was queer about you. All for that girl! But you can't have her. You'll never leave here alive. Give me that girl! Let me—get at her! She'll never win any more men in this camp."

She was a powerful woman, and it took all Duane's strength to ward off her onslaughts. She clawed at Jennie over his upheld arm. Every second her fury increased.

"HELP! HELP! HELP!" she shrieked, in a voice that must have penetrated to the remotest cabin in the valley.

"Let go! Let go!" cried Duane, low and sharp. He still held his gun in his right hand, and it began to be hard for him to ward the woman off. His coolness had gone with her shriek for help. "Let go!" he repeated, and he shoved her fiercely.

Suddenly she snatched a rifle off the wall and backed away, her strong hands fumbling at the lever. As she jerked it down, throwing a shell into the chamber and cocking the weapon, Duane leaped upon her. He struck up the rifle as it went off, the powder burning his face.

"Jennie, run out! Get on a horse!" he said.

Jennie flashed out of the door.

With an iron grasp Duane held to the rifle-barrel. He had grasped it with his left hand, and he gave such a pull that he swung the crazed woman off the floor. But he could not loose her grip. She was as strong as he.

"Kate! Let go!"

He tried to intimidate her. She did not see his gun thrust in her face, or reason had given way to such an extent to passion that she did not care. She cursed. Her husband had used the same curses, and from her lips they seemed strange, unsexed, more deadly. Like a tigress she fought him; her face no longer resembled a woman's. The evil of that outlaw life, the wildness and rage, the meaning to kill, was even in such a moment terribly impressed upon Duane.

He heard a cry from outside—a man's cry, hoarse and alarming.

It made him think of loss of time. This demon of a woman might yet block his plan.

"Let go!" he whispered, and felt his lips stiff. In the grimness of that instant he relaxed his hold on the rifle-barrel.

With sudden, redoubled, irresistible strength she wrenched the rifle down and discharged it. Duane felt a blow—a shock—a burning agony tearing through his breast. Then in a frenzy he jerked so powerfully upon the rifle that he threw the woman against the wall. She fell and seemed stunned.

Duane leaped back, whirled, flew out of the door to the porch. The sharp cracking of a gun halted him. He saw Jennie holding to the bridle of his bay horse. Euchre was astride the other, and he had a Colt leveled, and he was firing down the lane. Then came a single shot, heavier, and Euchre's ceased. He fell from the horse.

A swift glance back showed to Duane a man coming down the lane. Chess Alloway! His gun was smoking. He broke into a run. Then in an instant he saw Duane, and tried to check his pace as he swung up his arm. But that slight pause was fatal. Duane shot, and Alloway was falling when his gun went off. His bullet whistled close to Duane and thudded into the cabin.

Duane bounded down to the horses. Jennie was trying to hold the plunging bay. Euchre lay flat on his back, dead, a bullet-hole in his shirt, his face set hard, and his hands twisted round gun and bridle.

"Jennie, you've nerve, all right!" cried Duane, as he dragged down the horse she was holding. "Up with you now! There! Never mind—long stirrups! Hang on somehow!"

He caught his bridle out of Euchre's clutching grip and leaped astride. The frightened horses jumped into a run and thundered down the lane into the road. Duane saw men running from cabins. He heard shouts. But there were no shots fired. Jennie seemed able to stay on her horse, but without stirrups she was thrown about so much that Duane rode closer and reached out to grasp her arm.

Thus they rode through the valley to the trail that led up over, the steep and broken Rim Rock. As they began to climb Duane looked back. No pursuers were in sight.

"Jennie, we're going to get away!" he cried, exultation for her in his voice.

She was gazing horror-stricken at his breast, as in turning to look back he faced her.

"Oh, Duane, your shirt's all bloody!" she faltered, pointing with trembling fingers.

With her words Duane became aware of two things—the hand he instinctively placed to his breast still held his gun, and he had sustained a terrible wound.

Duane had been shot through the breast far enough down to give him grave apprehension of his life. The clean-cut hole made by the bullet bled freely both at its entrance and where it had come out, but with no signs of hemorrhage. He did not bleed at the mouth; however, he began to cough up a reddish-tinged foam.

As they rode on, Jennie, with pale face and mute lips, looked at him.

"I'm badly hurt, Jennie," he said, "but I guess I'll stick it out."

"The woman—did she shoot you?"

"Yes. She was a devil. Euchre told me to look out for her. I wasn't quick enough."

"You didn't have to—to—" shivered the girl.

"No! no!" he replied.

They did not stop climbing while Duane tore a scarf

and made compresses, which he bound tightly over his wounds. The fresh horses made fast time up the rough trail. From open places Duane looked down. When they surmounted the steep ascent and stood on top of the Rim Rock, with no signs of pursuit down in the valley, and with the wild, broken fastnesses before them, Duane turned to the girl and assured her that they now had every chance of escape.

"But—your—wound!" she faltered, with dark, troubled eyes. "I see—the blood—dripping from your back!"

"Jennie, I'll take a lot of killing," he said.

Then he became silent and attended to the uneven trail. He was aware presently that he had not come into Bland's camp by this route. But that did not matter; any trail leading out beyond the Rim Rock was safe enough. What he wanted was to get far away into some wild retreat where he could hide till he recovered from his wound. He seemed to feel a fire inside his breast, and his throat burned so that it was necessary for him to take a swallow of water every little while. He began to suffer considerable pain, which increased as the hours went by and then gave way to a numbness. From that time on he had need of his great strength and endurance. Gradually he lost his steadiness and his keen sight; and he realized that if he were to meet foes, or if pursuing outlaws should come up with him, he could make only a poor stand. So he turned off on a trail that appeared seldom traveled.

Soon after this move he became conscious of a further thickening of his senses. He felt able to hold on to his saddle for a while longer, but he was failing. Then he thought he ought to advise Jennie, so in case she was left alone she would have some idea of what to do.

"Jennie, I'll give out soon," he said. "No-I don't mean—what you think. But I'll drop soon. My strength's going. If I die—you ride back to the main trail. Hide and rest by day. Ride at night. That trail goes to water. I believe you could get across the Nueces, where some rancher will take you in."

Duane could not get the meaning of her incoherent reply. He rode on, and soon he could not see the trail or hear his horse. He did not know whether they traveled a mile or many times that far. But he was conscious when the horse stopped, and had a vague sense of falling and feeling Jennie's arms before all became dark to him.

When consciousness returned he found himself lying in a little hut of mesquite branches. It was well built and evidently some years old. There were two doors or openings, one in front and the other at the back. Duane imagined it had been built by a fugitive—one who meant to keep an eye both ways and not to be surprised. Duane felt weak and had no desire to move. Where was he, anyway? A strange, intangible sense of time, distance, of something far behind weighed upon him. Sight of the two packs Euchre had made brought his thought to Jennie. What had become of her? There was evidence of her work in a smoldering fire and a little blackened coffee-pot. Probably she was outside looking after the horses or getting water. He thought he heard a step and listened, but he felt tired, and presently his eyes closed and he fell into a doze.

Awakening from this, he saw Jennie sitting beside him. In some way she seemed to have changed. When he spoke she gave a start and turned eagerly to him.

"Duane!" she cried.

"Hello. How're you, Jennie, and how am I?" he said, finding it a little difficult to talk.

"Oh, I'm all right," she replied. "And you've come to—your wound's healed; but you've been sick. Fever, I guess. I did all I could."

Duane saw now that the difference in her was a whiteness and tightness of skin, a hollowness of eye, a look of strain.

"Fever? How long have we been here?" he asked.

She took some pebbles from the crown of his sombrero and counted them.

"Nine. Nine days," she answered.

"Nine days!" he exclaimed, incredulously. But another look at her assured him that she meant what she said. "I've been sick all the time? You nursed me?"

"Yes."

"Bland's men didn't come along here?"

"No."

"Where are the horses?"

"I keep them grazing down in a gorge back of here. There's good grass and water."

"Have you slept any?"

"A little. Lately I couldn't keep awake."

"Good Lord! I should think not. You've had a time

of it sitting here day and night nursing me, watching for the outlaws. Come, tell me all about it."

"There's nothing much to tell."

"I want to know, anyway, just what you did—how you felt."

"I can't remember very well," she replied, simply. "We must have ridden forty miles that day we got away. You bled all the time. Toward evening you lay on your horse's neck. When we came to this place you fell out of the saddle. I dragged you in here and stopped your bleeding. I thought you'd die that night. But in the morning I had a little hope. I had forgotten the horses. But luckily they didn't stray far. I caught them and kept them down in the gorge. When your wounds closed and you began to breathe stronger I thought you'd get well quick. It was fever that put you back. You raved a lot, and that worried me, because I couldn't stop you. Anybody trailing us could have heard you a good ways. I don't know whether I was scared most then or when you were quiet, and it was so dark and lonely and still all around. Every day I put a stone in your hat."

"Jennie, you saved my life," said Duane.

"I don't know. Maybe. I did all I knew how to do," she replied. "You saved mine—more than my life."

Their eyes met in a long gaze, and then their hands in a close clasp.

"Jennie, we're going to get away," he said, with gladness. "I'll be well in a few days. You don't know how strong I am. We'll hide by day and travel by night. I can get you across the river."

"And then?" she asked.

"We'll find some honest rancher."

"And then?" she persisted.

"Why," he began, slowly, "that's as far as my thoughts ever got. It was pretty hard, I tell you, to assure myself of so much. It means your safety. You'll tell your story. You'll be sent to some village or town and taken care of until a relative or friend is notified."

"And you?" she inquired, in a strange voice.

Duane kept silence.

"What will you do?" she went on.

"Jennie, I'll go back to the brakes. I daren't show my face among respectable people. I'm an outlaw."

"You're no criminal!" she declared, with deep passion.

"Jennie, on this border the little difference between an out law and a criminal doesn't count for much."

"You won't go back among those terrible men? You, with your gentleness and sweetness—all that's good about you? Oh, Duane, don't—don't go!"

"I can't go back to the outlaws, at least not Bland's band. No, I'll go alone. I'll lone-wolf it, as they say on the border. What else can I do, Jennie?"

"Oh, I don't know. Couldn't you hide? Couldn't you slip out of Texas—go far away?"

"I could never get out of Texas without being arrested. I could hide, but a man must live. Never mind about me, Jennie."

In three days Duane was able with great difficulty to mount his horse. During daylight, by short relays, he and Jennie rode back to the main trail, where they hid again till he had rested. Then in the dark they rode out of the canyons and gullies of the Rim Rock, and early in the morning halted at the first water to camp.

From that point they traveled after nightfall and went into hiding during the day. Once across the Nueces River, Duane was assured of safety for her and great danger for himself. They had crossed into a country he did not know. Somewhere east of the river there were scattered ranches. But he was as liable to find the rancher in touch with the outlaws as he was likely to find him honest. Duane hoped his good fortune would not desert him in this last service to Jennie. Next to the worry of that was realization of his condition. He had gotten up too soon; he had ridden too far and hard, and now he felt that any moment he might fall from his saddle. At last, far ahead over a barren mesquite-dotted stretch of dusty ground, he espied a patch of green and a little flat, red ranch-house. He headed his horse for it and turned a face he tried to make cheerful for Jennie's sake. She seemed both happy and sorry.

When near at hand he saw that the rancher was a thrifty farmer. And thrift spoke for honesty. There were fields of alfalfa, fruit-trees, corrals, windmill pumps, irrigation-ditches, all surrounding a neat little adobe house. Some children were playing in the yard. The way they ran at sight of Duane hinted of both the loneliness and the fear of their isolated lives. Duane saw a woman come to the door, then a man. The latter looked keenly, then stepped outside. He was a sandy-haired, freckled Texan.

"Howdy, stranger," he called, as Duane halted. "Get down, you an' your woman. Say, now, air you sick or shot or what? Let me—"

Duane, reeling in his saddle, bent searching eyes upon the rancher. He thought he saw good will, kindness, honesty. He risked all on that one sharp glance. Then he almost plunged from the saddle.

The rancher caught him, helped him to a bench.

"Martha, come out here!" he called. "This man's sick. No; he's shot, or I don't know blood-stains."

Jennie had slipped off her horse and to Duane's side. Duane appeared about to faint.

"Air you his wife?" asked the rancher.

"No. I'm only a girl he saved from outlaws. Oh, he's so paler Duane, Duane!"

"Buck Duane!" exclaimed the rancher, excitedly. "The man who killed Bland an' Alloway? Say, I owe him a good turn, an' I'll pay it, young woman."

The rancher's wife came out, and with a manner at once kind and practical essayed to make Duane drink from a flask. He was not so far gone that he could not recognize its contents, which he refused, and weakly asked for water. When that was given him he found his voice.

"Yes, I'm Duane. I've only overdone myself—just all in. The wounds I got at Bland's are healing. Will you take this girl in—hide her awhile till the excitement's over among the outlaws?"

"I shore will," replied the Texan.

"Thanks. I'll remember you—I'll square it."

"What 're you goin' to do?"

"I'll rest a bit—then go back to the brakes."

"Young man, you ain't in any shape to travel. See

here—any rustlers on your trail?"

"I think we gave Bland's gang the slip."

"Good. I'll tell you what. I'll take you in along with the girl, an' hide both of you till you get well. It'll be safe. My nearest neighbor is five miles off. We don't have much company."

"You risk a great deal. Both outlaws and rangers are hunting me," said Duane.

"Never seen a ranger yet in these parts. An' have always got along with outlaws, mebbe exceptin' Bland. I tell you I owe you a good turn."

"My horses might betray you," added Duane.

"I'll hide them in a place where there's water an' grass. Nobody goes to it. Come now, let me help you indoors."

Duane's last fading sensations of that hard day were the strange feel of a bed, a relief at the removal of his heavy boots, and of Jennie's soft, cool hands on his hot face.

He lay ill for three weeks before he began to mend, and it was another week then before he could walk out a little in the dusk of the evenings. After that his strength returned rapidly. And it was only at the end of this long siege that he recovered his spirits. During most of his illness he had been silent, moody.

"Jennie, I'll be riding off soon," he said, one evening. "I can't impose on this good man Andrews much longer. I'll never forget his kindness. His wife, too—she's been so good to us. Yes, Jennie, you and I will have to say good-by very soon."

"Don't hurry away," she replied.

Lately Jennie had appeared strange to him. She had changed from the girl he used to see at Mrs. Bland's house. He took her reluctance to say good-by as another indication of her regret that he must go back to the brakes. Yet somehow it made him observe her more closely. She wore a plain, white dress made from material Mrs. Andrews had given her. Sleep and good food had improved her. If she had been pretty out there in the outlaw den now she was more than that. But she had the same paleness, the same strained look, the same dark eyes full of haunting shadows. After Duane's realization of the change in her he watched her more, with a growing certainty that he would be sorry not to see her again.

"It's likely we won't ever see each other again," he said. "That's strange to think of. We've been through some hard days, and I seem to have known you a long time."

Jennie appeared shy, almost sad, so Duane changed the subject to something less personal.

Andrews returned one evening from a several days' trip to Huntsville.

"Duane, everybody's talkie' about how you cleaned up the Bland outfit," he said, important and full of news. "It's some exaggerated, accordin' to what you told me; but you've shore made friends on this side of the Nueces. I reckon there ain't a town where you wouldn't find people to welcome you. Huntsville, you know, is some divided in its ideas. Half the people are crooked. Likely enough, all them who was so loud in praise of you are the crookedest. For instance, I met

King Fisher, the boss outlaw of these parts. Well, King thinks he's a decent citizen. He was tellin' me what a grand job yours was for the border an' honest cattlemen. Now that Bland and Alloway are done for, King Fisher will find rustlin' easier. There's talk of Hardin movie' his camp over to Bland's. But I don't know how true it is. I reckon there ain't much to it. In the past when a big outlaw chief went under, his band almost always broke up an' scattered. There's no one left who could run thet outfit."

"Did you hear of any outlaws hunting me?" asked Duane.

"Nobody from Bland's outfit is huntin' you, thet's shore," replied Andrews. "Fisher said there never was a hoss straddled to go on your trail. Nobody had any use for Bland. Anyhow, his men would be afraid to trail you. An' you could go right in to Huntsville, where you'd be some popular. Reckon you'd be safe, too, except when some of them fool saloon loafers or bad cowpunchers would try to shoot you for the glory in it. Them kind of men will bob up everywhere you go, Duane."

"I'll be able to ride and take care of myself in a day or two," went on Duane. "Then I'll go—I'd like to talk to you about Jennie."

"She's welcome to a home here with us."

"Thank you, Andrews. You're a kind man. But I want Jennie to get farther away from the Rio Grande. She'd never be safe here. Besides, she may be able to find relatives. She has some, though she doesn't know where they are."

"All right, Duane. Whatever you think best. I reckon now you'd better take her to some town. Go north an' strike for Shelbyville or Crockett. Them's both good towns. I'll tell Jennie the names of men who'll help her. You needn't ride into town at all."

"Which place is nearer, and how far is it?"

"Shelbyville. I reckon about two days' ride. Poor stock country, so you ain't liable to meet rustlers. All the same, better hit the trail at night an' go careful."

At sunset two days later Duane and Jennie mounted their horses and said good-by to the rancher and his wife. Andrews would not listen to Duane's thanks.

"I tell you I'm beholden to you yet," he declared.

"Well, what can I do for you?" asked Duane. "I may come along here again some day."

"Get down an' come in, then, or you're no friend of mine. I reckon there ain't nothin' I can think of—I just happen to remember—" Here he led Duane out of earshot of the women and went on in a whisper. "Buck, I used to be well-to-do. Got skinned by a man named Brown—Rodney Brown. He lives in Huntsville, an' he's my enemy. I never was much on fightin', or I'd fixed him. Brown ruined me—stole all I had. He's a hoss an' cattle thief, an' he has pull enough at home to protect him. I reckon I needn't say any more."

"Is this Brown a man who shot an outlaw named Stevens?" queried Duane, curiously.

"Shore, he's the same. I heard thet story. Brown swears he plugged Stevens through the middle. But the outlaw rode off, an' nobody ever knew for shore."

"Luke Stevens died of that shot. I buried him," said Duane.

Andrews made no further comment, and the two men returned to the women.

"The main road for about three miles, then where it forks take the left-hand road and keep on straight. That what you said, Andrews?"

"Shore. An' good luck to you both!"

Duane and Jennie trotted away into the gathering twilight. At the moment an insistent thought bothered Duane. Both Luke Stevens and the rancher Andrews had hinted to Duane to kill a man named Brown. Duane wished with all his heart that they had not mentioned it, let alone taken for granted the execution of the deed. What a bloody place Texas was! Men who robbed and men who were robbed both wanted murder. It was in the spirit of the country. Duane certainly meant to avoid ever meeting this Rodney Brown. And that very determination showed Duane how dangerous he really was—to men and to himself. Sometimes he had a feeling of how little stood between his sane and better self and a self utterly wild and terrible. He reasoned that only intelligence could save him—only a thoughtful understanding of his danger and a hold upon some ideal.

Then he fell into low conversation with Jennie, holding out hopeful views of her future, and presently darkness set in. The sky was overcast with heavy clouds; there was no air moving; the heat and oppression threatened storm. By and by Duane could not see a rod in front of him, though his horse had no difficulty in keeping to the road. Duane was bothered by the blackness of the night. Traveling fast was impossible, and any moment he might miss the road that led off to the left. So he was compelled to give all his attention to peering into the thick shadows ahead. As good luck would have it, he came to higher ground where there was less mesquite, and therefore not such impenetrable darkness; and at this point he came to where the road split.

Once headed in the right direction, he felt easier in mind. To his annoyance, however, a fine, misty rain set in. Jennie was not well dressed for wet weather; and, for that matter, neither was he. His coat, which in that dry warm climate he seldom needed, was tied behind his saddle, and he put it on Jennie.

They traveled on. The rain fell steadily; if anything, growing thicker. Duane grew uncomfortably wet and chilly. Jennie, however, fared somewhat better by reason of the heavy coat. The night passed quickly despite the discomfort, and soon a gray, dismal, rainy dawn greeted the travelers.

Jennie insisted that he find some shelter where a fire could be built to dry his clothes. He was not in a fit condition to risk catching cold. In fact, Duane's teeth were chattering. To find a shelter in that barren waste seemed a futile task. Quite unexpectedly, however, they happened upon a deserted adobe cabin situated a little off the road. Not only did it prove to have a dry interior, but also there was firewood. Water was available in pools everywhere; however, there was no grass for the horses.

A good fire and hot food and drink changed the aspect of their condition as far as comfort went. And Jennie lay down to sleep. For Duane, however, there must be vigilance. This cabin was no hiding-place. The rain fell harder all the time, and the wind changed to the north. "It's a norther, all right," muttered Duane. "Two or three days." And he felt that his extraordinary luck had not held out. Still one point favored him, and it was that travelers were not likely to come along during the storm. Jennie slept while Duane watched. The saving of this girl meant more to him than any task he had ever assumed. First it had been partly from a human feeling to succor an unfortunate woman, and partly a motive to establish clearly to himself that he was no outlaw. Lately, however, had come a different sense, a strange one, with something personal and warm and protective in it.

As he looked down upon her, a slight, slender girl with bedraggled dress and disheveled hair, her face, pale and quiet, a little stern in sleep, and her long, dark lashes lying on her cheek, he seemed to see her fragility, her prettiness, her femininity as never before. But for him she might at that very moment have been a broken, ruined girl lying back in that cabin of the Blands'. The fact gave him a feeling of his importance in this shifting of her destiny. She was unharmed, still young; she would forget and be happy; she would live to be a good wife and mother. Somehow the thought swelled his heart. His act, death-dealing as it had been, was a noble one, and helped him to hold on to his drifting hopes. Hardly once since Jennie had entered into his thought had those ghosts returned to torment him.

To-morrow she would be gone among good, kind people with a possibility of finding her relatives. He thanked God for that; nevertheless, he felt a pang.

She slept more than half the day. Duane kept guard, always alert, whether he was sitting, standing, or walking. The rain pattered steadily on the roof and sometimes came in gusty flurries through the door. The horses were outside in a shed that afforded poor shelter, and they stamped restlessly. Duane kept them saddled and bridled.

About the middle of the afternoon Jennie awoke. They cooked a meal and afterward sat beside the little fire. She had never been, in his observation of her, anything but a tragic figure, an unhappy girl, the farthest removed from serenity and poise. That characteristic capacity for agitation struck him as stronger in her this day. He attributed it, however, to the long strain, the suspense nearing an end. Yet sometimes when her eyes were on him she did not seem to be thinking of her freedom, of her future.

"This time to-morrow you'll be in Shelbyville," he said.

"Where will you be?" she asked, quickly.

"Me? Oh, I'll be making tracks for some lonesome place," he replied.

The girl shuddered.

"I've been brought up in Texas. I remember what a hard lot the men of my family had. But poor as they were, they had a roof over their heads, a hearth with a fire, a warm bed—somebody to love them. And you, Duane—oh, my God! What must your life be? You must ride and hide and watch eternally. No decent food, no pillow, no friendly word, no clean clothes, no woman's hand! Horses, guns, trails, rocks, holes—these must be the important things in your life. You must go on riding, hiding, killing until you meet—"

She ended with a sob and dropped her head on her knees. Duane was amazed, deeply touched.

"My girl, thank you for that thought of me," he said, with a tremor in his voice. "You don't know how much that means to me."

She raised her face, and it was tear-stained, eloquent, beautiful.

"I've heard tell—the best of men go to the bad out there. You won't. Promise me you won't. I never—knew any man—like you. I—I—we may never see each other again—after to-day. I'll never forget you. I'll pray for you, and I'll never give up trying to—to do something. Don't despair. It's never too late. It was my hope that kept me alive—out there at Bland's—before you came. I was only a poor weak girl. But if I could hope—so can you. Stay away from men. Be a lone wolf. Fight for your life. Stick out your exile—and maybe—some day—"

Then she lost her voice. Duane clasped her hand and with feeling as deep as hers promised to remember her words. In her despair for him she had spoken wisdom—pointed out the only course.

Duane's vigilance, momentarily broken by emotion, had no sooner reasserted itself than he discovered the bay horse, the one Jennie rode, had broken his halter and gone off. The soft wet earth had deadened the sound of his hoofs. His tracks were plain in the mud. There were clumps of mesquite in sight, among which the horse might have strayed. It turned out, however, that he had not done so.

Duane did not want to leave Jennie alone in the cabin so near the road. So he put her up on his horse and bade her follow. The rain had ceased for the time being, though evidently the storm was not yet over. The tracks led up a wash to a wide flat where mesquite, prickly pear, and thorn-bush grew so thickly that Jennie could not ride into it. Duane was thoroughly concerned. He must have her horse. Time was flying. It would soon be night. He could not expect her to scramble quickly through that brake on foot. Therefore he decided to risk leaving her at the edge of the thicket and go in alone.

As he went in a sound startled him. Was it the breaking of a branch he had stepped on or thrust aside? He heard the impatient pound of his horse's hoofs. Then all was quiet. Still he listened, not wholly satisfied. He was never satisfied in regard to safety; he knew too well that there never could be safety for him in this country.

The bay horse had threaded the aisles of the thicket. Duane wondered what had drawn him there. Certainly it had not been grass, for there was none. Presently he heard the horse tramping along, and then he ran. The mud was deep, and the sharp thorns made going difficult. He came up with the horse, and at the same moment crossed a multitude of fresh horse-tracks.

He bent lower to examine them, and was alarmed to find that they had been made very recently, even since it had ceased raining. They were tracks of well-shod horses. Duane straightened up with a cautious glance all around. His instant decision was to hurry back to Jennie. But he had come a goodly way through the thicket, and it was impossible to rush back. Once or twice he imagined he heard crashings in the brush, but did not halt to make sure. Certain he was now that some kind of danger threatened.

Suddenly there came an unmistakable thump of horses' hoofs off somewhere to the fore. Then a scream rent the air. It ended abruptly. Duane leaped forward, tore his way through the thorny brake. He heard Jennie cry again—an appealing call quickly hushed. It seemed more to his right, and he plunged that way. He burst into a glade where a smoldering fire and ground covered with footprints and tracks showed that campers had lately been. Rushing across this, he broke his passage out to the open. But he was too late. His horse had disappeared. Jennie was gone. There were no riders in sight. There was no sound. There was a heavy trail of horses going north. Jennie had been carried off—probably by outlaws. Duane realized that pursuit was out of the question—that Jennie was lost.

CHAPTER X

A hundred miles from the haunts most familiar with Duane's deeds, far up where the Nueces ran a trickling clear stream between yellow cliffs, stood a small deserted shack of covered mesquite poles. It had been made long ago, but was well preserved. A door faced the overgrown trail, and another faced down into a gorge of dense thickets. On the border fugitives from law and men who hid in fear of some one they had wronged never lived in houses with only one door.

It was a wild spot, lonely, not fit for human habitation except for the outcast. He, perhaps, might have found it hard to leave for most of the other wild nooks in that barren country. Down in the gorge there was never-failing sweet water, grass all the year round, cool, shady retreats, deer, rabbits, turkeys, fruit, and miles and miles of narrow-twisting, deep canyon full of broken rocks and impenetrable thickets. The scream of the panther was heard there, the squall of the wildcat, the cough of the jaguar. Innumerable bees buzzed in the spring blossoms, and, it seemed, scattered honey to the winds. All day there was continuous song of birds, that of the mocking-bird loud and sweet and mocking above the rest.

On clear days—and rare indeed were cloudy days—with the subsiding of the wind at sunset a hush seemed to fall around the little hut. Far-distant dim-blue mountains stood gold-rimmed gradually to fade with the shading of light.

At this quiet hour a man climbed up out of the gorge and sat in the westward door of the hut. This lonely watcher of the west and listener to the silence was Duane. And this hut was the one where, three years before, Jennie had nursed him back to life.

The killing of a man named Sellers, and the combination of circumstances that had made the tragedy a memorable regret, had marked, if not a change, at least a cessation in Duane's activities. He had trailed Sellers to kill him for the supposed abducting of Jennie. He had trailed him long after he had learned Sellers traveled alone. Duane wanted absolute assurance of Jennie's death. Vague rumors, a few words here and there, unauthenticated stories, were all Duane had gathered in years to substantiate his belief—that Jennie died shortly after the beginning of her second captivity. But Duane did not know surely. Sellers might have told him. Duane expected, if not to force it from him at the end, to read it in his eyes. But the bullet went too unerringly; it locked his lips and fixed his eyes.

After that meeting Duane lay long at the ranchhouse of a friend, and when he recovered from the wound Sellers had given him he started with two horses and a pack for the lonely gorge on the Nueces. There he had been hidden for months, a prey to remorse, a dreamer, a victim of phantoms.

It took work for him to find subsistence in that rocky

fastness. And work, action, helped to pass the hours. But he could not work all the time, even if he had found it to do. Then in his idle moments and at night his task was to live with the hell in his mind.

The sunset and the twilight hour made all the rest bearable. The little hut on the rim of the gorge seemed to hold Jennie's presence. It was not as if he felt her spirit. If it had been he would have been sure of her death. He hoped Jennie had not survived her second misfortune; and that intense hope had burned into belief, if not surety. Upon his return to that locality, on the occasion of his first visit to the hut, he had found things just as they had left them, and a poor, faded piece of ribbon Jennie had used to tie around her bright hair. No wandering outlaw or traveler had happened upon the lonely spot, which further endeared it to Duane.

A strange feature of this memory of Jennie was the freshness of it—the failure of years, toil, strife, death-dealing to dim it—to deaden the thought of what might have been. He had a marvelous gift of visualization. He could shut his eyes and see Jennie before him just as clearly as if she had stood there in the flesh. For hours he did that, dreaming, dreaming of life he had never tasted and now never would taste. He saw Jennie's slender, graceful figure, the old brown ragged dress in which he had seen her first at Bland's, her little feet in Mexican sandals, her fine hands coarsened by work, her round arms and swelling throat, and her pale, sad, beautiful face with its staring dark eyes. He remembered every look she had given him, every word she had spoken to him, every time she had touched him. He thought of her beauty and sweetness, of the few things which had come to mean to him that she must have loved him; and he trained himself to think of these in preference to her life at Bland's, the escape with him, and then her recapture, because such memories led to bitter, fruitless pain. He had to fight suffering because it was eating out his heart.

Sitting there, eyes wide open, he dreamed of the old homestead and his white-haired mother. He saw the old home life, sweetened and filled by dear new faces and added joys, go on before his eyes with him a part of it.

Then in the inevitable reaction, in the reflux of bitter reality, he would send out a voiceless cry no less poignant because it was silent: "Poor fool! No, I shall never see mother again—never go home—never have a home. I am Duane, the Lone Wolf! Oh, God! I wish it were over! These dreams torture me! What have I to do with a mother, a home, a wife? No bright-haired boy, no dark-eyed girl will ever love me. I am an outlaw, an outcast, dead to the good and decent world. I am alone—alone. Better be a callous brute or better dead! I shall go mad thinking! Man, what is left to you? A hiding-place like a wolf's—lonely silent days, lonely nights with phantoms! Or the trail and the road with their bloody tracks, and then the hard ride, the sleepless, hungry ride to some hole in rocks or brakes. What hellish thing drives me? Why can't I end it all? What is left? Only that damned unquenchable spirit of the gun-fighter to live—to hang on to miserable life—to have no fear of death, yet to cling like a leach—to die as gun-fighters seldom die, with boots off! Bain, you were first, and you're long avenged. I'd change with you. And Sellers, you were last, and you're avenged. And you others—you're avenged. Lie quiet in your graves and give me peace!"

But they did not lie quiet in their graves and give him peace.

A group of specters trooped out of the shadows of dusk and, gathering round him, escorted him to his bed.

When Duane had been riding the trails passion-bent to escape pursuers, or passion-bent in his search, the constant action and toil and exhaustion made him sleep. But when in hiding, as time passed, gradually he required less rest and sleep, and his mind became more active. Little by little his phantoms gained hold on him, and at length, but for the saving power of his dreams, they would have claimed him utterly.

How many times he had said to himself: "I am an intelligent man. I'm not crazy. I'm in full possession of my faculties. All this is fancy—imagination—conscience. I've no work, no duty, no ideal, no hope—and my mind is obsessed, thronged with images. And these images naturally are of the men with whom I have dealt. I can't forget them. They come back to me, hour after hour; and when my tortured mind grows weak, then maybe I'm not just right till the mood wears out and lets me sleep."

So he reasoned as he lay down in his comfortable camp. The night was star-bright above the canyon-walls, darkly shadowing down between them. The insects hummed and chirped and thrummed a continuous thick song, low and monotonous. Slow-running water splashed softly over stones in the stream-bed. From far down the canyon came the mournful hoot of an owl. The moment he lay down, thereby giving up action for the day, all these things weighed upon him like a great heavy mantle of loneliness. In truth, they did not constitute loneliness.

And he could no more have dispelled thought than he could have reached out to touch a cold, bright star.

He wondered how many outcasts like him lay under this star-studded, velvety sky across the fifteen hundred miles of wild country between El Paso and the mouth of the river. A vast wild territory—a refuge for outlaws! Somewhere he had heard or read that the Texas Rangers kept a book with names and records of outlaws—three thousand known outlaws. Yet these could scarcely be half of that unfortunate horde which had been recruited from all over the states. Duane had traveled from camp to camp, den to den, hiding-place to hiding-place, and he knew these men. Most of them were hopeless criminals; some were avengers; a few were wronged wanderers; and among them occasionally was a man, human in his way, honest as he could be, not yet lost to good.

But all of them were akin in one sense—their outlawry; and that starry night they lay with their dark faces up, some in packs like wolves, others alone like the gray wolf who knew no mate. It did not make much difference in Duane's thought of them that the majority were steeped in crime and brutality, more often than not stupid from rum, incapable of a fine feeling, just lost wild dogs.

Duane doubted that there was a man among them who did not realize his moral wreck and ruin. He had met poor, half witted wretches who knew it. He believed he could enter into their minds and feel the truth of all their lives—the hardened outlaw, coarse, ignorant, bestial, who murdered as Bill Black had murdered, who stole for the sake of stealing, who craved money to gamble and drink, defiantly ready for death, and, like that terrible outlaw, Helm, who cried out on the scaffold, "Let her rip!"

The wild youngsters seeking notoriety and reckless adventure; the cowboys with a notch on their guns, with boastful pride in the knowledge that they were marked by rangers; the crooked men from the North, defaulters, forgers, murderers, all pale-faced, flat-chested men not fit for that wilderness and not surviving; the dishonest cattlemen, hand and glove with outlaws, driven from their homes; the old grizzled, bow-legged genuine rustlers—all these Duane had come in contact with, had watched and known, and as he felt with them he seemed to see that as their lives were bad, sooner or later to end dismally or tragically, so they must pay some kind of earthly penalty—if not of conscience, then of fear; if not of fear, then of that most terrible of all things to restless, active men—pain, the pang of flesh and bone.

Duane knew, for he had seen them pay. Best of all, moreover, he knew the internal life of the gun-fighter of that select but by no means small class of which he was representative. The world that judged him and his kind judged him as a machine, a killing-machine, with only mind enough to hunt, to meet, to slay another man. It had taken three endless years for Duane to understand his own father. Duane knew beyond all doubt that the gun-fighters like Bland, like Alloway, like Sellers, men who were evil and had no remorse, no spiritual accusing Nemesis, had something far more torturing to mind, more haunting, more murderous of rest and sleep and peace; and that something was abnormal fear of death. Duane knew this, for he had shot these men; he had seen the quick, dark shadow in eyes, the presentiment that the will could not control, and then the horrible certainty. These men must have been in agony at every meeting with a possible or certain foe—more agony than the hot rend of a bullet. They were haunted, too, haunted by this fear, by every victim calling from the grave that nothing was so inevitable as death, which lurked behind every corner, hid in every shadow, lay deep in the dark tube of every gun. These men could not have a friend; they could not love or trust a woman. They knew their one chance of holding on to life lay in their own distrust, watchfulness, dexterity, and that hope, by the very nature of their lives, could not be lasting. They had doomed themselves. What, then, could possibly have dwelt in the depths of their minds as they went to their beds on a starry night like this, with mystery in silence and shadow, with time passing surely, and the dark future and its secret approaching every hour—what, then, but hell?

The hell in Duane's mind was not fear of man or fear of death. He would have been glad to lay down the burden of life, providing death came naturally. Many times he had prayed for it. But that overdeveloped, superhuman spirit of defense in him precluded suicide or the inviting of an enemy's bullet. Sometimes he had a vague, scarcely analyzed idea that this spirit was what had made the Southwest habitable for the white man.

Every one of his victims, singly and collectively, returned to him for ever, it seemed, in cold, passionless, accusing domination of these haunted hours. They did not accuse him of dishonor or cowardice or brutality or murder; they only accused him of Death. It was as if they knew more than when they were alive, had learned that life was a divine mysterious gift not to be taken. They thronged about him with their voiceless clamoring, drifted around him with their fading eyes.

CHAPTER XI

After nearly six months in the Nueces gorge the loneliness and inaction of his life drove Duane out upon the trails seeking anything rather than to hide longer alone, a prey to the scourge of his thoughts. The moment he rode into sight of men a remarkable transformation occurred in him. A strange warmth stirred in him—a longing to see the faces of people, to hear their voices—a pleasurable emotion sad and strange. But it was only a precursor of his old bitter, sleepless, and eternal vigilance. When he hid alone in the brakes he was safe from all except his deeper, better self; when he escaped from this into the haunts of men his force and will went to the preservation of his life.

Mercer was the first village he rode into. He had many friends there. Mercer claimed to owe Duane a debt. On the outskirts of the village there was a grave overgrown by brush so that the rude-lettered post which marked it was scarcely visible to Duane as he rode by. He had never read the inscription. But he thought now of Hardin, no other than the erstwhile ally of Bland. For many years Hardin had harassed the stockmen and ranchers in and around Mercer. On an evil day for him he or his outlaws had beaten and robbed a man who once succored Duane when sore in need. Duane met Hardin in the little plaza of the village, called him every name known to border men, taunted him to draw, and killed him in the act.

Duane went to the house of one Jones, a Texan who had known his father, and there he was warmly received. The feel of an honest hand, the voice of a friend, the prattle of children who were not afraid of him or his gun, good wholesome food, and change of clothes—these things for the time being made a changed man of Duane. To be sure, he did not often speak. The price of his head and the weight of his burden made him silent. But eagerly he drank in all the news that was told him. In the years of his absence from home he had never heard a word about his mother or uncle. Those who were his real friends on the border would have been the last to make inquiries, to write or receive letters that might give a clue to Duane's whereabouts.

Duane remained all day with this hospitable Jones, and as twilight fell was loath to go and yielded to a pressing invitation to remain overnight. It was seldom indeed that Duane slept under a roof. Early in the evening, while Duane sat on the porch with two awed and hero-worshiping sons of the house, Jones returned from a quick visit down to the post-office. Summarily he sent the boys off. He labored under intense excitement.

"Duane, there's rangers in town," he whispered. "It's all over town, too, that you're here. You rode in long after sunup. Lots of people saw you. I don't believe there's a man or boy that 'd squeal on you. But the women might. They gossip, and these rangers are handsome fellows—devils with the women."

"What company of rangers?" asked Duane, quickly.

"Company A, under Captain MacNelly, that new ranger. He made a big name in the war. And since he's been in the ranger service he's done wonders. He's cleaned up some bad places south, and he's working north."

"MacNelly. I've heard of him. Describe him to me."

"Slight-built chap, but wiry and tough. Clean face, black mustache and hair. Sharp black eyes. He's got a look of authority. MacNelly's a fine man, Duane. Belongs to a good Southern family. I'd hate to have him look you up."

Duane did not speak.

"MacNelly's got nerve, and his rangers are all experienced men. If they find out you're here they'll come after you. MacNelly's no gun-fighter, but he wouldn't hesitate to do his duty, even if he faced sure death. Which he would in this case. Duane, you mustn't meet Captain MacNelly. Your record is clean, if it is terrible. You never met a ranger or any officer except a rotten sheriff now and then, like Rod Brown."

Still Duane kept silence. He was not thinking of danger, but of the fact of how fleeting must be his stay among friends.

"I've already fixed up a pack of grub," went on Jones. "I'll slip out to saddle your horse. You watch here."

He had scarcely uttered the last word when soft, swift footsteps sounded on the hard path. A man turned in at the gate. The light was dim, yet clean enough to disclose an unusually tall figure. When it appeared nearer he was seen to be walking with both arms raised, hands high. He slowed his stride.

"Does Burt Jones live here?" he asked, in a low, hurried voice.

"I reckon. I'm Burt. What can I do for you?" replied Jones.

The stranger peered around, stealthily came closer, still with his hands up.

"It is known that Buck Duane is here. Captain MacNelly's camping on the river just out of town. He sends word to Duane to come out there after dark."

The stranger wheeled and departed as swiftly and strangely as he had come.

"Bust me! Duane, whatever do you make of that?" exclaimed Jones.

"A new one on me," replied Duane, thoughtfully.

"First fool thing I ever heard of MacNelly doing. Can't make head nor tails of it. I'd have said offhand that MacNelly wouldn't double-cross anybody. He struck me as a square man, sand all through. But, hell! he must mean treachery. I can't see anything else in that deal."

"Maybe the Captain wants to give me a fair chance to surrender without bloodshed," observed Duane. "Pretty decent of him, if he meant that."

"He INVITES YOU out to his camp AFTER DARK. Something strange about this, Duane. But MacNelly's a new man out here. He does some queer things. Perhaps he's getting a swelled head. Well, whatever his intentions, his presence around Mercer is enough for us. Duane, you hit the road and put some miles between you the amiable Captain before daylight. To-morrow I'll go out there and ask him what in the devil he meant."

"That messenger he sent—he was a ranger," said Duane.

"Sure he was, and a nervy one! It must have taken sand to come bracing you that way. Duane, the fellow didn't pack a gun. I'll swear to that. Pretty odd, this trick. But you can't trust it. Hit the road, Duane."

A little later a black horse with muffled hoofs, bearing a tall, dark rider who peered keenly into every shadow, trotted down a pasture lane back of Jones's house, turned into the road, and then, breaking into swifter gait, rapidly left Mercer behind.

Fifteen or twenty miles out Duane drew rein in a forest of mesquite, dismounted, and searched about for a glade with a little grass. Here he staked his horse on a long lariat; and, using his saddle for a pillow, his saddle-blanket for covering, he went to sleep.

Next morning he was off again, working south. During the next few days he paid brief visits to several villages that lay in his path. And in each some one particular friend had a piece of news to impart that made Duane profoundly thoughtful. A ranger had made a quiet, unobtrusive call upon these friends and left this message, "Tell Buck Duane to ride into Captain MacNelly's camp some time after night."

Duane concluded, and his friends all agreed with him, that the new ranger's main purpose in the Nueces country was to capture or kill Buck Duane, and that this message was simply an original and striking ruse, the daring of which might appeal to certain outlaws.

But it did not appeal to Duane. His curiosity was aroused; it did not, however, tempt him to any foolhardy act. He turned southwest and rode a hundred miles until he again reached the sparsely settled country. Here he heard no more of rangers. It was a barren region he had never but once ridden through, and that ride had cost him dear. He had been compelled to shoot his way out. Outlaws were not in accord with the few ranchers and their cowboys who ranged there. He learned that both outlaws and Mexican raiders had long been at bitter enmity with these ranchers. Being unfamiliar with roads and trails, Duane had pushed on into the heart of this district, when all the time he really believed he was traveling around it. A rifle-shot from a ranch-house, a deliberate attempt to kill him because he was an unknown rider in those parts, discovered to Duane his mistake; and a hard ride to get away persuaded him to return to his old methods of hiding by day and traveling by night.

He got into rough country, rode for three days without covering much ground, but believed that he was getting on safer territory. Twice he came to a wide bottom-land green with willow and cottonwood and thick as chaparral, somewhere through the middle of which ran a river he decided must be the lower Nueces.

One evening, as he stole out from a covert where he had camped, he saw the lights of a village. He tried to pass it on the left, but was unable to because the brakes of this bottom-land extended in almost to the outskirts of the village, and he had to retrace his steps and go round to the right. Wire fences and horses in pasture made this a task, so it was well after midnight before he accomplished it. He made ten miles or more then by daylight, and after that proceeded cautiously along a road which appeared to be well worn from travel. He passed several thickets where he would have halted to hide during the day but for the fact that he had to find water.

He was a long while in coming to it, and then there was no thicket or clump of mesquite near the water-hole that would afford him covert. So he kept on.

The country before him was ridgy and began to show cottonwoods here and there in the hollows and yucca and mesquite on the higher ground. As he mounted a ridge he noted that the road made a sharp turn, and he could not see what was beyond it. He slowed up and was making the turn, which was down-hill between high banks of yellow clay, when his mettlesome horse heard something to frighten him or shied at something and bolted.

The few bounds he took before Duane's iron arm checked him were enough to reach the curve. One flashing glance showed Duane the open once more, a little valley below with a wide, shallow, rocky stream, a clump of cottonwoods beyond, a somber group of men facing him, and two dark, limp, strangely grotesque figures hanging from branches.

The sight was common enough in southwest Texas, but Duane had never before found himself so unpleasantly close.

A hoarse voice pealed out: "By hell! there's another one!"

"Stranger, ride down an' account fer yourself!" yelled another.

"Hands up!"

"Thet's right, Jack; don't take no chances. Plug him!"

These remarks were so swiftly uttered as almost to be continuous. Duane was wheeling his horse when a rifle cracked. The bullet struck his left forearm and he thought broke it, for he dropped the rein. The frightened horse leaped. Another bullet whistled past Duane. Then the bend in the road saved him probably from certain death. Like the wind his fleet steed wend down the long hill.

Duane was in no hurry to look back. He knew what to expect. His chief concern of the moment was for his injured arm. He found that the bones were still intact; but the wound, having been made by a soft bullet, was an exceedingly bad one. Blood poured from it. Giving the horse his head, Duane wound his scarf tightly round the holes, and with teeth and hand tied it tightly. That done, he looked back over his shoulder.

Riders were making the dust fly on the hillside road. There were more coming round the cut where the road curved. The leader was perhaps a quarter of a mile back, and the others strung out behind him. Duane needed only one glance to tell him that they were fast and hard-riding cowboys in a land where all riders were good. They would not have owned any but strong, swift horses. Moreover, it was a district where ranchers had suffered beyond all endurance the greed and brutality of outlaws. Duane had simply been so unfortunate as to run right into a lynching party at a time of all times when any stranger would be in danger and any outlaw put to his limit to escape with his life.

Duane did not look back again till he had crossed the ridgy piece of ground and had gotten to the level road. He had gained upon his pursuers. When he ascertained this he tried to save his horse, to check a little that killing gait. This horse was a magnificent animal, big, strong, fast; but his endurance had never been put to a grueling test. And that worried Duane. His life had made it impossible to keep one horse very long at a time, and this one was an unknown quantity.

Duane had only one plan—the only plan possible in this case—and that was to make the river-bottoms, where he might elude his pursuers in the willow brakes. Fifteen miles or so would bring him to the river, and this was not a hopeless distance for any good horse if not too closely pressed. Duane concluded presently that the cowboys behind were losing a little in the chase because they were not extending their horses. It was decidedly unusual for such riders to save their mounts. Duane pondered over this, looking backward several times to see if their horses were stretched out. They were not, and the fact was disturbing. Only one reason presented itself to Duane's conjecturing, and it was that with him headed straight on that road his pursuers were satisfied not to force the running. He began to hope and look for a trail or a road turning off to right or left. There was none. A rough, mesquite-dotted and yucca-spired country extended away on either side. Duane believed that he would be compelled to take to this hard going. One thing was certain—he had to go round the village. The river, however, was on the outskirts of the village; and once in the willows, he would be safe.

Dust-clouds far ahead caused his alarm to grow. He watched with his eyes strained; he hoped to see a wagon, a few stray cattle. But no, he soon descried several horsemen. Shots and yells behind him attested to the fact that his pursuers likewise had seen these new-comers on the scene. More than a mile separated these two parties, yet that distance did not keep them from soon understanding each other. Duane waited only to see this new factor show signs of sudden quick action, and then, with a muttered curse, he spurred his horse off the road into the brush.

He chose the right side, because the river lay nearer that way. There were patches of open sandy ground between clumps of cactus and mesquite, and he found that despite a zigzag course he made better time. It was impossible for him to locate his pursuers. They would come together, he decided, and take to his tracks.

What, then, was his surprise and dismay to run out of a thicket right into a low ridge of rough, broken rock, impossible to get a horse over. He wheeled to the left along its base. The sandy ground gave place to a harder soil, where his horse did not labor so. Here the growths of mesquite and cactus became scanter, affording better travel but poor cover. He kept sharp eyes ahead, and, as he had expected, soon saw moving dust-clouds and the dark figures of horses. They were half a mile away, and swinging obliquely across the flat, which fact proved that they had entertained a fair idea of the country and the fugitive's difficulty.

Without an instant's hesitation Duane put his horse to his best efforts, straight ahead. He had to pass those men. When this was seemingly made impossible by a deep wash from which he had to turn, Duane began to feel cold and sick. Was this the end? Always there had to be an end to an outlaw's career. He wanted then to ride straight at these pursuers. But reason outweighed instinct. He was fleeing for his life; nevertheless, the strongest instinct at the time was his desire to fight.

He knew when these three horsemen saw him, and a moment afterward he lost sight of them as he got into the mesquite again. He meant now to try to reach the road, and pushed his mount severely, though still saving him for a final burst. Rocks, thickets, bunches of cactus, washes—all operated against his following a straight line. Almost he lost his bearings, and finally would have ridden toward his enemies had not good fortune favored him in the matter of an open burned-over stretch of ground.

Here he saw both groups of pursuers, one on each side and almost within gun-shot. Their sharp yells, as much as his cruel spurs, drove his horse into that pace which now meant life or death for him. And never had Duane bestrode a gamer, swifter, stancher beast. He seemed about to accomplish the impossible. In the dragging sand he was far superior to any horse in pursuit, and on this sandy open stretch he gained enough to spare a little in the brush beyond. Heated now and thoroughly terrorized, he kept the pace through thickets that almost tore Duane from his saddle. Something weighty and grim eased off Duane. He was going to get out in front! The horse had speed, fire, stamina.

Duane dashed out into another open place dotted by few trees, and here, right in his path, within pistol-range, stood horsemen waiting. They yelled, they spurred toward him, but did not fire at him. He turned his horse—faced to the right. Only one thing kept him from standing his ground to fight it out. He remembered those dangling limp figures hanging from the cottonwoods. These ranchers would rather hang an outlaw than do anything. They might draw all his fire and then capture him. His horror of hanging was so great as to be all out of proportion compared to his gun-fighter's instinct of self-preservation.

A race began then, a dusty, crashing drive through gray mesquite. Duane could scarcely see, he was so blinded by stinging branches across his eyes. The hollow wind roared in his ears. He lost his sense of the nearness of his pursuers. But they must have been close. Did they shoot at him? He imagined he heard shots. But that might have been the cracking of dead snags. His left arm hung limp, almost useless; he handled the rein with his right; and most of the time he hung low over the pommel. The gray walls flashing by him, the whip of twigs, the rush of wind, the heavy, rapid pound of hoofs, the violent motion of his horse—these vied in sensation with the smart of sweat in his eyes, the rack of his wound, the cold, sick cramp in his stomach. With these also was dull, raging fury. He had to run when he wanted to fight. It took all his mind to force back that bitter hate of himself, of his pursuers, of this race for his useless life.

Suddenly he burst out of a line of mesquite into the road. A long stretch of lonely road! How fiercely, with hot, strange joy, he wheeled his horse upon it! Then he was sweeping along, sure now that he was out in front. His horse still had strength and speed, but showed signs of breaking. Presently Duane looked back. Pursuers—he could not count how many—were loping along in his rear. He paid no more attention to them, and with teeth set he faced ahead, grimmer now in his determination to foil them.

He passed a few scattered ranch-houses where horses whistled from corrals, and men curiously watched him fly past. He saw one rancher running, and he felt intuitively that this fellow was going to join in the chase. Duane's steed pounded on, not noticeably slower, but with a lack of former smoothness, with a strained, convulsive, jerking stride which showed he was almost done.

Sight of the village ahead surprised Duane. He had reached it sooner than he expected. Then he made a discovery—he had entered the zone of wire fences. As he dared not turn back now, he kept on, intending to ride through the village. Looking backward, he saw that his pursuers were half a mile distant, too far to alarm any villagers in time to intercept him in his flight. As he rode by the first houses his horse broke and began to labor. Duane did not believe he would last long enough to go through the village.

Saddled horses in front of a store gave Duane an idea, not by any means new, and one he had carried out successfully before. As he pulled in his heaving mount and leaped off, a couple of ranchers came out of the place, and one of them stepped to a clean-limbed, fiery bay. He was about to get into his saddle when he saw Duane, and then he halted, a foot in the stirrup.

Duane strode forward, grasped the bridle of this man's horse.

"Mine's done—but not killed," he panted. "Trade with me."

"Wal, stranger, I'm shore always ready to trade," drawled the man. "But ain't you a little swift?"

Duane glanced back up the road. His pursuers were entering the village.

"I'm Duane—Buck Duane," he cried, menacingly. "Will you trade? Hurry!"

The rancher, turning white, dropped his foot from the stirrup and fell back.

"I reckon I'll trade," he said.

Bounding up, Duane dug spurs into the bay's flanks. The horse snorted in fright, plunged into a run. He was fresh, swift, half wild. Duane flashed by the remaining houses on the street out into the open. But the road ended at that village or else led out from some other quarter, for he had ridden straight into the fields and from them into rough desert. When he reached the cover of mesquite once more he looked back to find six horsemen within rifle-shot of him, and more coming behind them.

His new horse had not had time to get warm before Duane reached a high sandy bluff below which lay the willow brakes. As far as he could see extended an immense flat strip of red-tinged willow. How welcome it was to his eye! He felt like a hunted wolf that, weary and lame, had reached his hole in the rocks. Zigzagging down the soft slope, he put the bay to the dense wall of leaf and branch. But the horse balked.

There was little time to lose. Dismounting, he dragged the stubborn beast into the thicket. This was harder and slower work than Duane cared to risk. If he had not been rushed he might have had better success. So he had to abandon the horse—a circumstance that only such sore straits could have driven him to. Then he went slipping swiftly through the narrow aisles.

He had not gotten under cover any too soon. For he heard his pursuers piling over the bluff, loud-voiced, confident, brutal. They crashed into the willows.

"Hi, Sid! Heah's your hoss!" called one, evidently to the man Duane had forced into a trade.

"Say, if you locoed gents'll hold up a little I'll tell you somethin'," replied a voice from the bluff.

"Come on, Sid! We got him corralled," said the first speaker.

"Wal, mebbe, an' if you hev it's liable to be damn hot. THET FELLER WAS BUCK DUANE!"

Absolute silence followed that statement. Presently it was broken by a rattling of loose gravel and then low voices.

"He can't git across the river, I tell you," came to Duane's ears. "He's corralled in the brake. I know thet hole."

Then Duane, gliding silently and swiftly through the willows, heard no more from his pursuers. He headed straight for the river. Threading a passage through a willow brake was an old task for him. Many days and nights had gone to the acquiring of a skill that might have been envied by an Indian.

The Rio Grande and its tributaries for the most of their length in Texas ran between wide, low, flat lands covered by a dense growth of willow. Cottonwood, mesquite, prickly pear, and other growths mingled with the willow, and altogether they made a matted, tangled copse, a thicket that an inexperienced man would have considered impenetrable. From above, these wild brakes looked green and red; from the inside they were gray and yellow—a striped wall. Trails and glades were scarce. There were a few deer-runways and sometimes little paths made by peccaries—the jabali, or wild pigs, of Mexico. The ground was clay and unusually dry, sometimes baked so hard that it left no imprint of a track. Where a growth of cottonwood had held back the encroachment of the willows there usually was thick grass and underbrush. The willows were short, slender poles with stems so close together that they almost touched, and with the leafy foliage forming a thick covering. The depths of this brake Duane had penetrated was a silent, dreamy, strange place. In the middle of the day the light was weird and dim. When a breeze fluttered the foliage, then slender shafts and spears of sunshine pierced the green mantle and danced like gold on the ground.

Duane had always felt the strangeness of this kind of place, and likewise he had felt a protecting, harboring something which always seemed to him to be the sympathy of the brake for a hunted creature. Any unwounded creature, strong and resourceful, was safe when he had glided under the low, rustling green roof of this wild covert. It was not hard to conceal tracks; the springy soil gave forth no sound; and men could hunt each other for weeks, pass within a few yards of each other and never know it. The problem of sustaining life was difficult; but, then, hunted men and animals survived on very little.

Duane wanted to cross the river if that was possible, and, keeping in the brake, work his way upstream till he had reached country more hospitable. Remembering what the man had said in regard to the river, Duane had his doubts about crossing. But he would take any chance to put the river between him and his hunters. He pushed on. His left arm had to be favored, as he could scarcely move it. Using his right to spread the willows, he slipped sideways between them and made fast time. There were narrow aisles and washes and holes low down and paths brushed by animals, all of which he took advantage of, running, walking, crawling, stooping any way to get along. To keep in a straight line was not easy—he did it by marking some bright sunlit stem or tree ahead, and when he reached it looked straight on to mark another. His progress necessarily grew slower, for as he advanced the brake became wilder, denser, darker. Mosquitoes began to whine about his head. He kept on without pause. Deepening shadows under the willows told him that the afternoon was far advanced. He began to fear he had wandered in a wrong direction. Finally a strip of light ahead relieved his anxiety, and after a toilsome penetration of still denser brush he broke through to the bank of the river.

He faced a wide, shallow, muddy stream with brakes on the opposite bank extending like a green and yellow wall. Duane perceived at a glance the futility of his trying to cross at this point. Everywhere the sluggish water raved quicksand bars. In fact, the bed of the river was all quicksand, and very likely there was not a foot of water anywhere. He could not swim; he could not crawl; he could not push a log across. Any solid thing touching that smooth yellow sand would be grasped and sucked down. To prove this he seized a long pole and, reaching down from the high bank, thrust it into the stream. Right there near shore there apparently was no bottom to the treacherous quicksand. He abandoned any hope of crossing the river. Probably for miles up and down it would be just the same as here. Before leaving the bank he tied his hat upon the pole and lifted enough water to quench his thirst. Then he worked his way back to where thinner growth made advancement easier, and kept on upstream till the shadows were so deep he could not see. Feeling around for a place big enough to stretch out on, he lay down. For the time being he was as safe there as he would have been beyond in the Rim Rock. He was tired, though not exhausted, and in spite of the throbbing pain in his arm he dropped at once into sleep.

CHAPTER XII

Some time during the night Duane awoke. A stillness seemingly so thick and heavy as to have substance blanketed the black willow brake. He could not see a star or a branch or tree-trunk or even his hand before his eyes. He lay there waiting, listening, sure that he had been awakened by an unusual sound. Ordinary noises of the night in the wilderness never disturbed his rest. His faculties, like those of old fugitives and hunted creatures, had become trained to a marvelous keenness. A long low breath of slow wind moaned through the willows, passed away; some stealthy, soft-footed beast trotted by him in the darkness; there was a rustling among dry leaves; a fox barked lonesomely in the distance. But none of these sounds had broken his slumber.

Suddenly, piercing the stillness, came a bay of a bloodhound. Quickly Duane sat up, chilled to his marrow. The action made him aware of his crippled arm. Then came other bays, lower, more distant. Silence enfolded him again, all the more oppressive and menacing in his suspense. Bloodhounds had been put on his trail, and the leader was not far away. All his life Duane had been familiar with bloodhounds; and he knew that if the pack surrounded him in this impenetrable darkness he would be held at bay or dragged down as wolves dragged a stag. Rising to his feet, prepared to flee as best he could, he waited to be sure of the direction he should take.

The leader of the hounds broke into cry again, a deep, full-toned, ringing bay, strange, ominous, terribly significant in its power. It caused a cold sweat to ooze out all over Duane's body. He turned from it, and with his uninjured arm outstretched to feel for the willows he groped his way along. As it was impossible to pick out the narrow passages, he had to slip and squeeze and plunge between the yielding stems. He made such a crashing that he no longer heard the baying of the hounds. He had no hope to elude them. He meant to climb the first cottonwood that he stumbled upon in his blind flight. But it appeared he never was going to be lucky enough to run against one. Often he fell, sometimes flat, at others upheld by the willows. What made the work so hard was the fact that he had only one arm to open a clump of close-growing stems and his feet would catch or tangle in the narrow crotches, holding him fast. He had to struggle desperately. It was as if the willows were clutching hands, his enemies, fiendishly impeding his progress. He tore his clothes on sharp branches and his flesh suffered many a prick. But in a terrible earnestness he kept on until he brought up hard against a cottonwood tree.

There he leaned and rested. He found himself as nearly exhausted as he had ever been, wet with sweat, his hands torn and burning, his breast laboring, his legs stinging from innumerable bruises. While he leaned there to catch his breath he listened for the pursuing hounds. For a long time there was no sound from them. This, however, did not deceive him into any hopefulness. There were bloodhounds that bayed often on a trail, and others that ran mostly silent. The former were more valuable to their owner and the latter more dangerous to the fugitive. Presently Duane's ears were filled by a chorus of short ringing yelps. The pack had found where he had slept, and now the trail was hot. Satisfied that they would soon overtake him, Duane set about climbing the cottonwood, which in his condition was difficult of ascent.

It happened to be a fairly large tree with a fork about fifteen feet up, and branches thereafter in succession. Duane climbed until he got above the enshrouding belt of blackness. A pale gray mist hung above the brake, and through it shone a line of dim lights. Duane decided these were bonfires made along the bluff to render his escape more difficult on that side. Away round in the direction he thought was north he imagined he saw more fires, but, as the mist was thick, he could not be sure. While he sat there pondering the matter, listening for the hounds, the mist and the gloom on one side lightened; and this side he concluded was east and meant that dawn was near. Satisfying himself on this score, he descended to the first branch of the tree.

His situation now, though still critical, did not appear to be so hopeless as it had been. The hounds would soon close in on him, and he would kill them or drive them away. It was beyond the bounds of possibility that any men could have followed running hounds through that brake in the night. The thing that worried Duane was the fact of the bonfires. He had gathered from the words of one of his pursuers that the brake was a kind of trap, and he began to believe there was only one way out of it, and that was along the bank where he had entered, and where obviously all night long his pursuers had kept fires burning. Further conjecture on this point, however, was interrupted by a crashing in the willows and the rapid patter of feet.

Underneath Duane lay a gray, foggy obscurity. He could not see the ground, nor any object but the black trunk of the tree. Sight would not be needed to tell him when the pack arrived. With a pattering rush through the willows the hounds reached the tree; and then high above crash of brush and thud of heavy paws rose a hideous clamor. Duane's pursuers far off to the south would hear that and know what it meant. And at daybreak, perhaps before, they would take a short cut across the brake, guided by the baying of hounds that had treed their quarry.

It wanted only a few moments, however, till Duane could distinguish the vague forms of the hounds in the gray shadow below. Still he waited. He had no shots to spare. And he knew how to treat bloodhounds. Gradually the obscurity lightened, and at length Duane had good enough sight of the hounds for his purpose. His first shot killed the huge brute leader of the pack. Then, with unerring shots, he crippled several others. That stopped the baying. Piercing howls arose. The pack took fright and fled, its course easily marked by the howls of the crippled members. Duane reloaded his gun, and, making certain all the hounds had gone, he descended to the ground and set off at a rapid pace to the northward.

The mist had dissolved under a rising sun when Duane made his first halt some miles north of the scene where he had waited for the hounds. A barrier to further progress, in shape of a precipitous rocky bluff, rose sheer from the willow brake. He skirted the base of the cliff, where walking was comparatively easy, around in the direction of the river. He reached the end finally to see there was absolutely no chance to escape from the brake at that corner. It took extreme labor, attended by some hazard and considerable pain to his arm, to get down where he could fill his sombrero with water. After quenching his thirst he had a look at his wound. It was caked over with blood and dirt. When washed off the arm was seen to be inflamed and swollen around the bullet-hole. He bathed it, experiencing a soothing relief in the cool water. Then he bandaged it as best he could and arranged a sling round his neck. This mitigated the pain of the injured member and held it in a quiet and restful position, where it had a chance to begin mending.

As Duane turned away from the river he felt refreshed. His great strength and endurance had always made fatigue something almost unknown to him. However, tramping on foot day and night was as unusual to him as to any other riders of the Southwest, and it had begun to tell on him. Retracing his steps, he reached the point where he had abruptly come upon the bluff, and here he determined to follow along its base in the other direction until he found a way out or discovered the futility of such effort.

Duane covered ground rapidly. From time to time he paused to listen. But he was always listening, and his eyes were ever roving. This alertness had become second nature with him, so that except in extreme cases of caution he performed it while he pondered his gloomy and fateful situation. Such habit of alertness and thought made time fly swiftly.

By noon he had rounded the wide curve of the brake and was facing south. The bluff had petered out from a high, mountainous wall to a low abutment of rock, but it still held to its steep, rough nature and afforded no crack or slope where quick ascent could have been possible. He pushed on, growing warier as he approached the danger-zone, finding that as he neared the river on this side it was imperative to go deeper into the willows. In the afternoon he reached a point where he could see men pacing to and fro on the bluff. This assured him that whatever place was guarded was one by which he might escape. He headed toward these men and approached to within a hundred paces of the bluff where they were. There were several men and several boys, all armed and, after the manner of Texans, taking their task leisurely. Farther down Duane made out black dots on the horizon of the bluff-line, and these he concluded were more guards stationed at another outlet. Probably all the available men in the district were on duty. Texans took a grim pleasure in such work. Duane remembered that upon several occasions he had served such duty himself.

Duane peered through the branches and studied the lay of the land. For several hundred yards the bluff could be climbed. He took stock of those careless guards. They had rifles, and that made vain any attempt to pass them in daylight. He believed an attempt by night might be successful; and he was swiftly coming to a determination to hide there till dark and then try it, when the sudden yelping of a dog betrayed him to the guards on the bluff.

The dog had likely been placed there to give an alarm, and he was lustily true to his trust. Duane saw the men run together and begin to talk excitedly and peer into the brake, which was a signal for him to slip away under the willows. He made no noise, and he assured himself he must be invisible. Nevertheless, he heard shouts, then the cracking of rifles, and bullets began to zip and swish through the leafy covert. The day was hot and windless, and Duane concluded that whenever he touched a willow stem, even ever so slightly, it vibrated to the top and sent a quiver among the leaves. Through this the guards had located his position. Once a bullet hissed by him; another thudded into the ground before him. This shooting loosed a rage in Duane. He had to fly from these men, and he hated them and himself because of it. Always in the fury of such moments he wanted to give back shot for shot. But he slipped on through the willows, and at length the rifles ceased to crack.

He sheered to the left again, in line with the rocky

barrier, and kept on, wondering what the next mile would bring.

It brought worse, for he was seen by sharp-eyed scouts, and a hot fusillade drove him to run for his life, luckily to escape with no more than a bullet-creased shoulder.

Later that day, still undaunted, he sheered again toward the trap-wall, and found that the nearer he approached to the place where he had come down into the brake the greater his danger. To attempt to run the blockade of that trail by day would be fatal. He waited for night, and after the brightness of the fires had somewhat lessened he assayed to creep out of the brake. He succeeded in reaching the foot of the bluff, here only a bank, and had begun to crawl stealthily up under cover of a shadow when a hound again betrayed his position. Retreating to the willows was as perilous a task as had ever confronted Duane, and when he had accomplished it, right under what seemed a hundred blazing rifles, he felt that he had indeed been favored by Providence. This time men followed him a goodly ways into the brake, and the ripping of lead through the willows sounded on all sides of him.

When the noise of pursuit ceased Duane sat down in the darkness, his mind clamped between two things—whether to try again to escape or wait for possible opportunity. He seemed incapable of decision. His intelligence told him that every hour lessened his chances for escape. He had little enough chance in any case, and that was what made another attempt so desperately hard. Still it was not love of life that bound him. There would come an hour, sooner or later, when he would wrench decision out of this chaos of emotion and thought. But that time was not yet. He had remained quiet long enough to cool off and recover from his run he found that he was tired. He stretched out to rest. But the swarms of vicious mosquitoes prevented sleep. This corner of the brake was low and near the river, a breeding-ground for the blood-suckers. They sang and hummed and whined around him in an ever-increasing horde. He covered his head and hands with his coat and lay there patiently. That was a long and wretched night. Morning found him still strong physically, but in a dreadful state of mind.

First he hurried for the river. He could withstand the pangs of hunger, but it was imperative to quench thirst. His wound made him feverish, and therefore more than usually hot and thirsty. Again he was refreshed. That morning he was hard put to it to hold himself back from attempting to cross the river. If he could find a light log it was within the bounds of possibility that he might ford the shallow water and bars of quicksand. But not yet! Wearily, doggedly he faced about toward the bluff.

All that day and all that night, all the next day and all the next night, he stole like a hunted savage from river to bluff; and every hour forced upon him the bitter certainty that he was trapped.

Duane lost track of days, of events. He had come to an evil pass. There arrived an hour when, closely pressed by pursuers at the extreme southern corner of the brake, he took to a dense thicket of willows, driven to what he believed was his last stand.

If only these human bloodhounds would swiftly close in on him! Let him fight to the last bitter gasp and have it over! But these hunters, eager as they were to get him, had care of their own skins. They took few risks. They had him cornered.

It was the middle of the day, hot, dusty, oppressive, threatening storm. Like a snake Duane crawled into a little space in the darkest part of the thicket and lay still. Men had cut him off from the bluff, from the river, seemingly from all sides. But he heard voices only from in front and toward his left. Even if his passage to the river had not been blocked, it might just as well have been.

"Come on fellers—down hyar," called one man from the bluff.

"Got him corralled at last," shouted another.

"Reckon ye needn't be too shore. We thought thet more'n once," taunted another.

"I seen him, I tell you."

"Aw, thet was a deer."

"But Bill found fresh tracks an' blood on the willows."

"If he's winged we needn't hurry."

"Hold on thar, you boys," came a shout in authoritative tones from farther up the bluff. "Go slow. You-all air gittin' foolish at the end of a long chase."

"Thet's right, Colonel. Hold 'em back. There's nothin' shorer than somebody'll be stoppin' lead pretty quick.

He'll be huntin' us soon!"

"Let's surround this corner an' starve him out."

"Fire the brake."

How clearly all this talk pierced Duane's ears! In it he seemed to hear his doom. This, then, was the end he had always expected, which had been close to him before, yet never like now.

"By God!" whispered Duane, "the thing for me to do now—is go out—meet them!"

That was prompted by the fighting, the killing instinct in him. In that moment it had almost superhuman power. If he must die, that was the way for him to die. What else could be expected of Buck Duane? He got to his knees and drew his gun. With his swollen and almost useless hand he held what spare ammunition he had left. He ought to creep out noiselessly to the edge of the willows, suddenly face his pursuers, then, while there was a beat left in his heart, kill, kill, kill. These men all had rifles. The fight would be short. But the marksmen did not live on earth who could make such a fight go wholly against him. Confronting them suddenly he could kill a man for every shot in his gun.

Thus Duane reasoned. So he hoped to accept his fate—to meet this end. But when he tried to step forward something checked him. He forced himself; yet he could not go. The obstruction that opposed his will was as insurmountable as it had been physically impossible for him to climb the bluff.

Slowly he fell back, crouched low, and then lay flat. The grim and ghastly dignity that had been his a moment before fell away from him. He lay there stripped of his last shred of self-respect. He wondered was he afraid; had he, the last of the Duanes—had he come to feel fear? No! Never in all his wild life had he so longed to go out and meet men face to face. It was not fear that held him back. He hated this hiding, this eternal vigilance, this hopeless life. The damnable paradox of the situation was that if he went out to meet these men there was absolutely no doubt of his doom. If he clung to his covert there was a chance, a merest chance, for his life. These pursuers, dogged and unflagging as they had been, were mortally afraid of him. It was his fame that made them cowards. Duane's keenness told him that at the very darkest and most perilous moment there was still a chance for him. And the blood in him, the temper of his father, the years of his outlawry, the pride of his unsought and hated career, the nameless, inexplicable something in him made him accept that slim chance.

Waiting then became a physical and mental agony. He lay under the burning sun, parched by thirst, laboring to breathe, sweating and bleeding. His uncared-for wound was like a red-hot prong in his flesh. Blotched and swollen from the never-ending attack of flies and mosquitoes his face seemed twice its natural size, and it ached and stung.

On one side, then, was this physical torture; on the other the old hell, terribly augmented at this crisis, in his mind. It seemed that thought and imagination had never been so swift. If death found him presently, how would it come? Would he get decent burial or be left for the peccaries and the coyotes? Would his people ever know where he had fallen? How wretched, how miserable his state! It was cowardly, it was monstrous for him to cling longer to this doomed life. Then the hate in his heart, the hellish hate of these men on his trail—that was like a scourge. He felt no longer human. He had degenerated into an animal that could think. His heart pounded, his pulse beat, his breast heaved; and this internal strife seemed to thunder into his ears. He was now enacting the tragedy of all crippled, starved, hunted wolves at bay in their dens. Only his tragedy was infinitely more terrible because he had mind enough to see his plight, his resemblance to a lonely wolf, bloody-fanged, dripping, snarling, fire-eyed in a last instinctive defiance.

Mounted upon the horror of Duane's thought was a watching, listening intensity so supreme that it registered impressions which were creations of his imagination. He heard stealthy steps that were not there; he saw shadowy moving figures that were only leaves. A hundred times when he was about to pull trigger he discovered his error. Yet voices came from a distance, and steps and crackings in the willows, and other sounds real enough. But Duane could not distinguish the real from the false. There were times when the wind which had arisen sent a hot, pattering breath down the willow aisles, and Duane heard it as an approaching army.

This straining of Duane's faculties brought on a reaction which in itself was a respite. He saw the sun darkened by thick slow spreading clouds. A storm appeared to be coming. How slowly it moved! The air was like steam. If there broke one of those dark, violent storms common though rare to the country, Duane believed he might slip away in the fury of wind and rain. Hope, that seemed unquenchable in him, resurged again. He hailed it with a bitterness that was sickening.

Then at a rustling step he froze into the old strained attention. He heard a slow patter of soft feet. A tawny shape crossed a little opening in the thicket. It was that of a dog. The moment while that beast came into full view was an age. The dog was not a bloodhound, and if he had a trail or a scent he seemed to be at fault on it. Duane waited for the inevitable discovery. Any kind of a hunting-dog could have found him in that thicket. Voices from outside could be heard urging on the dog. Rover they called him. Duane sat up at the moment the dog entered the little shaded covert. Duane expected a yelping, a baying, or at least a bark that would tell of his hiding-place. A strange relief swiftly swayed over Duane. The end was near now. He had no further choice. Let them come—a quick fierce exchange of shots—and then this torture past! He waited for the dog to give the alarm.

But the dog looked at him and trotted by into the thicket without a yelp. Duane could not believe the evidence of his senses. He thought he had suddenly gone deaf. He saw the dog disappear, heard him running to and fro among the willows, getting farther and farther away, till all sound from him ceased.

"Thar's Rover," called a voice from the bluff-side.

"He's been through thet black patch."

"Nary a rabbit in there," replied another.

"Bah! Thet pup's no good," scornfully growled another man. "Put a hound at thet clump of willows."

"Fire's the game. Burn the brake before the rain comes."

The voices droned off as their owners evidently walked up the ridge.

Then upon Duane fell the crushing burden of the old waiting, watching, listening spell. After all, it was not to end just now. His chance still persisted—looked a little brighter—led him on, perhaps, to forlorn hope.

All at once twilight settled quickly down upon the willow brake, or else Duane noted it suddenly. He imagined it to be caused by the approaching storm. But there was little movement of air or cloud, and thunder still muttered and rumbled at a distance. The fact was the sun had set, and at this time of overcast sky night was at hand.

Duane realized it with the awakening of all his old force. He would yet elude his pursuers. That was the moment when he seized the significance of all these fortunate circumstances which had aided him. Without haste and without sound he began to crawl in the direction of the river. It was not far, and he reached the bank before darkness set in. There were men up on the bluff carrying wood to build a bonfire. For a moment he half yielded to a temptation to try to slip along the river-shore, close in under the willows. But when he raised himself to peer out he saw that an attempt of this kind would be liable to failure. At the same moment he saw a rough-hewn plank lying beneath him, lodged against some willows. The end of the plank extended in almost to a point beneath him. Quick as a flash he saw where a desperate chance invited him. Then he tied his gun in an oilskin bag and put it in his pocket.

The bank was steep and crumbly. He must not break off any earth to splash into the water. There was a willow growing back some few feet from the edge of the bank. Cautiously he pulled it down, bent it over the water so that when he released it there would be no springing back. Then he trusted his weight to it, with his feet sliding carefully down the bank. He went into the water almost up to his knees, felt the quicksand grip his feet; then, leaning forward till he reached the plank, he pulled it toward him and lay upon it.

Without a sound one end went slowly under water and the farther end appeared lightly braced against the overhanging willows. Very carefully then Duane began to extricate his right foot from the sucking sand. It seemed as if his foot was incased in solid rock. But there was a movement upward, and he pulled with all the power he dared use. It came slowly and at length was free. The left one he released with less difficulty. The next few moments he put all his attention on the plank to ascertain if his weight would sink it into the sand. The far end slipped off the willows with a little splash and gradually settled to rest upon the bottom. But it sank no farther, and Duane's greatest concern was relieved. However, as it was manifestly impossible for him to keep his head up for long he carefully crawled out upon the plank until he could rest an arm and shoulder upon the willows.

When he looked up it was to find the night strangely luminous with fires. There was a bonfire on the extreme end of the bluff, another a hundred paces beyond. A great flare extended over the brake in that direction. Duane heard a roaring on the wind, and he knew his pursuers had fired the willows. He did not believe that would help them much. The brake was dry enough, but too green to burn readily. And as for the bonfires he discovered that the men, probably having run out of wood, were keeping up the light with oil and stuff from the village. A dozen men kept watch on the bluff scarcely fifty paces from where Duane lay concealed by the willows. They talked, cracked jokes, sang songs, and manifestly considered this outlaw-hunting a great lark. As long as the bright light lasted Duane dared not move. He had the patience and the endurance to wait for the breaking of the storm, and if that did not come, then the early hour before dawn when the gray fog and gloom were over the river.

Escape was now in his grasp. He felt it. And with that in his mind he waited, strong as steel in his conviction, capable of withstanding any strain endurable by the human frame.

The wind blew in puffs, grew wilder, and roared through the willows, carrying bright sparks upward. Thunder rolled down over the river, and lightning began to flash. Then the rain fell in heavy sheets, but not steadily. The flashes of lightning and the broad flares played so incessantly that Duane could not trust himself out on the open river. Certainly the storm rather increased the watchfulness of the men on the bluff. He knew how to wait, and he waited, grimly standing pain and cramp and chill. The storm wore away as desultorily as it had come, and the long night set in. There were times when Duane thought he was paralyzed, others when he grew sick, giddy, weak from the strained posture. The first paling of the stars quickened him with a kind of wild joy. He watched them grow paler, dimmer, disappear one by one. A shadow hovered down, rested upon the river, and gradually thickened. The bonfire on the bluff showed as through a foggy veil. The watchers were mere groping dark figures.

Duane, aware of how cramped he had become from long inaction, began to move his legs and uninjured arm and body, and at length overcame a paralyzing stiffness. Then, digging his hand in the sand and holding the plank with his knees, he edged it out into the river. Inch by inch he advanced until clear of the willows. Looking upward, he saw the shadowy figures of the men on the bluff. He realized they ought to see him, feared that they would. But he kept on, cautiously, noiselessly, with a heart-numbing slowness. From time to time his elbow made a little gurgle and splash in the water. Try as he might, he could not prevent this. It got to be like the hollow roar of a rapid filling his ears with mocking sound. There was a perceptible current out in the river, and it hindered straight advancement. Inch by inch he crept on, expecting to hear the bang of rifles, the spattering of bullets. He tried not to look backward, but failed. The fire appeared a little dimmer, the moving shadows a little darker.

Once the plank stuck in the sand and felt as if it were settling. Bringing feet to aid his hand, he shoved it over the treacherous place. This way he made faster progress. The obscurity of the river seemed to be enveloping him. When he looked back again the figures of the men were coalescing with the surrounding gloom, the fires were streaky, blurred patches of light. But the sky above was brighter. Dawn was not far off.

To the west all was dark. With infinite care and implacable spirit and waning strength Duane shoved the plank along, and when at last he discerned the black border of bank it came in time, he thought, to save him. He crawled out, rested till the gray dawn broke, and then headed north through the willows.

CHAPTER XIII

How long Duane was traveling out of that region he never knew. But he reached familiar country and found a rancher who had before befriended him. Here his arm was attended to; he had food and sleep; and in a couple of weeks he was himself again.

When the time came for Duane to ride away on his endless trail his friend reluctantly imparted the information that some thirty miles south, near the village of Shirley, there was posted at a certain cross-road a reward for Buck Duane dead or alive. Duane had heard of such notices, but he had never seen one. His friend's reluctance and refusal to state for what particular deed this reward was offered roused Duane's curiosity. He had never been any closer to Shirley than this rancher's home. Doubtless some post-office burglary, some gun-shooting scrape had been attributed to him. And he had been accused of worse deeds. Abruptly Duane decided to ride over there and find out who wanted him dead or alive, and why.

As he started south on the road he reflected that this was the first time he had ever deliberately hunted trouble. Introspection awarded him this knowledge; during that last terrible flight on the lower Nueces and while he lay abed recuperating he had changed. A fixed, immutable, hopeless bitterness abided with him. He had reached the end of his rope. All the power of his mind and soul were unavailable to turn him back from his fate.

That fate was to become an outlaw in every sense of the term, to be what he was credited with being—that is to say, to embrace evil. He had never committed a crime. He wondered now was crime close to him? He reasoned finally that the desperation of crime had been forced upon him, if not its motive; and that if driven, there was no limit to his possibilities. He understood now many of the hitherto inexplicable actions of certain noted outlaws—why they had returned to the scene of the crime that had outlawed them; why they took such strangely fatal chances; why life was no more to them than a breath of wind; why they rode straight into the jaws of death to confront wronged men or hunting rangers, vigilantes, to laugh in their very faces. It was such bitterness as this that drove these men.

Toward afternoon, from the top of a long hill, Duane saw the green fields and trees and shining roofs of a town he considered must be Shirley. And at the bottom of the hill he came upon an intersecting road. There was a placard nailed on the crossroad sign-post. Duane drew rein near it and leaned close to read the faded print. $1000 REWARD FOR BUCK DUANE DEAD OR ALIVE. Peering closer to read the finer, more faded print, Duane learned that he was wanted for the murder of Mrs. Jeff Aiken at her ranch near Shirley. The month September was named, but the date was illegible. The reward was offered by the woman's husband, whose name appeared with that of a sheriff's at the bottom of the placard.

Duane read the thing twice. When he straightened he was sick with the horror of his fate, wild with passion at those misguided fools who could believe that he had harmed a woman. Then he remembered Kate Bland, and, as always when she returned to him, he quaked inwardly. Years before word had gone abroad that he had killed her, and so it was easy for men wanting to fix a crime to name him. Perhaps it had been done often. Probably he bore on his shoulders a burden of numberless crimes.

A dark, passionate fury possessed him. It shook him like a storm shakes the oak. When it passed, leaving him cold, with clouded brow and piercing eye, his mind was set. Spurring his horse, he rode straight toward the village.

Shirley appeared to be a large, pretentious country town. A branch of some railroad terminated there. The main street was wide, bordered by trees and commodious houses, and many of the stores were of brick. A large plaza shaded by giant cottonwood trees occupied a central location.

Duane pulled his running horse and halted him, plunging and snorting, before a group of idle men who lounged on benches in the shade of a spreading cottonwood. How many times had Duane seen just that kind of lazy shirt-sleeved Texas group! Not often, however, had he seen such placid, lolling, good-natured men change their expression, their attitude so swiftly. His advent apparently was momentous. They evidently took him for an unusual visitor. So far as Duane could tell, not one of them recognized him, had a hint of his identity.

He slid off his horse and threw the bridle.

"I'm Buck Duane," he said. "I saw that placard—out there on a sign-post. It's a damn lie! Somebody find this man Jeff Aiken. I want to see him."

His announcement was taken in absolute silence. That was the only effect he noted, for he avoided looking at these villagers. The reason was simple enough; Duane felt himself overcome with emotion. There were tears in his eyes. He sat down on a bench, put his elbows on his knees and his hands to his face. For once he had absolutely no concern for his fate. This ignominy was the last straw.

Presently, however, he became aware of some kind of commotion among these villagers. He heard whisperings, low, hoarse voices, then the shuffle of rapid feet moving away. All at once a violent hand jerked his gun from its holster. When Duane rose a gaunt man, livid of face, shaking like a leaf, confronted him with his own gun.

"Hands up, thar, you Buck Duane!" he roared, waving the gun.

That appeared to be the cue for pandemonium to break loose. Duane opened his lips to speak, but if he had yelled at the top of his lungs he could not have made himself heard. In weary disgust he looked at the gaunt man, and then at the others, who were working themselves into a frenzy. He made no move, however, to hold up his hands. The villagers surrounded him, emboldened by finding him now unarmed. Then several men lay hold of his arms and pinioned them behind his back. Resistance was useless even if Duane had had the spirit. Some one of them fetched his halter from his saddle, and with this they bound him helpless.

People were running now from the street, the stores, the houses. Old men, cowboys, clerks, boys, ranchers came on the trot. The crowd grew. The increasing clamor began to attract women as well as men. A group of girls ran up, then hung back in fright and pity.

The presence of cowboys made a difference. They split up the crowd, got to Duane, and lay hold of him with rough, businesslike hands. One of them lifted his fists and roared at the frenzied mob to fall back, to stop the racket. He beat them back into a circle; but it was some little time before the hubbub quieted down so a voice could be heard.

“Shut up, will you-all?” he was yelling. “Give us a chance to hear somethin’. Easy now—soho. There ain’t nobody goin’ to be hurt. Thet’s right; everybody quiet now. Let’s see what’s come off.”

This cowboy, evidently one of authority, or at least one of strong personality, turned to the gaunt man, who still waved Duane’s gun.

“Abe, put the gun down,” he said. “It might go off. Here, give it to me. Now, what’s wrong? Who’s this roped gent, an’ what’s he done?”

The gaunt fellow, who appeared now about to collapse, lifted a shaking hand and pointed.

"Thet thar feller—he's Buck Duane!" he panted.

An angry murmur ran through the surrounding crowd.

"The rope! The rope! Throw it over a branch! String him up!" cried an excited villager.

"Buck Duane! Buck Duane!"

"Hang him!"

The cowboy silenced these cries.

"Abe, how do you know this fellow is Buck Duane?" he asked, sharply.

"Why—he said so," replied the man called Abe.

"What!" came the exclamation, incredulously.

"It's a tarnal fact," panted Abe, waving his hands importantly. He was an old man and appeared to be carried away with the significance of his deed. "He like to rid' his hoss right over us-all. Then he jumped off, says he was Buck Duane, an' he wanted to see Jeff Aiken bad."

This speech caused a second commotion as noisy though not so enduring as the first. When the cowboy, assisted by a couple of his mates, had restored order again some one had slipped the noose-end of Duane's rope over his head.

"Up with him!" screeched a wild-eyed youth.

The mob surged closer was shoved back by the cowboys.

"Abe, if you ain't drunk or crazy tell thet over," ordered Abe's interlocutor.

With some show of resentment and more of dignity Abe reiterated his former statement.

"If he's Buck Duane how'n hell did you get hold of

his gun?" bluntly queried the cowboy.

"Why—he set down thar—an' he kind of hid his face on his hand. An' I grabbed his gun an' got the drop on him."

What the cowboy thought of this was expressed in a laugh. His mates likewise grinned broadly. Then the leader turned to Duane.

"Stranger, I reckon you'd better speak up for yourself," he said.

That stilled the crowd as no command had done.

"I'm Buck Duane, all right." said Duane, quietly. "It was this way—"

The big cowboy seemed to vibrate with a shock. All the ruddy warmth left his face; his jaw began to bulge; the corded veins in his neck stood out in knots. In an instant he had a hard, stern, strange look. He shot out a powerful hand that fastened in the front of Duane's blouse.

"Somethin' queer here. But if you're Duane you're sure in bad. Any fool ought to know that. You mean it, then?"

"Yes."

"Rode in to shoot up the town, eh? Same old stunt of you gunfighters? Meant to kill the man who offered a reward? Wanted to see Jeff Aiken bad, huh?"

"No," replied Duane. "Your citizen here misrepresented things. He seems a little off his head."

"Reckon he is. Somebody is, that's sure. You claim Buck Duane, then, an' all his doings?"

"I'm Duane; yes. But I won't stand for the blame of things I never did. That's why I'm here. I saw that placard out there offering the reward. Until now I never was within half a day's ride of this town. I'm blamed for what I never did. I rode in here, told who I was, asked somebody to send for Jeff Aiken."

"An' then you set down an' let this old guy throw your own gun on you?" queried the cowboy in amazement.

"I guess that's it," replied Duane.

"Well, it's powerful strange, if you're really Buck Duane."

A man elbowed his way into the circle.

"It's Duane. I recognize him. I seen him in more'n one place," he said. "Sibert, you can rely on what I tell you. I don't know if he's locoed or what. But I do know he's the genuine Buck Duane. Any one who'd ever seen him onct would never forget him."

"What do you want to see Aiken for?" asked the cowboy Sibert.

"I want to face him, and tell him I never harmed his wife."

"Why?"

"Because I'm innocent, that's all."

"Suppose we send for Aiken an' he hears you an' doesn't believe you; what then?"

"If he won't believe me—why, then my case's so bad—I'd be better off dead."

A momentary silence was broken by Sibert.

"If this isn't a queer deal! Boys, reckon we'd better send for Jeff."

"Somebody went fer him. He'll be comin' soon," replied a man.

Duane stood a head taller than that circle of curious

faces. He gazed out above and beyond them. It was in this way that he chanced to see a number of women on the outskirts of the crowd. Some were old, with hard faces, like the men. Some were young and comely, and most of these seemed agitated by excitement or distress. They cast fearful, pitying glances upon Duane as he stood there with that noose round his neck. Women were more human than men, Duane thought. He met eyes that dilated, seemed fascinated at his gaze, but were not averted. It was the old women who were voluble, loud in expression of their feelings.

Near the trunk of the cottonwood stood a slender woman in white. Duane's wandering glance rested upon her. Her eyes were riveted upon him. A soft-hearted woman, probably, who did not want to see him hanged!

"Thar comes Jeff Aiken now," called a man, loudly.

The crowd shifted and trampled in eagerness.

Duane saw two men coming fast, one of whom, in the lead, was of stalwart build. He had a gun in his hand, and his manner was that of fierce energy.

The cowboy Sibert thrust open the jostling circle of men.

"Hold on, Jeff," he called, and he blocked the man with the gun. He spoke so low Duane could not hear what he said, and his form hid Aiken's face. At that juncture the crowd spread out, closed in, and Aiken and Sibert were caught in the circle. There was a pushing forward, a pressing of many bodies, hoarse cries and flinging hands—again the insane tumult was about to break out—the demand for an outlaw's blood, the call for a wild justice executed a thousand times before on Texas's bloody soil.

Sibert bellowed at the dark encroaching mass. The cowboys with him beat and cuffed in vain.

"Jeff, will you listen?" broke in Sibert, hurriedly, his hand on the other man's arm.

Aiken nodded coolly. Duane, who had seen many men in perfect control of themselves under circumstances like these, recognized the spirit that dominated Aiken. He was white, cold, passionless. There were lines of bitter grief deep round his lips. If Duane ever felt the meaning of death he felt it then.

"Sure this 's your game, Aiken," said Sibert. "But hear me a minute. Reckon there's no doubt about this man bein' Buck Duane. He seen the placard out at the cross-roads. He rides in to Shirley. He says he's Buck Duane an' he's lookin' for Jeff Aiken. That's all clear enough. You know how these gunfighters go lookin' for trouble. But here's what stumps me. Duane sits down there on the bench and lets old Abe Strickland grab his gun ant get the drop on him. More'n that, he gives me some strange talk about how, if he couldn't make you believe he's innocent, he'd better be dead. You see for yourself Duane ain't drunk or crazy or locoed. He doesn't strike me as a man who rode in here huntin' blood. So I reckon you'd better hold on till you hear what he has to say."

Then for the first time the drawn-faced, hungry-eyed giant turned his gaze upon Duane. He had intelligence which was not yet subservient to passion. Moreover, he seemed the kind of man Duane would care to have judge him in a critical moment like this.

"Listen," said Duane, gravely, with his eyes steady on Aiken's, "I'm Buck Duane. I never lied to any man in my life. I was forced into outlawry. I've never had a chance to leave the country. I've killed men to save my own life. I never intentionally harmed any woman. I rode thirty miles to-day—deliberately to see what this reward was, who made it, what for. When I read the placard I went sick to the bottom of my soul. So I rode in here to find you—to tell you this: I never saw Shirley before to-day. It was impossible for me to have—killed your wife. Last September I was two hundred miles north of here on the upper Nueces. I can prove that. Men who know me will tell you I couldn't murder a woman. I haven't any idea why such a deed should be laid at my hands. It's just that wild border gossip. I have no idea what reasons you have for holding me responsible. I only know—you're wrong. You've been deceived. And see here, Aiken. You understand I'm a miserable man. I'm about broken, I guess. I don't care any more for life, for anything. If you can't look me in the eyes, man to man, and believe what I say—why, by God! you can kill me!"

Aiken heaved a great breath.

"Buck Duane, whether I'm impressed or not by what you say needn't matter. You've had accusers, justly or unjustly, as will soon appear. The thing is we can prove you innocent or guilty. My girl Lucy saw my wife's assailant."

He motioned for the crowd of men to open up.

"Somebody—you, Sibert—go for Lucy. That'll settle this thing."

Duane heard as a man in an ugly dream. The faces around him, the hum of voices, all seemed far off. His life hung by the merest thread. Yet he did not think of that so much as of the brand of a woman-murderer which might be soon sealed upon him by a frightened, imaginative child.

The crowd trooped apart and closed again. Duane caught a blurred image of a slight girl clinging to Sibert's hand. He could not see distinctly. Aiken lifted the child, whispered soothingly to her not to be afraid. Then he fetched her closer to Duane.

"Lucy, tell me. Did you ever see this man before?" asked Aiken, huskily and low. "Is he the one—who came in the house that day—struck you down—and dragged mama—?"

Aiken's voice failed.

A lightning flash seemed to clear Duane's blurred sight. He saw a pale, sad face and violet eyes fixed in gloom and horror upon his. No terrible moment in Duane's life ever equaled this one of silence—of suspense.

"It's ain't him!" cried the child.

Then Sibert was flinging the noose off Duane's neck and unwinding the bonds round his arms. The spellbound crowd awoke to hoarse exclamations.

"See there, my locoed gents, how easy you'd hang the wrong man," burst out the cowboy, as he made the rope-end hiss. "You-all are a lot of wise rangers. Haw! haw!"

He freed Duane and thrust the bone-handled gun back in Duane's holster.

"You Abe, there. Reckon you pulled a stunt! But don't try the like again. And, men, I'll gamble there's a hell of a lot of bad work Buck Duane's named for—which all he never done. Clear away there. Where's his hoss? Duane, the road's open out of Shirley."

Sibert swept the gaping watchers aside and pressed Duane toward the horse, which another cowboy held. Mechanically Duane mounted, felt a lift as he went up. Then the cowboy's hard face softened in a smile.

"I reckon it ain't uncivil of me to say—hit that road quick!" he said, frankly.

He led the horse out of the crowd. Aiken joined him, and between them they escorted Duane across the plaza. The crowd appeared irresistibly drawn to follow.

Aiken paused with his big hand on Duane's knee. In it, unconsciously probably, he still held the gun.

"Duane, a word with you," he said. "I believe you're not so black as you've been painted. I wish there was time to say more. Tell me this, anyway. Do you know the Ranger Captain MacNelly?"

"I do not," replied Duane, in surprise.

"I met him only a week ago over in Fairfield," went on Aiken, hurriedly. "He declared you never killed my wife. I didn't believe him—argued with him. We almost had hard words over it. Now—I'm sorry. The last thing he said was: 'If you ever see Duane don't kill him. Send him into my camp after dark!' He meant something strange. What—I can't say. But he was right, and I was wrong. If Lucy had batted an eye I'd have killed you. Still, I wouldn't advise you to hunt up MacNelly's camp. He's clever. Maybe he believes there's no treachery in his new ideas of ranger tactics. I tell you for all it's worth. Good-by. May God help you further as he did this day!"

Duane said good-by and touched the horse with his spurs.

"So long, Buck!" called Sibert, with that frank smile breaking warm over his brown face; and he held his sombrero high.

CHAPTER XIV

When Duane reached the crossing of the roads the name Fairfield on the sign-post seemed to be the thing that tipped the oscillating balance of decision in favor of that direction.

He answered here to unfathomable impulse. If he had been driven to hunt up Jeff Aiken, now he was called to find this unknown ranger captain. In Duane's state of mind clear reasoning, common sense, or keenness were out of the question. He went because he felt he was compelled.

Dusk had fallen when he rode into a town which inquiry discovered to be Fairfield. Captain MacNelly's camp was stationed just out of the village limits on the other side.

No one except the boy Duane questioned appeared to notice his arrival. Like Shirley, the town of Fairfield was large and prosperous, compared to the innumerable hamlets dotting the vast extent of southwestern Texas. As Duane rode through, being careful to get off the main street, he heard the tolling of a church-bell that was a melancholy reminder of his old home.

There did not appear to be any camp on the outskirts of the town. But as Duane sat his horse, peering around and undecided what further move to make, he caught the glint of flickering lights through the darkness. Heading toward them, he rode perhaps a quarter of a mile to come upon a grove of mesquite. The brightness of several fires made the surrounding darkness all the blacker. Duane saw the moving forms of men and heard horses. He advanced naturally, expecting any moment to be halted.

"Who goes there?" came the sharp call out of the gloom.

Duane pulled his horse. The gloom was impenetrable.

"One man—alone," replied Duane.

"A stranger?"

"Yes."

"What do you want?"

"I'm trying to find the ranger camp."

"You've struck it. What's your errand?"

"I want to see Captain MacNelly."

"Get down and advance. Slow. Don't move your hands. It's dark, but I can see."

Duane dismounted, and, leading his horse, slowly advanced a few paces. He saw a dully bright object—a gun—before he discovered the man who held it. A few more steps showed a dark figure blocking the trail. Here Duane halted.

"Come closer, stranger. Let's have a look at you," the guard ordered, curtly.

Duane advanced again until he stood before the man. Here the rays of light from the fires flickered upon Duane's face.

"Reckon you're a stranger, all right. What's your name and your business with the Captain?"

Duane hesitated, pondering what best to say.

"Tell Captain MacNelly I'm the man he's been asking to ride into his camp—after dark," finally said Duane.

The ranger bent forward to peer hard at this night visitor. His manner had been alert, and now it became tense.

"Come here, one of you men, quick," he called, without turning in the least toward the camp-fire.

"Hello! What's up, Pickens?" came the swift reply. It was followed by a rapid thud of boots on soft ground. A dark form crossed the gleams from the fire-light. Then a ranger loomed up to reach the side of the guard. Duane heard whispering, the purport of which he could not catch. The second ranger swore under his breath. Then he turned away and started back.

"Here, ranger, before you go, understand this. My visit is peaceful—friendly if you'll let it be. Mind, I was asked to come here—after dark."

Duane's clear, penetrating voice carried far. The listening rangers at the camp-fire heard what he said.

"Ho, Pickens! Tell that fellow to wait," replied an authoritative voice. Then a slim figure detached itself from the dark, moving group at the camp-fire and hurried out.

"Better be foxy, Cap," shouted a ranger, in warning.

"Shut up—all of you," was the reply.

This officer, obviously Captain MacNelly, soon joined the two rangers who were confronting Duane. He had no fear. He strode straight up to Duane.

"I'm MacNelly," he said. "If you're my man, don't mention your name—yet."

All this seemed so strange to Duane, in keeping with much that had happened lately.

"I met Jeff Aiken to-day," said Duane. "He sent me—"

"You've met Aiken!" exclaimed MacNelly, sharp, eager, low. "By all that's bully!" Then he appeared to catch himself, to grow restrained.

"Men, fall back, leave us alone a moment."

The rangers slowly withdrew.

"Buck Duane! It's you?" he whispered, eagerly.

"Yes."

"If I give my word you'll not be arrested—you'll be treated fairly—will you come into camp and consult with me?"

"Certainly."

"Duane, I'm sure glad to meet you," went on MacNelly; and he extended his hand.

Amazed and touched, scarcely realizing this actuality, Duane gave his hand and felt no unmistakable grip of warmth.

"It doesn't seem natural, Captain MacNelly, but I believe I'm glad to meet you," said Duane, soberly.

"You will be. Now we'll go back to camp. Keep your identity mum for the present."

He led Duane in the direction of the camp-fire.

"Pickers, go back on duty," he ordered, "and, Beeson, you look after this horse."

When Duane got beyond the line of mesquite, which had hid a good view of the camp-site, he saw a group of perhaps fifteen rangers sitting around the fires, near a long low shed where horses were feeding, and a small adobe house at one side.

"We've just had grub, but I'll see you get some. Then we'll talk," said MacNelly. "I've taken up temporary quarters here. Have a rustler job on hand. Now, when you've eaten, come right into the house."

Duane was hungry, but he hurried through the ample supper that was set before him, urged on by curiosity and astonishment. The only way he could account for his presence there in a ranger's camp was that MacNelly hoped to get useful information out of him. Still that would hardly have made this captain so eager. There was a mystery here, and Duane could scarcely wait for it to be solved. While eating he had bent keen eyes around him. After a first quiet scrutiny the rangers apparently paid no more attention to him. They were all veterans in service—Duane saw that—and rugged, powerful men of iron constitution. Despite the occasional joke and sally of the more youthful members, and a general conversation of camp-fire nature, Duane was not deceived about the fact that his advent had been an unusual and striking one, which had caused an undercurrent of conjecture and even consternation among them. These rangers were too well trained to appear openly curious about their captain's guest. If they had not deliberately attempted to be oblivious of his presence Duane would have concluded they thought him an ordinary visitor, somehow of use to MacNelly. As it was, Duane felt a suspense that must have been due to a hint of his identity.

He was not long in presenting himself at the door of the house.

"Come in and have a chair," said MacNelly, motioning for the one other occupant of the room to rise. "Leave us, Russell, and close the door. I'll be through these reports right off."

MacNelly sat at a table upon which was a lamp and various papers. Seen in the light he was a fine-looking, soldierly man of about forty years, dark-haired and dark-eyed, with a bronzed face, shrewd, stern, strong, yet not wanting in kindliness. He scanned hastily over some papers, fussed with them, and finally put them in envelopes. Without looking up he pushed a cigar-case toward Duane, and upon Duane's refusal to smoke he took a cigar, rose to light it at the lamp-chimney, and then, settling back in his chair, he faced Duane, making a vain attempt to hide what must have been the fulfilment of a long-nourished curiosity.

"Duane, I've been hoping for this for two years," he began.

Duane smiled a little—a smile that felt strange on his face. He had never been much of a talker. And speech here seemed more than ordinarily difficult.

MacNelly must have felt that.

He looked long and earnestly at Duane, and his quick, nervous manner changed to grave thoughtfulness.

"I've lots to say, but where to begin," he mused. "Duane, you've had a hard life since you went on the dodge. I never met you before, don't know what you looked like as a boy. But I can see what—well, even ranger life isn't all roses."

He rolled his cigar between his lips and puffed clouds of smoke.

"Ever hear from home since you left Wellston?" he asked, abruptly.

"No."

"Never a word?"

"Not one," replied Duane, sadly.

"That's tough. I'm glad to be able to tell you that up to just lately your mother, sister, uncle—all your folks, I believe—were well. I've kept posted. But haven't heard lately."

Duane averted his face a moment, hesitated till the swelling left his throat, and then said, "It's worth what I went through to-day to hear that."

"I can imagine how you feel about it. When I was in the war—but let's get down to the business of this meeting."

He pulled his chair close to Duane's.

"You've had word more than once in the last two years that I wanted to see you?"

"Three times, I remember," replied Duane.

"Why didn't you hunt me up?"

"I supposed you imagined me one of those gun-fighters who couldn't take a dare and expected me to ride up to your camp and be arrested."

"That was natural, I suppose," went on MacNelly. "You didn't know me, otherwise you would have come. I've been a long time getting to you. But the nature of my job, as far as you're concerned, made me cautious. Duane, you're aware of the hard name you bear all over the Southwest?"

"Once in a while I'm jarred into realizing," replied Duane.

"It's the hardest, barring Murrell and Cheseldine, on the Texas border. But there's this difference. Murrell in his day was known to deserve his infamous name. Cheseldine in his day also. But I've found hundreds of men in southwest Texas who're your friends, who swear you never committed a crime. The farther south I get the clearer this becomes. What I want to know is the truth. Have you ever done anything criminal? Tell me the truth, Duane. It won't make any difference in my plan. And when I say crime I mean what I would call crime, or any reasonable Texan."

"That way my hands are clean," replied Duane.

"You never held up a man, robbed a store for grub, stole a horse when you needed him bad—never anything like that?"

"Somehow I always kept out of that, just when pressed the hardest."

"Duane, I'm damn glad!" MacNelly exclaimed, gripping Duane's hand. "Glad for you mother's sakel But, all the same, in spite of this, you are a Texas outlaw accountable to the state. You're perfectly aware that under existing circumstances, if you fell into the hands of the law, you'd probably hang, at least go to jail for a long term."

"That's what kept me on the dodge all these years," replied Duane.

"Certainly." MacNelly removed his cigar. His eyes narrowed and glittered. The muscles along his brown cheeks set hard and tense. He leaned closer to Duane, laid sinewy, pressing fingers upon Duane's knee.

"Listen to this," he whispered, hoarsely. "If I place a pardon in your hand—make you a free, honest citizen once more, clear your name of infamy, make your mother, your sister proud of you—will you swear yourself to a service, ANY service I demand of you?"

Duane sat stock still, stunned.

Slowly, more persuasively, with show of earnest agitation, Captain MacNelly reiterated his startling query.

"My God!" burst from Duane. "What's this? MacNelly, you CAN'T be in earnest!"

"Never more so in my life. I've a deep game. I'm playing it square. What do you say?"

He rose to his feet. Duane, as if impelled, rose with him. Ranger and outlaw then locked eyes that searched each other's souls. In MacNelly's Duane read truth, strong, fiery purpose, hope, even gladness, and a fugitive mounting assurance of victory.

Twice Duane endeavored to speak, failed of all save a hoarse, incoherent sound, until, forcing back a flood of speech, he found a voice.

"Any service? Every service! MacNelly, I give my word," said Duane.

A light played over MacNelly's face, warming out all the grim darkness. He held out his hand. Duane met it with his in a clasp that men unconsciously give in moments of stress.

When they unclasped and Duane stepped back to drop into a chair MacNelly fumbled for another cigar—he had bitten the other into shreds—and, lighting it as before, he turned to his visitor, now calm and cool. He had the look of a man who had justly won something at considerable cost. His next move was to take a long leather case from his pocket and extract from it several folded papers.

"Here's your pardon from the Governor," he said, quietly. "You'll see, when you look it over, that it's conditional. When you sign this paper I have here the condition will be met."

He smoothed out the paper, handed Duane a pen, ran his forefinger along a dotted line.

Duane's hand was shaky. Years had passed since he had held a pen. It was with difficulty that he achieved his signature. Buckley Duane—how strange the name looked!

"Right here ends the career of Buck Duane, outlaw and gunfighter," said MacNelly; and, seating himself, he took the pen from Duane's fingers and wrote several lines in several places upon the paper. Then with a smile he handed it to Duane.

"That makes you a member of Company A, Texas Rangers."

"So that's it!" burst out Duane, a light breaking in upon his bewilderment. "You want me for ranger service?"

"Sure. That's it," replied the Captain, dryly. "Now to hear what that service is to be. I've been a busy man since I took this job, and, as you may have heard, I've done a few things. I don't mind telling you that political influence put me in here and that up Austin way there's a good deal of friction in the Department of

State in regard to whether or not the ranger service is any good—whether it should be discontinued or not. I'm on the party side who's defending the ranger service. I contend that it's made Texas habitable. Well, it's been up to me to produce results. So far I have been successful. My great ambition is to break up the outlaw gangs along the river. I have never ventured in there yet because I've been waiting to get the lieutenant I needed. You, of course, are the man I had in mind. It's my idea to start way up the Rio Grande and begin with Cheseldine. He's the strongest, the worst outlaw of the times. He's more than rustler. It's Cheseldine and his gang who are operating on the banks. They're doing bank-robbing. That's my private opinion, but it's not been backed up by any evidence. Cheseldine doesn't leave evidences. He's intelligent, cunning. No one seems to have seen him—to know what he looks like. I assume, of course, that you are a stranger to the country he dominates. It's five hundred miles west of your ground. There's a little town over there called Fairdale. It's the nest of a rustler gang. They rustle and murder at will. Nobody knows who the leader is. I want you to find out. Well, whatever way you decide is best you will proceed to act upon. You are your own boss. You know such men and how they can be approached. You will take all the time needed, if it's months. It will be necessary for you to communicate with me, and that will be a difficult matter. For Cheseldine dominates several whole counties. You must find some way to let me know when I and my rangers are needed. The plan is to break up

Cheseldine's gang. It's the toughest job on the border. Arresting him alone isn't to be heard of. He couldn't be brought out. Killing him isn't much better, for his select men, the ones he operates with, are as dangerous to the community as he is. We want to kill or jail this choice selection of robbers and break up the rest of the gang. To find them, to get among them somehow, to learn their movements, to lay your trap for us rangers to spring—that, Duane, is your service to me, and God knows it's a great one!"

"I have accepted it," replied Duane.

"Your work will be secret. You are now a ranger in my service. But no one except the few I choose to tell will know of it until we pull off the job. You will simply be Buck Duane till it suits our purpose to acquaint Texas with the fact that you're a ranger. You'll see there's no date on that paper. No one will ever know just when you entered the service. Perhaps we can make it appear that all or most of your outlawry has really been good service to the state. At that, I'll believe it'll turn out so."

MacNelly paused a moment in his rapid talk, chewed his cigar, drew his brows together in a dark frown, and went on. "No man on the border knows so well as you the deadly nature of this service. It's a thousand to one that you'll be killed. I'd say there was no chance at all for any other man beside you. Your reputation will go far among the outlaws. Maybe that and your nerve and your gun-play will pull you through. I'm hoping so. But it's a long, long chance against your ever coming back."

"That's not the point," said Duane. "But in case I get killed out there—what—"

"Leave that to me," interrupted Captain MacNelly. "Your folks will know at once of your pardon and your ranger duty. If you lose your life out there I'll see your name cleared—the service you render known. You can rest assured of that."

"I am satisfied," replied Duane. "That's so much more than I've dared to hope."

"Well, it's settled, then. I'll give you money for expenses. You'll start as soon as you like—the sooner the better. I hope to think of other suggestions, especially about communicating with me."

Long after the lights were out and the low hum of voices had ceased round the camp-fire Duane lay wide awake, eyes staring into the blackness, marveling over the strange events of the day. He was humble, grateful to the depths of his soul. A huge and crushing burden had been lifted from his heart. He welcomed this hazardous service to the man who had saved him. Thought of his mother and sister and Uncle Jim, of his home, of old friends came rushing over him the first time in years that he had happiness in the memory. The disgrace he had put upon them would now be removed; and in the light of that, his wasted life of the past, and its probable tragic end in future service as atonement changed their aspects. And as he lay there, with the approach of sleep finally dimming the vividness of his thought, so full of mystery, shadowy faces floated in the blackness around him, haunting him as he had always been haunted.

It was broad daylight when he awakened. MacNelly was calling him to breakfast. Outside sounded voices of men, crackling of fires, snorting and stamping of horses, the barking of dogs. Duane rolled out of his blankets and made good use of the soap and towel and razor and brush near by on a bench—things of rare luxury to an outlaw on the ride. The face he saw in the mirror was as strange as the past he had tried so hard to recall. Then he stepped to the door and went out.

The rangers were eating in a circle round a tarpaulin spread upon the ground.

"Fellows," said MacNelly, "shake hands with Buck Duane. He's on secret ranger service for me. Service that'll likely make you all hump soon! Mind you, keep mum about it."

The rangers surprised Duane with a roaring greeting, the warmth of which he soon divined was divided between pride of his acquisition to their ranks and eagerness to meet that violent service of which their captain hinted. They were jolly, wild fellows, with just enough gravity in their welcome to show Duane their respect and appreciation, while not forgetting his lone-wolf record. When he had seated himself in that circle, now one of them, a feeling subtle and uplifting pervaded him.

After the meal Captain MacNelly drew Duane aside.

"Here's the money. Make it go as far as you can. Better strike straight for El Paso, snook around there and hear things. Then go to Valentine. That's near the river and within fifty miles or so of the edge of the

Rim Rock. Somewhere up there Cheseldine holds fort. Somewhere to the north is the town Fairdale. But he doesn't hide all the time in the rocks. Only after some daring raid or hold-up. Cheseldine's got border towns on his staff, or scared of him, and these places we want to know about, especially Fairdale. Write me care of the adjutant at Austin. I don't have to warn you to be careful where you mail letters. Ride a hundred, two hundred miles, if necessary, or go clear to El Paso."

MacNelly stopped with an air of finality, and then Duane slowly rose.

"I'll start at once," he said, extending his hand to the Captain. "I wish—I'd like to thank you."

"Hell, man! Don't thank me!" replied MacNelly, crushing the proffered hand. "I've sent a lot of good men to their deaths, and maybe you're another. But, as I've said, you've one chance in a thousand. And, by Heaven! I'd hate to be Cheseldine or any other man you were trailing. No, not good-by—Adios, Duane! May we meet again!"

BOOK II
THE RANGER

CHAPTER XV

West of the Pecos River Texas extended a vast wild region, barren in the north where the Llano Estacado spread its shifting sands, fertile in the south along the Rio Grande. A railroad marked an undeviating course across five hundred miles of this country, and the only villages and towns lay on or near this line of steel. Unsettled as was this western Texas, and despite the acknowledged dominance of the outlaw bands, the pioneers pushed steadily into it. First had come the lone rancher; then his neighbors in near and far valleys; then the hamlets; at last the railroad and the towns. And still the pioneers came, spreading deeper into the valleys, farther and wider over the plains. It was mesquite-dotted, cactus-covered desert, but rich soil upon which water acted like magic. There was little grass to an acre, but there were millions of acres. The climate was wonderful. Cattle flourished and ranchers prospered.

The Rio Grande flowed almost due south along the western boundary for a thousand miles, and then, weary of its course, turned abruptly north, to make what was called the Big Bend. The railroad, running west, cut across this bend, and all that country bounded on the north by the railroad and on the south by the river was as wild as the Staked Plains. It contained not one settlement. Across the face of this Big Bend, as if to isolate it, stretched the Ord mountain range, of which Mount Ord, Cathedral Mount, and Elephant Mount raised bleak peaks above their fellows. In the valleys of the foothills and out across the plains were ranches, and farther north villages, and the towns of Alpine and Marfa.

Like other parts of the great Lone Star State, this section of Texas was a world in itself—a world where the riches of the rancher were ever enriching the outlaw. The village closest to the gateway of this outlaw-infested region was a little place called Ord, named after the dark peak that loomed some miles to the south. It had been settled originally by Mexicans—there were still the ruins of adobe missions—but with the advent of the rustler and outlaw many inhabitants were shot or driven away, so that at the height of Ord's prosperity and evil sway there were but few Mexicans living there, and these had their choice between holding hand-and-glove with the outlaws or furnishing target practice for that wild element.

Toward the close of a day in September a stranger rode into Ord, and in a community where all men were remarkable for one reason or another he excited interest. His horse, perhaps, received the first and most engaging attention—horses in that region being apparently more important than men. This particular horse did not attract with beauty. At first glance he seemed ugly. But he was a giant, black as coal, rough despite the care manifestly bestowed upon him, long of body, ponderous of limb, huge in every way. A bystander remarked that he had a grand head. True, if only his head had been seen he would have been a beautiful horse. Like men, horses show what they are in the shape, the size, the line, the character of the head. This one denoted fire, speed, blood, loyalty, and his eyes were as soft and dark as a woman's. His face was solid black, except in the middle of his forehead, where there was a round spot of white.

"Say mister, mind tellin' me his name?" asked a ragged urchin, with born love of a horse in his eyes.

"Bullet," replied the rider.

"Thet there's fer the white mark, ain't it?" whispered the youngster to another. "Say, ain't he a whopper? Biggest hoss I ever seen."

Bullet carried a huge black silver-ornamented saddle of Mexican make, a lariat and canteen, and a small pack rolled into a tarpaulin.

This rider apparently put all care of appearances upon his horse. His apparel was the ordinary jeans of the cowboy without vanity, and it was torn and travel-stained. His boots showed evidence of an intimate acquaintance with cactus. Like his horse, this man was a giant in stature, but rangier, not so heavily built. Otherwise the only striking thing about him was his somber face with its piercing eyes, and hair white over the temples. He packed two guns, both low down—but that was too common a thing to attract notice in the Big Bend. A close observer, however, would have noted a singular fact—this rider's right hand was more bronzed, more weather-beaten than his left. He never wore a glove on that right hand!

He had dismounted before a ramshackle structure that bore upon its wide, high-boarded front the sign, "Hotel." There were horsemen coming and going down the wide street between its rows of old stores, saloons, and houses. Ord certainly did not look enterprising. Americans had manifestly assimilated much of the leisure of the Mexicans. The hotel had a wide platform in front, and this did duty as porch and sidewalk. Upon it, and leaning against a hitching-rail, were men of varying ages, most of them slovenly in old jeans and slouched sombreros. Some were booted, belted, and spurred. No man there wore a coat, but all wore vests. The guns in that group would have outnumbered the men.

It was a crowd seemingly too lazy to be curious. Good nature did not appear to be wanting, but it was not the frank and boisterous kind natural to the cowboy or rancher in town for a day. These men were idlers; what else, perhaps, was easy to conjecture. Certainly to this arriving stranger, who flashed a keen eye over them, they wore an atmosphere never associated with work.

Presently a tall man, with a drooping, sandy mustache, leisurely detached himself from the crowd.

"Howdy, stranger," he said.

The stranger had bent over to loosen the cinches; he straightened up and nodded. Then: "I'm thirsty!"

That brought a broad smile to faces. It was characteristic greeting. One and all trooped after the stranger into the hotel. It was a dark, ill-smelling barn of a place, with a bar as high as a short man's head. A bartender with a scarred face was serving drinks.

"Line up, gents," said the stranger.

They piled over one another to get to the bar, with coarse jests and oaths and laughter. None of them noted that the stranger did not appear so thirsty as he had claimed to be. In fact, though he went through the motions, he did not drink at all.

"My name's Jim Fletcher," said the tall man with the drooping, sandy mustache. He spoke laconically, nevertheless there was a tone that showed he expected to be known. Something went with that name. The stranger did not appear to be impressed.

"My name might be Blazes, but it ain't," he replied. "What do you call this burg?"

"Stranger, this heah me-tropoles bears the handle Ord. Is thet new to you?"

He leaned back against the bar, and now his little yellow eyes, clear as crystal, flawless as a hawk's, fixed on the stranger. Other men crowded close, forming a circle, curious, ready to be friendly or otherwise, according to how the tall interrogator marked the new-comer.

"Sure, Ord's a little strange to me. Off the railroad some, ain't it? Funny trails hereabouts."

"How fur was you goin'?"

"I reckon I was goin' as far as I could," replied the stranger, with a hard laugh.

His reply had subtle reaction on that listening circle. Some of the men exchanged glances. Fletcher stroked his drooping mustache, seemed thoughtful, but lost something of that piercing scrutiny.

"Wal, Ord's the jumpin'-off place," he said, presently. "Sure you've heerd of the Big Bend country?"

"I sure have, an' was makin' tracks fer it," replied the stranger.

Fletcher turned toward a man in the outer edge of the group. "Knell, come in heah."

This individual elbowed his way in and was seen to be scarcely more than a boy, almost pale beside those bronzed men, with a long, expressionless face, thin and sharp.

"Knell, this heah's—" Fletcher wheeled to the stranger. "What'd you call yourself?"

"I'd hate to mention what I've been callin' myself lately."

This sally fetched another laugh. The stranger appeared cool, careless, indifferent. Perhaps he knew, as the others present knew, that this show of Fletcher's, this pretense of introduction, was merely talk while he was looked over.

Knell stepped up, and it was easy to see, from the way Fletcher relinquished his part in the situation, that a man greater than he had appeared upon the scene.

"Any business here?" he queried, curtly. When he spoke his expressionless face was in strange contrast with the ring, the quality, the cruelty of his voice. This voice betrayed an absence of humor, of friendliness, of heart.

"Nope," replied the stranger.

"Know anybody hereabouts?"

"Nary one."

"Jest ridin' through?"

"Yep."

"Slopin' fer back country, eh?"

There came a pause. The stranger appeared to grow a little resentful and drew himself up disdainfully.

"Wal, considerin' you-all seem so damn friendly an' oncurious down here in this Big Bend country, I don't mind sayin' yes—I am in on the dodge," he replied, with deliberate sarcasm.

"From west of Ord—out El Paso way, mebbe?"

"Sure."

"A-huh! Thet so?" Knell's words cut the air, stilled the room. "You're from way down the river. Thet's what they say down there—'on the dodge.'... Stranger, you're a liar!"

With swift clink of spur and thump of boot the crowd split, leaving Knell and the stranger in the center.

Wild breed of that ilk never made a mistake in judging a man's nerve. Knell had cut out with the trenchant call, and stood ready. The stranger suddenly lost his every semblance to the rough and easy character before manifest in him. He became bronze. That situation seemed familiar to him. His eyes held a singular piercing light that danced like a compass-needle.

"Sure I lied," he said; "so I ain't takin' offense at the way you called me. I'm lookin' to make friends, not enemies. You don't strike me as one of them four-flushes, achin' to kill somebody. But if you are—

go ahead an' open the ball.... You see, I never throw a gun on them fellers till they go fer theirs."

Knell coolly eyed his antagonist, his strange face not changing in the least. Yet somehow it was evident in his look that here was metal which rang differently from what he had expected. Invited to start a fight or withdraw, as he chose, Knell proved himself big in the manner characteristic of only the genuine gunman.

"Stranger, I pass," he said, and, turning to the bar, he ordered liquor.

The tension relaxed, the silence broke, the men filled up the gap; the incident seemed closed. Jim Fletcher attached himself to the stranger, and now both respect and friendliness tempered his asperity.

"Wal, fer want of a better handle I'll call you Dodge," he said.

"Dodge's as good as any.... Gents, line up again—an' if you can't be friendly, be careful!"

Such was Buck Duane's debut in the little outlaw hamlet of Ord.

Duane had been three months out of the Nueces country. At El Paso he bought the finest horse he could find, and, armed and otherwise outfitted to suit him, he had taken to unknown trails. Leisurely he rode from town to town, village to village, ranch to ranch, fitting his talk and his occupation to the impression he wanted to make upon different people whom he met. He was in turn a cowboy, a rancher, a cattleman, a stock-buyer, a boomer, a land-hunter; and long before he reached the wild and inhospitable Ord he had acted the part of an outlaw, drifting into new territory. He passed on leisurely because he wanted to learn the lay of the country, the location of villages and ranches, the work, habit, gossip, pleasures, and fears of the people with whom he came in contact. The one subject most impelling to him—outlaws—he never mentioned; but by talking all around it, sifting the old ranch and cattle story, he acquired a knowledge calculated to aid his plot. In this game time was of no moment; if necessary he would take years to accomplish his task. The stupendous and perilous nature of it showed in the slow, wary preparation. When he heard Fletcher's name and faced Knell he knew he had reached the place he sought. Ord was a hamlet on the fringe of the grazing country, of doubtful honesty, from which, surely, winding trails led down into that free and never-disturbed paradise of outlaws—the Big Bend.

Duane made himself agreeable, yet not too much so, to Fletcher and several other men disposed to talk and drink and eat; and then, after having a care for his horse, he rode out of town a couple of miles to a grove he had marked, and there, well hidden, he prepared to spend the night. This proceeding served a double purpose—he was safer, and the habit would look well in the eyes of outlaws, who would be more inclined to see in him the lone-wolf fugitive.

Long since Duane had fought out a battle with himself, won a hard-earned victory. His outer life, the action, was much the same as it had been; but the inner life had tremendously changed. He could never become a happy man, he could never shake utterly those haunting phantoms that had once been his despair and madness; but he had assumed a task impossible for any man save one like him, he had felt the meaning of it grow strangely and wonderfully, and through that flourished up consciousness of how passionately he now clung to this thing which would blot out his former infamy. The iron fetters no more threatened his hands; the iron door no more haunted his dreams. He never forgot that he was free. Strangely, too, along with this feeling of new manhood there gathered the force of imperious desire to run these chief outlaws to their dooms. He never called them outlaws—but rustlers, thieves, robbers, murderers, criminals. He sensed the growth of a relentless driving passion, and sometimes he feared that, more than the newly acquired zeal and pride in this ranger service, it was the old, terrible inherited killing instinct lifting its hydra-head in new guise. But of that he could not be sure. He dreaded the thought. He could only wait.

Another aspect of the change in Duane, neither passionate nor driving, yet not improbably even more potent of new significance to life, was the imperceptible return of an old love of nature dead during his outlaw days.

For years a horse had been only a machine of locomotion, to carry him from place to place, to beat and spur and goad mercilessly in flight; now this giant black, with his splendid head, was a companion, a friend, a brother, a loved thing, guarded jealously, fed and trained and ridden with an intense appreciation of his great speed and endurance. For years the daytime, with its birth of sunrise on through long hours to the ruddy close, had been used for sleep or rest in some rocky hole or willow brake or deserted hut, had been hated because it augmented danger of pursuit, because it drove the fugitive to lonely, wretched hiding; now the dawn was a greeting, a promise of another day to ride, to plan, to remember, and sun, wind, cloud, rain, sky—all were joys to him, somehow speaking his freedom. For years the night had been a black space, during which he had to ride unseen along the endless trails, to peer with cat-eyes through gloom for the moving shape that ever pursued him; now the twilight and the dusk and the shadows of grove and canyon darkened into night with its train of stars, and brought him calm reflection of the day's happenings, of the morrow's possibilities, perhaps a sad, brief procession of the old phantoms, then sleep. For years canyons and valleys and mountains had been looked at as retreats that might be dark and wild enough to hide even an outlaw; now he saw these features of the great desert with something of the eyes of the boy who had once burned for adventure and life among them.

This night a wonderful afterglow lingered long in the west, and against the golden-red of clear sky the bold, black head of Mount Ord reared itself aloft, beautiful but aloof, sinister yet calling. Small wonder that Duane gazed in fascination upon the peak! Somewhere deep in its corrugated sides or lost in a rugged canyon was hidden the secret stronghold of the master outlaw Cheseldine. All down along the ride from El Paso Duane had heard of Cheseldine, of his band, his fearful deeds, his cunning, his widely separated raids, of his flitting here and there like a Jack-o'-lantern; but never a word of his den, never a word of his appearance.

Next morning Duane did not return to Ord. He struck off to the north, riding down a rough, slow-descending road that appeared to have been used occasionally for cattle-driving. As he had ridden in from the west, this northern direction led him into totally unfamiliar country. While he passed on, however, he exercised such keen observation that in the future he would know whatever might be of service to him if he chanced that way again.

The rough, wild, brush-covered slope down from the foothills gradually leveled out into plain, a magnificent grazing country, upon which till noon of that day Duane did not see a herd of cattle or a ranch. About that time he made out smoke from the railroad, and after a couple of hours' riding he entered a town which inquiry discovered to be Bradford. It was the largest town he had visited since Marfa, and he calculated must have a thousand or fifteen hundred inhabitants, not including Mexicans. He decided this would be a good place for him to hold up for a while, being the nearest town to Ord, only forty miles away. So he hitched his horse in front of a store and leisurely set about studying Bradford.

It was after dark, however, that Duane verified his suspicions concerning Bradford. The town was awake after dark, and there was one long row of saloons, dance-halls, gambling-resorts in full blast. Duane visited them all, and was surprised to see wildness and license equal to that of the old river camp of Bland's in its palmiest days. Here it was forced upon him that the farther west one traveled along the river the sparser the respectable settlements, the more numerous the hard characters, and in consequence the greater the element of lawlessness. Duane returned to his lodging-house with the conviction that MacNelly's task of cleaning up the Big Bend country was a stupendous one. Yet, he reflected, a company of intrepid and quick-shooting rangers could have soon cleaned up this Bradford.

The innkeeper had one other guest that night, a long black-coated and wide-sombreroed Texan who reminded Duane of his grandfather. This man had penetrating eyes, a courtly manner, and an unmistakable leaning toward companionship and mint-juleps. The gentleman introduced himself as Colonel Webb, of Marfa, and took it as a matter of course that Duane made no comment about himself.

"Sir, it's all one to me," he said, blandly, waving his hand. "I have traveled. Texas is free, and this frontier is one where it's healthier and just as friendly for a man to have no curiosity about his companion. You might be Cheseldine, of the Big Bend, or you might be Judge Little, of El Paso-it's all one to me. I enjoy drinking with you anyway."

Duane thanked him, conscious of a reserve and dignity that he could not have felt or pretended three months before. And then, as always, he was a good listener. Colonel Webb told, among other things, that he had come out to the Big Bend to look over the affairs of a deceased brother who had been a rancher and a sheriff of one of the towns, Fairdale by name.

"Found no affairs, no ranch, not even his grave," said Colonel Webb. "And I tell you, sir, if hell's any tougher than this Fairdale I don't want to expiate my sins there."

"Fairdale.... I imagine sheriffs have a hard row to hoe out here," replied Duane, trying not to appear curious.

The Colonel swore lustily.

"My brother was the only honest sheriff Fairdale ever had. It was wonderful how long he lasted. But he had nerve, he could throw a gun, and he was on the square. Then he was wise enough to confine his work to offenders of his own town and neighborhood. He let the riding outlaws alone, else he wouldn't have lasted at all.... What this frontier needs, sir, is about six companies of Texas Rangers."

Duane was aware of the Colonel's close scrutiny.

"Do you know anything about the service?" he asked.

"I used to. Ten years ago when I lived in San Antonio. A fine body of men, sir, and the salvation of Texas."

"Governor Stone doesn't entertain that opinion," said Duane.

Here Colonel Webb exploded. Manifestly the governor was not his choice for a chief executive of the great state. He talked politics for a while, and of the vast territory west of the Pecos that seemed never to get a benefit from Austin. He talked enough for Duane to realize that here was just the kind of intelligent, well-informed, honest citizen that he had been trying to meet. He exerted himself thereafter to be agreeable and interesting; and he saw presently that here was an opportunity to make a valuable acquaintance, if not a friend.

"I'm a stranger in these parts," said Duane, finally. "What is this outlaw situation you speak of?"

"It's damnable, sir, and unbelievable. Not rustling any more, but just wholesale herd-stealing, in which some big cattlemen, supposed to be honest, are equally guilty with the outlaws. On this border, you know, the rustler has always been able to steal cattle in any numbers. But to get rid of big bunches—that's the hard job. The gang operating between here and Valentine evidently have not this trouble. Nobody knows where the stolen stock goes. But I'm not alone in my opinion that most of it goes to several big stockmen. They ship to San Antonio, Austin, New Orleans, also to El Paso. If you travel the stock-road between here and Marfa and Valentine you'll see dead cattle all along the line and stray cattle out in the scrub. The herds have been driven fast and far, and stragglers are not rounded up."

"Wholesale business, eh?" remarked Duane. "Who are these—er—big stock-buyers?"

Colonel Webb seemed a little startled at the abrupt query. He bent his penetrating gaze upon Duane and thoughtfully stroked his pointed beard.

"Names, of course, I'll not mention. Opinions are one thing, direct accusation another. This is not a healthy country for the informer."

When it came to the outlaws themselves Colonel Webb was disposed to talk freely. Duane could not judge whether the Colonel had a hobby of that subject or the outlaws were so striking in personality and deed that any man would know all about them. The great name along the river was Cheseldine, but it seemed to be a name detached from an individual. No person of veracity known to Colonel Webb had ever seen Cheseldine, and those who claimed that doubtful honor varied so diversely in descriptions of the chief that they confused the reality and lent to the outlaw only further mystery. Strange to say of an outlaw leader, as there was no one who could identify him, so there was no one who could prove he had actually killed a man. Blood flowed like water over the Big Bend country, and it was Cheseldine who spilled it. Yet the fact remained there were no eye-witnesses to connect any individual called Cheseldine with these deeds of violence. But in striking contrast to this mystery was the person, character, and cold-blooded action of Poggin and Knell, the chief's lieutenants. They were familiar figures in all the towns within two hundred miles of Bradford. Knell had a record, but as gunman with an incredible list of victims Poggin was supreme. If Poggin had a friend no one ever heard of him. There were a hundred stories of his nerve, his wonderful speed with a gun, his passion for gambling, his love of a horse—his cold, implacable, inhuman wiping out of his path any man that crossed it.

"Cheseldine is a name, a terrible name," said Colonel Webb. "Sometimes I wonder if he's not only a name. In that case where does the brains of this gang come from? No; there must be a master craftsman behind this border pillage; a master capable of handling those terrors Poggin and Knell. Of all the thousands of outlaws developed by western Texas in the last twenty years these three are the greatest. In southern Texas, down between the Pecos and the Nueces, there have been and are still many bad men. But I doubt if any outlaw there, possibly excepting Buck Duane, ever equaled Poggin. You've heard of this Duane?"

"Yes, a little," replied Duane, quietly. "I'm from southern Texas. Buck Duane then is known out here?"

"Why, man, where isn't his name known?" returned Colonel Webb. "I've kept track of his record as I have all the others. Of course, Duane, being a lone outlaw, is somewhat of a mystery also, but not like Cheseldine. Out here there have drifted many stories of Duane, horrible some of them. But despite them a sort of romance clings to that Nueces outlaw. He's killed three great outlaw leaders, I believe—Bland, Hardin, and the other I forgot. Hardin was known in the Big Bend, had friends there. Bland had a hard name at Del Rio."

"Then this man Duane enjoys rather an unusual repute west of the Pecos?" inquired Duane.

"He's considered more of an enemy to his kind than to honest men. I understand Duane had many friends, that whole counties swear by him—secretly, of course, for he's a hunted outlaw with rewards on his head. His fame in this country appears to hang on his matchless gun-play and his enmity toward outlaw chiefs. I've heard many a rancher say: 'I wish to God that Buck Duane would drift out here! I'd give a hundred pesos to see him and Poggin meet.' It's a singular thing, stranger, how jealous these great outlaws are of each other."

"Yes, indeed, all about them is singular," replied Duane. "Has Cheseldine's gang been busy lately?"

"No. This section has been free of rustling for months, though there's unexplained movements of stock. Probably all the stock that's being shipped now was rustled long ago. Cheseldine works over a wide section, too wide for news to travel inside of weeks. Then sometimes he's not heard of at all for a spell. These lulls are pretty surely indicative of a big storm sooner or later. And Cheseldine's deals, as they grow fewer and farther between, certainly get bigger, more daring. There are some people who think Cheseldine had nothing to do with the bank-robberies and train-holdups during the last few years in this country. But that's poor reasoning. The jobs have been too well done, too surely covered, to be the work of greasers or ordinary outlaws."

"What's your view of the outlook? How's all this going to wind up? Will the outlaw ever be driven out?" asked Duane.

"Never. There will always be outlaws along the Rio Grande. All the armies in the world couldn't comb the wild brakes of that fifteen hundred miles of river. But the sway of the outlaw, such as is enjoyed by these great leaders, will sooner or later be past. The criminal element flock to the Southwest. But not so thick and fast as the pioneers. Besides, the outlaws kill themselves, and the ranchers are slowly rising in wrath, if not in action. That will come soon. If they only had a leader to start the fight! But that will come. There's talk of Vigilantes, the same hat were organized in California and are now in force in Idaho. So far it's only talk. But the time will come. And the days of Cheseldine and Poggin are numbered."

Duane went to bed that night exceedingly thoughtful. The long trail was growing hot. This voluble colonel had given him new ideas. It came to Duane in surprise that he was famous along the upper Rio Grande. Assuredly he would not long be able to conceal his identity. He had no doubt that he would soon meet the chiefs of this clever and bold rustling gang. He could not decide whether he would be safer unknown or known. In the latter case his one chance lay in the fatality connected with his name, in his power to look it and act it. Duane had never dreamed of any sleuth-hound tendency in his nature, but now he felt something like one. Above all others his mind fixed on Poggin—Poggin the brute, the executor of Cheseldine's will, but mostly upon Poggin the gunman. This in itself was a warning to Duane. He felt terrible forces at work within him. There was the stern and indomitable resolve to make MacNelly's boast good to the governor of the state—to break up Cheseldine's gang. Yet this was not in Duane's mind before a strange grim and deadly instinct—which he had to drive away for fear he would find in it a passion to kill Poggin, not for the state, nor for his word to MacNelly, but for himself. Had his father's blood and the hard years made Duane the kind of man who instinctively wanted to meet Poggin? He was sworn to MacNelly's service, and he fought himself to keep that, and that only, in his mind.

Duane ascertained that Fairdale was situated two days' ride from Bradford toward the north. There was a stage which made the journey twice a week.

Next morning Duane mounted his horse and headed for Fairdale. He rode leisurely, as he wanted to learn all he could about the country. There were few ranches. The farther he traveled the better grazing he encountered, and, strange to note, the fewer herds of cattle.

It was just sunset when he made out a cluster of adobe houses that marked the half-way point between Bradford and Fairdale. Here, Duane had learned, was stationed a comfortable inn for wayfarers.

When he drew up before the inn the landlord and his family and a number of loungers greeted him laconically.

"Beat the stage in, hey?" remarked one.

"There she comes now," said another. "Joel shore is drivin' to-night."

Far down the road Duane saw a cloud of dust and horses and a lumbering coach. When he had looked after the needs of his horse he returned to the group before the inn. They awaited the stage with that interest common to isolated people. Presently it rolled up, a large mud-bespattered and dusty vehicle, littered with baggage on top and tied on behind. A number of passengers alighted, three of whom excited Duane's interest. One was a tall, dark, striking-looking man, and the other two were ladies, wearing long gray ulsters and veils. Duane heard the proprietor of the inn address the man as Colonel Longstreth, and as the party entered the inn Duane's quick ears caught a few words which acquainted him with the fact that Longstreth was the Mayor of Fairdale.

Duane passed inside himself to learn that supper would soon be ready. At table he found himself opposite the three who had attracted his attention.

"Ruth, I envy the lucky cowboys," Longstreth was saying.

Ruth was a curly-headed girl with gray or hazel eyes.

"I'm crazy to ride bronchos," she said.

Duane gathered she was on a visit to western Texas. The other girl's deep voice, sweet like a bell, made Duane regard her closer. She had beauty as he had never seen it in another woman. She was slender, but the development of her figure gave Duane the impression she was twenty years old or more. She had the most exquisite hands Duane had ever seen. She did not resemble the Colonel, who was evidently her father. She looked tired, quiet, even melancholy. A finely chiseled oval face; clear, olive-tinted skin, long eyes set wide apart and black as coal, beautiful to look into; a slender, straight nose that had something nervous and delicate about it which made Duane think of a thoroughbred; and a mouth by no means small, but perfectly curved; and hair like jet—all these features proclaimed her beauty to Duane. Duane believed her a descendant of one of the old French families of eastern Texas. He was sure of it when she looked at him, drawn by his rather persistent gaze. There were pride, fire, and passion in her eyes. Duane felt himself blushing in confusion. His stare at her had been rude, perhaps, but unconscious. How many years had passed since he had seen a girl like her! Thereafter he kept his eyes upon his plate, yet he seemed to be aware that he had aroused the interest of both girls.

After supper the guests assembled in a big sitting-room where an open fire place with blazing mesquite sticks gave out warmth and cheery glow. Duane took a seat by a table in the corner, and, finding a paper, began to read. Presently when he glanced up he saw two dark-faced men, strangers who had not appeared before, and were peering in from a doorway. When they saw Duane had observed them they stepped back out of sight.

It flashed over Duane that the strangers acted suspiciously. In Texas in the seventies it was always bad policy to let strangers go unheeded. Duane pondered a moment. Then he went out to look over these two men. The doorway opened into a patio, and across that was a little dingy, dim-lighted bar-room. Here Duane found the innkeeper dispensing drinks to the two strangers. They glanced up when he entered, and one of them whispered. He imagined he had seen one of them before. In Texas, where outdoor men were so rough, bronzed, bold, and sometimes grim of aspect, it was no easy task to pick out the crooked ones. But Duane's years on the border had augmented a natural instinct or gift to read character, or at least to sense the evil in men; and he knew at once that these strangers were dishonest.

"Hey somethin'?" one of them asked, leering. Both looked Duane up and down.

"No thanks, I don't drink," Duane replied, and returned their scrutiny with interest. "How's tricks in the Big Bend?"

Both men stared. It had taken only a close glance for Duane to recognize a type of ruffian most frequently met along the river. These strangers had that stamp, and their surprise proved he was right. Here the innkeeper showed signs of uneasiness, and seconded the surprise of his customers. No more was said at the instant, and the two rather hurriedly went out.

"Say, boss, do you know those fellows?" Duane asked the innkeeper.

"Nope."

"Which way did they come?"

"Now I think of it, them fellers rid in from both corners today," he replied, and he put both hands on the bar and looked at Duane. "They nooned heah, comin' from Bradford, they said, an' trailed in after the stage."

When Duane returned to the sitting-room Colonel Longstreth was absent, also several of the other passengers. Miss Ruth sat in the chair he had vacated, and across the table from her sat Miss Longstreth. Duane went directly to them.

"Excuse me," said Duane, addressing them. "I want

to tell you there are a couple of rough-looking men here. I've just seen them. They mean evil. Tell your father to be careful. Lock your doors—bar your windows to-night."

"Oh!" cried Ruth, very low. "Ray, do you hear?"

"Thank you; we'll be careful," said Miss Longstreth, gracefully. The rich color had faded in her cheek. "I saw those men watching you from that door. They had such bright black eyes. Is there really danger—here?"

"I think so," was Duane's reply.

Soft swift steps behind him preceded a harsh voice: "Hands up!"

No man quicker than Duane to recognize the intent in those words! His hands shot up. Miss Ruth uttered a little frightened cry and sank into her chair. Miss Longstreth turned white, her eyes dilated. Both girls were staring at some one behind Duane.

"Turn around!" ordered the harsh voice.

The big, dark stranger, the bearded one who had whispered to his comrade in the bar-room and asked Duane to drink, had him covered with a cocked gun. He strode forward, his eyes gleaming, pressed the gun against him, and with his other hand dove into his inside coat pocket and tore out his roll of bills. Then he reached low at Duane's hip, felt his gun, and took it. Then he slapped the other hip, evidently in search of another weapon. That done, he backed away, wearing an expression of fiendish satisfaction that made Duane think he was only a common thief, a novice at this kind of game.

His comrade stood in the door with a gun leveled at two other men, who stood there frightened, speechless.

"Git a move on, Bill," called this fellow; and he took a hasty glance backward. A stamp of hoofs came from outside. Of course the robbers had horses waiting. The one called Bill strode across the room, and with brutal, careless haste began to prod the two men with his weapon and to search them. The robber in the doorway called "Rustle!" and disappeared.

Duane wondered where the innkeeper was, and Colonel Longstreth and the other two passengers. The bearded robber quickly got through with his searching, and from his growls Duane gathered he had not been well remunerated. Then he wheeled once more. Duane had not moved a muscle, stood perfectly calm with his arms high. The robber strode back with his bloodshot eyes fastened upon the girls. Miss Longstreth never flinched, but the little girl appeared about to faint.

"Don't yap, there!" he said, low and hard. He thrust the gun close to Ruth. Then Duane knew for sure that he was no knight of the road, but a plain cutthroat robber. Danger always made Duane exult in a kind of cold glow. But now something hot worked within him. He had a little gun in his pocket. The robber had missed it. And he began to calculate chances.

"Any money, jewelry, diamonds!" ordered the ruffian, fiercely.

Miss Ruth collapsed. Then he made at Miss Longstreth. She stood with her hands at her breast. Evidently the robber took this position to mean that she had valuables concealed there. But Duane fancied she had instinctively pressed her hands against a throbbing heart.

"Come out with it!" he said, harshly, reaching for her.

"Don't dare touch me!" she cried, her eyes ablaze. She did not move. She had nerve.

It made Duane thrill. He saw he was going to get a chance. Waiting had been a science with him. But here it was hard. Miss Ruth had fainted, and that was well. Miss Longstreth had fight in her, which fact helped Duane, yet made injury possible to her. She eluded two lunges the man made at her. Then his rough hand caught her waist, and with one pull ripped it asunder, exposing her beautiful shoulder, white as snow.

She cried out. The prospect of being robbed or even killed had not shaken Miss Longstreth's nerve as had this brutal tearing off of half her waist.

The ruffian was only turned partially away from Duane. For himself he could have waited no longer. But for her! That gun was still held dangerously upward close to her. Duane watched only that. Then a bellow made him jerk his head. Colonel Longstreth stood in the doorway in a magnificent rage. He had no weapon. Strange how he showed no fear! He bellowed something again.

Duane's shifting glance caught the robber's sudden movement. It was a kind of start. He seemed stricken. Duane expected him to shoot Longstreth. Instead the hand that clutched Miss Longstreth's torn waist loosened its hold. The other hand with its cocked weapon slowly dropped till it pointed to the floor. That was Duane's chance.

Swift as a flash he drew his gun and fired. Thud! went his bullet, and he could not tell on the instant whether it hit the robber or went into the ceiling. Then the robber's gun boomed harmlessly. He fell with blood spurting over his face. Duane realized he had hit him, but the small bullet had glanced.

Miss Longstreth reeled and might have fallen had Duane not supported her. It was only a few steps to a couch, to which he half led, half carried her. Then he rushed out of the room, across the patio, through the bar to the yard. Nevertheless, he was cautious. In the gloom stood a saddled horse, probably the one belonging to the fellow he had shot. His comrade had escaped. Returning to the sitting-room, Duane found a condition approaching pandemonium.

The innkeeper rushed in, pitchfork in hands. Evidently he had been out at the barn. He was now shouting to find out what had happened. Joel, the stage-driver, was trying to quiet the men who had been robbed. The woman, wife of one of the men, had come in, and she had hysterics. The girls were still and white. The robber Bill lay where he had fallen, and Duane guessed he had made a fair shot, after all. And, lastly, the thing that struck Duane most of all was Longstreth's rage. He never saw such passion. Like a caged lion Longstreth stalked and roared. There came a quieter moment in which the innkeeper shrilly protested:

"Man, what're you ravin' aboot? Nobody's hurt, an' thet's lucky. I swear to God I hadn't nothin' to do with them fellers!"

"I ought to kill you anyhow!" replied Longstreth. And his voice now astounded Duane, it was so full of power.

Upon examination Duane found that his bullet had furrowed the robber's temple, torn a great piece out of his scalp, and, as Duane had guessed, had glanced. He was not seriously injured, and already showed signs of returning consciousness.

"Drag him out of here!" ordered Longstreth; and he turned to his daughter.

Before the innkeeper reached the robber Duane had secured the money and gun taken from him; and presently recovered the property of the other men. Joel helped the innkeeper carry the injured man somewhere outside.

Miss Longstreth was sitting white but composed upon the couch, where lay Miss Ruth, who evidently had been carried there by the Colonel. Duane did not think she had wholly lost consciousness, and now she lay very still, with eyes dark and shadowy, her face pallid and wet. The Colonel, now that he finally remembered his women-folk, seemed to be gentle and kind. He talked soothingly to Miss Ruth, made light of the adventure, said she must learn to have nerve out here where things happened.

"Can I be of any service?" asked Duane, solicitously.

"Thanks; I guess there's nothing you can do. Talk to these frightened girls while I go see what's to be done with that thick-skulled robber," he replied, and, telling the girls that there was no more danger, he went out.

Miss Longstreth sat with one hand holding her torn waist in place; the other she extended to Duane. He took it awkwardly, and he felt a strange thrill.

"You saved my life," she said, in grave, sweet seriousness.

"No, no!" Duane exclaimed. "He might have struck you, hurt you, but no more."

"I saw murder in his eyes. He thought I had jewels under my dress. I couldn't bear his touch. The beast! I'd have fought. Surely my life was in peril."

"Did you kill him?" asked Miss Ruth, who lay listening.

"Oh no. He's not badly hurt."

"I'm very glad he's alive," said Miss Longstreth, shuddering.

"My intention was bad enough," Duane went on. "It was a ticklish place for me. You see, he was half drunk, and I was afraid his gun might go off. Fool careless he was!"

"Yet you say you didn't save me," Miss Longstreth returned, quickly.

"Well, let it go at that," Duane responded. "I saved you something."

"Tell me all about it?" asked Miss Ruth, who was fast recovering.

Rather embarrassed, Duane briefly told the incident from his point of view.

"Then you stood there all the time with your hands up thinking of nothing—watching for nothing except a little moment when you might draw your gun?" asked Miss Ruth.

"I guess that's about it," he replied.

"Cousin," said Miss Longstreth, thoughtfully, "it was fortunate for us that this gentleman happened to be here. Papa scouts—laughs at danger. He seemed to think there was no danger. Yet he raved after it came."

"Go with us all the way to Fairdale—please?" asked Miss Ruth, sweetly offering her hand. "I am Ruth Herbert. And this is my cousin, Ray Longstreth."

"I'm traveling that way," replied Duane, in great confusion. He did not know how to meet the situation.

Colonel Longstreth returned then, and after bidding Duane a good night, which seemed rather curt by contrast to the graciousness of the girls, he led them away.

Before going to bed Duane went outside to take a look at the injured robber and perhaps to ask him a few questions. To Duane's surprise, he was gone, and so was his horse. The innkeeper was dumfounded. He said that he left the fellow on the floor in the barroom.

"Had he come to?" inquired Duane.

"Sure. He asked for whisky."

"Did he say anything else?"

"Not to me. I heard him talkin' to the father of them girls."

"You mean Colonel Longstreth?"

"I reckon. He sure was some riled, wasn't he? Jest as if I was to blame fer that two-bit of a hold-up!"

"What did you make of the old gent's rage?" asked

Duane, watching the innkeeper. He scratched his head dubiously. He was sincere, and Duane believed in his honesty.

"Wal, I'm doggoned if I know what to make of it. But I reckon he's either crazy or got more nerve than most Texans."

"More nerve, maybe," Duane replied. "Show me a bed now, innkeeper."

Once in bed in the dark, Duane composed himself to think over the several events of the evening. He called up the details of the holdup and carefully revolved them in mind. The Colonel's wrath, under circumstances where almost any Texan would have been cool, nonplussed Duane, and he put it down to a choleric temperament. He pondered long on the action of the robber when Longstreth's bellow of rage burst in upon him. This ruffian, as bold and mean a type as Duane had ever encountered, had, from some cause or other, been startled. From whatever point Duane viewed the man's strange indecision he could come to only one conclusion—his start, his check, his fear had been that of recognition. Duane compared this effect with the suddenly acquired sense he had gotten of Colonel Longstreth's powerful personality. Why had that desperate robber lowered his gun and stood paralyzed at sight and sound of the Mayor of Fairdale? This was not answerable. There might have been a number of reasons, all to Colonel Longstreth's credit, but Duane could not understand. Longstreth had not appeared to see danger for his daughter, even though she had been roughly handled, and had advanced in front of a cocked gun. Duane probed deep into this singular fact, and he brought to bear on the thing all his knowledge and experience of violent Texas life. And he found that the instant Colonel Longstreth had appeared on the scene there was no further danger threatening his daughter. Why? That likewise Duane could not answer. Then his rage, Duane concluded, had been solely at the idea of HIS daughter being assaulted by a robber. This deduction was indeed a thought-disturber, but Duane put it aside to crystallize and for more careful consideration.

Next morning Duane found that the little town was called Sanderson. It was larger than he had at first supposed. He walked up the main street and back again. Just as he arrived some horsemen rode up to the inn and dismounted. And at this juncture the Longstreth party came out. Duane heard Colonel Longstreth utter an exclamation. Then he saw him shake hands with a tall man. Longstreth looked surprised and angry, and he spoke with force; but Duane could not hear what it was he said. The fellow laughed, yet somehow he struck Duane as sullen, until suddenly he espied Miss Longstreth. Then his face changed, and he removed his sombrero. Duane went closer.

"Floyd, did you come with the teams?" asked Longstreth, sharply.

"Not me. I rode a horse, good and hard," was the reply.

"Humph! I'll have a word to say to you later." Then Longstreth turned to his daughter. "Ray, here's the cousin I've told you about. You used to play with him ten years ago—Floyd Lawson. Floyd, my daughter—and my niece, Ruth Herbert."

Duane always scrutinized every one he met, and now with a dangerous game to play, with a consciousness of Longstreth's unusual and significant personality, he bent a keen and searching glance upon this Floyd Lawson.

He was under thirty, yet gray at his temples—dark, smooth-shaven, with lines left by wildness, dissipation, shadows under dark eyes, a mouth strong and bitter, and a square chin—a reckless, careless, handsome, sinister face strangely losing the hardness when he smiled. The grace of a gentleman clung round him, seemed like an echo in his mellow voice. Duane doubted not that he, like many a young man, had drifted out to the frontier, where rough and wild life had wrought sternly but had not quite effaced the mark of good family.

Colonel Longstreth apparently did not share the pleasure of his daughter and his niece in the advent of this cousin. Something hinged on this meeting. Duane grew intensely curious, but, as the stage appeared ready for the journey, he had no further opportunity to gratify it.

CHAPTER XVI

Duane followed the stage through the town, out into the open, on to a wide, hard-packed road showing years of travel. It headed northwest. To the left rose a range of low, bleak mountains he had noted yesterday, and to the right sloped the mesquite-patched sweep of ridge and flat. The driver pushed his team to a fast trot, which gait surely covered ground rapidly.

The stage made three stops in the forenoon, one at a place where the horses could be watered, the second at a chuck-wagon belonging to cowboys who were riding after stock, and the third at a small cluster of adobe and stone houses constituting a hamlet the driver called Longstreth, named after the Colonel. From that point on to Fairdale there were only a few ranches, each one controlling great acreage.

Early in the afternoon from a ridge-top Duane sighted Fairdale, a green patch in the mass of gray. For the barrens of Texas it was indeed a fair sight. But he was more concerned with its remoteness from civilization than its beauty. At that time, in the early seventies, when the vast western third of Texas was a wilderness, the pioneer had done wonders to settle there and establish places like Fairdale.

It needed only a glance for Duane to pick out Colonel Longstreth's ranch. The house was situated on the only elevation around Fairdale, and it was not high, nor more than a few minutes' walk from the edge of the town. It was a low, flat-roofed structure made of red adobe bricks, and covered what appeared to be fully an acre of ground. All was green about it, except where the fenced corrals and numerous barns or sheds showed gray and red.

Duane soon reached the shady outskirts of Fairdale, and entered the town with mingled feelings of curiosity, eagerness, and expectation. The street he rode down was a main one, and on both sides of the street was a solid row of saloons, resorts, hotels. Saddled horses stood hitched all along the sidewalk in two long lines, with a buckboard and team here and there breaking the continuity. This block was busy and noisy.

From all outside appearances Fairdale was no different from other frontier towns, and Duane's expectations were scarcely realized. As the afternoon was waning he halted at a little inn. A boy took charge of his horse. Duane questioned the lad about Fairdale and gradually drew to the subject most in mind.

"Colonel Longstreth has a big outfit, eh?"

"Reckon he has," replied the lad. "Doan know how many cowboys. They're always comin' and goin'. I ain't acquainted with half of them."

"Much movement of stock these days?"

"Stock's always movin'," he replied, with a queer look.

"Rustlers?"

But he did not follow up that look with the affirmative Duane expected.

"Lively place, I hear—Fairdale is?"

"Ain't so lively as Sanderson, but it's bigger."

"Yes, I heard it was. Fellow down there was talking about two cowboys who were arrested."

"Sure. I heered all about that. Joe Bean an' Brick Higgins—they belong heah, but they ain't heah much. Longstreth's boys."

Duane did not want to appear over-inquisitive, so he turned the talk into other channels.

After getting supper Duane strolled up and down the main street. When darkness set in he went into a hotel, bought cigars, sat around, and watched. Then he passed out and went into the next place. This was of rough crude exterior, but the inside was comparatively pretentious and ablaze with lights. It was full of men coming and going—a dusty-booted crowd that smelled of horses and smoke. Duane sat down for a while, with wide eyes and open ears. Then he hunted up the bar, where most of the guests had been or were going. He found a great square room lighted by six huge lamps, a bar at one side, and all the floor-space taken up by tables and chairs. This was the only gambling place of any size in southern Texas in which he had noted the absence of Mexicans. There was some card-playing going on at this moment. Duane stayed in there for a while, and knew that strangers were too common in Fairdale to be conspicuous. Then he returned to the inn where he had engaged a room.

Duane sat down on the steps of the dingy little restaurant. Two men were conversing inside, and they had not noticed Duane.

"Laramie, what's the stranger's name?" asked one.

"He didn't say," replied the other.

"Sure was a strappin' big man. Struck me a little odd, he did. No cattleman, him. How'd you size him?"

"Well, like one of them cool, easy, quiet Texans who's been lookin' for a man for years—to kill him when he found him."

"Right you are, Laramie; and, between you an' me, I hope he's lookin' for Long—"

"'S—sh!" interrupted Laramie. "You must be half drunk, to go talkie' that way."

Thereafter they conversed in too low a tone for Duane to hear, and presently Laramie's visitor left. Duane went inside, and, making himself agreeable, began to ask casual questions about Fairdale. Laramie was not communicative.

Duane went to his room in a thoughtful frame of mind. Had Laramie's visitor meant he hoped some one had come to kill Longstreth? Duane inferred just that from the interrupted remark. There was something wrong about the Mayor of Fairdale. Duane felt it. And he felt also, if there was a crooked and dangerous man, it was this Floyd Lawson. The innkeeper Laramie would be worth cultivating. And last in Duane's thoughts that night was Miss Longstreth. He could not help thinking of her—how strangely the meeting with her had affected him. It made him remember that long-past time when girls had been a part of his life. What a sad and dark and endless void lay between that past and the present! He had no right even to dream of a beautiful woman like Ray Longstreth. That conviction, however, did not dispel her; indeed, it seemed perversely to make her grow more fascinating. Duane grew conscious of a strange, unaccountable hunger, a something that was like a pang in his breast.

Next day he lounged about the inn. He did not make any overtures to the taciturn proprietor. Duane had no need of hurry now. He contented himself with watching and listening. And at the close of that day he decided Fairdale was what MacNelly had claimed it to be, and that he was on the track of an unusual adventure. The following day he spent in much the same way, though on one occasion he told Laramie he was looking for a man. The innkeeper grew a little less furtive and reticent after that. He would answer casual queries, and it did not take Duane long to learn that Laramie had seen better days—that he was now broken, bitter, and hard. Some one had wronged him.

Several days passed. Duane did not succeed in getting any closer to Laramie, but he found the idlers on the corners and in front of the stores unsuspicious and willing to talk. It did not take him long to find out that Fairdale stood parallel with Huntsville for gambling, drinking, and fighting. The street was always lined with dusty, saddled horses, the town full of strangers. Money appeared more abundant than in any place Duane had ever visited; and it was spent with the abandon that spoke forcibly of easy and crooked acquirement. Duane decided that Sanderson, Bradford, and Ord were but notorious outposts to this Fairdale, which was a secret center of rustlers and outlaws. And what struck Duane strangest of all was the fact that Longstreth was mayor here and held court daily. Duane knew intuitively, before a chance remark gave him proof, that this court was a sham, a farce. And he wondered if it were not a blind. This wonder of his was equivalent to suspicion of Colonel Longstreth, and Duane reproached himself. Then he realized that the reproach was because of the daughter. Inquiry had brought him the fact that Ray Longstreth had just come to live with her father. Longstreth had originally been a planter in Louisiana, where his family had remained after his advent in the West. He was a rich rancher; he owned half of Fairdale; he was a cattle-buyer on a large scale. Floyd Lawson was his lieutenant and associate in deals.

On the afternoon of the fifth day of Duane's stay in Fairdale he returned to the inn from his usual stroll, and upon entering was amazed to have a rough-looking young fellow rush by him out of the door. Inside Laramie was lying on the floor, with a bloody bruise on his face. He did not appear to be dangerously hurt.

"Bo Snecker! He hit me and went after the cash-drawer," said Laramie, laboring to his feet.

"Are you hurt much?" queried Duane.

"I guess not. But Bo needn't to have soaked me. I've been robbed before without that."

"Well, I'll take a look after Bo," replied Duane.

He went out and glanced down the street toward the center of the town. He did not see any one he could take for the innkeeper's assailant. Then he looked up the street, and he saw the young fellow about a block away, hurrying along and gazing back.

Duane yelled for him to stop and started to go after him. Snecker broke into a run. Then Duane set out to overhaul him. There were two motives in Duane's action—one of anger, and the other a desire to make a friend of this man Laramie, whom Duane believed could tell him much.

Duane was light on his feet, and he had a giant stride. He gained rapidly upon Snecker, who, turning this way and that, could not get out of sight. Then he took to the open country and ran straight for the green hill where Longstreth's house stood. Duane had almost caught Snecker when he reached the shrubbery and trees and there eluded him. But Duane kept him in sight, in the shade, on the paths, and up the road into the courtyard, and he saw Snecker go straight for Longstreth's house.

Duane was not to be turned back by that, singular as it was. He did not stop to consider. It seemed enough to know that fate had directed him to the path of this rancher Longstreth. Duane entered the first open door on that side of the court. It opened into a corridor which led into a plaza. It had wide, smooth stone porches, and flowers and shrubbery in the center. Duane hurried through to burst into the presence of Miss Longstreth and a number of young people. Evidently she was giving a little party.

Lawson stood leaning against one of the pillars that supported the porch roof; at sight of Duane his face changed remarkably, expressing amazement, consternation, then fear.

In the quick ensuing silence Miss Longstreth rose white as her dress. The young women present stared in astonishment, if they were not equally perturbed. There were cowboys present who suddenly grew intent and still. By these things Duane gathered that his appearance must be disconcerting. He was panting. He wore no hat or coat. His big gun-sheath showed plainly at his hip.

Sight of Miss Longstreth had an unaccountable effect upon Duane. He was plunged into confusion. For the moment he saw no one but her.

"Miss Longstreth—I came—to search—your house," panted Duane.

He hardly knew what he was saying, yet the instant he spoke he realized that that should have been the last thing for him to say. He had blundered. But he was not used to women, and this dark-eyed girl made him thrill and his heart beat thickly and his wits go scattering.

"Search my house!" exclaimed Miss Longstreth; and red succeeded the white in her cheeks. She appeared astonished and angry. "What for? Why, how dare you! This is unwarrantable!"

"A man—Bo Snecker—assaulted and robbed Jim Laramie," replied Duane, hurriedly. "I chased Snecker here—saw him run into the house."

"Here? Oh, sir, you must be mistaken. We have seen no one. In the absence of my father I'm mistress here. I'll not permit you to search."

Lawson appeared to come out of his astonishment.

He stepped forward.

"Ray, don't be bothered now," he said, to his cousin. "This fellow's making a bluff. I'll settle him. See here, Mister, you clear out!"

"I want Snecker. He's here, and I'm going to get him," replied Duane, quietly.

"Bah! That's all a bluff," sneered Lawson. "I'm on to your game. You just wanted an excuse to break in here—to see my cousin again. When you saw the company you invented that excuse. Now, be off, or it'll be the worse for you."

Duane felt his face burn with a tide of hot blood. Almost he felt that he was guilty of such motive. Had he not been unable to put this Ray Longstreth out of his mind? There seemed to be scorn in her eyes now. And somehow that checked his embarrassment.

"Miss Longstreth, will you let me search the house?" he asked.

"No."

"Then—I regret to say—I'll do so without your permission."

"You'll not dare!" she flashed. She stood erect, her bosom swelling.

"Pardon me, yes, I will."

"Who are you?" she demanded, suddenly.

"I'm a Texas Ranger," replied Duane.

"A TEXAS RANGER!" she echoed.

Floyd Lawson's dark face turned pale.

"Miss Longstreth, I don't need warrants to search houses," said Duane. "I'm sorry to annoy you. I'd prefer to have your permission. A ruffian has taken refuge here—in your father's house. He's hidden somewhere. May I look for him?"

"If you are indeed a ranger."

Duane produced his papers. Miss Longstreth haughtily refused to look at them.

"Miss Longstreth, I've come to make Fairdale a safer, cleaner, better place for women and children. I don't wonder at your resentment. But to doubt me—insult me. Some day you may be sorry."

Floyd Lawson made a violent motion with his hands.

"All stuff! Cousin, go on with your party. I'll take a couple of cowboys and go with this—this Texas Ranger."

"Thanks," said Duane, coolly, as he eyed Lawson. "Perhaps you'll be able to find Snecker quicker than I could."

"What do you mean?" demanded Lawson, and now he grew livid. Evidently he was a man of fierce quick passions.

"Don't quarrel," said Miss Longstreth. "Floyd, you go with him. Please hurry. I'll be nervous till—the man's found or you're sure there's not one."

They started with several cowboys to search the house. They went through the rooms searching, calling out, peering into dark places. It struck Duane more than forcibly that Lawson did all the calling. He was hurried, too, tried to keep in the lead. Duane wondered if he knew his voice would be recognized by the hiding man. Be that as it might, it was Duane who peered into a dark corner and then, with a gun leveled, said "Come out!"

He came forth into the flare—a tall, slim, dark-faced youth, wearing sombrero, blouse and trousers. Duane collared him before any of the others could move and held the gun close enough to make him shrink. But he did not impress Duane as being frightened just then; nevertheless, he had a clammy face, the pallid look of a man who had just gotten over a shock. He peered into Duane's face, then into that of the cowboy next to him, then into Lawson's, and if ever in Duane's life he beheld relief it was then. That was all Duane needed to know, but he meant to find out more if he could.

"Who're you?" asked Duane, quietly.

"Bo Snecker," he said.

"What'd you hide here for?"

He appeared to grow sullen.

"Reckoned I'd be as safe in Longstreth's as anywheres."

"Ranger, what'll you do with him?" Lawson queried, as if uncertain, now the capture was made.

"I'll see to that," replied Duane, and he pushed Snecker in front of him out into the court.

Duane had suddenly conceived the idea of taking Snecker before Mayor Longstreth in the court.

When Duane arrived at the hall where court was held there were other men there, a dozen or more, and all seemed excited; evidently, news of Duane had preceded him. Longstreth sat at a table up on a platform. Near him sat a thick-set grizzled man, with deep eyes, and this was Hanford Owens, county judge. To the right stood a tall, angular, yellow-faced fellow with a drooping sandy mustache. Conspicuous on his vest was a huge silver shield. This was Gorsech, one of Longstreth's sheriffs. There were four other men whom Duane knew by sight, several whose faces were familiar, and half a dozen strangers, all dusty horsemen.

Longstreth pounded hard on the table to be heard. Mayor or not, he was unable at once to quell the excitement. Gradually, however, it subsided, and from the last few utterances before quiet was restored Duane gathered that he had intruded upon some kind of a meeting in the hall.

"What'd you break in here for," demanded Longstreth.

"Isn't this the court? Aren't you the Mayor of Fairdale?" interrogated Duane. His voice was clear and loud, almost piercing.

"Yes," replied Longstreth. Like flint he seemed, yet Duane felt his intense interest.

"I've arrested a criminal," said Duane.

"Arrested a criminal!" ejaculated Longstreth. "You? Who're you?"

"I'm a ranger," replied Duane.

A significant silence ensued.

"I charge Snecker with assault on Laramie and attempted robbery—if not murder. He's had a shady past here, as this court will know if it keeps a record."

"What's this I hear about you, Bo? Get up and speak for yourself," said Longstreth, gruffly.

Snecker got up, not without a furtive glance at Duane, and he had shuffled forward a few steps toward the Mayor. He had an evil front, but not the boldness even of a rustler.

"It ain't so, Longstreth," he began, loudly. "I went in Laramie's place fer grub. Some feller I never seen before come in from the hall an' hit Laramie an' wrestled him on the floor. I went out. Then this big ranger chased me an' fetched me here. I didn't do nothin'. This ranger's hankerin' to arrest somebody. Thet's my hunch, Longstreth."

Longstreth said something in an undertone to Judge Owens, and that worthy nodded his great bushy head.

"Bo, you're discharged," said Longstreth, bluntly. "Now the rest of you clear out of here."

He absolutely ignored the ranger. That was his rebuff to Duane—his slap in the face to an interfering ranger service. If Longstreth was crooked he certainly had magnificent nerve. Duane almost decided he was above suspicion. But his nonchalance, his air of finality, his authoritative assurance—these to Duane's keen and practiced eyes were in significant contrast to a certain tenseness of line about his mouth and a slow paling of his olive skin. In that momentary lull Duane's scrutiny of Longstreth gathered an impression of the man's intense curiosity.

Then the prisoner, Snecker, with a cough that broke the spell of silence, shuffled a couple of steps toward the door.

"Hold on!" called Duane. The call halted Snecker, as if it had been a bullet.

"Longstreth, I saw Snecker attack Laramie," said Duane, his voice still ringing. "What has the court to say to that?"

"The court has this to say. West of the Pecos we'll not aid any ranger service. We don't want you out here. Fairdale doesn't need you."

"That's a lie, Longstreth," retorted Duane. "I've letters from Fairdale citizens all begging for ranger service."

Longstreth turned white. The veins corded at his temples. He appeared about to burst into rage. He was at a loss for quick reply.

Floyd Lawson rushed in and up to the table. The blood showed black and thick in his face; his utterance was incoherent, his uncontrollable outbreak of temper seemed out of all proportion to any cause he should reasonably have had for anger. Longstreth shoved him back with a curse and a warning glare.

"Where's your warrant to arrest Snecker?" shouted Longstreth.

"I don't need warrants to make arrests. Longstreth, you're ignorant of the power of Texas Rangers."

"You'll come none of your damned ranger stunts out here. I'll block you."

That passionate reply of Longstreth's was the signal Duane had been waiting for. He had helped on the crisis. He wanted to force Longstreth's hand and show the town his stand.

Duane backed clear of everybody.

"Men! I call on you all!" cried Duane, piercingly. "I call on you to witness the arrest of a criminal prevented by Longstreth, Mayor of Fairdale. It will be recorded in the report to the Adjutant-General at Austin. Longstreth, you'll never prevent another arrest."

Longstreth sat white with working jaw.

"Longstreth, you've shown your hand," said Duane, in a voice that carried far and held those who heard. "Any honest citizen of Fairdale can now see what's plain—yours is a damn poor hand! You're going to hear me call a spade a spade. In the two years you've been Mayor you've never arrested one rustler. Strange, when Fairdale's a nest for rustlers! You've never sent a prisoner to Del Rio, let alone to Austin. You have no jail. There have been nine murders during your office—innumerable street-fights and holdups. Not one arrest! But you have ordered arrests for trivial offenses, and have punished these out of all proportion. There have been lawsuits in your court-suits over water-rights, cattle deals, property lines. Strange how in these lawsuits you or Lawson or other men close to you were always involved! Strange how it seems the law was stretched to favor your interest!"

Duane paused in his cold, ringing speech. In the silence, both outside and inside the hall, could be heard the deep breathing of agitated men. Longstreth was indeed a study. Yet did he betray anything but rage at this interloper?

"Longstreth, here's plain talk for you and Fairdale," went on Duane. "I don't accuse you and your court of dishonesty. I say STRANGE! Law here has been a farce. The motive behind all this laxity isn't plain to me—yet. But I call your hand!"

CHAPTER XVII

Duane left the hall, elbowed his way through the crowd, and went down the street. He was certain that on the faces of some men he had seen ill-concealed wonder and satisfaction. He had struck some kind of a hot trait, and he meant to see where it led. It was by no means unlikely that Cheseldine might be at the other end. Duane controlled a mounting eagerness. But ever and anon it was shot through with a remembrance of Ray Longstreth. He suspected her father of being not what he pretended. He might, very probably would, bring sorrow and shame to this young woman. The thought made him smart with pain. She began to haunt him, and then he was thinking more of her beauty and sweetness than of the disgrace he might bring upon her. Some strange emotion, long locked inside Duane's heart, knocked to be heard, to be let out. He was troubled.

Upon returning to the inn he found Laramie there, apparently none the worse for his injury.

"How are you, Laramie?" he asked.

"Reckon I'm feelin' as well as could be expected," replied Laramie. His head was circled by a bandage that did not conceal the lump where he had been struck. He looked pale, but was bright enough.

"That was a good crack Snecker gave you," remarked

Duane.

"I ain't accusin' Bo," remonstrated Laramie, with eyes that made Duane thoughtful.

"Well, I accuse him. I caught him—took him to Longstreth's court. But they let him go."

Laramie appeared to be agitated by this intimation of friendship.

"See here, Laramie," went on Duane, "in some parts of Texas it's policy to be close-mouthed. Policy and health-preserving! Between ourselves, I want you to know I lean on your side of the fence."

Laramie gave a quick start. Presently Duane turned and frankly met his gaze. He had startled Laramie out of his habitual set taciturnity; but even as he looked the light that might have been amaze and joy faded out of his face, leaving it the same old mask. Still Duane had seen enough. Like a bloodhound he had a scent.

"Talking about work, Laramie, who'd you say Snecker worked for?"

"I didn't say."

"Well, say so now, can't you? Laramie, you're powerful peevish to-day. It's that bump on your head. Who does Snecker work for?"

"When he works at all, which sure ain't often, he rides for Longstreth."

"Humph! Seems to me that Longstreth's the whole circus round Fairdale. I was some sore the other day to find I was losing good money at Longstreth's faro game. Sure if I'd won I wouldn't have been sore—ha, ha! But I was surprised to hear some one say Longstreth owned the Hope So joint."

"He owns considerable property hereabouts," replied Laramie, constrainedly.

"Humph again! Laramie, like every other fellow I meet in this town, you're afraid to open your trap about Longstreth. Get me straight, Laramie. I don't care a damn for Colonel Mayor Longstreth. And for cause I'd throw a gun on him just as quick as on any rustler in Pecos."

"Talk's cheap," replied Laramie, making light of his bluster, but the red was deeper in his face.

"Sure. I know that," Duane said. "And usually I don't talk. Then it's not well known that Longstreth owns the Hope So?"

"Reckon it's known in Pecos, all right. But Longstreth's name isn't connected with the Hope So. Blandy runs the place."

"That Blandy. His faro game's crooked, or I'm a locoed bronch. Not that we don't have lots of crooked faro-dealers. A fellow can stand for them. But Blandy's mean, back-handed, never looks you in the eyes. That Hope So place ought to be run by a good fellow like you, Laramie."

"Thanks," replied he; and Duane imagined his voice a little husky. "Didn't you hear I used to run it?"

"No. Did you?" Duane said, quickly.

"I reckon. I built the place, made additions twice, owned it for eleven years."

"Well, I'll be doggoned." It was indeed Duane's turn to be surprised, and with the surprise came a glimmering. "I'm sorry you're not there now. Did you sell out?"

"No. Just lost the place."

Laramie was bursting for relief now—to talk, to tell. Sympathy had made him soft.

"It was two years ago-two years last March," he went on. "I was in a big cattle deal with Longstreth. We got the stock—an' my share, eighteen hundred head, was rustled off. I owed Longstreth. He pressed me. It come to a lawsuit—an' I—was ruined."

It hurt Duane to look at Laramie. He was white, and tears rolled down his cheeks. Duane saw the bitterness, the defeat, the agony of the man. He had failed to meet his obligations; nevertheless, he had been swindled. All that he suppressed, all that would have been passion had the man's spirit not been broken, lay bare for Duane to see. He had now the secret of his bitterness. But the reason he did not openly accuse Longstreth, the secret of his reticence and fear—these Duane thought best to try to learn at some later time.

"Hard luck! It certainly was tough," Duane said. "But you're a good loser. And the wheel turns! Now, Laramie, here's what. I need your advice. I've got a little money. But before I lose it I want to invest some. Buy some stock, or buy an interest in some rancher's herd. What I want you to steer me on is a good square rancher. Or maybe a couple of ranchers, if there happen to be two honest ones. Ha, ha! No deals with ranchers who ride in the dark with rustlers! I've a hunch Fairdale is full of them. Now, Laramie, you've been here for years. Sure you must know a couple of men above suspicion."

"Thank God I do," he replied, feelingly. "Frank Morton an' Si Zimmer, my friends an' neighbors all my prosperous days, an' friends still. You can gamble on Frank and Si. But if you want advice from me—don't invest money in stock now."

"Why?"

"Because any new feller buyin' stock these days will be rustled quicker 'n he can say Jack Robinson. The pioneers, the new cattlemen—these are easy pickin' for the rustlers. Lord knows all the ranchers are easy enough pickin'. But the new fellers have to learn the ropes. They don't know anythin' or anybody. An' the old ranchers are wise an' sore. They'd fight if they—"

"What?" Duane put in, as he paused. "If they knew who was rustling the stock?"

"Nope."

"If they had the nerve?"

"Not thet so much."

"What then? What'd make them fight?"

"A leader!"

"Howdy thar, Jim," boomed a big voice.

A man of great bulk, with a ruddy, merry face, entered the room.

"Hello, Morton," replied Laramie. "I'd introduce you to my guest here, but I don't know his name."

"Haw! Haw! Thet's all right. Few men out hyar go by their right names."

"Say, Morton," put in Duane, "Laramie gave me a hunch you'd be a good man to tie to. Now, I've a little money and before I lose it I'd like to invest it in stock."

Morton smiled broadly.

"I'm on the square," Duane said, bluntly. "If you fellows never size up your neighbors any better than you have sized me—well, you won't get any richer."

It was enjoyment for Duane to make his remarks to these men pregnant with meaning. Morton showed his pleasure, his interest, but his faith held aloof.

"I've got some money. Will you let me in on some kind of deal? Will you start me up as a stockman with a little herd all my own?"

"Wal, stranger, to come out flat-footed, you'd be foolish to buy cattle now. I don't want to take your money an' see you lose out. Better go back across the Pecos where the rustlers ain't so strong. I haven't had more'n twenty-five hundred herd of stock for ten years. The rustlers let me hang on to a breedin' herd. Kind of them, ain't it?"

"Sort of kind. All I hear is rustlers, Morton," replied Duane, with impatience. "You see, I haven't ever lived long in a rustler-run county. Who heads the gang, anyway?"

Morton looked at Duane with a curiously amused smile, then snapped his big jaw as if to shut in impulsive words.

"Look here, Morton. It stands to reason, no matter how strong these rustlers are, how hidden their work, however involved with supposedly honest men—they CAN'T last."

"They come with the pioneers, an' they'll last till thar's a single steer left," he declared.

"Well, if you take that view of circumstances I just figure you as one of the rustlers."

Morton looked as if he were about to brain Duane with the butt of his whip. His anger flashed by then, evidently as unworthy of him, and, something striking him as funny, he boomed out a laugh.

"It's not so funny," Duane went on. "If you're going to pretend a yellow streak, what else will I think?"

"Pretend?" he repeated.

"Sure. I know men of nerve. And here they're not any different from those in other places. I say if you show anything like a lack of sand it's all bluff. By nature you've got nerve. There are a lot of men around Fairdale who're afraid of their shadows—afraid to be out after dark—afraid to open their mouths. But you're not one. So I say if you claim these rustlers will last you're pretending lack of nerve just to help the popular idea along. For they CAN'T last. What you need out here is some new blood. Savvy what I mean?"

"Wal, I reckon I do," he replied, looking as if a storm had blown over him. "Stranger, I'll look you up the next time I come to town."

Then he went out.

Laramie had eyes like flint striking fire.

He breathed a deep breath and looked around the room before his gaze fixed again on Duane.

"Wal," he replied, speaking low. "You've picked the right men. Now, who in the hell are you?"

Reaching into the inside pocket of his buckskin vest, Duane turned the lining out. A star-shaped bright silver object flashed as he shoved it, pocket and all, under Jim's hard eyes.

"RANGER!" he whispered, cracking the table with his fist. "You sure rung true to me."

"Laramie, do you know who's boss of this secret gang of rustlers hereabouts?" asked Duane, bluntly. It was characteristic of him to come sharp to the point. His voice—something deep, easy, cool about him—seemed to steady Laramie.

"No," replied Laramie.

"Does anybody know?" went on Duane.

"Wal, I reckon there's not one honest native who KNOWS."

"But you have your suspicions?"

"We have."

"Give me your idea about this crowd that hangs round the saloons—the regulars."

"Jest a bad lot," replied Laramie, with the quick assurance of knowledge. "Most of them have been here years. Others have drifted in. Some of them work, odd times. They rustle a few steers, steal, rob, anythin' for a little money to drink an' gamble. Jest a bad lot!"

"Have you any idea whether Cheseldine and his gang are associated with this gang here?"

"Lord knows. I've always suspected them the same gang. None of us ever seen Cheseldine—an' thet's strange, when Knell, Poggin, Panhandle Smith, Blossom Kane, and Fletcher, they all ride here often. No, Poggin doesn't come often. But the others do. For thet matter, they're around all over west of the Pecos."

"Now I'm puzzled over this," said Duane. "Why do men—apparently honest men—seem to be so close-mouthed here? Is that a fact, or only my impression?"

"It's a sure fact," replied Laramie, darkly. "Men have lost cattle an' property in Fairdale—lost them honestly or otherwise, as hasn't been proved. An' in some cases when they talked—hinted a little—they was found dead. Apparently held up an robbed. But dead. Dead men don't talk! Thet's why we're close mouthed."

Duane felt a dark, somber sternness. Rustling cattle was not intolerable. Western Texas had gone on prospering, growing in spite of the hordes of rustlers ranging its vast stretches; but a cold, secret, murderous hold on a little struggling community was something too strange, too terrible for men to stand long.

The ranger was about to speak again when the clatter of hoofs interrupted him. Horses halted out in front, and one rider got down. Floyd Lawson entered. He called for tobacco.

If his visit surprised Laramie he did not show any evidence. But Lawson showed rage as he saw the ranger, and then a dark glint flitted from the eyes that shifted from Duane to Laramie and back again. Duane leaned easily against the counter.

"Say, that was a bad break of yours," Lawson said. "If you come fooling round the ranch again there'll be hell."

It seemed strange that a man who had lived west of the Pecos for ten years could not see in Duane something which forbade that kind of talk. It certainly was not nerve Lawson showed; men of courage were seldom intolerant. With the matchless nerve that characterized the great gunmen of the day there was a cool, unobtrusive manner, a speech brief, almost gentle, certainly courteous. Lawson was a hot-headed Louisianian of French extraction; a man, evidently, who had never been crossed in anything, and who was strong, brutal, passionate, which qualities in the face of a situation like this made him simply a fool.

"I'm saying again, you used your ranger bluff just to get near Ray Longstreth," Lawson sneered. "Mind you, if you come up there again there'll be hell."

"You're right. But not the kind you think," Duane retorted, his voice sharp and cold.

"Ray Longstreth wouldn't stoop to know a dirty blood-tracker like you," said Lawson, hotly. He did not seem to have a deliberate intention to rouse Duane; the man was simply rancorous, jealous. "I'll call you right. You cheap bluffer! You four-flush! You damned interfering, conceited ranger!"

"Lawson, I'll not take offense, because you seem to be championing your beautiful cousin," replied Duane, in slow speech. "But let me return your compliment. You're a fine Southerner! Why, you're only a cheap four-flush—damned, bull-headed RUSTLER!"

Duane hissed the last word. Then for him there was the truth in Lawson's working passion-blackened face.

Lawson jerked, moved, meant to draw. But how slow! Duane lunged forward. His long arm swept up. And Lawson staggered backward, knocking table and chairs, to fall hard, in a half-sitting posture against the wall.

"Don't draw!" warned Duane.

"Lawson, git away from your gun!" yelled Laramie.

But Lawson was crazed with fury. He tugged at his hip, his face corded with purple welts, malignant, murderous. Duane kicked the gun out of his hand. Lawson got up, raging, and rushed out.

Laramie lifted his shaking hands.

"What'd you wing him for?" he wailed. "He was drawin' on you. Kickin' men like him won't do out here."

"That bull-headed fool will roar and butt himself with all his gang right into our hands. He's just the man I've needed to meet. Besides, shooting him would have been murder."

"Murder!" exclaimed Laramie.

"Yes, for me," replied Duane.

"That may be true—whoever you are—but if Lawson's the man you think he is he'll begin thet secret underground bizness. Why, Lawson won't sleep of nights now. He an' Longstreth have always been after me."

"Laramie, what are your eyes for?" demanded Duane. "Watch out. And now here. See your friend Morton. Tell him this game grows hot. Together you approach four or five men you know well and can absolutely trust. I may need your help."

Then Duane went from place to place, corner to corner, bar to bar, watching, listening, recording. The excitement had preceded him, and speculation was rife. He thought best to keep out of it. After dark he stole up to Longstreth's ranch. The evening was warm; the doors were open; and in the twilight the only lamps that had been lit were in Longstreth's big sitting-room, at the far end of the house. When a buckboard drove up and Longstreth and Lawson alighted, Duane was well hidden in the bushes, so well screened that he could get but a fleeting glimpse of Longstreth as he went in. For all Duane could see, he appeared to be a calm and quiet man, intense beneath the surface, with an air of dignity under insult. Duane's chance to observe Lawson was lost. They went into the house without speaking and closed the door.

At the other end of the porch, close under a window, was an offset between step and wall, and there in the shadow Duane hid. So Duane waited there in the darkness with patience born of many hours of hiding.

Presently a lamp was lit; and Duane heard the swish of skirts.

"Something's happened surely, Ruth," he heard Miss Longstreth say, anxiously. "Papa just met me in the hall and didn't speak. He seemed pale, worried."

"Cousin Floyd looked like a thunder-cloud," said Ruth. "For once he didn't try to kiss me. Something's happened. Well, Ray, this had been a bad day."

"Oh, dear! Ruth, what can we do? These are wild men. Floyd makes life miserable for me. And he teases you unmer—"

"I don't call it teasing. Floyd wants to spoon," declared Ruth, emphatically. "He'd run after any woman."

"A fine compliment to me, Cousin Ruth," laughed Ray.

"I don't care," replied Ruth, stubbornly, "it's so. He's mushy. And when he's been drinking and tries to kiss me—I hate him!"

There were steps on the hall floor.

"Hello, girls!" sounded out Lawson's voice, minus its usual gaiety.

"Floyd, what's the matter?" asked Ray, presently. "I never saw papa as he is to-night, nor you so—so worried. Tell me, what has happened?"

"Well, Ray, we had a jar to-day," replied Lawson, with a blunt, expressive laugh.

"Jar?" echoed both the girls, curiously.

"We had to submit to a damnable outrage," added Lawson, passionately, as if the sound of his voice augmented his feeling. "Listen, girls; I'll tell you-all about it." He coughed, cleared his throat in a way that betrayed he had been drinking.

Duane sunk deeper into the shadow of his covert, and, stiffening his muscles for a protected spell of rigidity, prepared to listen with all acuteness and intensity. Just one word from this Lawson, inadvertently uttered in a moment of passion, might be the word Duane needed for his clue.

"It happened at the town hall," began Lawson, rapidly. "Your father and Judge Owens and I were there in consultation with three ranchers from out of town. Then that damned ranger stalked in dragging Snecker, the fellow who hid here in the house. He had arrested Snecker for alleged assault on a restaurant-keeper named Laramie. Snecker being obviously innocent, he was discharged. Then this ranger began shouting his insults. Law was a farce in Fairdale. The court was a farce. There was no law. Your father's office as mayor should be impeached. He made arrests only for petty offenses. He was afraid of the rustlers, highwaymen, murderers. He was afraid or—he just let them alone. He used his office to cheat ranchers and cattlemen in lawsuits. All this the ranger yelled for every one to hear. A damnable outrage. Your father, Ray, insulted in his own court by a rowdy ranger!"

"Oh!" cried Ray Longstreth, in mingled distress and anger.

"The ranger service wants to rule western Texas," went on Lawson. "These rangers are all a low set, many of them worse than the outlaws they hunt. Some of them were outlaws and gun-fighters before they became rangers. This is one of the worst of the lot. He's keen, intelligent, smooth, and that makes him more to be feared. For he is to be feared. He wanted to kill. He would kill. If your father had made the least move he would have shot him. He's a cold-nerved devil—the born gunman. My God, any instant I expected to see your father fall dead at my feet!"

"Oh, Floyd! The unspeakable ruffian!" cried Ray Longstreth, passionately.

"You see, Ray, this fellow, like all rangers, seeks notoriety. He made that play with Snecker just for a chance to rant against your father. He tried to inflame all Fairdale against him. That about the lawsuits was the worst! Damn him! He'll make us enemies."

"What do you care for the insinuations of such a man?" said Ray Longstreth, her voice now deep and rich with feeling. "After a moment's thought no one will be influenced by them. Do not worry, Floyd. Tell papa not to worry. Surely after all these years he can't be injured in reputation by—by an adventurer."

"Yes, he can be injured," replied Floyd, quickly. "The frontier is a queer place. There are many bitter men here—men who have failed at ranching. And your father has been wonderfully successful. The ranger has dropped poison, and it'll spread."

CHAPTER XVIII

Strangers rode into Fairdale; and other hard-looking customers, new to Duane if not to Fairdale, helped to create a charged and waiting atmosphere. The saloons did unusual business and were never closed. Respectable citizens of the town were awakened in the early dawn by rowdies carousing in the streets.

Duane kept pretty close under cover during the day. He did not entertain the opinion that the first time he walked down-street he would be a target for guns. Things seldom happened that way; and when they did happen so, it was more accident than design. But at night he was not idle. He met Laramie, Morton, Zimmer, and others of like character; a secret club had been formed; and all the members were ready for action. Duane spent hours at night watching the house where Floyd Lawson stayed when he was not up at Longstreth's. At night he was visited, or at least the house was, by strange men who were swift, stealthy, mysterious—all that kindly disposed friends or neighbors would not have been. Duane had not been able to recognize any of these night visitors; and he did not think the time was ripe for a bold holding-up of one of them. Nevertheless, he was sure such an event would discover Lawson, or some one in that house, to be in touch with crooked men.

Laramie was right. Not twenty-four hours after his last talk with Duane, in which he advised quick action, he was found behind the little bar of his restaurant with a bullet-hole in his breast, dead. No one could be found who had heard a shot. It had been deliberate murder, for upon the bar had been left a piece of paper rudely scrawled with a pencil: "All friends of rangers look for the same."

This roused Duane. His first move, however, was to bury Laramie. None of Laramie's neighbors evinced any interest in the dead man or the unfortunate family he had left. Duane saw that these neighbors were held in check by fear. Mrs. Laramie was ill; the shock of her husband's death was hard on her; and she had been left almost destitute with five children. Duane rented a small adobe house on the outskirts of town and moved the family into it. Then he played the part of provider and nurse and friend.

After several days Duane went boldly into town and showed that he meant business. It was his opinion that there were men in Fairdale secretly glad of a ranger's presence. What he intended to do was food for great speculation. A company of militia could not have had the effect upon the wild element of Fairdale that Duane's presence had. It got out that he was a gunman lightning swift on the draw. It was death to face him. He had killed thirty men—wildest rumor of all—it was actually said of him he had the gun-skill of Buck Duane or of Poggin.

At first there had not only been great conjecture among the vicious element, but also a very decided checking of all kinds of action calculated to be conspicuous to a keen-eyed ranger. At the tables, at the bars and lounging-places Duane heard the remarks: "Who's thet ranger after? What'll he do fust off? Is he waitin' fer somebody? Who's goin' to draw on him fust—an' go to hell? Jest about how soon will he be found somewheres full of lead?"

When it came out somewhere that Duane was openly cultivating the honest stay-at-home citizens to array them in time against the other element, then Fairdale showed its wolf-teeth. Several times Duane was shot at in the dark and once slightly injured. Rumor had it that Poggin, the gunman, was coming to meet him. But the lawless element did not rise up in a mass to slay Duane on sight. It was not so much that the enemies of the law awaited his next move, but just a slowness peculiar to the frontier. The ranger was in their midst. He was interesting, if formidable. He would have been welcomed at card-tables, at the bars, to play and drink with the men who knew they were under suspicion. There was a rude kind of good humor even in their open hostility.

Besides, one ranger or a company of rangers could not have held the undivided attention of these men from their games and drinks and quarrels except by some decided move. Excitement, greed, appetite were rife in them. Duane marked, however, a striking exception to the usual run of strangers he had been in the habit of seeing. Snecker had gone or was under cover. Again Duane caught a vague rumor of the coming of Poggin, yet he never seemed to arrive.

Moreover, the goings-on among the habitues of the resorts and the cowboys who came in to drink and gamble were unusually mild in comparison with former conduct. This lull, however, did not deceive Duane. It could not last. The wonder was that it had lasted so long.

Duane went often to see Mrs. Laramie and her children. One afternoon while he was there he saw Miss Longstreth and Ruth ride up to the door. They carried a basket. Evidently they had heard of Mrs. Laramie's trouble. Duane felt strangely glad, but he went into an adjoining room rather than meet them.

"Mrs. Laramie, I've come to see you," said Miss Longstreth, cheerfully.

The little room was not very light, there being only one window and the doors, but Duane could see plainly enough. Mrs. Laramie lay, hollow-checked and haggard, on a bed. Once she had evidently been a woman of some comeliness. The ravages of trouble and grief were there to read in her worn face; it had not, however, any of the hard and bitter lines that had characterized her husband's.

Duane wondered, considering that Longstreth had ruined Laramie, how Mrs. Laramie was going to regard the daughter of an enemy.

"So you're Granger Longstreth's girl?" queried the woman, with her bright, black eyes fixed on her visitor.

"Yes," replied Miss Longstreth, simply. "This is my cousin, Ruth Herbert. We've come to nurse you, take care of the children, help you in any way you'll let us."

There was a long silence.

"Well, you look a little like Longstreth," finally said Mrs. Laramie, "but you're not at ALL like him. You must take after your mother. Miss Longstreth, I don't know if I can—if I ought accept anything from you. Your father ruined my husband."

"Yes, I know," replied the girl, sadly. "That's all the more reason you should let me help you. Pray don't refuse. It will—mean so much to me."

If this poor, stricken woman had any resentment it speedily melted in the warmth and sweetness of Miss Longstreth's manner. Duane's idea was that the impression of Ray Longstreth's beauty was always swiftly succeeded by that of her generosity and nobility. At any rate, she had started well with Mrs. Laramie, and no sooner had she begun to talk to the children than both they and the mother were won. The opening of that big basket was an event. Poor, starved little beggars! Duane's feelings seemed too easily roused. Hard indeed would it have gone with Jim Laramie's slayer if he could have laid eyes on him then. However, Miss Longstreth and Ruth, after the nature of tender and practical girls, did not appear to take the sad situation to heart. The havoc was wrought in that household.

The needs now were cheerfulness, kindness, help, action—and these the girls furnished with a spirit that did Duane good.

"Mrs. Laramie, who dressed this baby?" presently asked Miss Longstreth. Duane peeped in to see a dilapidated youngster on her knee. That sight, if any other was needed, completed his full and splendid estimate of Ray Longstreth and wrought strangely upon his heart.

"The ranger," replied Mrs. Laramie.

"The ranger!" exclaimed Miss Longstreth.

"Yes, he's taken care of us all since—since—" Mrs. Laramie choked.

"Oh! So you've had no help but his," replied Miss Longstreth, hastily. "No women. Too bad! I'll send some one, Mrs. Laramie, and I'll come myself."

"It'll be good of you," went on the older woman. "You see, Jim had few friends—that is, right in town. And they've been afraid to help us—afraid they'd get what poor Jim—"

"That's awful!" burst out Miss Longstreth, passionately. "A brave lot of friends! Mrs. Laramie, don't you worry any more. We'll take care of you. Here, Ruth, help me. Whatever is the matter with baby's dress?"

Manifestly Miss Longstreth had some difficulty in subduing her emotion.

"Why, it's on hind side before," declared Ruth. "I guess Mr. Ranger hasn't dressed many babies."

"He did the best he could," said Mrs. Laramie. "Lord only knows what would have become of us!"

"Then he is—is something more than a ranger?" queried Miss Longstreth, with a little break in her voice.

"He's more than I can tell," replied Mrs. Laramie. "He buried Jim. He paid our debts. He fetched us here. He bought food for us. He cooked for us and fed us. He washed and dressed the baby. He sat with me the first two nights after Jim's death, when I thought

I'd die myself. He's so kind, so gentle, so patient. He has kept me up just by being near. Sometimes I'd wake from a doze, an', seeing him there, I'd know how false were all these tales Jim heard about him and believed at first. Why, he plays with the children just—just like any good man might. When he has the baby up I just can't believe he's a bloody gunman, as they say. He's good, but he isn't happy. He has such sad eyes. He looks far off sometimes when the children climb round him. They love him. His life is sad. Nobody need tell me—he sees the good in things. Once he said somebody had to be a ranger. Well, I say, 'Thank God for a ranger like him!'"

Duane did not want to hear more, so he walked into the room.

"It was thoughtful of you," Duane said. "Womankind are needed here. I could do so little. Mrs. Laramie, you look better already. I'm glad. And here's baby, all clean and white. Baby, what a time I had trying to puzzle out the way your clothes went on! Well, Mrs. Laramie, didn't I tell you—friends would come? So will the brighter side."

"Yes, I've more faith than I had," replied Mrs. Laramie. "Granger Longstreth's daughter has come to me. There for a while after Jim's death I thought I'd sink. We have nothing. How could I ever take care of my little ones? But I'm gaining courage to—"

"Mrs. Laramie, do not distress yourself any more," said Miss Longstreth. "I shall see you are well cared for. I promise you."

"Miss Longstreth, that's fine!" exclaimed Duane. "It's

what I'd have—expected of you."

It must have been sweet praise to her, for the whiteness of her face burned out in a beautiful blush.

"And it's good of you, too, Miss Herbert, to come," added Duane. "Let me thank you both. I'm glad I have you girls as allies in part of my lonely task here. More than glad for the sake of this good woman and the little ones. But both of you be careful about coming here alone. There's risk. And now I'll be going. Good-by, Mrs. Laramie. I'll drop in again to-night. Good-by."

"Mr. Ranger, wait!" called Miss Longstreth, as he went out. She was white and wonderful. She stepped out of the door close to him.

"I have wronged you," she said, impulsively.

"Miss Longstreth! How can you say that?" he returned.

"I believed what my father and Floyd Lawson said about you. Now I see—I wronged you."

"You make me very glad. But, Miss Longstreth, please don't speak of wronging me. I have been a—a gunman, I am a ranger—and much said of me is true. My duty is hard on others—sometimes on those who are innocent, alas! But God knows that duty is hard, too, on me."

"I did wrong you. If you entered my home again I would think it an honor. I—"

"Please—please don't, Miss Longstreth," interrupted Duane.

"But, sir, my conscience flays me," she went on. There was no other sound like her voice. "Will you take my hand? Will you forgive me?"

She gave it royally, while the other was there pressing at her breast. Duane took the proffered hand. He did not know what else to do.

Then it seemed to dawn upon him that there was more behind this white, sweet, noble intensity of her than just the making amends for a fancied or real wrong. Duane thought the man did not live on earth who could have resisted her then.

"I honor you for your goodness to this unfortunate woman," she said, and now her speech came swiftly. "When she was all alone and helpless you were her friend. It was the deed of a man. But Mrs. Laramie isn't the only unfortunate woman in the world. I, too, am unfortunate. Ah, how I may soon need a friend! Will you be my friend? I'm so alone. I'm terribly worried. I fear—I fear—Oh, surely I'll need a friend soon—soon. Oh, I'm afraid of what you'll find out sooner or later. I want to help you. Let us save life if not honor. Must I stand alone—all alone? Will you—will you be—" Her voice failed.

It seemed to Duane that she must have discovered what he had begun to suspect—that her father and Lawson were not the honest ranchers they pretended to be. Perhaps she knew more! Her appeal to Duane shook him deeply. He wanted to help her more than he had ever wanted anything. And with the meaning of the tumultuous sweetness she stirred in him there came realization of a dangerous situation.

"I must be true to my duty," he said, hoarsely.

"If you knew me you'd know I could never ask you to be false to it."

"Well, then—I'll do anything for you."

"Oh, thank you! I'm ashamed that I believed my cousin Floyd! He lied—he lied. I'm all in the dark, strangely distressed. My father wants me to go back home. Floyd is trying to keep me here. They've quarreled. Oh, I know something dreadful will happen. I know I'll need you if—if—Will you help me?"

"Yes," replied Duane, and his look brought the blood to her face.

CHAPTER XIX

After supper Duane stole out for his usual evening's spying. The night was dark, without starlight, and a stiff wind rustled the leaves. Duane bent his steps toward the Longstreth's ranchhouse. He had so much to think about that he never knew where the time went. This night when he reached the edge of the shrubbery he heard Lawson's well-known footsteps and saw Longstreth's door open, flashing a broad bar of light in the darkness. Lawson crossed the threshold, the door closed, and all was dark again outside. Not a ray of light escaped from the window.

Little doubt there was that his talk with Longstreth would be interesting to Duane. He tiptoed to the door and listened, but could hear only a murmur of voices. Besides, that position was too risky. He went round the corner of the house.

This side of the big adobe house was of much older construction than the back and larger part. There was a narrow passage between the houses, leading from the outside through to the patio.

This passage now afforded Duane an opportunity, and he decided to avail himself of it in spite of the very great danger. Crawling on very stealthily, he got under the shrubbery to the entrance of the passage. In the blackness a faint streak of light showed the location of a crack in the wall. He had to slip in sidewise. It was a tight squeeze, but he entered without the slightest noise. As he progressed the passage grew a very little wider in that direction, and that fact gave rise to the thought that in case of a necessary and hurried exit he would do best by working toward the patio. It seemed a good deal of time was consumed in reaching a vantage-point. When he did get there the crack he had marked was a foot over his head. There was nothing to do but find toe-holes in the crumbling walls, and by bracing knees on one side, back against the other, hold himself up Once with his eye there he did not care what risk he ran. Longstreth appeared disturbed; he sat stroking his mustache; his brow was clouded. Lawson's face seemed darker, more sullen, yet lighted by some indomitable resolve.

"We'll settle both deals to-night," Lawson was saying. "That's what I came for."

"But suppose I don't choose to talk here?" protested Longstreth, impatiently. "I never before made my house a place to—"

"We've waited long enough. This place's as good as any. You've lost your nerve since that ranger hit the town. First now, will you give Ray to me?"

"Floyd; you talk like a spoiled boy. Give Ray to you! Why, she's a woman, and I'm finding out that she's got a mind of her own. I told you I was willing for her to marry you. I tried to persuade her. But Ray hasn't any use for you now. She liked you at first. But now she doesn't. So what can I do?"

"You can make her marry me," replied Lawson.

"Make that girl do what she doesn't want to? It couldn't be done even if I tried. And I don't believe I'll try. I haven't the highest opinion of you as a prospective son-in-law, Floyd. But if Ray loved you I would consent. We'd all go away together before this damned miserable business is out. Then she'd never know. And maybe you might be more like you used to be before the West ruined you. But as matters stand, you fight your own game with her. And I'll tell you now you'll lose."

"What'd you want to let her come out here for?" demanded Lawson, hotly. "It was a dead mistake. I've lost my head over her. I'll have her or die. Don't you think if she was my wife I'd soon pull myself together? Since she came we've none of us been right. And the gang has put up a holler. No, Longstreth, we've got to settle things to-night."

"Well, we can settle what Ray's concerned in, right now," replied Longstreth, rising. "Come on; we'll ask her. See where you stand."

They went out, leaving the door open. Duane dropped down to rest himself and to wait. He would have liked to hear Miss Longstreth's answer. But he could guess what it would be. Lawson appeared to be all Duane had thought him, and he believed he was going to find out presently that he was worse.

The men seemed to be absent a good while, though that feeling might have been occasioned by Duane's thrilling interest and anxiety. Finally he heard heavy steps. Lawson came in alone. He was leaden-faced, humiliated. Then something abject in him gave place to rage. He strode the room; he cursed. Then Longstreth returned, now appreciably calmer. Duane could not but decide that he felt relief at the evident rejection of Lawson's proposal.

"Don't fuss about it, Floyd," he said. "You see I can't help it. We're pretty wild out here, but I can't rope my daughter and give her to you as I would an unruly steer."

"Longstreth, I can MAKE her marry me," declared Lawson, thickly.

"How?"

"You know the hold I got on you—the deal that made you boss of this rustler gang?"

"It isn't likely I'd forget," replied Longstreth, grimly.

"I can go to Ray, tell her that, make her believe I'd tell it broadcast—tell this ranger—unless she'd marry me."

Lawson spoke breathlessly, with haggard face and shadowed eyes. He had no shame. He was simply in the grip of passion. Longstreth gazed with dark, controlled fury at this relative. In that look Duane saw a strong, unscrupulous man fallen into evil ways, but still a man. It betrayed Lawson to be the wild and passionate weakling. Duane seemed to see also how during all the years of association this strong man had upheld the weak one. But that time had gone for ever, both in intent on Longstreth's part and in possibility. Lawson, like the great majority of evil and unrestrained men on the border, had reached a point where influence was futile. Reason had degenerated. He saw only himself.

"But, Floyd, Ray's the one person on earth who must never know I'm a rustler, a thief, a red-handed ruler of the worst gang on the border," replied Longstreth, impressively.

Floyd bowed his head at that, as if the significance had just occurred to him. But he was not long at a loss.

"She's going to find it out sooner or later. I tell you she knows now there's something wrong out here. She's got eyes. Mark what I say."

"Ray has changed, I know. But she hasn't any idea yet that her daddy's a boss rustler. Ray's concerned about what she calls my duty as mayor. Also I think she's not satisfied with my explanations in regard to certain property."

Lawson halted in his restless walk and leaned against the stone mantelpiece. He had his hands in his pockets. He squared himself as if this was his last stand. He looked desperate, but on the moment showed an absence of his usual nervous excitement.

"Longstreth, that may well be true," he said. "No doubt all you say is true. But it doesn't help me. I want the girl. If I don't get her—I reckon we'll all go to hell!"

He might have meant anything, probably meant the worst. He certainly had something more in mind. Longstreth gave a slight start, barely perceptible, like the switch of an awakening tiger. He sat there, head down, stroking his mustache. Almost Duane saw his thought. He had long experience in reading men under stress of such emotion. He had no means to vindicate his judgment, but his conviction was that

Longstreth right then and there decided that the thing to do was to kill Lawson. For Duane's part he wondered that Longstreth had not come to such a conclusion before. Not improbably the advent of his daughter had put Longstreth in conflict with himself.

Suddenly he threw off a somber cast of countenance, and he began to talk. He talked swiftly, persuasively, yet Duane imagined he was talking to smooth Lawson's passion for the moment. Lawson no more caught the fateful significance of a line crossed, a limit reached, a decree decided than if he had not been present. He was obsessed with himself. How, Duane wondered, had a man of his mind ever lived so long and gone so far among the exacting conditions of the Southwest? The answer was, perhaps, that Longstreth had guided him, upheld him, protected him. The coming of Ray Longstreth had been the entering-wedge of dissension.

"You're too impatient," concluded Longstreth. "You'll ruin any chance of happiness if you rush Ray. She might be won. If you told her who I am she'd hate you for ever. She might marry you to save me, but she'd hate you. That isn't the way. Wait. Play for time. Be different with her. Cut out your drinking. She despises that. Let's plan to sell out here—stock, ranch, property—and leave the country. Then you'd have a show with her."

"I told you we've got to stick," growled Lawson. "The gang won't stand for our going. It can't be done unless you want to sacrifice everything."

"You mean double-cross the men? Go without their

knowing? Leave them here to face whatever comes?"

"I mean just that."

"I'm bad enough, but not that bad," returned Longstreth. "If I can't get the gang to let me off, I'll stay and face the music. All the same, Lawson, did it ever strike you that most of the deals the last few years have been YOURS?"

"Yes. If I hadn't rung them in there wouldn't have been any. You've had cold feet, and especially since this ranger has been here."

"Well, call it cold feet if you like. But I call it sense. We reached our limit long ago. We began by rustling a few cattle—at a time when rustling was laughed at. But as our greed grew so did our boldness. Then came the gang, the regular trips, the one thing and another till, before we knew it—before I knew it—we had shady deals, holdups, and MURDERS on our record. Then we HAD to go on. Too late to turn back!"

"I reckon we've all said that. None of the gang wants to quit. They all think, and I think, we can't be touched. We may be blamed, but nothing can be proved. We're too strong."

"There's where you're dead wrong," rejoined Longstreth, emphatically. "I imagined that once, not long ago. I was bullheaded. Who would ever connect Granger Longstreth with a rustler gang? I've changed my mind. I've begun to think. I've reasoned out things. We're crooked, and we can't last. It's the nature of life, even here, for conditions to grow better. The wise deal for us would be to divide equally and leave the country, all of us."

"But you and I have all the stock—all the gain," protested Lawson.

"I'll split mine."

"I won't—that settles that," added Lawson, instantly.

Longstreth spread wide his hands as if it was useless to try to convince this man. Talking had not increased his calmness, and he now showed more than impatience. A dull glint gleamed deep in his eyes.

"Your stock and property will last a long time—do you lots of good when this ranger—"

"Bah!" hoarsely croaked Lawson. The ranger's name was a match applied to powder. "Haven't I told you he'd be dead soon—any time—same as Laramie is?"

"Yes, you mentioned the—the supposition," replied Longstreth, sarcastically. "I inquired, too, just how that very desired event was to be brought about."

"The gang will lay him out."

"Bah!" retorted Longstreth, in turn. He laughed contemptuously.

"Floyd, don't be a fool. You've been on the border for ten years. You've packed a gun and you've used it. You've been with rustlers when they killed their men. You've been present at many fights. But you never in all that time saw a man like this ranger. You haven't got sense enough to see him right if you had a chance. Neither have any of you. The only way to get rid of him is for the gang to draw on him, all at once. Then he's going to drop some of them."

"Longstreth, you say that like a man who wouldn't care much if he did drop some of them," declared Lawson; and now he was sarcastic.

"To tell you the truth, I wouldn't," returned the other, bluntly. "I'm pretty sick of this mess."

Lawson cursed in amazement. His emotions were all out of proportion to his intelligence. He was not at all quick-witted. Duane had never seen a vainer or more arrogant man.

"Longstreth, I don't like your talk," he said.

"If you don't like the way I talk you know what you can do," replied Longstreth, quickly. He stood up then, cool and quiet, with flash of eyes and set of lips that told Duane he was dangerous.

"Well, after all, that's neither here nor there," went on Lawson, unconsciously cowed by the other. "The thing is, do I get the girl?"

"Not by any means except her consent."

"You'll not make her marry me?"

"No. No," replied Longstreth, his voice still cold, low-pitched.

"All right. Then I'll make her."

Evidently Longstreth understood the man before him so well that he wasted no more words. Duane knew what Lawson never dreamed of, and that was that Longstreth had a gun somewhere within reach and meant to use it. Then heavy footsteps sounded outside tramping upon the porch. Duane might have been mistaken, but he believed those footsteps saved Lawson's life.

"There they are," said Lawson, and he opened the door.

Five masked men entered. They all wore coats hiding any weapons. A big man with burly shoulders shook hands with Longstreth, and the others stood back.

The atmosphere of that room had changed. Lawson might have been a nonentity for all he counted. Longstreth was another man—a stranger to Duane. If he had entertained a hope of freeing himself from this band, of getting away to a safer country, he abandoned it at the very sight of these men. There was power here, and he was bound.

The big man spoke in low, hoarse whispers, and at this all the others gathered around him close to the table. There were evidently some signs of membership not plain to Duane. Then all the heads were bent over the table. Low voices spoke, queried, answered, argued. By straining his ears Duane caught a word here and there. They were planning, and they were brief. Duane gathered they were to have a rendezvous at or near Ord.

Then the big man, who evidently was the leader of the present convention, got up to depart. He went as swiftly as he had come, and was followed by his comrades. Longstreth prepared for a quiet smoke. Lawson seemed uncommunicative and unsociable. He smoked fiercely and drank continually. All at once he straightened up as if listening.

"What's that?" he called, suddenly.

Duane's strained ears were pervaded by a slight rustling sound.

"Must be a rat," replied Longstreth.

The rustle became a rattle.

"Sounds like a rattlesnake to me," said Lawson.

Longstreth got up from the table and peered round the room.

Just at that instant Duane felt an almost inappreciable movement of the adobe wall which supported him. He could scarcely credit his senses. But the rattle inside Longstreth's room was mingling with little dull thuds of falling dirt. The adobe wall, merely dried mud, was crumbling. Duane distinctly felt a tremor pass through it. Then the blood gushed back to his heart.

"What in the hell!" exclaimed Longstreth.

"I smell dust," said Lawson, sharply.

That was the signal for Duane to drop down from his perch, yet despite his care he made a noise.

"Did you hear a step?" queried Longstreth.

No one answered. But a heavy piece of the adobe wall fell with a thud. Duane heard it crack, felt it shake.

"There's somebody between the walls!" thundered Longstreth.

Then a section of the wall fell inward with a crash. Duane began to squeeze his body through the narrow passage toward the patio.

"Hear him!" yelled Lawson. "This side!"

"No, he's going that way," yelled Longstreth.

The tramp of heavy boots lent Duane the strength of desperation. He was not shirking a fight, but to be cornered like a trapped coyote was another matter. He almost tore his clothes off in that passage. The dust nearly stifled him. When he burst into the patio it was not a single instant too soon. But one deep gasp of breath revived him and he was up, gun in hand, running for the outlet into the court. Thumping footsteps turned him back. While there was a chance to get away he did not want to fight. He thought he heard someone running into the patio from the other end. He stole along, and coming to a door, without any idea of where it might lead, he softly pushed it open a little way and slipped in.

CHAPTER XX

A low cry greeted Duane. The room was light. He saw Ray Longstreth sitting on her bed in her dressing-gown. With a warning gesture to her to be silent he turned to close the door. It was a heavy door without bolt or bar, and when Duane had shut it he felt safe only for the moment. Then he gazed around the room. There was one window with blind closely drawn. He listened and seemed to hear footsteps retreating, dying away.

Then Duane turned to Miss Longstreth. She had slipped off the bed, half to her knees, and was holding out trembling hands. She was as white as the pillow on her bed. She was terribly frightened. Again with warning hand commanding silence, Duane stepped softly forward, meaning to reassure her.

"Oh!" she whispered, wildly; and Duane thought she was going to faint. When he got close and looked into her eyes he understood the strange, dark expression in them. She was terrified because she believed he meant to kill her, or do worse, probably worse. Duane realized he must have looked pretty hard and fierce bursting into her room with that big gun in hand.

The way she searched Duane's face with doubtful, fearful eyes hurt him.

"Listen. I didn't know this was your room. I came

here to get away—to save my life. I was pursued. I was spying on—on your father and his men. They heard me, but did not see me. They don't know who was listening. They're after me now."

Her eyes changed from blank gulfs to dilating, shadowing, quickening windows of thought.

Then she stood up and faced Duane with the fire and intelligence of a woman in her eyes.

"Tell me now. You were spying on my father?"

Briefly Duane told her what had happened before he entered her room, not omitting a terse word as to the character of the men he had watched.

"My God! So it's that? I knew something was terribly wrong here—with him—with the place—the people. And right off I hated Floyd Lawson. Oh, it'll kill me if—if—It's so much worse than I dreamed. What shall I do?"

The sound of soft steps somewhere near distracted Duane's attention, reminded him of her peril, and now, what counted more with him, made clear the probability of being discovered in her room.

"I'll have to get out of here," whispered Duane.

"Wait," she replied. "Didn't you say they were hunting for you?"

"They sure are," he returned, grimly.

"Oh, then you mustn't go. They might shoot you before you got away. Stay. If we hear them you can hide. I'll turn out the light. I'll meet them at the door. You can trust me. Wait till all quiets down, if we have to wait till morning. Then you can slip out."

"I oughtn't to stay. I don't want to—I won't," Duane

replied, perplexed and stubborn.

"But you must. It's the only safe way. They won't come here."

"Suppose they should? It's an even chance Longstreth'll search every room and corner in this old house. If they found me here I couldn't start a fight. You might be hurt. Then—the fact of my being here—"

Duane did not finish what he meant, but instead made a step toward the door. White of face and dark of eye, she took hold of him to detain him. She was as strong and supple as a panther. But she need not have been either resolute or strong, for the clasp of her hand was enough to make Duane weak.

"Up yet, Ray?" came Longstreth's clear voice, too strained, too eager to be natural.

"No. I'm in bed reading. Good night," instantly replied Miss Longstreth, so calmly and naturally that Duane marveled at the difference between man and woman. Then she motioned for Duane to hide in the closet. He slipped in, but the door would not close altogether.

"Are you alone?" went on Longstreth's penetrating voice.

"Yes," she replied. "Ruth went to bed."

The door swung inward with a swift scrape and jar. Longstreth half entered, haggard, flaming-eyed. Behind him Duane saw Lawson, and indistinctly another man.

Longstreth barred Lawson from entering, which action showed control as well as distrust. He wanted to see into the room. When he had glanced around he went out and closed the door.

Then what seemed a long interval ensued. The house grew silent once more. Duane could not see Miss Longstreth, but he heard her quick breathing. How long did she mean to let him stay hidden there? Hard and perilous as his life had been, this was a new kind of adventure. He had divined the strange softness of his feeling as something due to the magnetism of this beautiful woman. It hardly seemed possible that he, who had been outside the pale for so many years, could have fallen in love. Yet that must be the secret of his agitation.

Presently he pushed open the closet door and stepped forth. Miss Longstreth had her head lowered upon her arms and appeared to be in distress. At his touch she raised a quivering face.

"I think I can go now—safely," he whispered.

"Go then, if you must, but you may stay till you're safe," she replied.

"I—I couldn't thank you enough. It's been hard on me—this finding out—and you his daughter. I feel strange. I don't understand myself well. But I want you to know—if I were not an outlaw—a ranger—I'd lay my life at your feet."

"Oh! You have seen so—so little of me," she faltered.

"All the same it's true. And that makes me feel more the trouble my coming caused you."

"You will not fight my father?"

"Not if I can help it. I'm trying to get out of his way.'

"But you spied upon him."

"I am a ranger, Miss Longstreth."

"And oh! I am a rustler's daughter," she cried. "That's so much more terrible than I'd suspected. It was tricky cattle deals I imagined he was engaged in. But only to-night I had strong suspicions aroused."

"How? Tell me."

"I overheard Floyd say that men were coming to-night to arrange a meeting for my father at a rendezvous near Ord. Father did not want to go. Floyd taunted him with a name."

"What name?" queried Duane.

"It was Cheseldine."

"CHESELDINE! My God! Miss Longstreth, why did you tell me that?"

"What difference does that make?"

"Your father and Cheseldine are one and the same," whispered Duane, hoarsely.

"I gathered so much myself," she replied, miserably. "But Longstreth is father's real name."

Duane felt so stunned he could not speak at once. It was the girl's part in this tragedy that weakened him. The instant she betrayed the secret Duane realized perfectly that he did love her. The emotion was like a great flood.

"Miss Longstreth, all this seems so unbelievable," he whispered. "Cheseldine is the rustler chief I've come out here to get. He's only a name. Your father is the real man. I've sworn to get him. I'm bound by more than law or oaths. I can't break what binds me. And I must disgrace you—wreck your lifer Why, Miss Longstreth, I believe I—I love you. It's all come in a rush.

I'd die for you if I could. How fatal—terrible—this is! How things work out!"

She slipped to her knees, with her hands on his.

"You won't kill him?" she implored. "If you care for me—you won't kill him?"

"No. That I promise you."

With a low moan she dropped her head upon the bed.

Duane opened the door and stealthily stole out through the corridor to the court.

When Duane got out into the dark, where his hot face cooled in the wind, his relief equaled his other feelings.

The night was dark, windy, stormy, yet there was no rain. Duane hoped as soon as he got clear of the ranch to lose something of the pain he felt. But long after he had tramped out into the open there was a lump in his throat and an ache in his breast. All his thought centered around Ray Longstreth. What a woman she had turned out to be! He seemed to have a vague, hopeless hope that there might be, there must be, some way he could save her.

CHAPTER XXI

Before going to sleep that night Duane had decided to go to Ord and try to find the rendezvous where Longstreth was to meet his men. These men Duane wanted even more than their leader. If Longstreth, or Cheseldine, was the brains of that gang, Poggin was the executor. It was Poggin who needed to be found and stopped. Poggin and his right-hand men! Duane experienced a strange, tigerish thrill. It was thought of Poggin more than thought of success for MacNelly's plan. Duane felt dubious over this emotion.

Next day he set out for Bradford. He was glad to get away from Fairdale for a while. But the hours and the miles in no wise changed the new pain in his heart. The only way he could forget Miss Longstreth was to let his mind dwell upon Poggin, and even this was not always effective.

He avoided Sanderson, and at the end of the day and a half he arrived at Bradford.

The night of the day before he reached Bradford, No. 6, the mail and express train going east, was held up by train-robbers, the Wells-Fargo messenger killed over his safe, the mail-clerk wounded, the bags carried away. The engine of No. 6 came into town minus even a tender, and engineer and fireman told conflicting stories. A posse of railroad men and citizens, led by a sheriff Duane suspected was crooked, was made up before the engine steamed back to pick up the rest of the train. Duane had the sudden inspiration that he had been cudgeling his mind to find; and, acting upon it, he mounted his horse again and left Bradford unobserved. As he rode out into the night, over a dark trail in the direction of Ord, he uttered a short, grim, sardonic laugh at the hope that he might be taken for a train-robber.

He rode at an easy trot most of the night, and when the black peak of Ord Mountain loomed up against the stars he halted, tied his horse, and slept until dawn. He had brought a small pack, and now he took his time cooking breakfast. When the sun was well up he saddled Bullet, and, leaving the trail where his tracks showed plain in the ground, he put his horse to the rocks and brush. He selected an exceedingly rough, roundabout, and difficult course to Ord, hid his tracks with the skill of a long-hunted fugitive, and arrived there with his horse winded and covered with lather. It added considerable to his arrival that the man Duane remembered as Fletcher and several others saw him come in the back way through the lots and jump a fence into the road.

Duane led Bullet up to the porch where Fletcher stood wiping his beard. He was hatless, vestless, and evidently had just enjoyed a morning drink.

"Howdy, Dodge," said Fletcher, laconically.

Duane replied, and the other man returned the greeting with interest.

"Jim, my hoss 's done up. I want to hide him from

any chance tourists as might happen to ride up curious-like."

"Haw! haw! haw!"

Duane gathered encouragement from that chorus of coarse laughter.

"Wal, if them tourists ain't too durned snooky the hoss'll be safe in the 'dobe shack back of Bill's here. Feed thar, too, but you'll hev to rustle water."

Duane led Bullet to the place indicated, had care of his welfare, and left him there. Upon returning to the tavern porch Duane saw the group of men had been added to by others, some of whom he had seen before. Without comment Duane walked along the edge of the road, and wherever one of the tracks of his horse showed he carefully obliterated it. This procedure was attentively watched by Fletcher and his companions.

"Wal, Dodge," remarked Fletcher, as Duane returned, "thet's safer 'n prayin' fer rain."

Duanes reply was a remark as loquacious as Fletcher's, to the effect that a long, slow, monotonous ride was conducive to thirst. They all joined him, unmistakably friendly. But Knell was not there, and most assuredly not Poggin. Fletcher was no common outlaw, but, whatever his ability, it probably lay in execution of orders. Apparently at that time these men had nothing to do but drink and lounge around the tavern. Evidently they were poorly supplied with money, though Duane observed they could borrow a peso occasionally from the bartender. Duane set out to make himself agreeable and succeeded. There was card-playing for small stakes, idle jests of coarse nature, much bantering among the younger fellows, and occasionally a mild quarrel. All morning men came and went, until, all told, Duane calculated he had seen at least fifty. Toward the middle of the afternoon a young fellow burst into the saloon and yelled one word:

"Posse!"

From the scramble to get outdoors Duane judged that word and the ensuing action was rare in Ord.

"What the hell!" muttered Fletcher, as he gazed down the road at a dark, compact bunch of horses and riders. "Fust time I ever seen thet in Ord! We're gettin' popular like them camps out of Valentine. Wish Phil was here or Poggy. Now all you gents keep quiet. I'll do the talkin'."

The posse entered the town, trotted up on dusty horses, and halted in a bunch before the tavern. The party consisted of about twenty men, all heavily armed, and evidently in charge of a clean-cut, lean-limbed cowboy. Duane experienced considerable satisfaction at the absence of the sheriff who he had understood was to lead the posse. Perhaps he was out in another direction with a different force.

"Hello, Jim Fletcher," called the cowboy.

"Howdy," replied Fletcher.

At his short, dry response and the way he strode leisurely out before the posse Duane found himself modifying his contempt for Fletcher. The outlaw was different now.

"Fletcher, we've tracked a man to all but three miles of this place. Tracks as plain as the nose on your face.

Found his camp. Then he hit into the brush, an' we lost the trail. Didn't have no tracker with us. Think he went into the mountains. But we took a chance an' rid over the rest of the way, seein' Ord was so close. Anybody come in here late last night or early this mornin'?"

"Nope," replied Fletcher.

His response was what Duane had expected from his manner, and evidently the cowboy took it as a matter of course. He turned to the others of the posse, entering into a low consultation. Evidently there was difference of opinion, if not real dissension, in that posse.

"Didn't I tell ye this was a wild-goose chase, comin' way out here?" protested an old hawk-faced rancher. "Them hoss tracks we follored ain't like any of them we seen at the water-tank where the train was held up."

"I'm not so sure of that," replied the leader.

"Wal, Guthrie, I've follored tracks all my life—'

"But you couldn't keep to the trail this feller made in the brush."

"Gimme time, an' I could. Thet takes time. An' heah you go hell-bent fer election! But it's a wrong lead out this way. If you're right this road-agent, after he killed his pals, would hev rid back right through town. An' with them mail-bags! Supposin' they was greasers? Some greasers has sense, an' when it comes to thievin' they're shore cute."

"But we sent got any reason to believe this robber who murdered the greasers is a greaser himself. I tell you it was a slick job done by no ordinary sneak. Didn't you hear the facts? One greaser hopped the engine an' covered the engineer an' fireman. Another greaser kept flashin' his gun outside the train. The big man who shoved back the car-door an' did the killin'—he was the real gent, an' don't you forget it."

Some of the posse sided with the cowboy leader and some with the old cattleman. Finally the young leader disgustedly gathered up his bridle.

"Aw, hell! Thet sheriff shoved you off this trail. Mebbe he hed reasons Savvy thet? If I hed a bunch of cowboys with me—I tell you what—I'd take a chance an' clean up this hole!"

All the while Jim Fletcher stood quietly with his hands in his pockets.

"Guthrie, I'm shore treasurin' up your friendly talk," he said. The menace was in the tone, not the content of his speech.

"You can—an' be damned to you, Fletcher!" called Guthrie, as the horses started.

Fletcher, standing out alone before the others of his clan, watched the posse out of sight.

"Luck fer you-all thet Poggy wasn't here," he said, as they disappeared. Then with a thoughtful mien he strode up on the porch and led Duane away from the others into the bar-room. When he looked into Duane's face it was somehow an entirely changed scrutiny.

"Dodge, where'd you hide the stuff? I reckon I git in on this deal, seein' I staved off Guthrie."

Duane played his part. Here was his a tiger after prey

he seized it. First he coolly eyed the outlaw and then disclaimed any knowledge whatever of the train-robbery other than Fletcher had heard himself. Then at Fletcher's persistence and admiration and increasing show of friendliness he laughed occasionally and allowed himself to swell with pride, though still denying. Next he feigned a lack of consistent will-power and seemed to be wavering under Fletcher's persuasion and grew silent, then surly. Fletcher, evidently sure of ultimate victory, desisted for the time being; however, in his solicitous regard and close companionship for the rest of that day he betrayed the bent of his mind.

Later, when Duane started up announcing his intention to get his horse and make for camp out in the brush, Fletcher seemed grievously offended.

"Why don't you stay with me? I've got a comfortable 'dobe over here. Didn't I stick by you when Guthrie an' his bunch come up? Supposin' I hedn't showed down a cold hand to him? You'd be swingin' somewheres now. I tell you, Dodge, it ain't square."

"I'll square it. I pay my debts," replied Duane. "But I can't put up here all night. If I belonged to the gang it 'd be different."

"What gang?" asked Fletcher, bluntly.

"Why, Cheseldine's."

Fletcher's beard nodded as his jaw dropped.

Duane laughed. "I run into him the other day. Knowed him on sight. Sure, he's the king-pin rustler. When he seen me an' asked me what reason I had for bein' on earth or some such like—why, I up an' told him."

Fletcher appeared staggered.

"Who in all-fired hell air you talkin' about?"

"Didn't I tell you once? Cheseldine. He calls himself Longstreth over there."

All of Fletcher's face not covered by hair turned a dirty white. "Cheseldine—Longstreth!" he whispered, hoarsely. "Gord Almighty! You braced the—" Then a remarkable transformation came over the outlaw. He gulped; he straightened his face; he controlled his agitation. But he could not send the healthy brown back to his face. Duane, watching this rude man, marveled at the change in him, the sudden checking movement, the proof of a wonderful fear and loyalty. It all meant Cheseldine, a master of men!

"WHO AIR YOU?" queried Fletcher, in a queer, strained voice.

"You gave me a handle, didn't you? Dodge. Thet's as good as any. Shore it hits me hard. Jim, I've been pretty lonely for years, an' I'm gettin' in need of pals. Think it over, will you? See you manana."

The outlaw watched Duane go off after his horse, watched him as he returned to the tavern, watched him ride out into the darkness—all without a word.

Duane left the town, threaded a quiet passage through cactus and mesquite to a spot he had marked before, and made ready for the night. His mind was so full that he found sleep aloof. Luck at last was playing his game. He sensed the first slow heave of a mighty crisis. The end, always haunting, had to be sternly blotted from thought. It was the approach that needed all his mind.

He passed the night there, and late in the morning, after watching trail and road from a ridge, he returned to Ord. If Jim Fletcher tried to disguise his surprise the effort was a failure. Certainly he had not expected to see Duane again. Duane allowed himself a little freedom with Fletcher, an attitude hitherto lacking.

That afternoon a horseman rode in from Bradford, an outlaw evidently well known and liked by his fellows, and Duane heard him say, before he could possibly have been told the train-robber was in Ord, that the loss of money in the holdup was slight. Like a flash Duane saw the luck of this report. He pretended not to have heard.

In the early twilight at an opportune moment he called Fletcher to him, and, linking his arm within the outlaw's, he drew him off in a stroll to a log bridge spanning a little gully. Here after gazing around, he took out a roll of bills, spread it out, split it equally, and without a word handed one half to Fletcher. With clumsy fingers Fletcher ran through the roll.

"Five hundred!" he exclaimed. "Dodge, thet's damn handsome of you, considerin' the job wasn't—"

"Considerin' nothin'," interrupted Duane. "I'm makin' no reference to a job here or there. You did me a good turn. I split my pile. If thet doesn't make us pards, good turns an' money ain't no use in this country."

Fletcher was won.

The two men spent much time together. Duane made up a short fictitious history about himself that satisfied the outlaw, only it drew forth a laughing jest upon Duane's modesty. For Fletcher did not hide his belief that this new partner was a man of achievements. Knell and Poggin, and then Cheseldine himself, would be persuaded of this fact, so Fletcher boasted. He had influence. He would use it. He thought he pulled a stroke with Knell. But nobody on earth, not even the boss, had any influence on Poggin. Poggin was concentrated ice part of the time; all the rest he was bursting hell. But Poggin loved a horse. He never loved anything else. He could be won with that black horse Bullet. Cheseldine was already won by Duane's monumental nerve; otherwise he would have killed Duane.

Little by little the next few days Duane learned the points he longed to know; and how indelibly they etched themselves in his memory! Cheseldine's hiding-place was on the far slope of Mount Ord, in a deep, high-walled valley. He always went there just before a contemplated job, where he met and planned with his lieutenants. Then while they executed he basked in the sunshine before one or another of the public places he owned. He was there in the Ord den now, getting ready to plan the biggest job yet. It was a bank-robbery; but where, Fletcher had not as yet been advised.

Then when Duane had pumped the now amenable outlaw of all details pertaining to the present he gathered data and facts and places covering a period of ten years Fletcher had been with Cheseldine. And herewith was unfolded a history so dark in its bloody regime, so incredible in its brazen daring, so appalling in its proof of the outlaw's sweep and grasp of the country from Pecos to Rio Grande, that Duane was stunned. Compared to this Cheseldine of the Big Bend, to this rancher, stock-buyer, cattle-speculator, property-holder, all the outlaws Duane had ever known sank into insignificance. The power of the man stunned Duane; the strange fidelity given him stunned Duane; the intricate inside working of his great system was equally stunning. But when Duane recovered from that the old terrible passion to kill consumed him, and it raged fiercely and it could not be checked. If that red-handed Poggin, if that cold-eyed, dead-faced Knell had only been at Ord! But they were not, and Duane with help of time got what he hoped was the upper hand of himself.

CHAPTER XXII

Again inaction and suspense dragged at Duane's spirit. Like a leashed hound with a keen scent in his face Duane wanted to leap forth when he was bound. He almost fretted. Something called to him over the bold, wild brow of Mount Ord. But while Fletcher stayed in Ord waiting for Knell and Poggin, or for orders, Duane knew his game was again a waiting one.

But one day there were signs of the long quiet of Ord being broken. A messenger strange to Duane rode in on a secret mission that had to do with Fletcher. When he went away Fletcher became addicted to thoughtful moods and lonely walks. He seldom drank, and this in itself was a striking contrast to former behavior. The messenger came again. Whatever communication he brought, it had a remarkable effect upon the outlaw. Duane was present in the tavern when the fellow arrived, saw the few words whispered, but did not hear them. Fletcher turned white with anger or fear, perhaps both, and he cursed like a madman. The messenger, a lean, dark-faced, hard-riding fellow reminding Duane of the cowboy Guthrie, left the tavern without even a drink and rode away off to the west. This west mystified and fascinated Duane as much as the south beyond Mount Ord. Where were Knell and Poggin? Apparently they were not at present with the leader on the mountain. After the messenger left Fletcher grew silent and surly. He had presented a variety of moods to Duane's observation, and this latest one was provocative of thought. Fletcher was dangerous. It became clear now that the other outlaws of the camp feared him, kept out of his way. Duane let him alone, yet closely watched him.

Perhaps an hour after the messenger had left, not longer, Fletcher manifestly arrived at some decision, and he called for his horse. Then he went to his shack and returned. To Duane the outlaw looked in shape both to ride and to fight. He gave orders for the men in camp to keep close until he returned. Then he mounted.

"Come here, Dodge," he called.

Duane went up and laid a hand on the pommel of the saddle. Fletcher walked his horse, with Duane beside him, till they reached the log bridge, when he halted.

"Dodge, I'm in bad with Knell," he said. "An' it 'pears I'm the cause of friction between Knell an' Poggy. Knell never had any use fer me, but Poggy's been square, if not friendly. The boss has a big deal on, an' here it's been held up because of this scrap. He's waitin' over there on the mountain to give orders to Knell or Poggy, an' neither one's showin' up. I've got to stand in the breach, an' I ain't enjoyin' the prospects."

"What's the trouble about, Jim?" asked Duane.

"Reckon it's a little about you, Dodge," said Fletcher, dryly. "Knell hadn't any use fer you thet day. He ain't got no use fer a man onless he can rule him. Some of the boys here hev blabbed before I edged in with my say, an' there's hell to pay. Knell claims to know somethin' about you that'll make both the boss an' Poggy sick when he springs it. But he's keepin' quiet. Hard man to figger, thet Knell. Reckon you'd better go back to Bradford fer a day or so, then camp out near here till I come back."

"Why?"

"Wal, because there ain't any use fer you to git in bad, too."

"The gang will ride over here any day. If they're friendly, I'll light a fire on the hill there, say three nights from to-night. If you don't see it thet night you hit the trail. I'll do what I can. Jim Fletcher sticks to his pals. So long, Dodge."

Then he rode away.

He left Duane in a quandary. This news was black. Things had been working out so well. Here was a setback. At the moment Duane did not know which way to turn, but certainly he had no idea of going back to Bradford. Friction between the two great lieutenants of Cheseldine! Open hostility between one of them and another of the chief's right-hand men! Among outlaws that sort of thing was deadly serious. Generally such matters were settled with guns. Duane gathered encouragement even from disaster. Perhaps the disintegration of Cheseldine's great band had already begun. But what did Knell know? Duane did not circle around the idea with doubts and hopes; if Knell knew anything it was that this stranger in Ord, this new partner of Fletcher's, was no less than

Buck Duane. Well, it was about time, thought Duane, that he made use of his name if it were to help him at all. That name had been MacNelly's hope. He had anchored all his scheme to Duane's fame. Duane was tempted to ride off after Fletcher and stay with him. This, however, would hardly be fair to an outlaw who had been fair to him. Duane concluded to await developments and when the gang rode in to Ord, probably from their various hiding-places, he would be there ready to be denounced by Knell. Duane could not see any other culmination of this series of events than a meeting between Knell and himself. If that terminated fatally for Knell there was all probability of Duane's being in no worse situation than he was now. If Poggin took up the quarrel! Here Duane accused himself again—tried in vain to revolt from a judgment that he was only reasoning out excuses to meet these outlaws.

Meanwhile, instead of waiting, why not hunt up Cheseldine in his mountain retreat? The thought no sooner struck Duane than he was hurrying for his horse.

He left Ord, ostensibly toward Bradford, but, once out of sight, he turned off the road, circled through the brush, and several miles south of town he struck a narrow grass-grown trail that Fletcher had told him led to Cheseldine's camp. The horse tracks along this trail were not less than a week old, and very likely much more. It wound between low, brush-covered foothills, through arroyos and gullies lined with mesquite, cottonwood, and scrub-oak.

In an hour Duane struck the slope of Mount Ord, and as he climbed he got a view of the rolling, black-spotted country, partly desert, partly fertile, with long, bright lines of dry stream-beds winding away to grow dim in the distance. He got among broken rocks and cliffs, and here the open, downward-rolling land disappeared, and he was hard put to it to find the trail. He lost it repeatedly and made slow progress. Finally he climbed into a region of all rock benches, rough here, smooth there, with only an occasional scratch of iron horseshoe to guide him. Many times he had to go ahead and then work to right or left till he found his way again. It was slow work; it took all day; and night found him half-way up the mountain. He halted at a little side-canyon with grass and water, and here he made camp. The night was clear and cool at that height, with a dark-blue sky and a streak of stars blinking across. With this day of action behind him he felt better satisfied than he had been for some time. Here, on this venture, he was answering to a call that had so often directed his movements, perhaps his life, and it was one that logic or intelligence could take little stock of. And on this night, lonely like the ones he used to spend in the Nueces gorge, and memorable of them because of a likeness to that old hiding-place, he felt the pressing return of old haunting things—the past so long ago, wild flights, dead faces—and the places of these were taken by one quiveringly alive, white, tragic, with its dark, intent, speaking eyes—Ray Longstreth's.

That last memory he yielded to until he slept.

In the morning, satisfied that he had left still fewer tracks than he had followed up this trail, he led his horse up to the head of the canyon, there a narrow crack in low cliffs, and with branches of cedar fenced him in. Then he went back and took up the trail on foot.

Without the horse he made better time and climbed through deep clefts, wide canyons, over ridges, up shelving slopes, along precipices—a long, hard climb—till he reached what he concluded was a divide. Going down was easier, though the farther he followed this dim and winding trail the wider the broken battlements of rock. Above him he saw the black fringe of pinon and pine, and above that the bold peak, bare, yellow, like a desert butte. Once, through a wide gateway between great escarpments, he saw the lower country beyond the range, and beyond this, vast and clear as it lay in his sight, was the great river that made the Big Bend. He went down and down, wondering how a horse could follow that broken trail, believing there must be another better one somewhere into Cheseldine's hiding-place.

He rounded a jutting corner, where view had been shut off, and presently came out upon the rim of a high wall. Beneath, like a green gulf seen through blue haze, lay an amphitheater walled in on the two sides he could see. It lay perhaps a thousand feet below him; and, plain as all the other features of that wild environment, there shone out a big red stone or adobe cabin, white water shining away between great borders, and horses and cattle dotting the levels. It was a peaceful, beautiful scene. Duane could not help grinding his teeth at the thought of rustlers living there in quiet and ease.

Duane worked half-way down to the level, and, well hidden in a niche, he settled himself to watch both trail and valley. He made note of the position of the sun and saw that if anything developed or if he decided to descend any farther there was small likelihood of his getting back to his camp before dark. To try that after nightfall he imagined would be vain effort.

Then he bent his keen eyes downward. The cabin appeared to be a crude structure. Though large in size, it had, of course, been built by outlaws.

There was no garden, no cultivated field, no corral. Excepting for the rude pile of stones and logs plastered together with mud, the valley was as wild, probably, as on the day of discovery. Duane seemed to have been watching for a long time before he saw any sign of man, and this one apparently went to the stream for water and returned to the cabin.

The sun went down behind the wall, and shadows were born in the darker places of the valley. Duane began to want to get closer to that cabin. What had he taken this arduous climb for? He held back, however, trying to evolve further plans.

While he was pondering the shadows quickly gathered and darkened. If he was to go back to camp he must set out at once. Still he lingered. And suddenly his wide-roving eye caught sight of two horsemen riding up the valley. The must have entered at a point below, round the huge abutment of rock, beyond

Duane's range of sight. Their horses were tired and stopped at the stream for a long drink.

Duane left his perch, took to the steep trail, and descended as fast as he could without making noise. It did not take him long to reach the valley floor. It was almost level, with deep grass, and here and there clumps of bushes. Twilight was already thick down there. Duane marked the location of the trail, and then began to slip like a shadow through the grass and from bush to bush. He saw a bright light before he made out the dark outline of the cabin. Then he heard voices, a merry whistle, a coarse song, and the clink of iron cooking-utensils. He smelled fragrant wood-smoke. He saw moving dark figures cross the light. Evidently there was a wide door, or else the fire was out in the open.

Duane swerved to the left, out of direct line with the light, and thus was able to see better. Then he advanced noiselessly but swiftly toward the back of the house. There were trees close to the wall. He would make no noise, and he could scarcely be seen—if only there was no watch-dog! But all his outlaw days he had taken risks with only his useless life at stake; now, with that changed, he advanced stealthy and bold as an Indian. He reached the cover of the trees, knew he was hidden in their shadows, for at few paces' distance he had been able to see only their tops. From there he slipped up to the house and felt along the wall with his hands.

He came to a little window where light shone through. He peeped in. He saw a room shrouded in shadows, a lamp turned low, a table, chairs. He saw an open door, with bright flare beyond, but could not see the fire. Voices came indistinctly. Without hesitation Duane stole farther along—all the way to the end of the cabin. Peeping round, he saw only the flare of light on bare ground. Retracing his cautious steps, he paused at the crack again, saw that no man was in the room, and then he went on round that end of the cabin. Fortune favored him. There were bushes, an old shed, a wood-pile, all the cover he needed at that corner. He did not even need to crawl.

Before he peered between the rough corner of wall and the bush growing close to it Duane paused a moment. This excitement was different from that he had always felt when pursued. It had no bitterness, no pain, no dread. There was as much danger here, perhaps more, yet it was not the same. Then he looked.

He saw a bright fire, a red-faced man bending over it, whistling, while he handled a steaming pot. Over him was a roofed shed built against the wall, with two open sides and two supporting posts. Duane's second glance, not so blinded by the sudden bright light, made out other men, three in the shadow, two in the flare, but with backs to him.

"It's a smoother trail by long odds, but ain't so short as this one right over the mountain," one outlaw was saying.

"What's eatin' you, Panhandle?" ejaculated another. "Blossom an' me rode from Faraway Springs, where Poggin is with some of the gang."

"Excuse me, Phil. Shore I didn't see you come in, an'

Boldt never said nothin.'"

"It took you a long time to get here, but I guess that's just as well," spoke up a smooth, suave voice with a ring in it.

Longstreth's voice—Cheseldine's voice!

Here they were—Cheseldine, Phil Knell, Blossom Kane, Panhandle Smith, Boldt—how well Duane remembered the names!—all here, the big men of Cheseldine's gang, except the biggest—Poggin. Duane had holed them, and his sensations of the moment deadened sight and sound of what was before him. He sank down, controlled himself, silenced a mounting exultation, then from a less-strained position he peered forth again.

The outlaws were waiting for supper. Their conversation might have been that of cowboys in camp, ranchers at a roundup. Duane listened with eager ears, waiting for the business talk that he felt would come. All the time he watched with the eyes of a wolf upon its quarry. Blossom Kane was the lean-limbed messenger who had so angered Fletcher. Boldt was a giant in stature, dark, bearded, silent. Panhandle Smith was the red-faced cook, merry, profane, a short, bow-legged man resembling many rustlers Duane had known, particularly Luke Stevens. And Knell, who sat there, tall, slim, like a boy in build, like a boy in years, with his pale, smooth, expressionless face and his cold, gray eyes. And Longstreth, who leaned against the wall, handsome, with his dark face and beard like an aristocrat, resembled many a rich Louisiana planter Duane had met. The sixth man sat so much in the shadow that he could not be plainly discerned, and, though addressed, his name was not mentioned.

Panhandle Smith carried pots and pans into the cabin, and cheerfully called out: "If you gents air hungry fer grub, don't look fer me to feed you with a spoon."

The outlaws piled inside, made a great bustle and clatter as they sat to their meal. Like hungry men, they talked little.

Duane waited there awhile, then guardedly got up and crept round to the other side of the cabin. After he became used to the dark again he ventured to steal along the wall to the window and peeped in. The outlaws were in the first room and could not be seen.

Duane waited. The moments dragged endlessly. His heart pounded. Longstreth entered, turned up the light, and, taking a box of cigars from the table, he carried it out.

"Here, you fellows, go outside and smoke," he said. "Knell, come on in now. Let's get it over."

He returned, sat down, and lighted a cigar for himself. He put his booted feet on the table.

Duane saw that the room was comfortably, even luxuriously furnished. There must have been a good trail, he thought, else how could all that stuff have been packed in there. Most assuredly it could not have come over the trail he had traveled. Presently he heard the men go outside, and their voices became indistinct. Then Knell came in and seated himself without any of his chief's ease. He seemed preoccupied and, as always, cold.

"What's wrong, Knell? Why didn't you get here sooner?" queried Longstreth.

"Poggin, damn him! We're on the outs again."

"What for?"

"Aw, he needn't have got sore. He's breakin' a new hoss over at Faraway, an you know him where a hoss 's concerned. That kept him, I reckon, more than anythin'."

"What else? Get it out of your system so we can go on to the new job."

"Well, it begins back a ways. I don't know how long ago—weeks—a stranger rode into Ord an' got down easy-like as if he owned the place. He seemed familiar to me. But I wasn't sure. We looked him over, an' I left, tryin' to place him in my mind."

"What'd he look like?"

"Rangy, powerful man, white hair over his temples, still, hard face, eyes like knives. The way he packed his guns, the way he walked an' stood an' swung his right hand showed me what he was. You can't fool me on the gun-sharp. An' he had a grand horse, a big black."

"I've met your man," said Longstreth.

"No!" exclaimed Knell. It was wonderful to hear surprise expressed by this man that did not in the least show it in his strange physiognomy. Knell laughed a short, grim, hollow laugh. "Boss, this here big gent drifts into Ord again an' makes up to Jim Fletcher. Jim, you know, is easy led. He likes men. An' when a posse come along trailin' a blind lead, huntin' the wrong way for the man who held up No. 6, why, Jim—he up an' takes this stranger to be the fly road-agent an' cottons to him. Got money out of him sure. An' that's what stumps me more. What's this man's game? I happen to know, boss, that he couldn't have held up No. 6."

"How do you know?" demanded Longstreth.

"Because I did the job myself."

A dark and stormy passion clouded the chief's face.

"Damn you, Knell! You're incorrigible. You're unreliable. Another break like that queers you with me. Did you tell Poggin?"

"Yes. That's one reason we fell out. He raved. I thought he was goin' to kill me."

"Why did you tackle such a risky job without help or plan?"

"It offered, that's all. An' it was easy. But it was a mistake. I got the country an' the railroad hollerin' for nothin'. I just couldn't help it. You know what idleness means to one of us. You know also that this very life breeds fatality. It's wrong—that's why. I was born of good parents, an' I know what's right. We're wrong, an' we can't beat the end, that's all. An' for my part I don't care a damn when that comes."

"Fine wise talk from you, Knell," said Longstreth, scornfully. "Go on with your story."

"As I said, Jim cottons to the pretender, an' they get chummy. They're together all the time. You can gamble Jim told all he knew an' then some. A little liquor loosens his tongue. Several of the boys rode over from Ord, an' one of them went to Poggin an' says Jim Fletcher has a new man for the gang. Poggin, you know, is always ready for any new man. He says if one doesn't turn out good he can be shut off easy. He rather liked the way this new part of Jim's was boosted. Jim an' Poggin always hit it up together. So until I got on the deal Jim's pard was already in the gang, without Poggin or you ever seein' him. Then I got to figurin' hard. Just where had I ever seen that chap? As it turned out, I never had seen him, which accounts for my bein' doubtful. I'd never forget any man I'd seen. I dug up a lot of old papers from my kit an' went over them. Letters, pictures, clippin's, an' all that. I guess I had a pretty good notion what I was lookin' for an' who I wanted to make sure of. At last I found it. An' I knew my man. But I didn't spring it on Poggin. Oh no! I want to have some fun with him when the time comes. He'll be wilder than a trapped wolf. I sent Blossom over to Ord to get word from Jim, an' when he verified all this talk I sent Blossom again with a message calculated to make Jim hump. Poggin got sore, said he'd wait for Jim, an' I could come over here to see you about the new job. He'd meet me in Ord."

Knell had spoken hurriedly and low, now and then with passion. His pale eyes glinted like fire in ice, and now his voice fell to a whisper.

"Who do you think Fletcher's new man is?"

"Who?" demanded Longstreth.

"BUCK DUANE!"

Down came Longstreth's boots with a crash, then his body grew rigid.

"That Nueces outlaw? That two-shot ace-of-spades gun-thrower who killed Bland, Alloway—?"

"An' Hardin." Knell whispered this last name with more feeling than the apparent circumstance demanded.

"Yes; and Hardin, the best one of the Rim Rock fellows—Buck Duane!"

Longstreth was so ghastly white now that his black mustache seemed outlined against chalk. He eyed his grim lieutenant. They understood each other without more words. It was enough that Buck Duane was there in the Big Bend. Longstreth rose presently and reached for a flask, from which he drank, then offered it to Knell. He waved it aside.

"Knell," began the chief, slowly, as he wiped his lips, "I gathered you have some grudge against this Buck Duane."

"Yes."

"Well, don't be a fool now and do what Poggin or almost any of you men would—don't meet this Buck Duane. I've reason to believe he's a Texas Ranger now."

"The hell you say!" exclaimed Knell.

"Yes. Go to Ord and give Jim Fletcher a hunch. He'll get Poggin, and they'll fix even Buck Duane."

"All right. I'll do my best. But if I run into Duane—"

"Don't run into him!" Longstreth's voice fairly rang with the force of its passion and command. He wiped his face, drank again from the flask, sat down, resumed his smoking, and, drawing a paper from his vest pocket he began to study it.

"Well, I'm glad that's settled," he said, evidently referring to the Duane matter. "Now for the new job. This is October the eighteenth. On or before the twenty-fifth there will be a shipment of gold reach the Rancher's Bank of Val Verde. After you return to Ord give Poggin these orders. Keep the gang quiet. You, Poggin, Kane, Fletcher, Panhandle Smith, and Boldt to be in on the secret and the job. Nobody else. You'll leave Ord on the twenty-third, ride across country by the trail till you get within sight of Mercer. It's a hundred miles from Bradford to Val Verde—about the same from Ord. Time your travel to get you near Val Verde on the morning of the twenty-sixth. You won't have to more than trot your horses. At two o'clock in the afternoon, sharp, ride into town and up to the Rancher's Bank. Val Verde's a pretty big town. Never been any holdups there. Town feels safe. Make it a clean, fast, daylight job. That's all. Have you got the details?"

Knell did not even ask for the dates again.

"Suppose Poggin or me might be detained?" he asked.

Longstreth bent a dark glance upon his lieutenant.

"You never can tell what'll come off," continued Knell. "I'll do my best."

"The minute you see Poggin tell him. A job on hand steadies him. And I say again—look to it that nothing happens. Either you or Poggin carry the job through. But I want both of you in it. Break for the hills, and when you get up in the rocks where you can hide your tracks head for Mount Ord. When all's quiet again I'll join you here. That's all. Call in the boys."

Like a swift shadow and as noiseless Duane stole across the level toward the dark wall of rock. Every nerve was a strung wire. For a little while his mind was cluttered and clogged with whirling thoughts, from which, like a flashing scroll, unrolled the long, baffling order of action. The game was now in his hands. He must cross Mount Ord at night. The feat was improbable, but it might be done. He must ride into Bradford, forty miles from the foothills before eight o'clock next morning. He must telegraph MacNelly to be in Val Verde on the twenty-fifth. He must ride back to Ord, to intercept Knell, face him be denounced, kill him, and while the iron was hot strike hard to win Poggin's half-won interest as he had wholly won Fletcher's. Failing that last, he must let the outlaws alone to bide their time in Ord, to be free to ride on to their new job in Val Verde. In the mean time he must plan to arrest Longstreth. It was a magnificent outline, incredible, alluring, unfathomable in its nameless certainty. He felt like fate. He seemed to be the iron consequences falling upon these doomed outlaws.

Under the wall the shadows were black, only the tips of trees and crags showing, yet he went straight to the trail. It was merely a grayness between borders of black. He climbed and never stopped. It did not seem steep. His feet might have had eyes. He surmounted the wall, and, looking down into the ebony gulf pierced by one point of light, he lifted a menacing arm and shook it. Then he strode on and did not falter till he reached the huge shelving cliffs. Here he lost the trail; there was none; but he remembered the shapes, the points, the notches of rock above.

Before he reached the ruins of splintered ramparts and jumbles of broken walls the moon topped the eastern slope of the mountain, and the mystifying blackness he had dreaded changed to magic silver light. It seemed as light as day, only soft, mellow, and the air held a transparent sheen. He ran up the bare ridges and down the smooth slopes, and, like a goat, jumped from rock to rock. In this light he knew his way and lost no time looking for a trail. He crossed the divide and then had all downhill before him. Swiftly he descended, almost always sure of his memory of the landmarks. He did not remember having studied them in the ascent, yet here they were, even in changed light, familiar to his sight. What he had once seen was pictured on his mind. And, true as a deer striking for home, he reached the canyon where he had left his horse.

Bullet was quickly and easily found. Duane threw on the saddle and pack, cinched them tight, and resumed his descent. The worst was now to come. Bare downward steps in rock, sliding, weathered slopes, narrow black gullies, a thousand openings in a maze of broken stone—these Duane had to descend in fast time, leading a giant of a horse. Bullet cracked the loose fragments, sent them rolling, slid on the scaly slopes, plunged down the steps, followed like a faithful dog at Duane's heels.

Hours passed as moments. Duane was equal to his great opportunity. But he could not quell that self in him which reached back over the lapse of lonely, searing years and found the boy in him. He who had been worse than dead was now grasping at the skirts of life—which meant victory, honor, happiness. Duane knew he was not just right in part of his mind. Small wonder that he was not insane, he thought! He tramped on downward, his marvelous faculty for covering rough ground and holding to the true course never before even in flight so keen and acute. Yet all the time a spirit was keeping step with him. Thought of Ray Longstreth as he had left her made him weak. But now, with the game clear to its end, with the trap to spring, with success strangely haunting him, Duane could not dispel memory of her. He saw her white face, with its sweet sad lips and the dark eyes so tender and tragic. And time and distance and risk and toil were nothing.

The moon sloped to the west. Shadows of trees and crags now crossed to the other side of him. The stars dimmed. Then he was out of the rocks, with the dim trail pale at his feet. Mounting Bullet, he made short work of the long slope and the foothills and the rolling land leading down to Ord. The little outlaw camp, with its shacks and cabins and row of houses, lay silent and dark under the paling moon. Duane passed by on the lower trail, headed into the road, and put Bullet to a gallop. He watched the dying moon, the waning stars, and the east. He had time to spare, so he saved the horse. Knell would be leaving the rendezvous about the time Duane turned back toward Ord. Between noon and sunset they would meet.

The night wore on. The moon sank behind low mountains in the west. The stars brightened for a while, then faded. Gray gloom enveloped the world, thickened, lay like smoke over the road. Then shade by shade it lightened, until through the transparent obscurity shone a dim light.

Duane reached Bradford before dawn. He dismounted some distance from the tracks, tied his horse, and then crossed over to the station. He heard the clicking of the telegraph instrument, and it thrilled him. An operator sat inside reading. When Duane tapped on the window he looked up with startled glance, then went swiftly to unlock the door.

"Hello. Give me paper and pencil. Quick," whispered Duane.

With trembling hands the operator complied. Duane wrote out the message he had carefully composed.

"Send this—repeat it to make sure—then keep mum. I'll see you again. Good-by."

The operator stared, but did not speak a word.

Duane left as stealthily and swiftly as he had come. He walked his horse a couple miles back on the road and then rested him till break of day. The east began to redden, Duane turned grimly in the direction of Ord.

When Duane swung into the wide, grassy square on the outskirts of Ord he saw a bunch of saddled horses hitched in front of the tavern. He knew what that meant. Luck still favored him. If it would only hold! But he could ask no more. The rest was a matter of how greatly he could make his power felt. An open conflict against odds lay in the balance. That would be fatal to him, and to avoid it he had to trust to his name and a presence he must make terrible. He knew outlaws. He knew what qualities held them. He knew what to exaggerate.

There was not an outlaw in sight. The dusty horses had covered distance that morning. As Duane dismounted he heard loud, angry voices inside the tavern. He removed coat and vest, hung them over the pommel. He packed two guns, one belted high on the left hip, the other swinging low on the right side. He neither looked nor listened, but boldly pushed the door and stepped inside.

The big room was full of men, and every face pivoted toward him. Knell's pale face flashed into Duane's swift sight; then Boldt's, then Blossom Kane's, then Panhandle Smith's, then Fletcher's, then others that were familiar, and last that of Poggin. Though Duane had never seen Poggin or heard him described, he knew him. For he saw a face that was a record of great and evil deeds.

There was absolute silence. The outlaws were lined back of a long table upon which were papers, stacks of silver coin, a bundle of bills, and a huge gold-mounted gun.

"Are you gents lookin' for me?" asked Duane. He gave his voice all the ringing force and power of which he was capable. And he stepped back, free of anything, with the outlaws all before him.

Knell stood quivering, but his face might have been a mask. The other outlaws looked from him to Duane. Jim Fletcher flung up his hands.

"My Gawd, Dodge, what'd you bust in here fer?"

he said, plaintively, and slowly stepped forward. His action was that of a man true to himself. He meant he had been sponsor for Duane and now he would stand by him.

"Back, Fletcher!" called Duane, and his voice made the outlaw jump.

"Hold on, Dodge, an' you-all, everybody," said Fletcher. "Let me talk, seein' I'm in wrong here."

His persuasions did not ease the strain.

"Go ahead. Talk," said Poggin.

Fletcher turned to Duane. "Pard, I'm takin' it on myself thet you meet enemies here when I swore you'd meet friends. It's my fault. I'll stand by you if you let me."

"No, Jim," replied Duane.

"But what'd you come fer without the signal?" burst out Fletcher, in distress. He saw nothing but catastrophe in this meeting.

"Jim, I ain't pressin' my company none. But when I'm wanted bad—"

Fletcher stopped him with a raised hand. Then he turned to Poggin with a rude dignity.

"Poggy, he's my pard, an' he's riled. I never told him a word thet'd make him sore. I only said Knell hadn't no more use fer him than fer me. Now, what you say goes in this gang. I never failed you in my life. Here's my pard. I vouch fer him. Will you stand fer me? There's goin' to be hell if you don't. An' us with a big job on hand!"

While Fletcher toiled over his slow, earnest persuasion Duane had his gaze riveted upon Poggin. There was something leonine about Poggin. He was tawny. He blazed. He seemed beautiful as fire was beautiful. But looked at closer, with glance seeing the physical man, instead of that thing which shone from him, he was of perfect build, with muscles that swelled and rippled, bulging his clothes, with the magnificent head and face of the cruel, fierce, tawny-eyed jaguar.

Looking at this strange Poggin, instinctively divining his abnormal and hideous power, Duane had for the first time in his life the inward quaking fear of a man. It was like a cold-tongued bell ringing within him and numbing his heart. The old instinctive firing of blood followed, but did not drive away that fear. He knew. He felt something here deeper than thought could go. And he hated Poggin.

That individual had been considering Fletcher's appeal.

"Jim, I ante up," he said, "an' if Phil doesn't raise us out with a big hand—why, he'll get called, an' your pard can set in the game."

Every eye shifted to Knell. He was dead white. He laughed, and any one hearing that laugh would have realized his intense anger equally with an assurance which made him master of the situation.

"Poggin, you're a gambler, you are—the ace-high, straight-flush hand of the Big Bend," he said, with stinging scorn. "I'll bet you my roll to a greaser peso that I can deal you a hand you'll be afraid to play."

"Phil, you're talkin' wild," growled Poggin, with both advice and menace in his tone.

"If there's anythin' you hate it's a man who pretends

to be somebody else when he's not. Thet so?"

Poggin nodded in slow-gathering wrath.

"Well, Jim's new pard—this man Dodge—he's not who he seems. Oh-ho! He's a hell of a lot different. But I know him. An' when I spring his name on you, Poggin, you'll freeze to your gizzard. Do you get me? You'll freeze, an' your hand'll be stiff when it ought to be lightnin'—All because you'll realize you've been standin' there five minutes—five minutes ALIVE before him!"

If not hate, then assuredly great passion toward Poggin manifested itself in Knell's scornful, fiery address, in the shaking hand he thrust before Poggin's face. In the ensuing silent pause Knell's panting could be plainly heard. The other men were pale, watchful, cautiously edging either way to the wall, leaving the principals and Duane in the center of the room.

"Spring his name, then, you—" said Poggin, violently, with a curse.

Strangely Knell did not even look at the man he was about to denounce. He leaned toward Poggin, his hands, his body, his long head all somewhat expressive of what his face disguised.

"BUCK DUANE!" he yelled, suddenly.

The name did not make any great difference in Poggin. But Knell's passionate, swift utterance carried the suggestion that the name ought to bring Poggin to quick action. It was possible, too, that Knell's manner, the import of his denunciation the meaning back of all his passion held Poggin bound more than the surprise. For the outlaw certainly was surprised, perhaps staggered at the idea that he, Poggin, had been about to stand sponsor with Fletcher for a famous outlaw hated and feared by all outlaws.

Knell waited a long moment, and then his face broke its cold immobility in an extraordinary expression of devilish glee. He had hounded the great Poggin into something that gave him vicious, monstrous joy.

"BUCK DUANE! Yes," he broke out, hotly. "The Nueces gunman! That two-shot, ace-of-spades lone wolf! You an' I—we've heard a thousand times of him—talked about him often. An' here he IN FRONT of you! Poggin, you were backin' Fletcher's new pard, Buck Duane. An' he'd fooled you both but for me. But I know him. An' I know why he drifted in here. To flash a gun on Cheseldine—on you—on me! Bah! Don't tell me he wanted to join the gang. You know a gunman, for you're one yourself. Don't you always want to kill another man? An' don't you always want to meet a real man, not a four-flush? It's the madness of the gunman, an' I know it. Well, Duane faced you—called you! An' when I sprung his name, what ought you have done? What would the boss—anybody—have expected of Poggin? Did you throw your gun, swift, like you have so often? Naw; you froze. An' why? Because here's a man with the kind of nerve you'd love to have. Because he's great—meetin' us here alone. Because you know he's a wonder with a gun an' you love life. Because you an' I an' every damned man here had to take his front, each to himself. If we all drew we'd kill him. Sure! But who's goin' to lead? Who was goin' to be first? Who was goin' to make him draw? Not you, Poggin! You leave that for a lesser man—me—who've lived to see you a coward. It comes once to every gunman. You've met your match in Buck Duane. An', by God, I'm glad! Here's once I show you up!"

The hoarse, taunting voice failed. Knell stepped back from the comrade he hated. He was wet, shaking, haggard, but magnificent.

"Buck Duane, do you remember Hardin?" he asked, in scarcely audible voice.

"Yes," replied Duane, and a flash of insight made clear Knell's attitude.

"You met him—forced him to draw—killed him?"

"Yes."

"Hardin was the best pard I ever had."

His teeth clicked together tight, and his lips set in a thin line.

The room grew still. Even breathing ceased. The time for words had passed. In that long moment of suspense Knell's body gradually stiffened, and at last the quivering ceased. He crouched. His eyes had a soul-piercing fire.

Duane watched them. He waited. He caught the thought—the breaking of Knell's muscle-bound rigidity. Then he drew.

Through the smoke of his gun he saw two red spurts of flame. Knell's bullets thudded into the ceiling. He fell with a scream like a wild thing in agony.

Duane did not see Knell die. He watched Poggin. And Poggin, like a stricken and astounded man, looked down upon his prostrate comrade.

Fletcher ran at Duane with hands aloft.

"Hit the trail, you liar, or you'll hev to kill me!" he yelled.

With hands still up, he shouldered and bodied Duane out of the room.

Duane leaped on his horse, spurred, and plunged away.

CHAPTER XXIII

Duane returned to Fairdale and camped in the mesquite till the twenty-third of the month. The few days seemed endless. All he could think of was that the hour in which he must disgrace Ray Longstreth was slowly but inexorably coming. In that waiting time he learned what love was and also duty. When the day at last dawned he rode like one possessed down the rough slope, hurdling the stones and crashing through the brush, with a sound in his ears that was not all the rush of the wind. Something dragged at him.

Apparently one side of his mind was unalterably fixed, while the other was a hurrying conglomeration of flashes of thought, reception of sensations. He could not get calmness. By and by, almost involuntarily, he hurried faster on. Action seemed to make his state less oppressive; it eased the weight. But the farther he went on the harder it was to continue. Had he turned his back upon love, happiness, perhaps on life itself?

There seemed no use to go on farther until he was absolutely sure of himself. Duane received a clear warning thought that such work as seemed haunting and driving him could never be carried out in the mood under which he labored. He hung on to that thought. Several times he slowed up, then stopped, only to go on again. At length, as he mounted a low ridge, Fairdale lay bright and green before him not far away, and the sight was a conclusive check. There were mesquites on the ridge, and Duane sought the shade beneath them. It was the noon-hour, with hot, glary sun and no wind. Here Duane had to have out his fight. Duane was utterly unlike himself; he could not bring the old self back; he was not the same man he once had been. But he could understand why. It was because of Ray Longstreth. Temptation assailed him. To have her his wife! It was impossible. The thought was insidiously alluring. Duane pictured a home. He saw himself riding through the cotton and rice and cane, home to a stately old mansion, where long-eared hounds bayed him welcome, and a woman looked for him and met him with happy and beautiful smile. There might—there would be children. And something new, strange, confounding with its emotion, came to life deep in Duane's heart. There would be children! Ray their mother! The kind of life a lonely outcast always yearned for and never had! He saw it all, felt it all.

But beyond and above all other claims came Captain MacNelly's. It was then there was something cold and death-like in Duane's soul. For he knew, whatever happened, of one thing he was sure—he would have to kill either Longstreth or Lawson. Longstreth might be trapped into arrest; but Lawson had no sense, no control, no fear. He would snarl like a panther and go for his gun, and he would have to be killed. This, of all consummations, was the one to be calculated upon.

Duane came out of it all bitter and callous and sore—in the most fitting of moods to undertake a difficult and deadly enterprise. He had fallen upon his old strange, futile dreams, now rendered poignant by reason of love. He drove away those dreams. In their places came the images of the olive-skinned Longstreth with his sharp eyes, and the dark, evil-faced Lawson, and then returned tenfold more thrilling and sinister the old strange passion to meet Poggin.

It was about one o'clock when Duane rode into Fairdale. The streets for the most part were deserted. He went directly to find Morton and Zimmer. He found them at length, restless, somber, anxious, but unaware of the part he had played at Ord. They said Longstreth was home, too. It was possible that Longstreth had arrived home in ignorance.

Duane told them to be on hand in town with their men in case he might need them, and then with teeth locked he set off for Longstreth's ranch.

Duane stole through the bushes and trees, and when nearing the porch he heard loud, angry, familiar voices. Longstreth and Lawson were quarreling again. How Duane's lucky star guided him! He had no plan of action, but his brain was equal to a hundred lightning-swift evolutions. He meant to take any risk rather than kill Longstreth. Both of the men were out on the porch. Duane wormed his way to the edge of the shrubbery and crouched low to watch for his opportunity.

Longstreth looked haggard and thin. He was in his shirt-sleeves, and he had come out with a gun in his hand. This he laid on a table near the wall. He wore no belt.

Lawson was red, bloated, thick-lipped, all fiery and sweaty from drink, though sober on the moment, and he had the expression of a desperate man in his last stand. It was his last stand, though he was ignorant of that.

"What's your news? You needn't be afraid of my feelings," said Lawson.

"Ray confessed to an interest in this ranger," replied Longstreth.

Duane thought Lawson would choke. He was thick-necked anyway, and the rush of blood made him tear at the soft collar of his shirt. Duane awaited his chance, patient, cold, all his feelings shut in a vise.

"But why should your daughter meet this ranger?" demanded Lawson, harshly.

"She's in love with him, and he's in love with her."

Duane reveled in Lawson's condition. The statement might have had the force of a juggernaut. Was Longstreth sincere? What was his game?

Lawson, finding his voice, cursed Ray, cursed the ranger, then Longstreth.

"You damned selfish fool!" cried Longstreth, in deep bitter scorn. "All you think of is yourself—your loss of the girl. Think once of ME—my home—my life!"

Then the connection subtly put out by Longstreth apparently dawned upon the other. Somehow through this girl her father and cousin were to be betrayed. Duane got that impression, though he could not tell how true it was. Certainly Lawson's jealousy was his paramount emotion.

"To hell with you!" burst out Lawson, incoherently. He was frenzied. "I'll have her, or nobody else will!"

"You never will," returned Longstreth, stridently. "So help me God I'd rather see her the ranger's wife than yours!"

While Lawson absorbed that shock Longstreth leaned toward him, all of hate and menace in his mien.

"Lawson, you made me what I am," continued Longstreth. "I backed you—shielded you. YOU'RE Cheseldine—if the truth is told! Now it's ended. I quit you. I'm done!"

Their gray passion-corded faces were still as stones.

"GENTLEMEN!" Duane called in far-reaching voice as he stepped out. "YOU'RE BOTH DONE!"

They wheeled to confront Duane.

"Don't move! Not a muscle! Not a finger!" he warned.

Longstreth read what Lawson had not the mind to read. His face turned from gray to ashen.

"What d'ye mean?" yelled Lawson, fiercely, shrilly. It was not in him to obey a command, to see impending death.

All quivering and strung, yet with perfect control, Duane raised his left hand to turn back a lapel of his open vest. The silver star flashed brightly.

Lawson howled like a dog. With barbarous and insane fury, with sheer impotent folly, he swept a clawing hand for his gun. Duane's shot broke his action.

Before Lawson ever tottered, before he loosed the gun, Longstreth leaped behind him, clasped him with left arm, quick as lightning jerked the gun from both clutching fingers and sheath. Longstreth protected himself with the body of the dead man. Duane saw red flashes, puffs of smoke; he heard quick reports. Something stung his left arm. Then a blow like wind, light of sound yet shocking in impact, struck him, staggered him. The hot rend of lead followed the blow. Duane's heart seemed to explode, yet his mind kept extraordinarily clear and rapid.

Duane heard Longstreth work the action of Lawson's gun. He heard the hammer click, fall upon empty shells. Longstreth had used up all the loads in Lawson's gun. He cursed as a man cursed at defeat. Duane waited, cool and sure now. Longstreth tried to lift the dead man, to edge him closer toward the table where his own gun lay. But, considering the peril of exposing himself, he found the task beyond him. He bent peering at Duane under Lawson's arm, which flopped out from his side. Longstreth's eyes were the eyes of a man who meant to kill. There was never any mistaking the strange and terrible light of eyes like those. More than once Duane had a chance to aim at them, at the top of Longstreth's head, at a strip of his side.

Longstreth flung Lawson's body off. But even as it dropped, before Longstreth could leap, as he surely intended, for the gun, Duane covered him, called piercingly to him:

"Don't jump for the gun! Don't! I'll kill you! Sure as God I'll kill you!"

Longstreth stood perhaps ten feet from the table

where his gun lay Duane saw him calculating chances. He was game. He had the courage that forced Duane to respect him. Duane just saw him measure the distance to that gun. He was magnificent. He meant to do it. Duane would have to kill him.

"Longstreth, listen," cried Duane, swiftly. "The game's up. You're done. But think of your daughter! I'll spare your life—I'll try to get you freedom on one condition. For her sake! I've got you nailed—all the proofs. There lies Lawson. You're alone. I've Morton and men to my aid. Give up. Surrender. Consent to demands, and I'll spare you. Maybe I can persuade MacNelly to let you go free back to your old country. It's for Ray's sake! Her life, perhaps her happiness, can be saved! Hurry, man! Your answer!"

"Suppose I refuse?" he queried, with a dark and terrible earnestness.

"Then I'll kill you in your tracks! You can't move a hand! Your word or death! Hurry, Longstreth! Be a man! For her sake! Quick! Another second now—I'll kill you!"

"All right, Buck Duane, I give my word," he said, and deliberately walked to the chair and fell into it.

Longstreth looked strangely at the bloody blot on Duane's shoulder.

"There come the girls!" he suddenly exclaimed. "Can you help me drag Lawson inside? They mustn't see him."

Duane was facing down the porch toward the court and corrals. Miss Longstreth and Ruth had come in sight, were swiftly approaching, evidently alarmed.

The two men succeeded in drawing Lawson into the house before the girls saw him.

"Duane, you're not hard hit?" said Longstreth.

"Reckon not," replied Duane.

"I'm sorry. If only you could have told me sooner! Lawson, damn him! Always I've split over him!"

"But the last time, Longstreth."

"Yes, and I came near driving you to kill me, too. Duane, you talked me out of it. For Ray's sake! She'll be in here in a minute. This'll be harder than facing a gun."

"Hard now. But I hope it'll turn out all right."

"Duane, will you do me a favor?" he asked, and he seemed shamefaced.

"Sure."

"Let Ray and Ruth think Lawson shot you. He's dead. It can't matter. Duane, the old side of my life is coming back. It's been coming. It'll be here just about when she enters this room. And, by God, I'd change places with Lawson if I could!"

"Glad you—said that, Longstreth," replied Duane. "And sure—Lawson plugged me. It's our secret."

Just then Ray and Ruth entered the room. Duane heard two low cries, so different in tone, and he saw two white faces. Ray came to his side, She lifted a shaking hand to point at the blood upon his breast. White and mute, she gazed from that to her father.

"Papa!" cried Ray, wringing her hands.

"Don't give way," he replied, huskily. "Both you girls will need your nerve. Duane isn't badly hurt. But Floyd is—is dead. Listen. Let me tell it quick. There's been a fight. It—it was Lawson—it was Lawson's gun that shot Duane. Duane let me off. In fact, Ray, he saved me. I'm to divide my property—return so far as possible what I've stolen—leave Texas at once with Duane, under arrest. He says maybe he can get MacNelly, the ranger captain, to let me go. For your sake!"

She stood there, realizing her deliverance, with the dark and tragic glory of her eyes passing from her father to Duane.

"You must rise above this," said Duane to her. "I expected this to ruin you. But your father is alive. He will live it down. I'm sure I can promise you he'll be free. Perhaps back there in Louisiana the dishonor will never be known. This country is far from your old home. And even in San Antonio and Austin a man's evil repute means little. Then the line between a rustler and a rancher is hard to draw in these wild border days. Rustling is stealing cattle, and I once heard a well-known rancher say that all rich cattlemen had done a little stealing Your father drifted out here, and, like a good many others, he succeeded. It's perhaps just as well not to split hairs, to judge him by the law and morality of a civilized country. Some way or other he drifted in with bad men. Maybe a deal that was honest somehow tied his hands. This matter of land, water, a few stray head of stock had to be decided out of court. I'm sure in his case he never realized where he was drifting. Then one thing led to another, until he was face to face with dealing that took on crooked form. To protect himself he bound men to him. And so the gang developed. Many powerful gangs have developed that way out here. He could not control them. He became involved with them. And eventually their dealings became deliberately and boldly dishonest. That meant the inevitable spilling of blood sooner or later, and so he grew into the leader because he was the strongest. Whatever he is to be judged for, I think he could have been infinitely worse."

CHAPTER XXIV

On the morning of the twenty-sixth Duane rode into Bradford in time to catch the early train. His wounds did not seriously incapacitate him. Longstreth was with him. And Miss Longstreth and Ruth Herbert would not be left behind. They were all leaving Fairdale for ever. Longstreth had turned over the whole of his property to Morton, who was to divide it as he and his comrades believed just. Duane had left Fairdale with his party by night, passed through Sanderson in the early hours of dawn, and reached Bradford as he had planned.

That fateful morning found Duane outwardly calm, but inwardly he was in a tumult. He wanted to rush to Val Verde. Would Captain MacNelly be there with his rangers, as Duane had planned for them to be? Memory of that tawny Poggin returned with strange passion. Duane had borne hours and weeks and months of waiting, had endured the long hours of the outlaw, but now he had no patience. The whistle of the train made him leap.

It was a fast train, yet the ride seemed slow.

Duane, disliking to face Longstreth and the passengers in the car, changed his seat to one behind his prisoner. They had seldom spoken. Longstreth sat with bowed head, deep in thought. The girls sat in a seat near by and were pale but composed. Occasionally the train halted briefly at a station. The latter half of that ride Duane had observed a wagon-road running parallel with the railroad, sometimes right alongside, at others near or far away. When the train was about twenty miles from Val Verde Duane espied a dark group of horsemen trotting eastward. His blood beat like a hammer at his temples. The gang! He thought he recognized the tawny Poggin and felt a strange inward contraction. He thought he recognized the clean-cut Blossom Kane, the black-bearded giant Boldt, the red-faced Panhandle Smith, and Fletcher. There was another man strange to him. Was that Knell? No! it could not have been Knell.

Duane leaned over the seat and touched Longstreth on the shoulder.

"Look!" he whispered. Cheseldine was stiff. He had already seen.

The train flashed by; the outlaw gang receded out of range of sight.

"Did you notice Knell wasn't with them?" whispered Duane.

Duane did not speak to Longstreth again till the train stopped at Val Verde.

They got off the car, and the girls followed as naturally as ordinary travelers. The station was a good deal larger than that at Bradford, and there was considerable action and bustle incident to the arrival of the train.

Duane's sweeping gaze searched faces, rested upon a man who seemed familiar. This fellow's look, too, was that of one who knew Duane, but was waiting for a sign, a cue. Then Duane recognized him—MacNelly, clean-shaven. Without mustache he appeared different, younger.

When MacNelly saw that Duane intended to greet him, to meet him, he hurried forward. A keen light flashed from his eyes. He was glad, eager, yet suppressing himself, and the glances he sent back and forth from Duane to Longstreth were questioning, doubtful. Certainly Longstreth did not look the part of an outlaw.

"Duane! Lord, I'm glad to see you," was the Captain's greeting. Then at closer look into Duane's face his warmth fled—something he saw there checked his enthusiasm, or at least its utterance.

"MacNelly, shake hand with Cheseldine," said Duane, low-voiced.

The ranger captain stood dumb, motionless. But he saw Longstreth's instant action, and awkwardly he reached for the outstretched hand.

"Any of your men down here?" queried Duane, sharply.

"No. They're up-town."

"Come. MacNelly, you walk with him. We've ladies in the party. I'll come behind with them."

They set off up-town. Longstreth walked as if he were with friends on the way to dinner. The girls were mute. MacNelly walked like a man in a trance. There was not a word spoken in four blocks.

Presently Duane espied a stone building on a corner of the broad street. There was a big sign, "Rancher's Bank."

"There's the hotel," said MacNelly. "Some of my men are there. We've scattered around."

They crossed the street, went through office and lobby, and then Duane asked MacNelly to take them to a private room. Without a word the Captain complied. When they were all inside Duane closed the door, and, drawing a deep breath as if of relief, he faced them calmly.

"Miss Longstreth, you and Miss Ruth try to make yourselves comfortable now," he said. "And don't be distressed." Then he turned to his captain. "MacNelly, this girl is the daughter of the man I've brought to you, and this one is his niece."

Then Duane briefly related Longstreth's story, and, though he did not spare the rustler chief, he was generous.

"When I went after Longstreth," concluded Duane, "it was either to kill him or offer him freedom on conditions. So I chose the latter for his daughter's sake. He has already disposed of all his property. I believe he'll live up to the conditions. He's to leave Texas never to return. The name Cheseldine has been a mystery, and now it'll fade."

A few moments later Duane followed MacNelly to a large room, like a hall, and here were men reading and smoking. Duane knew them—rangers!

MacNelly beckoned to his men.

"Boys, here he is."

"How many men have you?" asked Duane.

"Fifteen."

MacNelly almost embraced Duane, would probably

have done so but for the dark grimness that seemed to be coming over the man. Instead he glowed, he sputtered, he tried to talk, to wave his hands. He was beside himself. And his rangers crowded closer, eager, like hounds ready to run. They all talked at once, and the word most significant and frequent in their speech was "outlaws."

MacNelly clapped his fist in his hand.

"This'll make the adjutant sick with joy. Maybe we won't have it on the Governor! We'll show them about the ranger service. Duane! how'd you ever do it?"

"Now, Captain, not the half nor the quarter of this job's done. The gang's coming down the road. I saw them from the train. They'll ride into town on the dot—two-thirty."

"How many?" asked MacNelly.

"Poggin, Blossom Kane, Panhandle Smith, Boldt, Jim Fletcher, and another man I don't know. These are the picked men of Cheseldine's gang. I'll bet they'll be the fastest, hardest bunch you rangers ever faced."

"Poggin—that's the hard nut to crack! I've heard their records since I've been in Val Verde. Where's Knell? They say he's a boy, but hell and blazes!"

"Knell's dead."

"Ah!" exclaimed MacNelly, softly. Then he grew businesslike, cool, and of harder aspect. "Duane, it's your game to-day. I'm only a ranger under orders. We're all under your orders. We've absolute faith in you. Make your plan quick, so I can go around and post the boys who're not here."

"You understand there's no sense in trying to arrest

Poggin, Kane, and that lot?" queried Duane.

"No, I don't understand that," replied MacNelly, bluntly.

"It can't be done. The drop can't be got on such men. If you meet them they shoot, and mighty quick and straight. Poggin! That outlaw has no equal with a gun—unless—He's got to be killed quick. They'll all have to be killed. They're all bad, desperate, know no fear, are lightning in action."

"Very well, Duane; then it's a fight. That'll be easier, perhaps. The boys are spoiling for a fight. Out with your plan, now."

"Put one man at each end of this street, just at the edge of town. Let him hide there with a rifle to block the escape of any outlaw that we might fail to get. I had a good look at the bank building. It's well situated for our purpose. Put four men up in that room over the bank—four men, two at each open window. Let them hide till the game begins. They want to be there so in case these foxy outlaws get wise before they're down on the ground or inside the bank. The rest of your men put inside behind the counters, where they'll hide. Now go over to the bank, spring the thing on the bank officials, and don't let them shut up the bank. You want their aid. Let them make sure of their gold. But the clerks and cashier ought to be at their desks or window when Poggin rides up. He'll glance in before he gets down. They make no mistakes, these fellows. We must be slicker than they are, or lose. When you get the bank people wise, send your men over one by one. No hurry, no excitement, no unusual thing to attract notice in the bank."

"All right. That's great. Tell me, where do you intend to wait?"

Duane heard MacNelly's question, and it struck him peculiarly. He had seemed to be planning and speaking mechanically. As he was confronted by the fact it nonplussed him somewhat, and he became thoughtful, with lowered head.

"Where'll you wait, Duane?" insisted MacNelly, with keen eyes speculating.

"I'll wait in front, just inside the door," replied Duane, with an effort.

"Why?" demanded the Captain.

"Well," began Duane, slowly, "Poggin will get down first and start in. But the others won't be far behind. They'll not get swift till inside. The thing is—they MUSTN'T get clear inside, because the instant they do they'll pull guns. That means death to somebody. If we can we want to stop them just at the door."

"But will you hide?" asked MacNelly.

"Hide!" The idea had not occurred to Duane.

"There's a wide-open doorway, a sort of round hall, a vestibule, with steps leading up to the bank. There's a door in the vestibule, too. It leads somewhere. We can put men in there. You can be there."

Duane was silent.

"See here, Duane," began MacNelly, nervously. "You shan't take any undue risk here. You'll hide with the rest of us?"

"No!" The word was wrenched from Duane.

MacNelly stared, and then a strange, comprehending light seemed to flit over his face.

"Duane, I can give you no orders to-day," he said, distinctly. "I'm only offering advice. Need you take any more risks? You've done a grand job for the service—already. You've paid me a thousand times for that pardon. You've redeemed yourself.—The Governor, the adjutant-general—the whole state will rise up and honor you. The game's almost up. We'll kill these outlaws, or enough of them to break for ever their power. I say, as a ranger, need you take more risk than your captain?"

Still Duane remained silent. He was locked between two forces. And one, a tide that was bursting at its bounds, seemed about to overwhelm him. Finally that side of him, the retreating self, the weaker, found a voice.

"Captain, you want this job to be sure?" he asked.

"Certainly."

"I've told you the way. I alone know the kind of men to be met. Just WHAT I'll do or WHERE I'll be I can't say yet. In meetings like this the moment decides. But I'll be there!"

MacNelly spread wide his hands, looked helplessly at his curious and sympathetic rangers, and shook his head.

"Now you've done your work—laid the trap—is this strange move of yours going to be fair to Miss Longstreth?" asked MacNelly, in significant low voice.

Like a great tree chopped at the roots Duane vibrated to that. He looked up as if he had seen a ghost.

Mercilessly the ranger captain went on: "You can

win her, Duane! Oh, you can't fool me. I was wise in a minute. Fight with us from cover—then go back to her. You will have served the Texas Rangers as no other man has. I'll accept your resignation. You'll be free, honored, happy. That girl loves you! I saw it in her eyes. She's—"

But Duane cut him short with a fierce gesture. He lunged up to his feet, and the rangers fell back. Dark, silent, grim as he had been, still there was a transformation singularly more sinister, stranger.

"Enough. I'm done," he said, somberly. "I've planned. Do we agree—or shall I meet Poggin and his gang alone?"

MacNelly cursed and again threw up his hands, this time in baffled chagrin. There was deep regret in his dark eyes as they rested upon Duane.

Duane was left alone.

Never had his mind been so quick, so clear, so wonderful in its understanding of what had heretofore been intricate and elusive impulses of his strange nature. His determination was to meet Poggin; meet him before any one else had a chance—Poggin first—and then the others! He was as unalterable in that decision as if on the instant of its acceptance he had become stone.

Why? Then came realization. He was not a ranger now. He cared nothing for the state. He had no thought of freeing the community of a dangerous outlaw, of ridding the country of an obstacle to its progress and prosperity. He wanted to kill Poggin. It was significant now that he forgot the other outlaws. He was the gunman, the gun-thrower, the gun-fighter, passionate and terrible. His father's blood, that dark and fierce strain, his mother's spirit, that strong and unquenchable spirit of the surviving pioneer—these had been in him; and the killings, one after another, the wild and haunted years, had made him, absolutely in spite of his will, the gunman. He realized it now, bitterly, hopelessly. The thing he had intelligence enough to hate he had become. At last he shuddered under the driving, ruthless inhuman blood-lust of the gunman. Long ago he had seemed to seal in a tomb that horror of his kind—the need, in order to forget the haunting, sleepless presence of his last victim, to go out and kill another. But it was still there in his mind, and now it stalked out, worse, more powerful, magnified by its rest, augmented by the violent passions peculiar and inevitable to that strange, wild product of the Texas frontier—the gun-fighter. And those passions were so violent, so raw, so base, so much lower than what ought to have existed in a thinking man. Actual pride of his record! Actual vanity in his speed with a gun. Actual jealousy of any rival!

Duane could not believe it. But there he was, without a choice. What he had feared for years had become a monstrous reality. Respect for himself, blindness, a certain honor that he had clung to while in outlawry—all, like scales, seemed to fall away from him. He stood stripped bare, his soul naked—the soul of Cain. Always since the first brand had been forced and burned upon him he had been ruined. But now with conscience flayed to the quick, yet utterly powerless over this tiger instinct, he was lost. He said it. He admitted it. And at the utter abasement the soul he despised suddenly leaped and quivered with the thought of Ray Longstreth.

Then came agony. As he could not govern all the chances of this fatal meeting—as all his swift and deadly genius must be occupied with Poggin, perhaps in vain—as hard-shooting men whom he could not watch would be close behind, this almost certainly must be the end of Buck Duane. That did not matter. But he loved the girl. He wanted her. All her sweetness, her fire, and pleading returned to torture him.

At that moment the door opened, and Ray Longstreth entered.

"Duane," she said, softly. "Captain MacNelly sent me to you."

"But you shouldn't have come," replied Duane.

"As soon as he told me I would have come whether he wished it or not. You left me—all of us—stunned. I had no time to thank you. Oh, I do-with all my soul. It was noble of you. Father is overcome. He didn't expect so much. And he'll be true. But, Duane, I was told to hurry, and here I'm selfishly using time."

"Go, then—and leave me. You mustn't unnerve me now, when there's a desperate game to finish."

"Need it be desperate?" she whispered, coming close to him.

"Yes; it can't be else."

MacNelly had sent her to weaken him; of that Duane was sure. And he felt that she had wanted to come.

Her eyes were dark, strained, beautiful, and they shed a light upon Duane he had never seen before.

"You're going to take some mad risk," she said. "Let me persuade you not to. You said—you cared for me—and I—oh, Duane—don't you—know—?"

The low voice, deep, sweet as an old chord, faltered and broke and failed.

Duane sustained a sudden shock and an instant of paralyzed confusion of thought.

She moved, she swept out her hands, and the wonder of her eyes dimmed in a flood of tears.

"My God! You can't care for me?" he cried, hoarsely.

Then she met him, hands outstretched.

"But I do-I do!"

Swift as light Duane caught her and held her to his breast. He stood holding her tight, with the feel of her warm, throbbing breast and the clasp of her arms as flesh and blood realities to fight a terrible fear. He felt her, and for the moment the might of it was stronger than all the demons that possessed him. And he held her as if she had been his soul, his strength on earth, his hope of Heaven, against his lips.

The strife of doubt all passed. He found his sight again. And there rushed over him a tide of emotion unutterably sweet and full, strong like an intoxicating wine, deep as his nature, something glorious and terrible as the blaze of the sun to one long in darkness. He had become an outcast, a wanderer, a gunman, a victim of circumstances; he had lost and suffered worse than death in that loss; he had gone down the endless bloody trail, a killer of men, a fugitive whose mind slowly and inevitably closed to all except the instinct to survive and a black despair; and now, with this woman in his arms, her swelling breast against his, in this moment almost of resurrection, he bent under the storm of passion and joy possible only to him who had endured so much.

"Do you care—a little?" he whispered, unsteadily.

He bent over her, looking deep into the dark wet eyes.

She uttered a low laugh that was half sob, and her arms slipped up to his neck.

"A littler Oh, Duane—Duane—a great deal!"

Their lips met in their first kiss. The sweetness, the fire of her mouth seemed so new, so strange, so irresistible to Duane. His sore and hungry heart throbbed with thick and heavy beats. He felt the outcast's need of love. And he gave up to the enthralling moment. She met him half-way, returned kiss for kiss, clasp for clasp, her face scarlet, her eyes closed, till, her passion and strength spent, she fell back upon his shoulder.

Duane suddenly thought she was going to faint. He divined then that she had understood him, would have denied him nothing, not even her life, in that moment. But she was overcome, and he suffered a pang of regret at his unrestraint.

Presently she recovered, and she drew only the closer, and leaned upon him with her face upturned. He felt her hands on his, and they were soft, clinging, strong, like steel under velvet. He felt the rise and fall, the warmth of her breast. A tremor ran over him. He tried to draw back, and if he succeeded a little her form swayed with him, pressing closer. She held her face up, and he was compelled to look. It was wonderful now: white, yet glowing, with the red lips parted, and dark eyes alluring. But that was not all. There was passion, unquenchable spirit, woman's resolve deep and mighty.

"I love you, Duane!" she said. "For my sake don't go out to meet this outlaw face to face. It's something wild in you. Conquer it if you love me."

Duane became suddenly weak, and when he did take her into his arms again he scarcely had strength to lift her to a seat beside him. She seemed more than a dead weight. Her calmness had fled. She was throbbing, palpitating, quivering, with hot wet cheeks and arms that clung to him like vines. She lifted her mouth to his, whispering, "Kiss me!" She meant to change him, hold him.

Duane bent down, and her arms went round his neck and drew him close. With his lips on hers he seemed to float away. That kiss closed his eyes, and he could not lift his head. He sat motionless holding her, blind and helpless, wrapped in a sweet dark glory. She kissed him—one long endless kiss—or else a thousand times. Her lips, her wet cheeks, her hair, the softness, the fragrance of her, the tender clasp of her arms, the swell of her breast—all these seemed to inclose him.

Duane could not put her from him. He yielded to her lips and arms, watching her, involuntarily returning her caresses, sure now of her intent, fascinated by the sweetness of her, bewildered, almost lost. This was what it was to be loved by a woman. His years of outlawry had blotted out any boyish love he might have known. This was what he had to give up—all this wonder of her sweet person, this strange fire he feared yet loved, this mate his deep and tortured soul recognized. Never until that moment had he divined the meaning of a woman to a man. That meaning was physical inasmuch that he learned what beauty was, what marvel in the touch of quickening flesh; and it was spiritual in that he saw there might have been for him, under happier circumstances, a life of noble deeds lived for such a woman.

"Don't go! Don't go!" she cried, as he started violently.

"I must. Dear, good-by! Remember I loved you."

He pulled her hands loose from his, stepped back.

"Ray, dearest—I believe—I'll come back!" he whispered.

These last words were falsehood.

He reached the door, gave her one last piercing glance, to fix for ever in memory that white face with its dark, staring, tragic eyes.

"DUANE!"

He fled with that moan like thunder, death, hell in his ears.

To forget her, to get back his nerve, he forced into mind the image of Poggin-Poggin, the tawny-haired, the yellow-eyed, like a jaguar, with his rippling muscles. He brought back his sense of the outlaw's wonderful presence, his own unaccountable fear and hate. Yes, Poggin had sent the cold sickness of fear to his marrow. Why, since he hated life so? Poggin was his supreme test. And this abnormal and stupendous instinct, now deep as the very foundation of his life, demanded its wild and fatal issue. There was a horrible thrill in his sudden remembrance that Poggin likewise had been taunted in fear of him.

So the dark tide overwhelmed Duane, and when he left the room he was fierce, implacable, steeled to any outcome, quick like a panther, somber as death, in the thrall of his strange passion.

There was no excitement in the street. He crossed to the bank corner. A clock inside pointed the hour of two. He went through the door into the vestibule, looked around, passed up the steps into the bank. The clerks were at their desks, apparently busy. But they showed nervousness. The cashier paled at sight of Duane. There were men—the rangers—crouching down behind the low partition. All the windows had been removed from the iron grating before the desks. The safe was closed. There was no money in sight. A customer came in, spoke to the cashier, and was told to come to-morrow.

Duane returned to the door. He could see far down the street, out into the country. There he waited, and minutes were eternities. He saw no person near him; he heard no sound. He was insulated in his unnatural strain.

At a few minutes before half past two a dark, compact body of horsemen appeared far down, turning into the road. They came at a sharp trot—a group that would have attracted attention anywhere at any time. They came a little faster as they entered town; then faster still; now they were four blocks away, now three, now two. Duane backed down the middle of the vestibule, up the steps, and halted in the center of the wide doorway.

There seemed to be a rushing in his ears through which pierced sharp, ringing clip-clop of iron hoofs. He could see only the corner of the street. But suddenly into that shot lean-limbed dusty bay horses. There was a clattering of nervous hoofs pulled to a halt.

Duane saw the tawny Poggin speak to his companions. He dismounted quickly. They followed suit. They had the manner of ranchers about to conduct some business. No guns showed. Poggin started leisurely for the bank door, quickening step a little. The others, close together, came behind him. Blossom Kane had a bag in his left hand. Jim Fletcher was left at the curb, and he had already gathered up the bridles.

Poggin entered the vestibule first, with Kane on one side, Boldt on the other, a little in his rear.

As he strode in he saw Duane.

"HELL'S FIRE!" he cried.

Something inside Duane burst, piercing all of him with cold. Was it that fear?

"BUCK DUANE!" echoed Kane.

One instant Poggin looked up and Duane looked down.

Like a striking jaguar Poggin moved. Almost as quickly Duane threw his arm.

The guns boomed almost together.

Duane felt a blow just before he pulled trigger. His thoughts came fast, like the strange dots before his eyes. His rising gun had loosened in his hand. Poggin had drawn quicker! A tearing agony encompassed his breast. He pulled—pulled—at random. Thunder of booming shots all about him! Red flashes, jets of smoke, shrill yells! He was sinking. The end; yes, the end! With fading sight he saw Kane go down, then Boldt. But supreme torture, bitterer than death, Poggin stood, mane like a lion's, back to the wall, bloody-faced, grand, with his guns spouting red!

All faded, darkened. The thunder deadened. Duane fell, seemed floating. There it drifted—Ray Longstreth's sweet face, white, with dark, tragic eyes, fading from his sight... fading.. . fading...

CHAPTER XXV

Light shone before Duane's eyes—thick, strange light that came and went. For a long time dull and booming sounds rushed by, filling all. It was a dream in which there was nothing; a drifting under a burden; darkness, light, sound, movement; and vague, obscure sense of time—time that was very long. There was fire—creeping, consuming fire. A dark cloud of flame enveloped him, rolled him away.

He saw then, dimly, a room that was strange, strange people moving about over him, with faint voices, far away, things in a dream. He saw again, clearly, and consciousness returned, still unreal, still strange, full of those vague and far-away things. Then he was not dead. He lay stiff, like a stone, with a weight ponderous as a mountain upon him and all his bound body racked in slow, dull-beating agony.

A woman's face hovered over him, white and tragic-eyed, like one of his old haunting phantoms, yet sweet and eloquent. Then a man's face bent over him, looked deep into his eyes, and seemed to whisper from a distance: "Duane—Duane! Ah, he knew me!"

After that there was another long interval of darkness. When the light came again, clearer this time, the same earnest-faced man bent over him. It was MacNelly. And with recognition the past flooded back.

Duane tried to speak. His lips were weak, and he could scarcely move them.

"Poggin!" he whispered. His first real conscious thought was for Poggin. Ruling passion—eternal instinct!

"Poggin is dead, Duane; shot to pieces," replied MacNelly, solemnly. "What a fight he made! He killed two of my men, wounded others. God! he was a tiger. He used up three guns before we downed him."

"Who-got—away?"

"Fletcher, the man with the horses. We downed all the others. Duane, the job's done—it's done! Why, man, you're—"

"What of—of—HER?"

"Miss Longstreth has been almost constantly at your bedside. She helped the doctor. She watched your wounds. And, Duane, the other night, when you sank low—so low—I think it was her spirit that held yours back. Oh, she's a wonderful girl. Duane, she never gave up, never lost her nerve for a moment. Well, we're going to take you home, and she'll go with us. Colonel Longstreth left for Louisiana right after the fight. I advised it. There was great excitement. It was best for him to leave."

"Have I—a—chance—to recover?"

"Chance? Why, man," exclaimed the Captain, "you'll get well! You'll pack a sight of lead all your life. But you can stand that. Duane, the whole Southwest knows your story. You need never again be ashamed of the name Buck Duane. The brand outlaw is washed out. Texas believes you've been a secret ranger all the time.

You're a hero. And now think of home, your mother, of this noble girl—of your future."

The rangers took Duane home to Wellston.

A railroad had been built since Duane had gone into exile. Wellston had grown. A noisy crowd surrounded the station, but it stilled as Duane was carried from the train.

A sea of faces pressed close. Some were faces he remembered—schoolmates, friends, old neighbors. There was an upflinging of many hands. Duane was being welcomed home to the town from which he had fled. A deadness within him broke. This welcome hurt him somehow, quickened him; and through his cold being, his weary mind, passed a change. His sight dimmed.

Then there was a white house, his old home. How strange, yet how real! His heart beat fast. Had so many, many years passed? Familiar yet strange it was, and all seemed magnified.

They carried him in, these ranger comrades, and laid him down, and lifted his head upon pillows. The house was still, though full of people. Duane's gaze sought the open door.

Some one entered—a tall girl in white, with dark, wet eyes and a light upon her face. She was leading an old lady, gray-haired, austere-faced, somber and sad. His mother! She was feeble, but she walked erect. She was pale, shaking, yet maintained her dignity.

The some one in white uttered a low cry and knelt by Duane's bed. His mother flung wide her arms with a strange gesture.

"This man! They've not brought back my boy. This man's his father! Where is my son? My son—oh, my son!"

When Duane grew stronger it was a pleasure to lie by the west window and watch Uncle Jim whittle his stick and listen to his talk. The old man was broken now. He told many interesting things about people Duane had known—people who had grown up and married, failed, succeeded, gone away, and died. But it was hard to keep Uncle Jim off the subject of guns, outlaws, fights. He could not seem to divine how mention of these things hurt Duane. Uncle Jim was childish now, and he had a great pride in his nephew. He wanted to hear of all of Duane's exile. And if there was one thing more than another that pleased him it was to talk about the bullets which Duane carried in his body.

"Five bullets, ain't it?" he asked, for the hundredth time.

"Five in that last scrap! By gum! And you had six before?"

"Yes, uncle," replied Duane.

"Five and six. That makes eleven. By gum! A man's a man, to carry all that lead. But, Buck, you could carry more. There's that nigger Edwards, right here in Wellston. He's got a ton of bullets in him. Doesn't seem to mind them none. And there's Cole Miller. I've seen him. Been a bad man in his day. They say he packs twenty-three bullets. But he's bigger than you—got more flesh.... Funny, wasn't it, Buck, about the doctor only bein' able to cut one bullet out of you—that one in your breastbone? It was a forty-one caliber, an unusual cartridge. I saw it, and I wanted it, but Miss Longstreth wouldn't part with it. Buck, there was a bullet left in one of Poggin's guns, and that bullet was the same kind as the one cut out of you. By gum! Boy, it'd have killed you if it'd stayed there."

"It would indeed, uncle," replied Duane, and the old, haunting, somber mood returned.

But Duane was not often at the mercy of childish old hero-worshiping Uncle Jim. Miss Longstreth was the only person who seemed to divine Duane's gloomy mood, and when she was with him she warded off all suggestion.

One afternoon, while she was there at the west window, a message came for him. They read it together.

You have saved the ranger service to the Lone Star State

MACNELLEY.

Ray knelt beside him at the window, and he believed she meant to speak then of the thing they had shunned. Her face was still white, but sweeter now, warm with rich life beneath the marble; and her dark eyes were still intent, still haunted by shadows, but no longer tragic.

"I'm glad for MacNelly's sake as well as the state's," said Duane.

She made no reply to that and seemed to be thinking deeply. Duane shrank a little.

"The pain—Is it any worse to-day?" she asked, instantly.

"No; it's the same. It will always be the same. I'm full

of lead, you know. But I don't mind a little pain."

"Then—it's the old mood—the fear?" she whispered. "Tell me."

"Yes. It haunts me. I'll be well soon—able to go out. Then that—that hell will come back!"

"No, no!" she said, with emotion.

"Some drunken cowboy, some fool with a gun, will hunt me out in every town, wherever I go," he went on, miserably. "Buck Duane! To kill Buck Duane!"

"Hush! Don't speak so. Listen. You remember that day in Val Verde, when I came to you—plead with you not to meet Poggin? Oh, that was a terrible hour for me. But it showed me the truth. I saw the struggle between your passion to kill and your love for me. I could have saved you then had I known what I know now. Now I understand that—that thing which haunts you. But you'll never have to draw again. You'll never have to kill another man, thank God!"

Like a drowning man he would have grasped at straws, but he could not voice his passionate query.

She put tender arms round his neck. "Because you'll have me with you always," she replied. "Because always I shall be between you and that—that terrible thing."

It seemed with the spoken thought absolute assurance of her power came to her. Duane realized instantly that he was in the arms of a stronger woman that she who had plead with him that fatal day.

"We'll—we'll be married and leave Texas," she said, softly, with the red blood rising rich and dark in her cheeks.

"Ray!"

"Yes we will, though you're laggard in asking me, sir."

"But, dear—suppose," he replied, huskily, "suppose there might be—be children—a boy. A boy with his father's blood!"

"I pray God there will be. I do not fear what you fear. But even so—he'll be half my blood."

Duane felt the storm rise and break in him. And his terror was that of joy quelling fear. The shining glory of love in this woman's eyes made him weak as a child. How could she love him—how could she so bravely face a future with him? Yet she held him in her arms, twining her hands round his neck, and pressing close to him. Her faith and love and beauty—these she meant to throw between him and all that terrible past. They were her power, and she meant to use them all. He dared not think of accepting her sacrifice.

"But Ray—you dear, noble girl—I'm poor. I have nothing. And I'm a cripple."

"Oh, you'll be well some day," she replied. "And listen. I have money. My mother left me well off. All she had was her father's—Do you understand? We'll take Uncle Jim and your mother. We'll go to Louisiana—to my old home. It's far from here. There's a plantation to work. There are horses and cattle—a great cypress forest to cut. Oh, you'll have much to do. You'll forget there. You'll learn to love my home. It's a beautiful old place. There are groves where the gray moss blows all day and the nightingales sing all night."

"My darling!" cried Duane, brokenly. "No, no, no!"

Yet he knew in his heart that he was yielding to her, that he could not resist her a moment longer. What was this madness of love?

"We'll be happy," she whispered. "Oh, I know. Come!—come!-come!"

Her eyes were closing, heavy-lidded, and she lifted sweet, tremulous, waiting lips.

With bursting heart Duane bent to them. Then he held her, close pressed to him, while with dim eyes he looked out over the line of low hills in the west, down where the sun was setting gold and red, down over the Nueces and the wild brakes of the Rio Grande which he was never to see again.

It was in this solemn and exalted moment that Duane accepted happiness and faced a new life, trusting this brave and tender woman to be stronger than the dark and fateful passion that had shadowed his past.

It would come back—that wind of flame, that madness to forget, that driving, relentless instinct for blood. It would come back with those pale, drifting, haunting faces and the accusing fading eyes, but all his life, always between them and him, rendering them powerless, would be the faith and love and beauty of this noble woman.

Zane Grey—A True Colossus of American Literary Culture

Born Pearl Grey, Zane Grey is the man credited by many for forging the timeless literally genre now commonly called Western. A trained and practicing dentist, Grey is better known for his prolific writing which continues to influence a swathe of both performing and literary arts to date. A true prodigy in the classic sense of the word, Grey was not only a dentist but also a successful baseball player and a game fishing.

Nativity and Childhood

Grey was born in Zanesville, Ohio, on January 31, 1872, and died aged 67 at Altadena, California on October 23, 1939. It has been suggested that Grey earned the name Pearl early in life from newspaper references to Queen Victoria's "pearl grey" mourning clothes (grey is the British spelling of the color gray). The credence of this theory is strengthened by the fact that his family changed the family name from Gray to Grey soon after Zane was born. However, it is unclear when Grey changed his first name to Zane, the maiden name of his mother.

The city of Grey's birth, Zanesville, was named after his maternal great-grandfather, Ebenezer Zane, who was a veteran of the American Civil War. Growing up in a largely rural area of Ohio, Grey led an active and exuberant early life. He was fascinated by the great outdoors—a major element of his later literary works. He grew avid interests in fishing and baseball, preoccupations which would continue to inspire him well into his adulthood.

Grey's keenest interest was however in writing, and it all started from an early age. He found inspiration from historic retellings of the American civil war. The raw accounts of heroism that comes out in his early novels about the civil war come directly from the accounts which he was regaled with during his childhood. With several ancestors actively involved in this seismic era of American history, the young Grey had no dearth of inspiration.

Zane Grey the Dentist

Zane Grey trained as a dentist in order to please his father who was a practicing dentist, too. It was always an unexciting pursuit to him. Even in college, his grades were never impressive. He was by far more interested in writing and baseball. However, as he juggled all the options available to him, he opted to go into dentistry, convinced it was the safer career path.

In 1896, after graduating from his university, Grey moved to New York where he set up a practice. His choice of New York, as competitive for clinical practice as it was, was based more on his desire to be near publishers who would help with his fledgling writing career. After the tedium of dental practice, Grey would withdraw to his study in the evening to write.

Zane Grey the Baseball Player

As a youngster, Grey played summer baseball for Columbus Capitols (by then the family had moved from Zanesville to Columbus). He had ambitions to join Major League Baseball. He was a prodigious pitcher and was soon spotted by scouts, leading to a plethora of offers from colleges with a tradition of baseball success.

Grey subsequently earned a baseball scholarship and opted to go study dentistry at the University of Pennsylvania. On his very first game for the Penn, he was instrumental in his team's eventual win over the Riverton Club, producing a double in the tenth.

As a reliable pitcher and solid hitter, Grey remained a popular baseballer throughout his university days. However, the effectiveness of his method suffered considerably when the standard distance from the pitcher's mound to the plate was increased by ten feet in 1894.

After college, Grey was enlisted by a few Minor League Baseball teams but his game did not make enough of an impression as to advance his playing career. By 1902 Grey had given up on baseball as a prospective career.

Zane Grey and Game Fishing

Perhaps the most understated aspect of Zane Grey was his passion for game fishing. Indeed, Grey called fishing his "first and greatest passion", esteemed above baseball, writing, or dentistry. He gained plenty of inspiration for his literary creations from the adventures and escapades he had on fishing expeditions.

Grey was instrumental in the popularization of the sports hunting of dolphins and porpoises around the Americas. He is widely regarded in many quarters as the "Father of Modern Big Game Fishing". His son

Loren claims that his father would fish for an average of three hundred days a year throughout his adulthood.

Using his keen interest and innovative mind, Grey invented tackle and fishing equipment still widely used today. His most prolific fishing took place in the Pacific, especially the waters off Tahiti. It was there where he captured what he claimed was the "greatest marlin of all time". It was the first ever recorded game fish to exceed one thousand pounds in weight.

Family Life

During one of the summer breaks from college, Grey was confronted with a paternity suit which he quietly settled with financial help from his father.

While canoeing and fishing in the Delaware River with his brother in 1900, Grey met and fell in love with Lina "Dolly" Roth. Lina came from a family of physicians and was training to be a schoolteacher. The couple married in 1905. They settled at Lackawaxen, Pennsylvania. The family home, a picturesque farmhouse at the confluence of the Delaware and Lackawaxen rivers is today the location of the Zane Grey Museum and is listed in the national U.S. National Register of Historic Places.

Zane and Lina went on to have three children: Romer, Betty, and Loren. After marriage, Lina left her teaching career. She was instrumental in the management of her husband's career. It was she who negotiated contracts with publishers, literary agents and movie studios. Lina used her keen eye and sense of prose to proofread and copy edit her husband's manuscripts. This was crucial in developing Zane's writing style in the formative years of his career.

Despite his wife's devotion to his career, Zane Grey was a serial philanderer. He was constantly on the travel and openly flaunted his mistresses. Lina may not have been entirely at ease with her husband's disloyalty but she never stood up to him. Insights in her letters show that she took his affairs more as a result of a handicap in his character, rather than a consequence of choices he made.

Literary Inspiration and Style

From an early age, Grey was a voracious reader of adventure novels. His personal favorites included Robinson Crusoe and The Leatherstocking Tales. Later in life when he took to fishing and expeditions in the American West as well as the open seas. These turned out to be fertile grounds for the budding writer's creative instinct.

Before writing his first novel, he studied Owen Wister's great western novel, The Virginian. He attempted to incorporate Wister's structure and plot strategy in his first novel, Betty Zane. Harper & Brothers rejected the manuscript. He later self-published it, possibly with financial assistance from his wife who had just received her inheritance.

Literary Breakthrough

Grey penned his first novel, *Jim of the Cave*, as a fifteen-year-old boy. When his father, who was convinced writing books was a worthless pursuit, found out he was furious. He tore up young Zane's manuscript and administered a thorough beating.

By the end of the first decade of the twentieth century, Grey looked set to become a career dentist, if a half-hearted one at that. His first published work was the aforementioned *Betty Zane*, a historical novel about one of his own female ancestors. It did not showcase the makings of a bestselling author.

The event which turned the fortunes of Grey's writing career came in 1908 when he was requested to write the biography of Colonel C. J. "Buffalo" Jones. As he gathered material for the novel, Grey accompanied Jones west. Grey was fascinated and captivated by the people, culture, and landscapes of the region.

While Colonel Jones' biography, The Last of the Plainsmen, did not make much of a mark, the inspiration for the great wilds of the west had been planted in Grey's mind. He embarked on penning western historical romances. The first one to become a literary success was Heritage of the Desert, published in 1910. His place in the history of American literature was however sealed by the publication of Riders of the Purple Sage in 1912. To this day it is Zane Grey's most popular literary work.

Career Success as a Writer

Having discovered his path, Grey moved his family to Altadena, California. He also bought a hunting lodge on the Mogollon Rim near Payson, Arizona. Settled in the west for good, Grey also started his avid game fishing career at this time. The precocious adventurer also acquired a schooner and embarked on one of the most remarkable sea game careers ever recorded.

Grey was the quintessential writer adventurer. He wrote to live and lived to write. Today there are over ninety Zane Greys books in print. Several of these were published posthumously. Over sixty of his works are westerns.

As a writer, Grey was intense, meticulous, and authentic to the last detail. He connected easily with diverse readers around the world. His books sold fast in both peacetime and war. In his most prolific years, from 1917 and 1926, Grey was perennially in the annual top ten list of bestselling authors. He not only made a name for himself but considerable fortune as well.

Ranking in the top ten bestseller list at the time required that one have sales exceeding one hundred thousand a year. It is a testament to Grey's prodigious talent that he continued to churn world-class books even as he led such an active life as an adventurer. A true pioneer, Grey was among the first millionaire authors.

It is estimated that Grey was such a prolific writer that he wrote over nine million words in his career. Indeed, he was so productive that after he died in 1939, his publishers Harper & Brothers continued to publish his works annually up to 1963.

Zane Grey's Legacy and Place in History

Zane Grey is, without doubt, one of the great colossuses of American culture and philosophy of freedom. His overarching themes of adventure, oneness with nature and irrepressible spirit ring true with many readers around the world.

Grey's novels were among the first to be adapted into feature-length Hollywood films. By his death, over a hundred western films were spawned from his literary works.

Today, the legacy of Zane Grey is celebrated in several museums and national monuments erected in his honor. His literary influence is clear in many western movies and television shows depicted on screens around the world today. He was a truly larger-than-life character whose ideas, inventions and worldview continue to inspire literary figures to this day.

Other Books by Sastrugi Press

2024 Total Eclipse State Series by Aaron Linsdau

Sastrugi Press has published state-specific guides for the 2024 total eclipse crossing over the United States. Check the Sastrugi Press website for the available state eclipse books: www.sastrugipress.com/eclipse

Along the Sylvan Trail by Julianne Couch

Along the Sylvan Trail dips into the lives of linked characters as they confront futures that aren't clearly dictated by conventional planning. The conflicts of the small town change and pressure residents of Sylvan Grove to look beyond their world to the outside.

Antarctic Tears by Aaron Linsdau

What would make someone give up a high-paying career to ski alone across Antarctica to the South Pole? This inspirational true story will make readers both cheer and cry. Discover what drives someone to the brink of destruction to pursue a dream.

Sagebrush Alley by Patricia Jones

What's worse than having a stalker? Being pursued by a second one who has already killed. Attempting to complete her studies, Dana Cameron has to avoid becoming a murder victim. She becomes tangled in a struggle for life trapped in a claustrophobic nightmare.

Sleeping Dogs Don't Lie by Michael McCoy

A young Native American boy is taken from his home after tragedy strikes, grows up in middle America, and through his first real adult summer searches for Wyoming artifacts, falls in with the subversive Dog Soldiers Resurrected, and attempts single-handedly to solve the mystery behind the murder of his treasured coworker.

The Diary of a Dude Wrangler by Struthers Burt

The dude ranch world of Struthers Burt was a romantic destination in the early twentieth century. They transported people back to the Wild West. These ranches were and still are popular destinations. Experience the old west through this dude rancher's writing.

Voices at Twilight by Lori Howe, Ph.D.

Voices at Twilight is a guide takes readers on a visual tour of twelve past and present Wyoming ghost towns. Contained within are travel directions, GPS coordinates, and tips for intrepid readers.

Sastrugi Press has a classic series just for you. Visit our webpage and find more quality books like this one at www.sastrugipress.com/classics/.

Visit Sastrugi Press on the web at www.sastrugipress.com to purchase the above titles in bulk. They are also available from your local bookstore or online retailers in print, e-book, or audiobook form. Thank you for choosing Sastrugi Press.

www.sastrugipress.com

"Turn the Page Loose"

www.ingramcontent.com/pod-product-compliance
Lightning Source LLC
Chambersburg PA
CBHW030549310726
48979CB00010B/2089/J

* 9 7 8 1 6 4 9 2 2 0 3 9 4 *